TEOTWAWKI

The
End of the World
as
We Know It

C.A. Bailes

Fulton Books
Meadville, PA

Published by Fulton Books 2023

ISBN 979-8-88505-814-8 (paperback)
ISBN 979-8-88505-815-5 (digital)

Printed in the United States of America

PREFACE

THIS BOOK HAS been a long road for me. I began writing this book in 2009 with hopes and dreams of finally having a concrete idea. Thirteen years later, my dream is becoming a reality. I initially intended this to be two separate books. However, like a lot of readers, I hate waiting for a sequel. After completing the first part, I dove right into the sequel. I didn't want my readers to have to wait to find out what happens.

I would like to thank my second-grade teacher, Mrs. Janac, for introducing me to the world of creative writing, and my favorite teacher of all time, Mr. Mack Hall, for always bleeding all over my papers in red ink to make me a better writer. I would like to recognize my parents for their undying love and support. To my girls, Jessica and Katie, I love you both so much. Never give up on your dreams. To my stepson, Mark, thank you for your editing skills and suggestions. Finally, to my sweet husband, Gator Bait, I couldn't have done any of this without you. Your love, support, and encouragement got me through this. Thank you for loving me for who I am and giving me the encouragement to reach my lifelong dream.

T HE NASA SPACE Center of Houston reverberated with activity. People dashed in and out of rooms and sprinted down hallways. On any other day, they would be welcoming visitors and giving guests tours. However, unbeknownst to many people, today was a day of crisis. It was going to be one of those days you train and prepare for your entire career. Then when the moment finds you, all you want to do is find a dark corner and hide.

NASA administrator, Bradley Rogers, met National Security administrator, Mr. Daniel Tonahill, in the hallway. It was Tonahill's job to alert the president of the outcome of today's mission. They exchanged a fast but vigorous handshake before they disappeared to the control room in a shroud of secrecy.

Freddie Twynkle ran from the bathroom, fastening his pants as he stumbled out the door. He had unfortunately become well acquainted with the porcelain throne. Ever since the Alpine Confirmation, Freddie had lived on coffee, caffeine pills, and Red Bull; none of which did much to help his multiple stomach ulcers or irritable bowel syndrome. He had thought more than once about placing a potty chair at his station in the control room. The same kind old people used in the nursing homes. He probably would have if it had not been for the horrible smell. He had worked twenty-hour days for over a month, putting the final touches on his Trajectory and Damage Assessment Prediction Program. For once, he was proud to be a little nerd from Katy, Texas. It was NASA who had searched him out. Word of mouth had somehow traveled about his prediction program. He showed them what it could do. He did not understand too much of what was going on. He believed it was some sort of training exercise. He assumed that most information was on a need-to-know basis, and he did not need to know anything except his own little piece of the puzzle. He was proud that all these people had turned out for the test run of his program. He would let everyone do their part, and when his new friend Alex said to run the numbers, that was his cue to show off what he could do.

Freddie entered the control room and took his seat. "Where are we at, Alex?"

Alex Ross never took his eyes off the multiple large screens in front of him. "The bunker busters are two minutes out."

Freddie sat with his fingers poised, ready to attack the keyboard. If the bombs Alex spoke of didn't take out the comet as all the bigwigs predicted, he would have to quickly recalculate its trajectory. For now, all he could do was keep his fingers crossed and hold his breath. For the first time in his life, he was a part of something big.

He looked around the room. It was full of people. Most were the usual NASA employees he had seen day in and day out for the past month. Something was different about today. The entire NEO Committee was there, along with many men in military attire. The NASA director stood beside another man dressed in a fine-looking suit. Between them was the legendary red phone line to the president. Freddie noticed the looks in their eyes. The tension was high and thick in the room.

Finally, the countdown began. Ten seconds till the impact of the nuclear bombs on some big rock hurtling through space. The room drew very quiet. The only sounds were the humming of the computers and the animated voice conducting the countdown. All eyes were glued to the screen. The countdown continued: *5, 4, 3, 2, 1.* The bombs hit the massive rock in succession. Everyone cheered. People were patting one another on the back, hugging one another, and passing out high fives like candy on Halloween. Smiles were big, and hopes were high. The picture was lost in the blast. Freddie was confused. He couldn't understand why everyone was cheering. There was no need for him to be here. There was no need for his program. Why had he worked so many long hours for nothing? He looked around at all the happy, relieved faces, and it hit him. This wasn't a training mission. This was reality. There really was a huge rock out there, and they had just bombed the hell out of it. The only reason Freddie was there was for a backup. If the rock wasn't destroyed, he could run his program and properly inform them of the details of the impending impact.

Freddie refreshed his computer. His eyes widened and chin dropped as he saw the results. "Hey, umm, Alex."

Alex was by his side in a flash. "I see it too." He patted Freddie on the back. "Run the numbers, man. Do your thing. I'll get the administrator."

Freddy's fingers flew across the keyboard. This was his time, his whole reason for being there. This was his little piece of the puzzle. He quickly entered the new information. The picture returned to the screen. A solemn hush fell over the room. The high fives were quickly replaced with looks of worry and confusion.

"What do you have for me, Mr. Tinkle?" Mr. Tonahill asked eagerly.

Freddy never looked up or stopped. He was tired of correcting the pronunciation of his name. It was something he had done since elementary school. Luckily, Alex came to his rescue. "His name is Twine-kle, sir. And as soon as he has the correct information, he will give it to you. He will want to check and recheck." Alex looked at Freddie with a look that ensured him that he had better be certain.

Freddie looked at the screen and shook his head. "This isn't going to make the bigwigs happy," he mumbled. "Impact scenario coming up now, sir." Freddie couldn't help but smile at his accomplishment. Now he was able to see it on the big screen in real time. He turned to the National Security administrator. "The program will show you down to the street where the impacts will be and then what damage you can expect to happen."

Freddie vibrated with anticipation and anxiety. He rose from his chair and reluctantly smiled. The impending disaster calculation took on a life of its own as the screen illuminated. Freddy looked around at the emotionally charged room. Faces of fear and anger, worry and anxiety were all around. The final scenario began to display. The point of impact looked familiar. Freddie removed his thick black-rimmed Coke bottle glasses and scrubbed them off on his shirt tail. Returning them to his head, he squinted as he looked at the screen again. The model showed impact to occur only five miles from his current location, the NASA Space Center.

People in the room came to life around him. They began running around and shouting orders. He could tell from their horrified expression that this was for real. He knew his numbers were correct. He stood and watched as the scenario replayed. A magnitude of realization hit him. They were all about to die.

He stood in horrific disbelief. The moment he had worked so hard for, the one he thought would be the highlight of his whole nerdy career was the same one that was leading him to his own death.

"What the hell is that smell?" Alex yelled out.

Freddie's eyes never left the screen. He could feel the warmth of the fresh, loose fecal matter running down his leg. He simply raised his hand like a schoolchild. "It's me. I think I just shit my pants."

Part I

CHAPTER 1

MY NAME IS Ashley Reese. I was a typical thirty-five-year-old hardworking, honest woman. There was nothing special or specific about me as far as I could tell, except perhaps my irrational fear of frogs. I was a divorced mother of two little girls. My oldest, Harley, was sixteen, and she had the attitude to match. Katherine, or Kat, as I nicknamed her, was an average nine-year-old who enjoyed her television time and was still enthused with toys. She was an easygoing kid who could keep herself entertained for hours on end. Harley, on the other hand, relied on the latest technology to get through the day. Her new cell phone was now a permanent accessory to her wardrobe. I worked the night shift as an emergency room nurse for the local hospital. I have always enjoyed my work. I have always been a simple country girl who loved the outdoors and watched professional wrestling on television the day I was born.

I had been married for fourteen years to Aaron Reese till the day he decided not to come home. Without a phone call, text message, or Dear John email, he just left. The memory of having to officially report him missing wasn't a fond one I cared to let linger in my brain. He was eventually found at his girlfriend's house. It was the lowest point in my life thus far. As it turned out, I was amazingly resilient. I picked up the pieces and started over. Even though I felt broken inside, I refused to allow my divorce to be the single most important event of my life. I wasn't about to let it define who I was going to be for the rest of my life. I wasn't going to live in bitterness. However, it was Harley and Kat who were most affected. They both were devastated by the absence of their father. Since the divorce, they had only seen their father four times. He had moved to New Orleans to pursue a new life for himself. He had a new girlfriend who was currently pregnant with his baby. He called his girls once every two weeks to make sure they got the menial child support check. In his mind, that was what he considered supporting them.

I moved on with my life as well. I moved in with my parents, Charles and Joan Williams. I was fortunate to make enough money to support Harley, Kat, and myself, but because of the hours I worked, I still needed someone to help police the girls at night. The thought of dating again honestly scared the hell out of me. I refused the idea of the whole bar scene. In my mind, whatever came out of a bar would go back into the bar. I had been active in my little small-town church. Sadly, the only two single men were ages eighteen and eighty. There was absolutely no middle ground to work with.

Reluctantly, I resorted to the internet dating sites. I wasn't out to get married. I wasn't trying to find a man to take care of me or be a daddy to my babies. I just wanted to find someone nice to go out with for nothing more than a type of companionship that went a step beyond friends with benefits. It seemed like a desperate search for the proverbial needle in the haystack. Most of the men who contacted me were on disability, unemployed, or barely spoke English. One guy had been married six times. All sorts of red flags were going up. I was about to give up and declare a life of celibacy. It was then that Dallas Blackwolf sent me a message. I had seen his add but didn't think we were in the same league. He seemed a little too posh for my country girl side, one of the "too good to be true" types. He was in my age bracket, gainfully employed, spoke English, and didn't need booze or medication to get through the day. Second most importantly, he made me laugh. In one of our first emails, I asked him a basic get-to-know-you question, "What do you consider an ideal first date?" His response was, "On a first date, I like to go out and rob a bank and allow my date to be the getaway driver. It seems like a dramatic start, but it really establishes trust." I could tell he had a great sense of humor to top off his other great assets.

Dallas was a native of Browning, Montana. He was an American Indian born into the Blackfeet Tribe who had left home, determined to attend law school. He had only returned to his tribe once since he left. His father passed away a few years before we met, and Dallas went home for his funeral. He stayed in constant contact with his mother, Greta Blackwolf, and her twin sister, Frances Two Feathers, by phone and email. His mother and aunt owned a lodge and tried everything possible to get their beloved long-lost boy to come home and run it for them. They complained of being too old and not being able to keep things up as they should be. Their complaints fell on deaf ears. Dallas had no intention of going back to the small community to live. Dallas had a son named Marcus, who was the same age as Harley. Marcus lived with his mother, Makayla, in Austin. Makayla was a short, arrogant woman with intense beige eyes. She and Dallas had been divorced for about three years and was self-sufficient.

Dallas had worked long and hard to finish his law degree. He was now a partner in a successful firm in Austin. He could have easily hired a maid to help with cooking, cleaning, and laundry. However, he didn't see such work at being above him and chose to do it himself.

From our first date, we each knew we had something special. I thought Dallas was as beautiful as the sunset. He was a deep golden tan in color with big brown eyes and black hair that he kept cut short and neat. He was almost six feet tall with broad shoulders. I felt a little self-conscious next to him. I myself only stood five feet, two inches and was slightly overweight. I disagreed, snickering when Dallas suggested I was just curvy. And he obviously liked my curves. I was constantly asking questions regarding his lineage. I found it extremely interesting. I even learned a few words in his native tongue. We only had a handful of actual dates, growing comfortable with each other quickly. We spent many nights on the phone for hours. There were times when I felt like a silly teenager again. I was happy and looked forward to seeing Dallas every chance I got. Because of our schedules, our time was limited to me traveling to his home in Austin once every two weeks for the weekend. Once I was comfortable with the idea, I started bringing Harley and Kat with me on my weekend expeditions. The girls liked Dallas from the start, or at least his rather large swimming pool complete with slide, diving board, and hot tub.

After about a year of this, Dallas came to a conclusion. He could no longer handle only seeing me once every two weeks. A total of four or five days a month just wasn't enough. He made a decision that would affect the both of us for the rest of our lives. He surprised me with tickets to a live wrestling event. During the event, he astonished me further by asking for my hand in marriage. It was a televised event, and even though the cameramen weren't a part of Dallas's plan, they quickly found our special moment transpiring in the crowd. It wasn't a traditional proposal. Most people wouldn't even call it special. I thought it was perfect. I was exhilarated and scared to death but accepted his proposal. It felt natural, and I honestly couldn't imagine my life without him in it. We decided to move in together. I wasn't sure about it at first. I was raised old-fashioned. There was a particular order in which things were supposed to happen. I was throwing all caution into the wind. I was taking a chance on love, a chance on him, and a chance on us.

He sold his small home and bought a larger family home in Cedar Park, a nice little suburb of Austin. It was a total change for me. Aaron and I always rented and never had enough money to buy a home. I never dreamed I would have something this extravagant. I was never really able to plant the flowers or trees that I wanted. Everything I had ever grown had been in pots, something portable in case we moved. I fell in love with it. It was close to the Texas Hill Country, which allowed me a combination of suburban life and outdoor attractions. It wasn't far away from my parents and my brother, all of whom lived in a small town a little less than an hour away. I had always wanted a place my kids could call home. When you walked through the door and said aloud, "I'm home," it had a real meaning, and it felt really good. The proudest moment of my life was when Dallas handed me the house keys, kissed me on the cheek, and softly said, "Welcome home." He had no idea how much this home meant to me. It wasn't just a structure with walls and a ceiling; it was an investment of our future together.

Even though Dallas made enough money to support his new ready-made family, I refused to quit working. I enjoyed my job and got great satisfaction doing it. I decided to only work part-time though. I wanted to devote as much time as possible into making my impending nuptials successful. The whole family fell into a nice routine. Harley and Kat even found their new private school intriguing, except for the uniforms of course. Harley earned a spot on the volleyball team, and Kat loved her small class and was excelling academically. Dallas enjoyed finding any reason to dote upon his new family. He bought and set up a volleyball net and helped Harley practice every evening, weather permitting. And he promised Kat that when summer came around, she would have a swimming pool again.

On the night before my world ended, I had tucked Harley in and said good night. I was closing her door when I heard Dallas's voice. He was in Kat's room telling her a Native American story. She truly loved to hear the stories of his tribe. She found his history as interesting as I did. She had even gone as far as to stop greeting people with hello and started saying *oki*, which meant the same thing in Blackfeet. I could see her happily dancing around a campfire and singing a Native song.

Dallas continued as I stood outside the door and listened. "There was an Indian chief who had four sons. He wanted his sons to learn not to judge things too quickly, so he sent them each on a quest, in turn, to go and look at a pear tree that was a great distance away. The first son went in winter, the second in spring, the third in summer, and the youngest son in the fall. When they had all gone and come back, he called them together to describe what they had seen. The first son said the tree was ugly, bent, and twisted. The second son said no, it was covered with green buds and full of promise. The third son disagreed. He said the tree was laden with blossoms that smelled sweet and looked beautiful. It was the most graceful thing he had ever seen. The last son disagreed with all of them. He said it was ripe and drooping with fruit, full of life and fulfillment.

"The man then explained to his sons that they were all right, because they had each seen but only one season in the tree's life. He told them that they can't judge a tree, or a person, by only one season and that the essence of who they are and the pleasure, joy, and love that come from that life can only be measured at the end, when all the seasons are up. If you give up when it's winter, you will miss the promise of your spring, the beauty of your summer, the fulfillment of your fall. And the moral of the story is, don't let the pain of one season destroy the joy of all the rest. Don't judge life by one difficult season. Persevere through the difficult patches, and better times are sure to come." Dallas paused and took a breath. "Now do you think you can go to sleep?" I guess Kat nodded. Dallas tucked her in and came out, leaving the door cracked a little bit.

"Good night, Daddy D.," I heard Kat say. Dallas waved through the cracked door.

Dallas came to bed and lay there silently for a few minutes with his eyes closed. I smiled seeing him lying there barely covered with a sheet, his bronze body basking in the bright moonlight that was breaking through the sheer curtains.

His eyes fluttered open, obviously feeling my gaze. His smile matched mine. "What are you smiling at?"

"Nothing. Just admiring." I scooted closer and rested my head on the arm he offered to me.

"Admiring what?" he asked.

I looked deep into his eyes and cupped his face with my hand. "Only the most beautiful, handsome man in the world."

I could have sworn in that very moment, he blushed. "Well, you better tell him to leave because I would really like to have some private time with my wife-to-be."

Our lips met and our bodies intertwined as we shared a magnificent night together. I'm thankful that neither of us knew it would be our last one.

The next morning started out like any other late October day. The sun radiated in the brilliant blue sky. White clouds billowed overhead like giant cotton balls. There was no sign of the impending doom that was about to transpire. I crawled out of bed and got dressed and opened the curtains to my luscious bedroom. I felt lucky to have such a wonderful day off from work. I had wanted to get some landscaping done around my new home. I saw Dallas off to work, speaking briefly about what to have for supper and a fast reminder of a business dinner he had Friday night. I got the girls up, ready, and off to school. However, it didn't happen without fighting over the cell phone bill and cleaning their rooms. Soon, they were out the door running to catch the bus. We lived close enough to the school that most kids in the neighborhood rode their bikes or walked; however, I didn't feel comfortable allowing my girls to do that just yet. It only gave Harley another reason to hate me, but at least she was safe.

I put the breakfast dishes in the dishwasher and headed outside. I worked most of the morning planting the flower beds that ran along the entire front of the house. I carefully planted elephant ear bulbs near the drain spouts and also planted mums, sunflowers, calendulas, and a running rosebush so it would grow up the piece of latticework that Dallas had hung up for me. I had big plans to get a concrete water fountain in the middle of the horseshoe drive. I stood up from my planting spot and stretched and looked at the huge house. I never dreamed that I would live in a home like this. Even though it was in a subdivision, it was private. Our home set off the road at least fifty yards at the end of a cul-de-sac. There was a long driveway that I eventually wanted lined with flowering pear trees. We had plenty of land to do anything we wanted with. I loved the wraparound porch. The thought crossed my mind that a few Boston ferns to hang in between the porch post and maybe a couple of white rocking chairs would look nice. Our bedroom was a work of art. Dallas had a four-posted Paul Bunyan bed shipped in from Colorado with a sheer canopy hanging down. I felt like a true princess when I sank into the plush mattress. There was a sitting area in the window that overlooked the driveway; it was perfect for reading on a sunny day. There were double french doors that opened to a balcony that overlooked the backyard. My kitchen was a gourmet's dream come true. It had been stocked with every new-age gadget and gizmo. Most of them were smarter than I was. I loved the island with attached bar and large walk-in pantry.

Harley's room was her favorite colors of black and hot pink and completely decorated in peace signs. Kat and Dallas worked for two weeks painting a castle mural on her wall. Her bed was suspended from the ceiling and looked like an actual drawbridge. Almost every night, he told her stories from his people that had been passed down from generations. She loved hearing them. I think it amused him to know she was so enthused about his heritage. Marcus didn't want any part of it. The only inherited trait he embraced was his long black hair. He detested his beautiful bronze skin. It inhibited him to fully achieve the dark, gothic vampire look he was currently going for.

Dallas, although of Indian descent, found the Chinese culture interesting. Particularly, their early inventions intrigued him. He often to included me. "Did you know the Chinese were the first to invent the umbrella?" He was full of senseless facts such as this. I would only grin, nod, and give a simulated fascinated "awe" escape my lips. As an agreement when we bought our home, Dallas was in charge of decorating the living room. He took great pride in placing his intricate Chinese artifacts about the room. It housed only one replicated artifact that I found remotely attractive. It was called a *didong yi*. It was the first seismograph dating back to AD 132. The didong yi was an ornate vase with eight evenly spaced dragons encircling the side representing a different direction. Each dragon held a metal ball in its mouth. Below each dragon was a toad with its mouth open unusually wide. Inside the vase was a sophisticated series of cogs, levers, and a long metal pendulum. The pendulum would vibrate and swing in the direction in which a quake occurred. The ball would dislodge from its resting place and fall from the dragon's mouth. Theoretically, it would land in the frog's mouth, thus revealing the direction of the quake. Since there were no methods of accelerated communication, this would let authorities know in what direction to send help and supplies. The original didong yi measured over six feet in diameter. I was very happy Dallas had settled on a smaller tabletop version. It was one of his prized possessions and a great conversation piece at dinner parties.

I looked around again. The yard, once completely landscaped, would be beautiful. Although it still needed a lot of work, I would take my time in doing it correctly. I had it all pictured in my mind. You could look to the south and just see the tops of the skyscrapers in the horizon. I twirled around in a circle. I felt like I was living in

a fantasy world. I took a deep breath and sighed in deep appreciation for the gifts I had been blessed with. I had just crossed over the
threshold of the kitchen to fix lunch when the phone rang.

A prerecorded voiced echoed in response to my gallant "Hello."

"Attention. There is immediate danger to your area. Please tune
your television to your local news station for further instructions.
Attention. There is immediate danger to your area. Please tune your
television to your local news station for further instructions." A deafening silence was followed by a dial tone.

I stood still for just a moment, then quickly sprinted to the
television in the living room and turned the station to KVAE, news
out of Austin. I expected to hear reports of a possible terrorist attack
on the scale of 9/11 or perhaps even bigger. Perhaps maybe a wild-
fire had been started. Instead, the news anchor was stating that the
president of the United States would be addressing the nation in a
few moments.

"We here at KVAE have not been made aware as to the nature
of the address. Moments ago, the National Communication Board
jammed phone lines and rang every landline in the continental
United States with a message to tune in to your local news. We are
just as lost as the rest of you. Okay, we are now going to a live feed."
The television displayed a small podium with the presidential seal
behind it, on the wall.

Watching, confused and a little scared, I knew this had to be
something big. My stomach began to knot up. My mind raced.
Were we at war? Was there a new viral pandemic? What could be so
important? Whatever it was, I knew it had to be something life-altering for the president to be addressing the nation. The air in the
room seemed to get dense. My foot tapped on the finely polished
hardwood floors. My eyes remained glued to the television. I perked
up when I could see the president coming into view and turning to
face the camera.

The thin-faced man looked worn out. The camera zoomed in
on his face. His eyes were swollen and looked wet, and he was apparently shaken. Had he been crying? What representative of the free
world cries? I leaned back into the velvety hunter-green sofa, pulling

my knees to my chest while wrapping my arms around them. This was something I had done as a child to feel secure. However, I hadn't felt the need to do this in years. I wished Dallas was home to hold me in his big brawny arms.

The president started in a shaky voice, "My fellow Americans, I have a major announcement to make. It will take some time to get through it. I will be feeding a lot of important information and details. So please bear with me. I will not take any questions because there is simply no time.

"About two months ago at the McDonald Observatory in Alpine, Texas, a group of college students found something disturbing. They collected and sent their data to NASA, who confirmed their findings. What those students discovered is nothing short of life-altering—a comet on a collision course with Earth. This comet was approximately one and a half miles wide in diameter. If it were to hit Earth, it would be an extinction level event.

"So for the last two months, the Near-Earth Object Monitoring Committee, or NEO, has worked diligently to keep this quiet. At least until we could come up with a plan. A satellite already in orbit around Earth was equipped and programmed to launch bunker buster nuclear bombs. We had to wait until the comet was closer to maximize the effectiveness of the bombs. And that is what brings me here before you today.

"Our warheads were both a success and a failure. They failed to obliterate the comet as we had hoped. However, it was successful in breaking the comet into three manageable pieces. The first piece, named Alpine One, is three-quarters of a mile wide in diameter. It will hit about one hundred miles north of Haiti in the Atlantic Ocean. It will flash boil millions of gallons of water. The impact will cause a tsunami fifty to seventy-five feet tall that will rush across the Atlantic Seaboard. Impact is to be in approximately three hours."

A wave of gasps spread across the room. Reporters mumbled in hushed, worried tones. The president raised his hands in an attempt to keep order in the room.

"The second piece, Alpine Two, is approximately half a mile wide in diameter. It will ironically hit the Galveston Bay area in

Texas, about twenty miles from the NASA Space Center of Houston. This will be a land hit. However, we believe that considering the low elevation of the area, the impact will generate another tsunami that will be between twenty-five and fifty feet tall. It will wash over the state of Florida, destroying homes and businesses, anyone and anything in its way. It will destroy oil refineries as well as offshore drilling rigs. New Orleans will once again be flooded. Impact of Alpine Two will be in four hours.

"The third piece, sequentially named Alpine Three, is the smallest piece. It is a little more than a quarter mile in diameter. It will make impact in the area in San Bernadino, California. This hit will contribute to a dust cloud that will block some sunlight for several months. Most current plant life will wilt and die within a few weeks. However, the sky should be clear enough to plant spring crops. Our biggest fear is that the magnitude of the impact will trigger the San Andreas Fault. If this happens, the effects will be catastrophic. We will simply have to wait and see. Impact of Alpine Three will occur in about four and a half hours."

The president took a deep breath and gripped the sides of the podium to steady his trembling small frame before beginning again.

"Over the last month, you may have noticed a recall of American troops from abroad. We felt it was in the best interest of Homeland Security to have our troops home to assist in the aftermath of the Alpine comets. Evacuations of oil rigs are completed, and evacuations of the coastal cities along the Atlantic Seaboard, including the entire state of Florida, will commence as soon as this broadcast is over. If you reside in Florida or a coastal city, you need to go to your nearest bus station or airport within one hour of the conclusion of this broadcast. You will be taken to a safer location. Because of limited space, you are allowed one bag per person.

"At this time, I'm declaring a state of national emergency and signing several executive orders, including, but not limited to, nationalizing the transportation industry. All railroads, cruise ships, trucking lines, bus lines, and airlines are under government control. This will include the nationalizing of all utility companies. All US cargo vessels, oil tankers have been rerouted to a more secure area out of harm's way. They, too, are under federal control. Our naval fleet, including, but not limited to, submarines, aircraft carriers, and battleships, have also been rerouted to a safer location. I have ordered all cruise ships out of areas of immediate danger. Upon their return to our shores, they will be facilitated as hospitals.

"I'm suspending the stock market until further notice. I'm freezing all prices and all wages. All public servants—such as doctors, firefighters, and police officers—will be expected to continue to serve their communities to the best of their abilities.

"The company known as Walmart is now under government contract. This is one of the largest and best organized distribution centers in the world. We will utilize their skills and resources to better serve the American people.

"To confirm rumors of the past, there are several underground military bases across the United States. Members of my cabinet and the joint chiefs are currently en route to a secure location. Carefully selected teachers, doctors, and scientists have already been evacuated. Please understand, we don't believe their lives are of more importance than anyone else's, but we have to ensure we can maintain our continuity of life.

"After the Alpine comets have hit and imminent danger has passed, tent cities will be set up outside every military base. Supplies will be delivered and distributed from Red Cross and Salvation Army stations, as well as all Walmart Supercenters.

"This is not a perfect plan, and not everyone will escape or survive. And I'm sure some will be left behind. This is all we have and the best we can do. As your president, I intend to do everything in my power to provide help and hope to the American people. I implore every American to be a Good Samaritan. Do what you can to help your neighbors. At this time, I would like to say that I welcome any help from other countries. In the past, the US has given help to countries in need. I hope we can now count on our friends to help us in our time of need. Therefore, with that said, any foreign country that lends aid will be given first priority in any future debt forgiveness. I would like to announce that Fort Leavenworth, Kansas, is the new acting national capital.

"Crimes against man and property will be dealt with swiftly and harshly. If you choose to abandon your home, please mark it with a red flag. This will indicate that it's vacant.

"The United States will unfortunately lose a large portion of our population in just a few hours. We have never known the kind of death and destruction that we are about to witness. However, life will continue. The effects of the Alpine comets will be felt for years to come. My heart goes out to each and every one of you. My thoughts and prayers are with each of you. May God be with you."

The president briefly straightened his tie, turned, and disappeared.

I sat deathly quiet for just a moment, then jumped up. My mind was swimming. I wasn't sure which way to run first. My first thought was to my girls. I had to go get my girls from school. They would be scared to death. I picked up the phone to call the school just as the phone rang, and I inadvertently threw it up in the air like it was a hot potato. I quickly retrieved the phone, and the school was sending out a prerecorded message saying they were loading the buses up and would have the children home within the hour. I hung up, and the phone rang again. "Hello," I cried.

"Ash, it's me. Did you hear? Did you see the news?" Dallas exclaimed in a frantic voice I had never heard.

"Yes, I saw it. The school just called and said they would have the children home within the hour. Dal, what do I do? Are you coming home?" I could feel the tears of panic creeping into my eyes.

"Listen to me carefully. When I got to the office this morning, they sent me to meet with a client in Houston. I'm in the impact zone. I am trying to make it home, but the traffic is already terrible, and it's only going to get worse. People are already showing signs of panic and distress. I'm doing my best to make it to you and the kids. However, if I don't make it, you still have another option. If worse comes to worst, you can always go to my mother's home in Montana. Whatever you do, don't wait for me to show up. Once it is safe to travel, leave. I'll get home when I can. I'm going to try to check on Marcus. Leave me a note telling me where you are and where you are going. Do you understand that?" Dallas was out of breath, and

15

I could hear the engine of the car as it revved up. I knew he had the needle buried in an attempt to get home.

"What do I do, Dal? Tell me what to do," I pleaded. I was scared to death. He was right in the area that was going to be hit. He was right in harm's way. How far away would he get?"

"Get some necessities together. Box up food, toiletries, batteries, clothes. Remember, it's likely to be colder with the dust cloud. You will need warmer clothes. Pack up utility stuff, like rope, a shovel, toolboxes, and get the hurricane lamps and any extra lamp oil, things like that, anything you can think of. Go to an ATM and get cash out as soon as you can. I know it's a lot to put on you. Can you handle all this?"

"Yes, I can handle it. I just want you to be careful and get out of there."

"I'll be careful, honey. But promise me, if I don't make it back home, don't wait for me. Head to Montana and get to my family. It's the White Pine Lodge in Browning. They will protect you, and the kids will have food and shelter. Please promise me. I will be right behind you and will catch up. I will find you. Do you understand?"

My heart was breaking. "Yes, I understand. I will get it all done, and we will leave once it is safe and the roads open. I love you." The tears began to fall now as the severity of the whole ordeal was creeping. People were going to die, a lot of people, and he might be one of them.

"I have to call my mom and tell her we may be coming before the lines get jammed. I love you so much, and I will see you soon. Remember, no matter what happens, I love you and I will find you. Do you hear me? I will find you. I love you, Ash." And just like that, the line went dead.

I dropped to my knees and had a brief private moment in a fit of tears. I clung to the phone as if it were a lifeline. My stomach was heavy with a feeling that it was the last time I would hear his tender voice. I sat quietly, trying to soak in everything that was going on and what I had to do. I quickly pulled myself together when I heard the front door open and the fast-approaching pitter-patter footsteps of my girls. Obviously, all the disaster drills at school had paid off.

They were home a lot sooner than I expected. I looked up and saw the fear in their faces.

Harley stated in rampant speech, "They let us watch the news, Mama. Are we going to die?"

My youngest, Kat, looked up with wonder and fear in her eyes.

I looked at my two angels. I pulled them both over to the sofa and hugged and kissed them. I was fighting back my own tears to soothe theirs. I knew that I couldn't allow them to see me break down. I had no choice but to hold it together. I had a lot of work to do and very little time to do it in.

"I need you both to listen to me carefully. Something very bad is going to happen. I need you girls to be good and work with me. I have some work to do to prepare, and I need you to stay quiet. I will explain everything later, but first, we have to go to the bank."

I got my girls gathered up and into the van. I could already hear the horns honking with road rage on the highway. I made sure the girls were buckled up and began to drive.

People were insane. Most were driving way too fast. They were cutting one another off and pulling out in front of other cars. Finger gestures were flying freely. I waited for my light to turn green then went. I was almost broadsided by a large truck that ran the red light. He honked, cursing at me, shaking his fist in my direction, as if it were my fault.

I pulled into the bank. The lines at the drive-through seemed too long, so I left Harley and Kat in the van. I instructed Harley to lock the doors and open them only for me, then went into the bank. I knew how much money we had in the bank, but I wasn't sure how much to take out. I didn't want to leave Dallas without any resources. I waited patiently for my turn at the teller's window. I was able to see the van and kept a vigilant eye on my kids, who were under orders to honk the horn if they absolutely needed me. They must have been scared to death because neither of them had said a word since they left the house. I could see that Harley was on her cell phone, probably talking to the little boy she considered her boyfriend. I could only guess as to what was running through their little imaginations.

"How can I help you?" the teller asked courteously.

My attention popped back to the moment. "I would like to get some cash, please." I handed the withdraw slip to the teller. She fiddled on the computer and began to count out the money. I would leave two thousand in the bank in case Dallas needed it. I took out six thousand. Hopefully, that would be enough to see him through. I would have to be diligent. I remembered what the president said about using a barter system. I made a mental note to pack extra stuff to be able to barter with.

"Did the kids get home from school okay, Ms. Reese?" the teller asked.

Suddenly, I recognized her. It was my neighbor Mrs. Bradley. Her son was in the same class as Harley. She was stuck here working while her son was home alone. "Yes, Amanda, they got home. Do you want Jimmy to come stay at our house till you get home? How much longer is the bank going to be open?"

Amanda smiled. "My husband is on his way home now. We will only be open for another thirty minutes, then we are shutting down the doors. Thank you for the offer."

"If we can do anything, let us know. Dallas is on his way home. He is coming from Houston. He said the traffic was terrible. I hope he makes it home in time." I felt my voice start to break and swallowed hard.

"Oh, honey, I'm sure he will. If you need anything, just let us know, all right?" She finished counting out the money and put it in an envelope. She reached under the counter and handed me a leather bank envelope that had a lock on it. "Here you go. Take this. You can never to be too careful."

I expressed my gratitude and made my way back to the van. We stopped and filled the van up with gas. Amazingly, there was hardly anyone in line. I pulled into the grocery store. It, too, was oddly quiet. I got the girls out of the van with strict instructions to stay close to me. I got a buggy and allowed Harley to get a second buggy. We hit the water aisle first. That was going to be one of the most important commodities. Next, we hit the canned meat. I wasn't sure how much to buy, but I would rather have too much than not enough. I allowed the girls to pick out a few things they liked to eat. Raviolis were always a big hit with them. Kat talked me into getting a big jar of pickles. I got plenty of dried beans. They were one thing that would last a long time, and we could get several meals from them. We walked up and down every aisle of the store, snatching things of interest. I grabbed whatever I thought we might need. It was like we were starting another household. I glanced up and became more aware of my surroundings. The store was starting to get busy, and I didn't want to be around when people were fighting over the last loaf of bread. I quickly finished up getting a few last-minute split-decision items and went to the checkout line. I got them each a soda and candy bar that Kat had her hopeful eyes on. That kid loved chocolate.

When we got out to the van, two men were verbally assaulting each other over something as trivial as a parking space. I made the girls get into the van and buckle up. I was hoping that neither of the men had a gun. But just in case, I didn't want to stick around to find out. I loaded the groceries quickly, not even bothering to stack them. Wherever they landed was good enough for now. Leaving the shopping cart beside the van, I got in and began to drive. We only lived ten minutes from the store, but it took almost forty-five minutes to drive home. The traffic was getting horrible, and I could only imagine what it was like for Dallas right now.

I pulled into the driveway, unrealistically hoping to see his car. Naturally, I was disappointed. Harley and Kat both helped get the groceries in without being asked. If I weren't already halfway in shock, that alone would have put me there. I usually have to beg them to help me. I was so grateful to be off the road. I had never seen people act in such manners. Panic was setting in, and people were reacting as such. I could only imagine what it was like for Dallas. Nothing had any sense or reason. I guessed the instinct of survival had kicked in. That word stuck in my head. I contemplated the meaning of the word *survival*. That was what we were doing now. From this point forward, no matter what hand fate dealt us, we were no longer living. We were surviving. I hoped.

Once safely inside our home, I called both Harley and Kat into the kitchen. I let them sit at the bar with their candy bar and soda.

I looked at their little faces and had no idea what to say or how to say it.

"There isn't a lot of time for me to go into a lot of detail here, girls, so I am asking that you be understanding and work with me." They both looked at me attentively. I briefly prayed to whatever god was listening to give me strength to get through this without breaking down. "You know what an asteroid is, right?" They both nodded. "Well, there are three coming toward Earth, and they're going to hit us. Two are going to hit land, and one is going to hit the ocean. There is going to be a big wave. A lot of people who live on the coastlines are going to die or be washed out to sea. The second is going to hit around Houston. And the third is going to hit over in California." I knew I sounded harsh and cold and was probably scaring them to death, but I wanted them to grasp the intensity of the situation and make them realize that it was serious. "Now I think we will be pretty safe here. However, the lights are going to go out. We will have to cook outside and use oil lamps to see after the sun goes down. I am going to need you girls to work with me. I have to get some supplies together. I am going to be pretty busy for a while. And, Harley, I may ask you to help me from time to time. Is that understood?" Harley nodded in agreement. "Kat, I need you to get your backpack and put some toys in it. Only pack the special things you want to keep close to you. Do you understand?" She nodded. Her little wide eyes seemed to wobble in their sockets. I could tell they were scared. I hugged them tightly. "We are going to be fine, girls. You just have to do what I tell you when I tell you. It could be a matter of life and death."

Soon, Kat was headed off to her princess room to gather her belongings. It was then that Harley turned to me. "Mama," she said.

"Yes, baby, what is it?" At this point, I was prepared for almost anything. Harley had never been the brightest crayon in the box. I never knew what to expect of her.

"What about Daddy D.? Is he coming home?" That was Harley's nickname for Dallas. When Dallas and I had first gotten together, she just called him Mr. Dallas. Now Dallas had been more of a father than her biological father ever was; she didn't feel like it was enough.

We encouraged her to call him whatever she was comfortable with. She searched her heart for about a week and finally came up with Daddy D., and they were both comfortable with it.

I knew she could see my facial expressions, and I didn't want her to see my dismay. "Honey, Daddy D. is on his way home from Houston right now. But there is a lot of traffic. Hopefully, he will be here in time." Harley nodded, showing her understanding. "Now I want you to do the same thing I told Kat to do. I want you to get a backpack, something you can carry, and put all your special things in it. Remember, we probably won't have electricity, so don't pack anything electronic. Just anything you want to save." Harley nodded. At that moment, she seemed a little more mature. Maybe the intensity in the air was making her understand that the events transpiring were crucial.

I spent the next half hour quickly digging out winter clothes, oil lamps, and extra oil. I got the sleeping bags and camping gear. Our camping gas stove was in need of a good cleaning, but for now, it would have to do. I was lucky in my thinking that we had enough gas for the stove was correct. I knew I wouldn't need them right away, but I wanted them handy. I took the back seat out of the van to make more room. My mind was spinning in every direction. There was so much I needed to get.

I grabbed a backpack of my own and packed my special jewelry box that held my special treasures. I packed all our photos in a water-tight container. I tried to stay busy and not to think about Dallas too much. I feared I would go certifiably insane if I thought of him out on the road. I sent Harley to the bathrooms with a container. I told her to pack all toilet paper, soaps, razors, and other toiletries, even the little ones we had taken from hotels over the years. I would, of course, go behind her to make sure she didn't skip anything. Kat was playing in the living room, watching what would prove to be one of her last cartoons in a very long time.

I was packing food into containers when the phone rang, startling me so fiercely that I dropped everything I was holding. Harley was first to the phone as usual. I had stopped trying to beat her to the phone a long time ago. Harley talked for a few minutes and handed the phone to Kat. Kat kept her eyes on the television and muttered a few yeses and nos. "I love you, Meme. See you soon." Kat gave the phone back to Harley.

Harley, with the phone to her ear, simply stated, "Okay, hold on." She paused. "I love you too, Meme." Harley handed me the phone and went out on the porch.

I took the phone. "Hello."

"Ashley, it's Mom. Honey, are you doing okay?"

"Yes, Mama, we are doing fine. I'm just trying to get things packed up. What are you guys going to do?" It was killing me to know that I could not spend a few minutes with my mother. I was wishing I had time to go see my mama and daddy.

"Well, we have some stuff packed up and in the garage. Max has gotten most of his house packed up. Monica is frazzled. She is not holding it together very well at all. She is crying and don't want to put Dannie down. She sat for an hour just holding him and rocking him. When he fell asleep, she did manage to get all of his little stuff packed."

My brother Max was nine years younger than me. When we were younger, we had fought like cats and dogs. Max was your typical annoying little brother. He thought he was as big as I was and wanted to be on my skirt tail every time I turned around. I found it extremely exasperating trying to come up with new ways to ditch him whenever my friends came over. Once, when Max was about five, I tried to deter him from wanting to spend time with me. My best friend and I had pulled him into my bedroom and put makeup and a dress on him, then took pictures. Oddly enough, we all had a good time with it. It was one of Max's earliest memories, and he still had the photo. He held on to it for sentimental reasons. In his mind, it was the first time I acted like I liked him. Over the years, we had both matured. We were very close and saw each other regularly. Now he was a strapping six-foot-tall, clean-cut, good-looking man who made a good living working at the local mill.

Monica had been my babysitter when the girls were younger. She and Max had met through me and hit it off from the beginning. She was a tall, slender-built girl with reddish-blond hair. They were married two years later. I couldn't have been happier with Max's choice of bride. Even though there was a big age difference, I always held Monica as a close friend. I relied on her and confided in her a lot during the divorce. I wanted to be there and help her get through this. Monica had an intense fear of thunderstorms. I could only imagine what her state of mind was at this time.

"What is Dallas doing?" my mother inquired, interrupting my private thoughts.

I hesitated for a moment and sighed deeply. "He is trying to get home, Mama. He was sent to Houston this morning. He called right after the broadcast and told me that he was on his way home. Traffic was bad, and he didn't know if he would make it in time." My voice broke off. I was choking back the tears. "The cell phone lines are jammed right now. I can't get through to him to even know how close he is."

"Oh, honey, I know Dallas. He will make it," she said reassuringly. "I wanted to call and tell you something, Ashley," she said in a somber voice.

"What is it, Mama?"

"I just wanted to say that I love you. I am so proud of you for being so strong. You are one of the strongest women I have ever known. You remind me so much of your grandmother. She would be proud of you. You take everything thrown at you and deal with it. I just wanted to say that if ever you are lost, just pray, honey, and you will know what to do."

I was quiet for a moment. I didn't want to get into a religious debate with my mother when there was a comet on its way to destroy life as we knew it. I was in no mood to endure a lecture on prayer. I thought it best to humor her at this point. The fact that God would provide, and all we had to do was have faith. I couldn't help but think to myself no matter how sacrilegious it was that if there were a god and if he did provide, he would let my future husband walk through the door at that very moment. I couldn't help but look at the door; it didn't open. I simply replied, "I know, Mama."

"You're tough. You're a survivor. You have proven that time and time again. You are going to do just fine. As a kid, you went hunting and fishing. You have it in you. You just have to believe in yourself as much as I believe in you. You have to for the sake of my grandbabies."

I sighed heavily. "That's the only thing keeping me going right now, Mama." I told my mother of our plans to possibly travel to Montana, and she was in approval. We exchanged a few more pleasantries before we said our final "I love you." I briefly spoke with my father, mainly just stating that we loved each other. We ended the conversation not by saying goodbye; instead, we said, "See you later." The plan was, when it was safe and the dust had settled, I would go check on my brother. Then Max and I would go check on our parents together. It all seemed so trivial in the grand scheme of things, but I went along with it, making notes. I knew I would never remember everything.

I could feel my heart racing. I looked at the clock; it was now 4:30 p.m. I only had maybe forty-five minutes left at most. Time was going by too fast. Kat was still watching cartoons. Harley was outside trying to reach her father on the cell phone. I knew she was worried about him. She knew the risk of living in New Orleans. God could flood that city with a teardrop. I wasn't totally heartless toward Aaron; I did hope he survived.

Throwing a bag around my shoulders, I took off and practically ran upstairs, double-checking the bathrooms. Harley had done a great job packing all the toiletries. The nurse inside me took over. I grabbed my big first aid kit, which was actually a large tackle box. It held all our household medications. I always had the essentials on hand. I went to the medicine cabinet and emptied it into the bag. Antibiotics would probably come in handy at some point. I even grabbed a bottle of nerve pills. Normally, I would have overlooked it. I had tried to stop smoking a few months ago. This particular exploit was one that I wasn't successful at. The doctor had prescribed them to me for my nerves. I only took a few but never liked how they made me feel. With the stress of the current state of affairs, I may be wishing I had them. At this point, it may be hazardous to everyone's health if I stopped smoking.

I went into my bedroom. I already packed clothes and had them waiting by the back door to put in the van. I rummaged through my closet. Looking up, I saw a little wooden lockbox. I hadn't thought about this thing in years. I opened the box, revealing a 9 mm semi-automatic pistol. My dad had given me this as a special gift when I graduated nursing school. I had only fired it a few times and had plenty of ammunition. I closed the box and shoved it down into my shoulder bag. I hoped I would never have to use it. I headed back downstairs to get some of the stuff packed into the van before I ran out of time. Briefly checking on the girls and knowing they were okay, I headed to the van.

I stacked the supplies in the van. Looking up at the garage door, I had an epiphany. If we lost power, I wouldn't be able to get the garage door open. The van would be stuck inside the garage. I was grateful for the common sense that had kicked in even though it baffled me as to where it came from. I fetched my keys out of my pocket, opened the garage door, and pulled the van out into the middle of the drive. I pushed my pistol as far under the driver's seat as it would go. As I got out of the van, I saw Harley running toward me holding out her phone. "Daddy wants to talk to you. Kat and I have both already talked to him." I could tell that she had been crying.

"Okay, baby. Go check on Kat for me." One of the last things I wanted to do was to talk to Aaron. Harley nodded and disappeared inside the house. I put the phone up to my ear. "Hello."

"Ashley, we are still in New Orleans. There was no way we were going to get out in time. I just wanted to say that." He paused. "Well, I'm sorry for everything I have ever done that hurt you. We know our fate here. I just wanted to say that I was sorry for everything and that you have done a great job with the girls. They…" His voice was breaking.

In a small way, I felt sorry for him, but I didn't want to stay on the phone and chitchat either. "Aaron, I don't have long because I'm trying to get things packed up. We are going to Montana, to the reservation. Dallas was sent to Houston this morning, so he is still trying to get home. He probably won't make it in time. But we are supposed to meet up at the reservation. His family has property there. We will be safe. I wish there was some way you could get out of there for the girls' sake."

"I know. Me too. I'm not sure what is going to happen or how it's going to happen. Just…just always tell my girls that I love them," he stuttered. I could tell he was crying now.

"I will, Aaron. Try to be safe, won't you?" Even though I hated him for everything he had put me and the girls through, a small part of me couldn't help but feel sorry for him, and an even bigger part felt pain for my girls. They were about to lose their father. One part of me felt that all his bad deeds were catching up to him all at once. He was sitting in his little apartment waiting to die.

"I will. Just take care of my girls. Bye, Ashley." Then the line went dead.

I shoved the phone in my pocket and went into the house. Kat was whining about the television going out. I looked up to see a blue screen flashing with an annoying sound. It was the alert system. The news abruptly came on. A shaken anchor was at his desk.

"Good evening. We have an update on the Alpine comets that are headed toward us. We will be on the air with you as long as we safely can. There may be some interruptions in our broadcast, but please bear with us. Several radio stations will also continue broadcasting news and conducting briefings as well. The first piece has made impact. Please understand, this was a small piece that was dislodged from the main asteroid when our rockets hit it this morning. We were told that it landed in the ocean where it was expected to hit, which is located off the coast of Haiti. We have lost communications in that area, but our last word was from a news helicopter that simply stated, and I quote, 'It's all gone.' We are trying to get word on the wave that we know is coming."

Harley interrupted my concentration. "Come on, Kat. Let's go get our radios and flashlights. We can take batteries out of our other toys." Harley went upstairs. Kat looked at me, waiting for approval.

"You can go. Just hurry up and come right back here." Kat nodded and was chasing after her sister.

I turned back to the television.

"We want to talk about safety for a moment. It is a good idea to be on the lowest level of your home. If you're right on the coastline, then you want to be on the highest level. If you have a life jacket, put it on. Turn off all natural and propane gas lines. Our government is asking that you write you Social Security number on your arm. It sounds like a morbid thing, but it will be easier to identify." The screen went black, interrupting the reporter.

I stood up and looked at the time. I scrambled upstairs and helped the girls get a few things. They both ended up with another shoulder bag full of stuff. I instructed them to get downstairs and see if the television came back on. At least that would keep them busy. Harley took her small handheld radio and shoved it down into the bag. I ran to the kitchen. The house was all electric, so I didn't have anything gas to turn off. I had left the garage door open. There was a cooler to put cold stuff in. Luckily, we had bags of ice in the freezer. Every time the ice maker was full, we dumped it into a bag in the freezer. All the canned food was packed and in the van along with the camping gear. My first aid and medical stuff was all packed. I heard Harley scream at the top of her lungs. The sound pierced my thoughts. I spun around like I had been shot. She was pointing outside.

"You can see it coming."

Dusk was approaching; the sky looked dark and ominous. In the middle of the darkness was a bright light. A bright fireball with swirling colors of red and orange was hurtling toward us. Trailing behind was a tail of black smoke with even blacker specks of rocky debris. It was traveling in the east sky. Harley was breathing fast; I could almost feel her heart beating. She reached for my hand, a gesture she hadn't done in a long time. Kat was soon beside me, holding on to the back of my pants leg, taking a peek. "What do we do, Mama?"

We all stood staring, unable to turn away. It was truly a beautiful sight. I had difficulty understanding how something so beautiful was going to leave nothing but doom and destruction in its wake. We were watching the world as we knew it end. Things would never be the same. In this very instant, their father was facing his impending death. My fiancé was still on the road and his exact whereabouts, as well as his mortality, was unknown. I hugged my girls closely. The wind started blowing, light at first, then stronger and stronger, till it was a full gust of at least sixty miles per hour.

"Get inside now!" I yelled as reality hit me. We ran inside the house. I purposely left the front door open. I wanted to see it happen. I didn't want to miss any part of this tragedy. "Get under the table now!" Amazingly, my normally unruly children did exactly what I told them to do, grabbing their backpacks and shoulder bags along the way. The table was well-built and made of oak. Hopefully, it would be strong enough. I crawled under the table with my girls. "I want you girls to put on your headphones." I didn't want them to hear anything that would produce nightmares later on. They fished around in their bag, and each found their headphones. They put the music as loud as they could stand it.

The television was still black. I knew that I would not be receiving another news report anytime soon. "I'll be right back." I motioned for the girls to stay put. I went to the door to take a peek. I could still see the rock of doom. It seemed closer to the ground and traveling very fast. I watched it, horrified, till it was gone. It had hit. A bright flash of light made me turn my head and shield my eyes. I glanced at my girls. Harley, who had tears streaming down her face, sadly hung her head down.

I stood there staring into the skyline. I was beginning to think we were going to get lucky and not feel any of the effects of this disaster. I quickly found out that I was wrong. Staring out, I felt a strong breeze coming from the direction of the impact. The cosmic blast was definitely going to reach us. I began to run across the living room toward the table. The initial blast knocked me off my feet and pushed me forward into the table. My chest crushed against it, knocking the air from my lungs. I lay on the floor gasping for air. Opening my eyes, I saw Harley was looking at me, petrified. Kat was hiding her face onto her knees. I struggled to my knees and crawled toward my kids. I was holding my chest with one arm. I lay under the table and held Harley and Kat close to me. I could still see through the hole that was once my front door. The door itself was gone, leaving a gaping void of hinges and exposed wood. I could faintly hear people screaming. I didn't know if it was from pain or fear. My gasping slowed as the air flowed more easily.

I sat up, pulling Kat into my lap; she was crying now. I held her with one hand and held Harley close to me with the other. I could hear a distant roaring sound that gradually got louder and seemingly closer. The sound grew to the point that Harley and Kat covered their ears. Soon, another blast of air tore through the house. I heard a ripping sound. Harley screamed in fear. Holding her closer, I kissed the top of her head, attempting to soothe her in some small way. Kat threw her arms around my neck. She was shaking. I kissed her too. I had no idea how to soothe my kids, to calm their fears, especially when I myself was scared to death.

The roaring suddenly slacked off then stopped altogether. The wind died down to a steady gusty breeze of about thirty miles per hour. I looked up abruptly. Was this it? Was it over? I looked through what was left of our doorway. There was a cloud that resembled a mushroom cloud from an atomic blast, the kind we would see on television. I moved Kat from my lap. "I have to go see if that's all, honey. I'll be right back."

"Mom, wait! Please wait just a few more minutes," Harley pleaded. "It may not be safe yet." To appease her, I waited. Time meant nothing; I had no idea how much time had already passed.

Finally, without any more blasting air or deafening roar, I crawled out from under the table. I walked softly to the doorway and peeked out, not knowing what to expect. Looking down, I saw the porch was detached about two feet from the rest of the house. I stepped widely onto the porch, testing each step for security. I rubbed my chest as the air flowed freely through my lungs. I had no pains on either side, so I assumed there were no broken ribs.

Our home was one of the few left standing. I glimpsed around the yard and saw a few things I recognized. As I looked closer, I observed Harley's dresser in the yard. "How in the hell…" I walked down the cracked and chipped brick steps. Once in the yard, I looked up at the house. I gasped and covered my mouth with my hand. The entire roof was gone, exposing the second floor. Things were strewn about. Curtains flapped freely where windows once where. I shook my head in disbelief. *My house…my home…it's totaled!* I thought to myself, not being able to force the words out. Only a short time ago, I was working in my yard, admiring my splendor.

The ageless verse crossed my mind, *The Lord giveth, and he taketh away.* My knees got weak, and I collapsed. I braced myself up with my hands. I felt myself getting mad. Anger moved like a wave washing through my body. I wanted to hit, kick, punch, and scream. I felt like a time bomb ready to explode. Grabbing a double handful of earth, I threw it toward the house. "God dammit!" I yelled as the anger found a portal of escape. I felt tears welling in my eyes. I rested on my knees and pounded my fist on the ground. I sat up on my knees and stopped crying suddenly. I felt something strange. The ground itself seemed to be slightly vibrating. "I didn't hit it that hard," I comically said to myself. I stood up thinking of everything it could be, *The tsunami, pipelines?* My mind snapped. "Earthquake," I allowed the word to escape my lips. It was a small simple word with so much meaning. The asteroid hit with such force that it burrowed into Earth's surface. Not only was there a tsunami wave that would flood the entire coast but the impact might have also triggered an earthquake, opening fault lines. With a comet this size, it could open faults that had been dormant for centuries.

I bolted back into the house, jumping over the gap. Harley saw my expression. "What? What is it?"

"There may be an earthquake," I explained.

"What? Isn't it bad enough that a big rock just fell out of the sky and killed my daddy? What else is going to happen?" Harley was on the verge of tears again.

I started toward her to console her when I heard a distinctive *plink,* the sound that occurs when metal lightly taps another metal. I stopped to listen closely. *Plink.*

"What is that sound?" I asked.

"It's Dallas's Chinese thingy. It has already lost two of the little ball bearings. I guess it's falling apart too. Why should it be any different?" she said sarcastically, folding her arms across her chest.

"What?" I didn't fully understand her. She had always had a hard time trying to explain things so other people could understand them. Then it hit me—the didong yi. I went over to the vase of doom. Four balls had already been expelled. As I watched, another dropped. *Plink.* This made no sense. The balls were supposed to drop in the direction of the quake. At that point, the remaining three balls were expelled simultaneously and went directly into their toad's awaiting mouth.

"Oh my god…" I looked up, understanding its meaning. "It's everywhere." I understood that this comet wasn't considered a global killer. However, it was conceivable that with three impacts so close together, a massive earthquake was imminent.

I looked at Harley, who was still crying. Grabbing her shoulders, I shook her gently. "Honey, there is nothing we can do about it but endure it and survive it. Now I'm going to need your help. Open the back door going into the garage and all the windows." I went over to the table and tried to lure Kat out. She was staring forward and rocking back and forth. "Kat, Kat, can you hear me?" She didn't answer me as I cautiously looked her over. There were no signs of injury anywhere. I looked into her eyes. I had seen this before. The lights were on, but no one was home. "Oh my god, you're in shock." As a defense mechanism, her little body had shut down. This was her way of dealing with the trauma. I wrapped my arms around my baby and dragged her out from under the table. I carried her to the couch and wrapped her in a thin throw blanket.

"Okay, doors and windows are open. What's wrong with her?" Harley said, coming back into the room and motioning toward Kat.

"She's in shock. I need you to sit here with your arm around her, okay? I have to move the table."

"And you plan to do this by yourself? Mom, it took four grown men to move it in there," Harley reminded me with a little attitude behind it.

"I know, but I have to try. I want to get the table by the door so if the quake does come, we can be safe under the table but beside a door in case the rest of the top floor comes down on us." I remembered seeing the exposed walls of our second story. That seemed like a long time ago instead of just a few minutes.

"What do you mean the rest of the second story?"

31

"I mean the roof is missing, Harley. You can see later. Right now, I'm trying to keep us from dying. Now sit down and keep your sister warm." Harley did as she was told.

I knew I would have more luck pushing than pulling. I grabbed the side of the table and began to push. I pushed till my face was red with strain. The table only moved inches. Suddenly, I found myself wishing I had a smaller house. If I did, I wouldn't have far to move it. "Damn English oak. Come on, *move*, you big bastard!" I groaned, pushing. The table began to slide. My face started turning red. My legs were shaking. I closed my eyes knowing the direction I had to go. I grunted, almost growling, against the table. I was doing well enough to be able to take a few steps with it. My face felt as if it would explode. I could feel the veins in my neck straining against the skin. I wasn't stopping, in fear that I would never get it started again. It was steadily moving, then suddenly stopped. I looked up, adjusting my eyes. I was seeing stars from the strain I had put on myself. I had done it, though my legs were still shaking.

"Mom, the floor, look," Harley sounded terrified.

I looked down. The floor was visibly quivering. I could hear a slight growling sound that seemed like it was coming from the ground. "Harley, get the bags and get under the table!" I had quickly determined that my legs weren't shaking from the strain; it was the entire floor that was quivering madly.

Harley ran toward the table, grabbed the bags, and dove under it. I ran to the couch to retrieve Kat. I snatched her up, blanket and all, and ran back to the table. I slid under it with Kat in my arms. She curled up in a tight ball on my lap. Covering her with the blanket, her little body continued to shake. Tears streaked down her face while no sound escaped her lips. Harley rested on her knees, leaning forward, covering her head with her hands. I hugged them both as tightly as I could. Tears began rolling down my cheeks. I could hear people screaming again. The distinct sounds of explosions echoed in the air. Drywall was falling off the walls and ceiling in chunks. The floorboards shook violently, looking like giant teeth trying to bite us. I jumped at the sound of glass shattering around us. Harley let out a piercing scream when she was hit by the falling shards of glass.

"Hang on, baby. It will be over in a minute!" I hollered over the growling roar, praying I wasn't lying. I cupped my hand over the bleeding cut on her arm and applied pressure by pulling her toward me, continuing to hold her. She was crying uncontrollably. "It's going to be okay." I didn't know if she could hear me, but I needed to hear it too, even if it was my own voice. I buried my face down closer to my kids. "It will be over in a minute." I didn't want to see anymore. I heard glass shattering, cracking, crumbling, and ripping sounds coming from all around me. It seemed like the house itself had come alive in reaction to the events unfolding around us. I didn't pray for death, but if death was going to find us, it was going to find us together, and with a little luck, it would come quickly.

After what seemed like forever, the shaking eased back to a slight rumble. The rumbling faded to a growl, then it was gone. Outside, the screams were fading as well. It was almost dark. I knew I had to get myself together and take care of a few things in order to make us safe for the night.

"Harley, do you still have your flashlight?"

She was sniffling. "Yeah, why?"

"Because, baby, I need it for a few minutes. We have to get out of this house or what's left of it, and I have to see where we are going to spend the night," I explained as Harley produced her light. I slid Kat from my lap and onto the floor where she cried and reclaimed her fetal position. As I crawled out, I could no longer see the hole that was now the front door or even where it was supposed to be. The exit was now blocked by something massive. I retreated back to our stronghold.

"What is it?" Harley asked, still holding her arm. Blood was oozing between her fingers, and she continued to apply pressure.

"The front door is blocked. We can't get out that way. I will have to go out the back and go around." I pointed to the back door that was now beside our oak fortress. The back door was opened halfway off its hinges and housed no glass panes. This was probably the glass that cut Harley. I looked back at Harley, who had lain down next to her sister. "I will be right back. Just let me see what is going on. I want to get you somewhere safe, and then we can get your arm bandaged." I paused. The wind cooled my tearstained cheeks. "Harley, I know your arm hurts. You're being brave and a very big help. Just keep applying pressure on your arm, and I will be back in just a minute."

"Watch out for the glass," Harley warned me.

I nodded and stepped cautiously over the glass. I found my way around the house. Thankfully, the van was still there and in one piece. I laid down the driver's seat. I had one oil lamp ready so I could see to bandage Harley's arm. I didn't want to waste the van battery, and the dome light wouldn't give me what I needed to properly dress a wound. I dug out a few blankets so we wouldn't be cold through the night. The lamp was the only thing we had to be extremely careful with. When I felt like I had things ready, I ran back to my girls.

Harley screamed and jumped. "Oh, Mama, I'm glad it's you." She leaned forward and hugged me tight.

"Who else would it be?" I said jokingly.

"I heard a growling sound. I thought it may be a dog." She gave a small giggle as she pointed to the glass. "It's not like we could shut the door."

"A growling sound, huh." I gave her the look of nonsense. "Come on, let's get you out of here." I took her good arm and helped her up. "Watch your head, baby." My biggest fear was that the growling sound she heard was the remainder of the house that was inevitably going to come down. Once Harley was safely outside, I turned to get Kat. I picked up her body and held her close, scooting on one knee toward the doorway. I could feel the glass piercing through my pants and prickling my skin. I winced at the slight pain but never stopped moving. I had to get my baby out of there. Harley reached back and grabbed the bags and first aid kit, then followed me to the van.

She opened the driver's side door at my request and without question. I laid Kat in the driver's seat and covered her up. "You will be safe now, baby. Just try to get some sleep. "Harley, get in the back seat so I can look at your arm." I went around and got in behind her.

The lamp illuminated the van very well. The cut wasn't deep enough for stitches. There didn't seem to be any glass remaining in her arm. I cleaned it, then applied sterile strips to close the wound and wrapped it up. I gave Harley a pain reliever and kissed her. "You did good today. I'm very proud of you." I hung my head down but continued, "Harley, I don't know what lies ahead for us. I don't know what is going to happen to the world or to us. I do know that I am going to need your help and understanding. We are going to have to work together if we are going to make it through this. I love you, girl." I reached out and hugged my daughter tightly.

When our embrace broke, Harley climbed over into the passenger seat. "I love you too. What about Kat? What's wrong with her, Mama?" She actually seemed concerned over her annoying little sister.

"I'm going to pull her back here with me for the night. She is in shock, which means she got so scared her body shut down. She will be okay. It is just her way of dealing with the trauma of everything." I truly hoped I was right. I lifted Kat up and laid her on my chest as I lay on the long seat of the van. It was extremely uncomfortable, but I held her close to my chest and covered us both up. I was grateful that we were all safe. I extinguished the lamp and shut the door. I whispered to Kat, "It's going to be okay now, honey. We are just having a really bad day. But we are safe now." She buried her face in my neck. I could feel her hot little tears dampening my hair. "Shh," I hushed her, "it's all right, baby. You're safe." I consoled her till I somehow drifted off to sleep.

CHAPTER 2

I DREAMED OF DALLAS and our wedding that now most likely wasn't going to happen. His face lit up as he watched me make my descent down the aisle. Lifting my arms, I reached out for him. We joined hands and lovingly stared into each other's eyes. His face changed; his skin went pale and cracked. It reminded me of an old porcelain doll. His usually plump lips turned black and began to crumble. Pieces of his face began to crack, chip, and fall away. His hands soon followed, crumbling into mine. I jumped back and began shaking my head. "No! No!" I repeated. Was this a premonition? Was Dallas dead? "No!" I awakened by sitting straight up. My panic breathing quickened as I looked around.

"Mama, wake up!" Harley shouted as she shook my arm.

"What?" I looked around in an attempt to reorient myself.

"It's happening again," Harley cried out.

Then I noticed the shaking. It wasn't as strong as the original quake. "It will be all right. Just hold on to something." I held on to the sides of the seat. I noticed Harley did the same. Looking down, Kat was behind the driver's seat with her head resting on her knees. She rocked back and forth, trying to block out everything else around her. Although violent, the shaking didn't last long, then everything went back to the same stillness.

"What was that, Mama?" Harley inquired.

"It was an aftershock. We will have them off and on, honey. It is normal to have aftershocks after an earthquake." I secretly hoped we wouldn't have very many. "It's okay now." I sat up and rubbed my eyes.

Harley was quiet for a few minutes. It seemed for once she was at a loss for words. "You were having a nightmare." Harley moved to the console between the front seats of the van and looked up at me.

"Yeah, I was. I was just dreaming. It was just a dream." I looked out the window. The sun was a shadowed red glow rising in the east sky, the dust and debris left behind by the comets still lingering. Kat was awake but cowering on the floor behind the driver's seat. She stared straight ahead now, only occasionally blinking.

"What are we going to do now, Mama?" Harley sniped.

"I don't know yet, Harley! Give me time to wake up! I have to figure out a few things," I snapped at her. Reaching for my purse that I placed in the van earlier, I retrieved my cigarettes.

I climbed out of the van, lit up a cigarette, and fished Harley's cell phone out of my pocket. Inhaling deeply, I savored the sweet nicotine as I looked at the cell phone. The time displayed was 7:30 a.m. I didn't need to be psychic to know what it was going to say when I tried to make a call. It didn't keep me from trying it. I found Dallas's number and hit dial. I looked down with hopeful eyes, then my physic mind was confirmed as the words "No Service" displayed across the screen. "Worthless piece of shit technology." I tossed the cell phone into the van, not caring where it landed.

Harley's head rested on her knees. She had been really good through everything so far.

"How is your arm, kiddo?"

"I think I'll live. It doesn't hurt very much anymore." She paused and looked up at me. "I don't want to get on your nerves, but how long do we have to wait before we go to Uncle Max's house?"

I put my arm around her. "You're not getting on my nerves, baby. You have done very well. I appreciate everything you have done and for not giving me a hard time. I love you, baby." I leaned over and kissed her on the forehead. "The truth is, I have no idea what to do next. I'm as lost as a white goose in a snowstorm." We took in deep breaths and sighed, then giggled at each other.

"Mama, I have to tell you something. Please don't get mad." Harley looked at me with hopeful eyes.

"What is it, Harley?" Lord only knows what this kid was going to tell me. With Harley, you could never be sure.

"I don't want to annoy you or press my luck." She paused. "But I really have to pee."

I laughed and hugged her close. "You know, I think I do too. Let's go get a place ready."

I quickly dug through the van and found a roll of toilet paper. I got Kat by the hand and coerced her out of the van. We walked to the back of the house. I found a five-gallon bucket and placed the bucket behind the small toolshed. We took turns using the bucket. I found a small shovel and dug a hole. When we were through, I emptied the waste into the hole and covered it up.

"I will fix up a better spot later." I paused and looked at my girls. They looked dirty and tired despite the night's sleep. However, if their sleep was anything like mine, I could rightfully understand why they looked so tired. I clapped my hands to get their attention. "Okay, girls, first things first, let's find you something to eat for breakfast." We walked in a line back to the van. I opened the back of the van and found a box of cereal. "The milk is still in the house—" I glanced back toward the ruble that was once our home. "You will have to eat it without milk for now." Harley was taking a bowl and getting a juice box.

I looked around the van, and Kat had moved to the doorway and had her little shoeless feet dangling. At this point, I had no idea where the child's shoes were. "Harley, stay here and give me a moment with Kat." I made my way over to Kat. I felt like I was sneaking up on her. One false move and she was going to bolt like a scared rabbit. I eased down beside her. "You know, we have already gone through a lot, honey. I don't know what is running through your mind. I know you have to be thinking about your daddy. And the fact is, we don't know anything yet, baby. We don't know what has happened, and we don't know what the condition of anything is. I know you are worried, scared, and sad, and that's perfectly okay to feel that way. However, you still have to eat and drink. You have to live. You have to go on. What would happen if your daddy comes to find you and he finds you sick because you won't eat? You have to do what you think will make people proud. You have to keep going for them, honey. You can't give up, and you can't give in." I had no idea how to convey to her the importance of going on. We couldn't then let our loved ones die in vain. How was I supposed to explain this to a nine-year-old?

She was still holding her head down; she hadn't even acknowledged that I was sitting there. I had no idea if she even heard me. So I tried another approach. "Now," I spoke in a harsher tone, "I want you to get back there and eat some cereal and drink some juice. You never have to speak again if you don't want to, but you will eat and sleep, or I will spank you so hard you won't be able to sit down for a week." I stood up and noticed I had gotten her attention. She was now looking at me with sad puppy dog eyes. "Go on, get back there!" Kat turned and went to the back of the van. Harley had already fixed her something to eat. Kat never spoke but took the bowl of cereal and juice and sat in the van and ate silently.

The sun was broadcasting a red-orange glow. It was enough to see clearly. I looked at my demolished home. The second story had completely collapsed onto the first. The entire house was moved about a yard off the foundation piers. The garage was totally detached from the rest of the house, leaving a large jagged gaping hole in its wake. I shook my head negatively. I couldn't even recognize the house.

"Harley, when you two get through eating, find the tent and get it out of the van. We will have to set it up for a few days." Kat was shivering. "And if you will be so kind, please try to find her a jacket of some sorts to keep her warm and her shoes." I extinguished my cigarette.

"Okay. Where are you going?" Harley inquired.

"I'm just going into the house to see if I missed anything important we can use. I think I got everything in the van." Even though I was sure I had everything, I mainly wanted to see the inside of what was only a few hours ago my home. "I'll be right back."

Walking around the house, I entered the same way we came out. My scratched knees still ached from the trip out. The water lines were obviously ruptured. Water spewed from the kitchen faucet like a small geyser. It dripped down the broken, cracked walls and pooled onto the floor. I picked up a dishrag and wiped pieces of cracked drywall off the cabinets. I laughed in spite of myself, looking down at my cracked, chipped ocean-blue tiled countertop.

"Like it matters now," I spoke out loud with only myself to hear. Walking over to the end table, I picked up the didong yi. "You're coming with me." This replicated relic obviously worked just as it was supposed to. With a quake of this magnitude, I felt for sure there would be more aftershocks, and maybe this would give us a heads-up. If nothing else, when Dallas came home, I could tell him it worked and that I had saved at least one of his priceless trinkets. I shook the thought of Dallas out of my head. I had no idea where he was. I didn't know if he was alive or dead. I would stick to the plan by waiting for a week, then move on to Montana. Surely he would catch up to me.

I caught a glimpse of something familiar near a collapsed wall. I eased over to it. I laughed when I picked up Harley's old stuffed animal. It was a little stuffed dog she had named Puppy. Harley never was original when it came to naming animals, stuffed or otherwise. She truly had never been the sharpest cheese on the cracker. Her daddy had given her this on her first Christmas. She slept with it every night and carried it with her everywhere. This small stuffed animal had almost caused me to get in a fight one time when Harley accidentally left it behind at the doctor's office. A rather large African American woman had found it in the waiting room, and when Harley asked nicely to get it back, the woman refused. I remember how Harley looked at me with hurt in her eyes. She turned to the woman, and the look on Harley's face quickly changed from innocence to one of rage. She stared at the woman intently for about a full second, then hauled off and kicked the woman in the leg with all her might. The momentary shock gave Harley the split second she needed to snatch the puppy out of the woman's hands and run behind me. The woman stood up. She was all of six feet and at least three hundred pounds. She could have easily taken me down. She pushed herself up from the chair, turning sideways, to make sure her hips cleared the chair. She walked toward me. I wanted so badly to giggle at her. She was a large woman, and her walk was more of a waddle. There wasn't one part of her body that didn't jiggle like Jell-O with each step she took toward me. When her big ass was in front of me, her hands placed firmly on her hips, she gruffly said, "Are you going to do anything about that?"

I stared at her, scared to death. My legs were shaking, and I could admit now that I felt a little faint. But I was the mama, the protector, the rescuer of Puppy and my daughter. I firmly stood my ground. "No, I'm not. She asked you politely, and you crudely refused a child. You may as well be taking candy from a baby. You are nothing but a big bully, and if you don't sit your ass back down and stop torturing my baby, I'm going to kick your other leg." The woman stood staring at me with her mouth gaping open in shock. I got Harley by the hand and left the doctor's office.

This little dog had been dropped behind a Coke display at a grocery store, puked on, peed on, cried on, and dropped in the mud repeatedly. He'd been through hell. And if I were going to go through hell, I wanted someone with me who knew the way.

I retrieved the milk from the fridge and smelled it. It seemed fine. Looking around, there was nothing else that would be beneficial for me to bring along, so I headed out. Stopping by the garage, I grabbed my little garden cart. I placed a hoe, a shovel, a toolbox, a cord of rope, and a cooler in it. I would have to reorganize the van to make more room for everything. All the stuff was thrown in with no organization whatsoever.

"Mom!" I heard Harley crying out. "Are you okay in there?"

"Yeah, I'm coming out." I exited the garage, pushing my garden cart.

Harley had found the tent and had it on the ground waiting for me. Kat had on a jacket and was lying in the back seat of the van.

"Thank you, Harley. You are a big help." I smiled as I saw Harley beam with pride. She helped me unload the rest of the van, and then we set up the tent. Harley took some of the rocks from my new flower garden to make a fire ring. She then took it upon herself to get the beds made up in the tent while I took a hammer and a crowbar to the porch. I pried the wooden planks up for firewood. By noon, we had ourselves a very classy-looking campsite. The kids ate cereal again for lunch with a promise that I would have something better for supper.

Kat reclaimed her horizontal position inside the tent. I organized the groceries a little better in watertight containers. I patted the top of the last container.

"Mom!" Harley yelled. "Someone is coming. It looks like Uncle Max."

I jumped from my position. It wasn't time for us to meet yet. I was supposed to go to his house tomorrow. From there, we were both going to our parents' to check on them. I looked down the driveway, and sure enough, Max was driving slowly down the drive on his motorcycle. Monica was on the back, holding Dannie tightly in her arms. Their big dumb dog, a boxer, ironically named Rocky, was in the sidecar with his tongue hanging out. Something was obviously wrong. Max pulled up beside the van. I assisted Monica off the bike with the baby. Rocky jumped out, looked around, and went straight for Kat in the tent. He stood over her and licked the side of her face. Kat smiled ever so slightly as he lay down beside her. It was as if Rocky were saying that he was protecting her. I asked Harley if she would get him some water.

"Hey, guys, I thought we were supposed to come to your house tomorrow," I clarified.

"What house? It's gone, totally demolished, collapsed." Max sounded exhausted and at the end of his rope. "We were lucky to crawl out alive. The parts of the roof that didn't cave in are resting on the hood of the truck, pinning it down. I couldn't get it out right away, and all of our stuff is in it, so I thought I would bring Monica and the baby up here and go back tomorrow. I will have to use jacks or something to get it out with. I can do it, but I wanted to get them out and safe first. I hope you don't mind," Max explained.

"Well, of course, I don't care. I'm glad you came. We have the tent set up, and there is plenty of room for all of us." I was glad to have adult company and help. "I have to ask though. Why didn't you go to Mama and Daddy's? Wouldn't it have been a little closer?"

"The road is blocked. I can make it on the bike part of the way and on foot the rest of the way, but it would be rough. I didn't want to make it any harder on Monica and Dannie, so we just came here." Max stopped and looked at me. Controlled panic was in his eyes. The only thing keeping him from breaking down was his wife and baby. "Sissy, it's bad. There are bodies lining the streets—"

I interrupted him, "Why don't we get things situated around here? We can sit up tonight around the campfire after the kids have gone to sleep. You can tell me about it then." I looked over at Kat in the tent. "Harley has done pretty well with everything. She got a large cut on her arm from some glass. But Kat"—I shook my head— "she won't speak. She is barely functioning. I had to threaten her just to get her to eat. All she does is lie around. I'm scared." I stopped and turned away, choking back the tears. What if she never spoke again? How would that affect her life in the long run?

Max put his arms around me. "Do you need a time-out?"

I giggled. "No, I will be fine. I'm just really glad you are here and safe. But when you have time, I have a small job for you."

"What?" Max looked at me inquisitively.

"I have a shovel over there. If it wouldn't be asking too much, could you go behind the house somewhere and dig a hole just large enough to fit a five-gallon bucket over? Keep it fairly deep though. And then cut the bottom out of a five-gallon bucket," I explained.

"Umm, okay. May I ask why?" I could tell he wasn't following my ideas.

"That will be our toilet. When we leave, we can just cover it up."

"Ah, I understand now. Yeah, I can do that with no problem. But where in the world did you get the idea for that?" Max laughed at my innovative ideas.

I smiled. "Well, it wasn't my idea. You were too young to remember, but one Christmas, we were at Grandma's house, and all the aunts, uncles, and cousins were there. There must have been fifty people in that small house. Then the toilet clogged up, and no plumber was going to come out on Christmas. So Granny took a five-gallon bucket and cut the bottom out of it. She took it to the chicken yard, which, at the time, luckily, housed no live chickens. She dug a hole and put that bucket over the hole. She marched back into the house and explained to everyone what she had done. She told everybody that if they were too stuck up to use that bucket and still enjoy their holiday together that they could just go home and they were no kids of hers." I loved my grandmother. She could be rude and abrasive but still make you feel loved.

Max laughed out loud and rubbed his head. "Yeah, that sounds like Grandma."

Monica eased into the tent with Dannie and laid him down for a nap.

The evening went by without any problems. Max got our toilet put together, and I made a stew over the fire. It wasn't the best in the world. I was definitely going to have to get accustomed to cooking over an open fire. With no way to keep leftovers from going bad, we ate our fill, then allowed Rocky to enjoy the leftovers. I found that my outside water faucet was still intact and working. I got some water and heated it up over the fire. I helped the girls to get washed up. Monica did the same thing for Dannie. We got all the kids inside the tent and got them bedded down for the night. Kat gave me no problems; she lay there silently. Harley wanted to stay up and listen to the radio.

"Honey, I'm sure you are going to see and hear a few things that are going to be bad. But for right now, with everything still fresh, please just humor me and do what I say. Things are bad all over, and I don't want you to hear something you don't need to."

Harley protested, but in the end, she went to sleep. She had been such a big girl and helped out so much today. I hated not letting her sit up for a little while, but for the time, I wanted to shield her from as much information as possible.

Max, Monica, and I sat around the fire.

"Okay, Max, how bad is it?"

He brought his head down. "I don't even know where to start, sissy. Buildings are all crumpled. We didn't see one that wasn't damaged. But most of them were unrecognizable. People are running around half crazed. It's mass hysteria out there." He pointed in no general direction, but I knew what he meant. Past my property line, the world had gone crazy. He continued, "I am scared of what we may find tomorrow when we go to Mama's."

Monica whimpered. She had been almost as quiet as Kat all day.

"What about you?" I looked at her. "How are you holding up? I know you have been quiet, but how are you really doing?"

Monica just shook her head negatively as Max placed his arm around her shoulders.

"Max, what's the plan for tomorrow?" I inquired.

"Monica will stay here with the kids. You and I can go to Mama's. That is, if you don't mind riding on the bike. We can drive the truck back here."

"That sounds good. Let's turn on the radio for a little while and see what they are saying." I had wanted to turn the radio on all day but wouldn't because of the kids. We sat in silence as Max found a station that came in.

The radio announcer sounded exhausted himself. We listened closely, keeping the volume down so we wouldn't disturb the kids.

"Information we are getting is scarce and widely unconfirmed. The only confirmed reports are that all three Alpine comets have hit. Alpine One hit the water approximately one hundred miles south of Haiti. The heat blast obliterated Haiti, Jamaica, the Dominican Republic, and most of the other smaller islands in the area. The tsunami took out Cuba and the Cayman Islands. It is not known at this time how far inland the wave washed once it hit the United States. It is known that the wave slowed down as it got into more shallow water but grew taller. We understand the wave was at least fifty feet. The main problem from the tsunami was not only the flooding but also the fires. The wave destroyed fuel tanks that were covered in oil. The wave itself appeared to be on fire. When it moved inland, the fire spread along with the water. Homes, business, and people perished.

"Another confirmed report is of the earthquakes. Some of these quakes went over a 10 on the Richter scale. The devastation is unimaginable. We were lucky enough to be able to load up the internet for about an hour last night. Los Angeles has separated from mainland. I think that was almost expected from an earthquake of this size. Untold number of lives has been lost. We will most likely never have an exact number.

"Locally, there is no electricity or running water. Most cell phones are not working because of cell towers being toppled. Fire and police departments, as well as health-care facilities, are strained to the breaking point. Within one hour, phone lines were jammed, and the phone system actually shut down from the massive number of calls. Most buildings are damaged or totally demolished. Citizens are panic-stricken. Survival instinct mixed with stupidity and selfishness has kicked in. Large amounts of looting of businesses and homes have been reported. Some people are just taking what they think they need. Others are being downright ignorant and greedy. They are taking televisions and other electronics when there is no electricity to run them. We are being told that military units are dealing with the looting in an extreme manner. One eyewitness report said that a group of what appeared to be teenage boys were found ransacking a local store. The National Guard unit fired a warning shot and shouted at the boys to stop. The boys took off running, still carrying their stolen merchandise. Another warning shot was fired, and they continued to flee, so the National Guard shot them down. Other reports are of mercy killings, people found so severely injured, unable to be transported. There is a lack of available health care, so they are being shot and killed to end their suffering.

"We have an unconfirmed report that several volcanoes have started to vent. It wouldn't surprise me with the magnitude of the earthquakes for the volcanoes to be triggered. However, we don't have specific reports of which ones are now being considered active.

"We will be going off the air soon. We are running off a generator, and we want to save our gas so we will be able to bring you the news as we have it. We will broadcast every night at seven and give you whatever information we have."

Max turned the radio off. We didn't need to hear any more. We sat looking at each other. My mouth hung open like a flytrap. I couldn't believe it. I shook my head in disbelief; I felt sick to my stomach. I closed my eyes and tried to keep haunting images from attacking me in the darkness. I heard Monica sniffle. I looked up, and Max was holding her in his lap. They loved each other so much. That was going to be the one thing that was going to help them get through this.

"Okay, so things are really bad. We are still going to be all right. We have to be. We will go on. We will live. No," I corrected myself, "we will survive. We will take what we have and make the best of it. We will learn to make do with what we have. We will make it to Montana and live, and things will work out." I stated this, attempting to convince myself too. I felt the tears welling up inside me; this time, there was no holding them back. The tears flowed like water being busted from a dam. "We are going to have to be tough. We have to work together."

I fell to my knees. I had a flood of emotions coming out with the tears. Through the slobbery tears, I screeched whatever came into my mind, "I want Dallas. I want him to hold me and console me and reassure me. I want his arms around me, protecting me from all the atrocities in the world. I want to look up and see him pulling into the driveway. I want to be his wife. I want to know my mama and daddy are alive. I want my daughter to speak." I sobbed like a baby for what seemed like forever. Wave after wave of emotion crashed over me. When I opened my eyes, Max was on one side of me and Monica was on the other. They both had their arms around me. I quickly glanced around and noticed Harley and Kat peeking out of the tent. I must have made enough noise to wake them up. I could only imagine what was running through their little minds seeing me in such a state.

With my brother's help, I stood up. I regained my composure and wiped away my tears. "Thanks you, guys," I said in a straight, calm voice as if nothing had happened. "I appreciate your help. That won't happen again."

"Sissy, we understand. We all need that every once in a while," Max said.

"Yeah, with everything going on, I can't see how you haven't broken down before now," Monica spoke softly.

"I don't know either. But I can tell you this. It won't happen again. I have two little girls in there." I pointed toward the tent. "They are depending on me. I can't afford the luxury of breaking down. I have to be strong and give them the hope and reassurance they need to get through this. If it means me becoming a complete hard ass with no emotions, then so be it. I will cut off all emotions till a time when it's safe for me and my family to feel again," I explained.

Max shook his head. "That's not healthy either, sissy."

"I don't really care about my health right now. I have to go by what Dallas told me. I will give him six more days, then I will leave for Montana. I want you guys to come with me. Now are y'all up for it?" I stood firm with my hands on my hips.

Monica nodded at Max. Max, with his broad shoulders, stated firmly, "Yeah, we're up for it."

"Good. I'm going to bed, and I will see y'all in the morning. Good night."

I entered the tent. Harley had put my bed between her and Kat. I had to move Rocky over, but I lay down and pulled Kat close. I looked over at Harley, who was staring at me.

"Are you okay, Mama?"

"Yes, baby, I am fine. I hope I didn't scare you. I'm sorry you saw that, but it won't happen again. Now I want both of you to get some sleep. I love you." I rolled onto my side and wrapped my arm around Kat to keep her warm.

"Good night, Mama. I love you too." Harley closed her eyes, retiring for the night, with her arm around me.

I lay still and quiet as I listened to the sounds of my children breathing. As their breathing deepened, I knew they were sleeping. I focused my attention toward my brother talking with Monica. I struggled to keep my own eyes opened. I overheard Max talking.

"No, it's going to be a long trip. It's going to be scary at times. We don't know what we are going to encounter. There are going to be hardships. I know gas is going to be hard to come by without electricity. But who knows, farther north, they may have power and gas may be easier to come by. It will be getting cold soon, and when I say cold, you have no idea how cold. Montana has some of the coldest winters. I just hope we get there before it starts snowing," he explained to Monica.

"We will be fine. I have to keep faith in that. Things will work out." Monica took a deep breath. "It has been a long day, and tomorrow will be a long one too. Let's go to bed."

I watched their silhouettes as they shared a kiss in front of the fire. I shut my eyes quickly as they entered the tent and drifted into a peaceful slumber.

I entered a brightly lit area that appeared to have no boundaries. As I became more aware, I noticed that I had on a white robe that hung to my ankles. There was almost a fog that covered the entire area around me. It limited my sight to only a few feet in front of me. Nothing looked familiar. Then I heard his voice.

"It's about time you made it."

The voice belonged to Dallas. I turned in a circle; I couldn't determine where the voice was coming from. "Dallas, where are you?" I called out into the illuminated oblivion.

"I'm here. I wasn't sure you would make it. What took you so long? The wedding is about to start." The voice definitely belonged to Dallas.

"What are you talking about? Dallas, where are you? I can't see you. I'm scared. What's going on? I don't understand any of this." I felt myself allowing a small panic to sink its way into my mind.

"I'm right here. And I'm talking about our wedding, silly." Dallas came into my line of sight wearing a black suit.

I looked at him in horror. He looked as if he had stepped out of a horror movie. He was scratched up with chucks of flesh missing from his arms, hands, and neck. His skin seemed to have a pale gray color. His neck was obviously broken in half, allowing his head to topple over to rest on his right shoulder. He reached his arms out to me, giving him the appearance of a zombie out of an old movie. I screamed and turned away; I didn't want to see this. Feeling his hand on my shoulder, I jumped and screamed. I was grateful when I looked around. Reality came flooding back to me, and I became aware of my surroundings. I couldn't tell what time it was, but I knew that smell. I crawled from the tent and went to the fire ring.

CHAPTER 3

MAX POURED ME a cup of coffee. "Good morning."

"Well, that remains to be seen. Forgive me if I'm not as optimistic as you are. I will just say *morning*." I cocked my head to the side and cheerfully stressed the word *morning*. I was assured that it looked goofy, which was what I was going for. "What time is it?"

"It's almost seven. I was going to come wake you and Monica up in a few minutes. I wasn't sure when you wanted to leave out to go to Mama's." Max offered me the cream and sugar.

I took them with a grateful hand and added it to my coffee. I sipped it slowly, allowing the flavor to be savored. "Mama always made the best coffee over a fire." I chuckled. "But yours is pretty close." Max smiled and nodded. "What do you think we will find when we get to Mama's?"

"I don't know, sissy, but I have a sinking feeling in the pit of my stomach that it won't be good." He took another sip. "I just want us both to be mentally prepared for what we'll find. I should have taken Monica and Dannie over there when all this crap started. But we were selfish and didn't want to leave our home. And—"

I interrupted him, "Max, if they didn't make it, do you realize you, Monica, and Dannie may have been killed along with them? Everything happens for a reason. I have to believe that. We were all right where we should have been."

He nodded as Monica exited the tent. "Morning. I know you don't drink coffee, so I made you some hot cocoa. I have plenty for Kat and Harley too." Max nodded toward me.

"They will like that, I'm sure." I smiled, thinking about how much Kat loved her chocolate.

Monica took a seat beside Max and snuggled under his left arm while she sipped her hot chocolate. She had never been much of a morning person. Having a baby changes everything, including your sleeping habits. I believed the fact was that none of us had slept well in the past two nights.

"Dannie didn't keep you up last night, did he, Ashley?" Monica asked.

"Honestly, I don't even remember closing my eyes. I'm not sure if I even moved all night. I don't think I could have moved much if I wanted to. Being between Harley and Kat didn't leave me much wiggle room."

Monica giggled sweetly. "Yeah, you didn't look too comfortable."

"Well, sleeping with those two is like trying to sleep with two jackasses." I laughed briefly. It felt good. For a second, my sprits lifted. I was elated when Max and Monica followed suit and laughed with me. Winking at Monica, I stated, "I don't think you will have a problem out of Kat today. Harley was a big help to me yesterday, so just give her a few chores and tell her you need some help. She can make up the bed in the tent and a few little things."

Monica nodded. "When we get the truck, we'll have Rocky's bed. Maybe he will sleep in it and leave ours alone."

We sat and passed around small talk for a little while. I got some things together and cooked breakfast. I fried bacon then scrambled some eggs in a cast-iron skillet that was passed down to me from my grandmother. I put bread on some tin foil and laid it on some hot coals. It didn't toast like I had wanted, but it warmed it enough to melt some butter. One thing was for sure—we wouldn't go hungry. I had meat from the freezer that we would have to cook this week.

The kids got up, dressed, and came to eat. Harley was her usually bubbly self. She only whined when I changed the dressing on her arm and made her take an antibiotic. Kat sat quietly as she ate and silently returned to the tent. Rocky quickly followed her. It amazed me to see how he was looking after her. She didn't show signs of being sleepy. She simply sat in the tent and stared into space. Monica fed Dannie some eggs and got him dressed. When everyone was ready, Max and I nodded to each other, knowing it was time.

I told Harley to help Monica and do whatever she told her to and instructed Kat to be good. She didn't even seem to notice that I was there. I kissed each of them on the forehead. "I will be back soon. Y'all don't give Monica a hard time."

Harley waved vigorously, as did Monica after giving Max a brief kiss goodbye. We all had an understanding. Knowing how bad things were, there was a slight chance we wouldn't be coming back. If that were the case, Monica was going to inherit my two girls. From there, she would have to do the best she could. It was a responsibility that she took on as we drove away. I looked back at my babies and shut my eyes, silently praying to whatever god was listening that I would see them again.

It didn't take us too long to get into town, or what was left of it. I could no longer see the skyline of Austin. The only thing left was smoke rising where tops of buildings used to be. It was my first look of what was left of my little neighborhood. The bank and grocery store were leveled. Paper littered the streets, catching a breeze and flying onward. I hoped they didn't have anybody's bank account information on them. Although at this point, I'm not sure they would even care. There weren't too many people on the streets, so at least we had that in our favor. I noticed that I didn't see any cops either. I couldn't imagine where they all would be. As we went on, I began to notice landmarks where things stood only two days before. At the movie store, ripped posters hung from the remnant of walls, flapping in the breeze. Restaurants, car washes, banks, and business—they were all gone. You could tell people had tried to get into the stores, most likely to pillage and plunder whatever they could.

A military jeep passed, then turned around and began to flag us down. A young man shouted from the jeep, "Pull over!" He held a gun of some kind. Max had brought his own pistol, but we weren't about to argue with these guys. Max pulled over as the jeep pulled about eight feet ahead of us. The soldier got out and made his way to us. Max and I held up our hands to show him we meant him no harm. Thankfully, the soldier lowered his weapon. "Do you have any identification?" We pulled out our licenses and handed it to the soldier, who couldn't have been any older than twenty.

"I'm Officer McDaniels, mind if I ask what you doing out here?" The soldier spoke as gruff as he could.

"This is my sister, and we are going to check on our parents. They live in Round Rock. We were just going to see if they made it and, if not, then take care of them and go back to my sister's in Cedar Park. Is everything okay, Officer?" Max was trying to read the soldier.

"As good as it can be, I suppose. We are trying to keep down the looting. I have been instructed to tell you that there is an information center down at the city park on Laurel Street. If they have confirmed information, they are posting it on a board. Some people are bringing food and grills and cooking what is left in their freezers. It's going to go to waste soon, so we are trying to feed as many as we can for as long as we can."

"Thank you very much, sir. We will check out the park. We will be leaving town in a few days. We are going to Montana," I explained. "I want to thank you for your service. Just in case no one ever tells you this, you deserve it, so thank you." I know it sounded corny, but I did appreciate our soldiers attempting to protect us. I'm sure most of these guys had their own families and wanted nothing more than to be with them.

The soldier smiled a little crooked smile. "Thank you, and I'll pass that along to my troops. You take care, and I hope you find your family safe." He turned on his heel and marched double-time back to the truck.

We made it to my parents' neighborhood and soon realized we were not going to make it on the bike. Rubble flowed onto the streets like a river. Bricks, mortar, and wood, along with remnants of people's homes and lives, littered the streets. A black-and-white photo of a little boy beside an older man blew across the street as if it were running away. There were no people out. I couldn't imagine where everyone was, and I wasn't sure I wanted to. I was expecting to find people standing outside their homes, huddling together for support. I expected to see more tents in yards. There was nothing that resembled that life was continuing here. The majority of the population in this community was elderly. Realization sank into my brain. I had a macabre curiosity of how many people might still be trapped inside their home. A cold chill ran down my spine as I attempted to put the thoughts out of my head.

We found a safe place to park, and Max chained the bike to the bumper of an abandoned car. "We will have to walk from here, I'm afraid."

"It's okay. It's not that far." We walked side by side, knowing the way by heart even if nothing was recognizable. Every house was crumbling beneath itself. Garages collapsed onto the tops of cars, and large sinkholes dented the ground; several homes were disappearing into them. We walked around a curve and looked where my parents' home should have been. I would have given anything to look up and see my parents' single-level ranch-style home untouched by catastrophe. I wanted to see them come running out of the house with arms open wide, ready to embrace us. I looked with widened eyes and gaping mouth. Max hung his head down and shook it in disbelief. At that point, we both knew what we would inevitably find; however, neither of us was going to say it out loud.

We looked at the piece of land where we had grown up. The roof had slid off to the side of the house. My heart sank, and my pulse quickened. Max and I looked at each other and took off running toward the heap of broken debris. Max stopped short. "Where could they be?" he said frantically as he cautiously stepped over the bricks.

I thought about our steps in general. With each one we took, we could be literally stepping on top of our parents and not even know it. The debris was deep; our parents could very well be buried alive. I could only hope to get that lucky.

"Mama! Daddy!" he called repeatedly. "I'll search over here. You go over there. Just look around and see if you can find anything."

My heart was aching. Where could they have been? I looked around the debris. I recognized some of the furniture that was protruding from the rubble—the arm of the couch, the stove. I followed with my eyes and thought to myself. "That means the table would have been over here," I whispered to myself. I made my way over to the dining room area. Max was about where their bedroom would have been. I could tell that grim look on his face was the same as mine. I found the table and began to move debris off it. I slung it away, not caring where it landed. After a few seconds, I could see the top of the table. It had withstood all the debris piled on top of it. I began working on the side. I was digging through the brick and Sheetrock. I felt the jagged shards of brick slicing my fingers and hands as I tossed them over my shoulders. Then I heard my brother shout with an agonizing tone that pierced the silence.

"No!"

My head snapped up to find my brother collapsing to his knees. "Max!" I shouted. Pulling myself up, I used my hands as a brace. I quickly crawled over the debris. As I got to Max, I placed my hands on his shoulders. I saw the sight that held his attention—my mother's cyanotic hand protruding from the rubble. I closed my eyes. "Dammit." I pushed past Max and reached my mother. I picked up her hand and held it close to my cheek. I didn't need to feel for a pulse. Her skin was a purplish blue and cold and stiff to the touch. I began picking up bricks and tossing them to the side. I could go slower and more cautiously now that I knew my parents weren't trapped alive, waiting for us to rescue them. I could afford to take my time and handle this situation in a more delicate manner. My mother deserved that. Max rose up and silently went to work uncovering my father. I could hear him sniffling and occasionally wiping his eyes.

My mom had on a beautiful peach-colored nightgown with intricate lace around the neck. She lay on her right side facing my father, who was lying on his left side. My father was dressed in slacks and dress shirt with a jacket. It looked as if they had gone to bed dressed for their funeral. They either knew they wouldn't survive this ordeal or never intended on surviving it. They chose to die together, in love, side by side rather than in a state of panic and mayhem. I had an admiration for that. They felt their chances for survival were slim and chose to go out their own way.

Max went to retrieve the shovels from where we had dropped them at the street. I looked at my peaceful mother. She almost had a smile on her face. I lightly brushed off some of the dust from her face. She had a few scratches around her forehead from the bricks but otherwise looked perfectly intact. It was torture for me to stand there looking at my dead parents. I was about to dig a hole and put my parents into the earth forever. At the same time, I felt a little relieved. They weren't going to have to fight and scrimp to make it through this aftermath. I leaned over and kissed my mother on her cold dead cheek. Stepping over the rubble, I made my way over to my father. I looked at him. He, too, looked happy. He had always been such a strong-willed man, a Marine who volunteered for three tours in Vietnam. He always worked so hard to give us everything we ever wanted. "I love you, Daddy." I leaned over and kissed him on his iron cheek. "I will do my best to make you proud."

"Where should we bury them?" Max asked as he returned.

"Um, I think we should bury them under the oak tree in the backyard." Mama had her daylilies planted there, and she would like that. "I wanted to bring something up before we bury them." Max looked at me questioningly. "We need to take their wedding rings off. I don't want this to sound horrible, but I thought about grave robbers. If someone finds the graves, they could think there may be something to take. I don't want someone to dig them up over a piece of metal."

Max only nodded in agreement. We took off their wedding rings and put them away for safekeeping. One by one, we tightly wrapped our parents in a sheet and tied it up. We worked together and carried their bodies to the oak tree in the backyard. We worked for several hours digging, and when we thought it was sufficient, we placed their bodies in the dark, bleak hole. We positioned them just as we had found them on their bed, on their side facing each other. We did this with as much dignity as we possibly could have. Our parents deserved nothing less. Our hearts were breaking. This wasn't how it was supposed to be. They were supposed to have nice caskets, and all their friends and family were supposed to be here. Instead, their two kids wrapped them in sheets and stuck them in a dark hole. My stomach flopped over inside. My throat was dry, and my chest felt heavy. I wanted to throw up at the sight of my parents in this hole.

We stood side by side at their covered grave. Max made a makeshift tombstone and carved their last name into it. He looked down at the ground. I took his hand lovingly. "We knew what we were going to find, Max. We have done all we can do." I tried to give him encouragement and reassurance. I knew he was feeling the same way I was.

"I know, sissy. I just don't understand. When Monica talked to Mama, she told her that they had everything packed in the garage. Why would they pack if they never intended on surviving this thing?" A lonely tear rolled down Max's face. "It just doesn't make any sense."

"Well, let's go inspect the garage. Let's see what they packed."

We walked through the rubble to where the garage should have been. The crinkled and crunched garage door marked the spot. I crawled under the twisted metal and found my parents' car. There was indeed packed food and water, as well as a suitcase, in the car. I found a small familiar box in the driver's seat. I handed it off to Max, then made my way back out. Max and I sat on a pile of debris and opened the box. Inside were my father's Purple Hearts and my mother's small jewelry box. The jewelry box held her rings. Each ring was labeled with the name of one of the grandkids. This box was basically their will. Small mementos such as old family photos held value only to us. Also, there was a piece of paper that was folded with our names on it. We slowly opened the letter and read silently to ourselves.

Dearest Max and Ashley,

I'm sure this isn't what you intended on finding. I had most of our stuff packed up and in the car, ready to go. Then something changed at the last minute that changed my mind. Your daddy had a heart attack. I knew there was no way we would get an ambulance or a cop here with everything that was going on. He died in my arms. I dressed him in his best suit and placed him in his favorite sleeping position. I put together some sentimental things for you two, and if you are reading this letter, then I suppose you found it.

Max, you are going to have to be strong. I know you can do this. Your job is to take care of Monica and Dannie.

Ashley, honey, it is a long road to Montana. Be strong for the girls and for yourself. I know you can do it. You have too much of your grandmother in you. She was the strongest, most stubborn, most bullheaded woman I have ever known, with the exception of you. If anyone can handle the trials that lay ahead, you can.

You two work together.

I have taken some sleeping pills. I don't want to wake up when hell comes off the hinges. I don't know what morning will bring, if anything. If God intends for me to wake up, then I will. I want you to understand that I have not killed myself by taking the pills. I simply want to lie down next to your daddy and go to sleep. If I wake up after everything is said and done, then I will deal with it.

I love you both very much. Take care of my grandbabies. Always let them know that I love them.

With all the love I have to give,
Mama

Max inhaled deeply and shut the box and nodded. "I don't know about you, but I'm ready to go." He was mentally exacerbated. He wanted to break down and cry, kick, or scream. His insides felt twisted, worn, and ripped apart. He loved his parents. He was especially close to his daddy. Max and Daddy always held a special bond, one that went beyond father and son—they were friends. I looked into his eyes and saw a man who looked beat. It looked as if he should fall to the ground and yell, "Uncle!"

"Sounds good, Max." I wrapped my arm around his. "Let's go to your house and work on getting your truck." We solemnly walked back to where we had left the motorcycle. I held on to Max's arm, leaning my head on his shoulder, silently telling him that he wasn't alone. I want to break down crying; however, I refused to allow myself that luxury. My stomach churned and twisted. I felt nauseated. The thought of putting my mother wrapped up in a sheet in the dark earth and covering her up with dirt made me want to puke. She and Daddy deserved so much more than that. Daddy was a veteran. He fought in Vietnam for our country. He earned three Purple Hearts in his service. He deserved a proper funeral. My mother had been a stay-at-home mom. She was there to cook and clean. She was there when we needed a Band-Aid or help with homework. She always let us know that she loved us. Even when she was mad, we never doubted her love. I knew in my heart that Max and I had done what we could. We did right by our parents. We came to find them as soon as it was safe and gave them a decent burial. I knew even if we had come a day earlier, it wouldn't have changed what we found or what we had to do. I shook the thoughts out of my head. I had to stop thinking about it, or I would lose control. I could feel the tears welling up, and I couldn't allow that right now. I had to be strong for my family. We still had the unfortunate task of going home without Mama and Daddy and explaining to Monica and my girls what we found.

All of a sudden, a hellacious sound robbed me of my thoughts. I promptly looked up and noticed a group of rather large dogs rounding the corner, running and barking ferociously. Right off, I recognized a Doberman and German shepherd; the two others were mixed breeds.

Upon closer inspection, they were chasing a smaller dog. This smaller dog was bite-size for some of these bigger ones. Going several days without someone to feed them, I was sure of what the bigger dogs had in mind. They were hungry, and this small long-haired Chihuahua was a nice little meal. The Chihuahua was literally running for its life and headed right toward us at a blazing speed. It looked as if its little feet weren't even touching the ground. Max grabbed his pistol, firing one shot in the air. The bigger dogs stopped in their tracks while the Chihuahua kept going. It was almost as if he knew, or at least hoped, we would protect him. And if not, at least a single gunshot would be fast and easy, nothing compared to being ripped apart or chewed on. The beasts before us took a guarded position, growling, snarling, showing their teeth in retaliation. They looked vicious enough to be able to take us down. The little Chihuahua jumped into my arms and buried his head between the trunk of my body and my arm. His little body was shaking almost to the point of vibrating. I looked at Max and smiled. I climbed on the bike holding the dog. I knew I shouldn't take in another mouth to feed, but I wasn't about to throw this innocent little dog to the proverbial wolves. He wouldn't eat much, and I knew Kat would love it. Maybe it would help bring her out of her current state.

It took us about an hour to drive to Max's house. The trip would only normally take about twenty minutes. I tried to keep my attention on the little canine that was still nestled safely in my arms. The few times I did look up, I saw the same destruction. It was probably best that I didn't pay too close attention. I had seen a lot of bad things in my experience as a nurse, but this was beyond my comprehension. The human part of me wanted to stop at every house and see if anyone was left alive. I wanted to see if I could help in some way to improve someone's situation. The rational part of me knew there was no way I could do this. I had to take control and take care of myself and my family. Everyone was on their own now. I looked at the Chihuahua intently. The bigger dogs had it right; it was now a dog-eat-dog world. I refused to be the Chihuahua in this world. I was going to have to step up and be a Doberman. I snickered silently to myself at my crude comparison.

Max pulled into his driveway. I looked up in disbelief. The walls were completely disintegrated. You couldn't determine where they should have been. The roof was lying on top of the ground. It gave the effect that the actual rooms would have been underground. I shook my head. "My god, Max, how did y'all get out of there?" I looked up at him. His face was red, and his eyes were a little swollen. He had most likely been crying the entire ride over. I put the shaking Chihuahua in the sidecar. "Stay," I commanded. I leaned over and hugged Max. I wasn't sure what to say to him. What could I possibly say to give him peace of mind? "Max—" I started.

"I'll be fine," he interrupted. "I'm just taking it all in. It just got to be a little overwhelming." Max wiped his eyes and got off the cycle. He pointed to the dilapidated house "We crawled through the attic and got out through the outside vents. Dannie cried the entire time. There was a brief time where I wondered if we would get out alive. I knew I couldn't give up. I had to keep us moving. Monica was scared to the point where she couldn't move at times. The shaking got so intense I had to yell at her, and I even slapped her once and told her if she didn't move, she would be the one killing Dannie. It seemed cruel, but it got her moving. Once we were safe outside, I hugged them both close and explained myself. The last thing I want is for her to hate me." Max shrugged his shoulders. I could tell he was close to tears again.

"I'm sure she doesn't hate you, Max. She understands you were only doing what you had to in order to keep them alive." I couldn't imagine Monica's shock and horror as Max slapped her. My feeble attempt of reassurance fell on deaf ears.

Max shook his head and threw up his arms. He held a strong resentment toward himself for his actions toward Monica, even if she had already forgiven him. He would never forgive himself for hitting her. That was one thing we were always taught as children—never hit a woman. And as a woman, never allow a man to hit you. However, this was no case of spouse abuse; it was a case of survival. Striking Monica was never a thing Max would normally do. He would never hit her out of anger.

"I'll go get my jacks and start to work on the truck." I only nodded in agreement. I knew there was nothing that could be said. This was something that they would have to work out for themselves. I wasn't going to interfere, or at least try not to. It was getting late, and we needed to hurry to get back to Monica and the kids before dark.

Max diligently went to work. He strategically placed the jacks on the hood of the truck under the debris. He carefully and slowly jacked the debris up. I climbed in the truck and started the engine. I eased the truck into reverse, holding my foot on the brake. When Max gave me the signal, I pressed down on the accelerator, increasing the pressure on the gas till I heard the engine whine. I released the brake and floored the accelerator simultaneously. The truck broke free from the debris. I slammed on the brake when I felt I was a safe distance away, throwing myself forward into the steering wheel. I looked up and caught a glimpse of the side of the house sliding to the ground. The sound of glass breaking and wood cracking was all too familiar. Max ran up to the truck. "Are you all right?"

"Yeah, I'm fine." I actually felt great. The sudden rush of adrenaline was exhilarating. "The truck is free. It's getting dark. We need to get going. Do you want to drive the cycle back to my house or just take the truck?"

"We can take the truck. I don't suppose I will have much use for the motorcycle anymore." Max loved that motorcycle. I knew he hated to leave it behind. "Can you drive the truck, or do you want me to drive?" he asked.

"No, I can drive." I looked toward the cycle and saw the little Chihuahua sticking its head up, looking at me. I patted my leg. "Come on, Taco." The little dog jumped out of the cycle, ran across the yard, and jumped into the truck.

Max laughed. "Taco?" he said inquisitively.

"Well, if we hadn't saved him, he would have been a little snack for those bigger dogs." I snickered and smiled. "Stop laughing and get in the truck." Still laughing, Max got in the truck. Taco sat on the vinyl seat between us.

We carefully drove through the streets of death and destruction with a heavy heart. We were just beginning to breathe a little easier when the ground began to shake again. The truck vibrated and began sliding to one side. Max looked over his right shoulder and saw a huge sinkhole forming behind us. It was widening at a rapid pace and beginning to expand down the street.

"Sissy," Max yelled, "go!"

I looked back and saw the sinkhole. It looked like a wide mouth opening, ready to swallow us. The back passenger tire began to spin without traction; nothing but open air supported it. I turned the wheel and stomped on the gas, feeling a slight bump when the tire was back on solid ground. The hole, still widening, was running almost parallel to us. There were about thirty people on the street ahead of us who were now running for their lives. One man attempted to grab the side of the truck as we passed by, an action that unfortunately proved to be his last bad decision as he lost his grip. I heard a distinct thud as the back tires rolled over his body. I glanced up in the rearview mirror just as the truck spat his bloody, crumpled body out the back like a bad seed. Seconds later, the sinkhole swallowed him, disposing of his body into the vast darkness below. I gasped and squeezed my eyes shut momentarily. "Oh *god*, I killed him."

"No, sissy. He killed himself. And you are trying not to kill us. Now drive!" he forcefully commanded.

There was a part of me that wanted to stop to help, but the realistic part knew that I had to get off this road. I looked around for the nearest escape route. People behind us were now disappearing into the sinkhole as it swallowed them. My eyes widened in horror.

I whipped the truck around the next corner. Taco slid across the seat, whimpering. I punched the accelerator to the floor. The tires spun and slung rocks. The engine whined under the strain. There was a low grumbling sound coming from the earth below us, like a monster ready to snatch us. What few bricks remained standing was now taking their place on the streets below. I dodged debris like a barrel racer at a rodeo.

"Whooo-hooo! Yeah, you can drive. I knew my sister wouldn't disappoint me," Max shouted in displaced excitement.

Allowing a smile to cross my lips, I continued to dodge debris with the vibrating truck. I kept my attention focused on getting home while never looking back. I knew Monica and the girls would be scared. Max looked back and saw the remaining buildings collapse into a smoldering pile of rubble. A large explosion rocked the truck, giving us a boost forward. I screamed and ducked in surprise.

"Gas station," Max said.

"You think," I sarcastically responded loudly. My ears were ringing from the explosion. I held a tight grin on my face; feeling the speed was exhilarating. It seemed that I was developing an uncanny addiction to what I would normally call reckless driving. It wasn't unnatural for me to get a momentary high from intense situations. I suppose that was why I loved working in the emergency room.

"I was just letting you know," he said, laughing. "What were you ducking from?"

"I don't know. I was just ducking. Who knows, maybe shell shock runs in our family too." Max continued to laugh. I had never liked loud noises. Ever since I was a child, I hated the fire trucks in parade because of the sirens; I even hated fireworks. I giggled under my breath as I remembered a particular Fourth of July. I was probably seventeen. Max had begged Daddy and me to watch the fireworks he had gotten. Reluctantly, Daddy and I went. Everything seemed to be going just fine until Max lit a particular explosive device. It was supposed to shoot straight into the air and explode into beautiful colors. Instead, the whole thing blew up with a loud boom. I don't remember much except covering my ears and shutting my eyes. When I opened them, I was looking right into Daddy's eyes. We both apparently had jumped under the tailgate of the truck in refuge of the explosion. I looked up at Daddy, and we both had a good laugh over it. It was understandable that he would have shell shock because of his three tours in Vietnam. But there was absolutely no reason for me to have jumped other than I just detested loud noises.

Shaking my head, I looked in the rearview mirror to see a large fireball and black cloud rising into the air. I shook my head. I briefly wondered how long it would take the fire to spread and how far it would go. We got to the subdivision entrance. I entered the open gates, doing sixty. The tires skidded as I took the turn. Taco slid across the seat in the opposite direction, his little nails gripping the vinyl seats in an attempt to steady himself. I could imagine the poor thing had to be wondering if he hadn't been better off taking his chances with the big dogs. Downed trees now littered the road, their roots disturbed by small fissures. I didn't feel the least bit insensitive as I jumped the curb and drove over lawns and sidewalks. My neighbors, or at least the ones who were still alive, probably didn't think having tire tracks in their yard was a big deal. Max had his window down, and he had a hold on the top of the truck, allowing his elbow to swing freely. I got to my driveway and slowed down as the rumbling and shaking died out. We looked around cautiously till we saw Monica stirring about in the distance. We both breathed a little easier then.

We pulled into the driveway slower now. Monica smiled, then looked behind us. I knew she was looking for Mama and Daddy. Her hand cupped her mouth as she began shaking her head. Max motioned for her to meet the truck. We stopped a little farther down the drive. Monica came running to meet us halfway.

Max got out. "We will walk from here."

I only nodded. I knew he would take this opportunity to explain things to Monica. I pulled the truck up next to my van and got out. Harley came running out to meet me.

"Mama, we had another quake." She seemed oddly excited about it.

"I know, baby. I felt it." I knew I had to tell her about her grandparents. However, I had no idea how to do it. How does a child perceive death? How do you explain death to a kid?

"Mama, where is Meme and Poppy? Are they going to come later tonight?" She was looking down the driveway.

"I need to talk to you and Kat. Come on in the tent." I allowed her to go in the tent first, then I followed behind her. Kat was still there on her bed, Rocky by her side. I doubted that she ever moved. Harley sat beside Kat; she hung her head down. I had a feeling she knew exactly what I was about to say. She looked like she was as much as a guardian as Rocky.

"I have bad news, girls." I looked at them. They both stared at me intently. I knew what I was about to say was going to crush their spirits. "Max and I got to Meme and Poppy's house. Their house was just like ours. It was all broken apart. We looked for Meme and Poppy and finally found them lying on their bed." I took a deep breath. "They were dead. They didn't make it." I found no reason to explain to them about my daddy having a heart attack and Mama taking the pills. This was going to be enough for them to handle. "We buried them in the backyard under the oak tree. You know that was Meme's favorite place."

Kat lay back down without speaking a word. Harley came over to me and hugged me tight. "I'm so sorry, Mama."

"Oh, honey, it's going to be fine." I tried to reassure her.

"I'm going to miss Meme." I felt her hot tears dousing my shoulder. I hugged her and patted her head, holding her close and allowing her to cry it out. When Max and Monica came into the tent, Harley went to Max and cried on his shoulder.

I picked up Kat and looked at her. "Are you all right?"

She stood before me and shook her head. Her hair was matted to her head in places, her face was dirty, and her clothes astray. She looked like a throwaway stepchild. Kat looked at me. Her eyes looked lost inside themselves. A single tear dripped like honey from her right eye.

"It is all right for you to cry, Kat. They were your grandparents. You should feel something."

Kat fell into my arms with a whimper. She let loose and let her tears flow. I held her tight and rocked back and forth. I was hoping, as traumatic as it was, maybe this would be a breaking point for Kat. Maybe she would talk. As a few minutes passed, I realized I was wrong. If anything, she was taking the news as an excuse to retreat further into whatever mental fantasy world she was creating for herself. She never spoke a word, only cried silently and shook. Her shaking reminded me about Taco, who was still in the truck. I allowed her to calm down.

"Hey, I found something for you. Do you want to see it?" She nodded affirmatively. I took her by the hand and led her to the truck. "Max and I rescued this little guy from a bunch of big dogs that was going to have him for lunch." I opened the door and picked up

Taco, passing him to Kat, whose eyes lit up in a brief moment of excitement. "I named him Taco." I watched her pet the little dog. He seemed to take to her. "You can take him into the tent. He should make a nice bed partner for you. But you have to take care of him. I have enough to handle, so he will have to be your responsibility." Kat nodded and smiled as she went into the tent.

Monica walked up to me and hugged me close. "I'm so sorry, Ashley."

I solemnly nodded. "We knew it was a possibility when we went. We knew what we may find." I choked back my tears. I couldn't allow myself to show the emotion that I so readily thought was healthy for everyone else to show. I would have my time later. I needed to change the subject though. "So what are we going to fix for dinner?"

Monica looked at me, a little shocked. "Umm, I have thrown some stuff in a pot. It is a soup-type thing," Monica stammered out. The uncertainty in her voice revealed that she wasn't for sure what it was. However, it was food, and it was hot. For the first time today, I felt a little hungry. "It's ready for you two. We already ate. Harley was a big help today. I was quite impressed with her."

I looked over at Harley, who seemed to have a prideful glow about her. At that brief moment, I noticed something. I really began looking hard at her. She was smiling and seemed almost grown up. She was helping out. She had washed her hands and commenced to fixing Max and me a plate of soup. She had a certain maturity about her that wasn't there before. In the past, I had to fight with her to keep her room clean or do the dishes. Now she was helping to cook supper, making beds, and helping care for her sister. In the last few days, a change had come over her. In my eyes, it was for the better. I had to keep in mind that she was only sixteen. She needed to be more mature, but I realized the importance of her enjoying the everyday kid things.

As the sun, or at least what we could see of it, began to set, we sat around the fire while Max and I ate. Kat quietly played with Taco. The two were getting along as if they were lifelong friends. Rocky had moved away from Kat's side and was now standing over Harley. When we had finished, I took Harley and Kat to our makeshift toilet for a final time before bed. I had to hold Taco for Kat. I was sure she didn't want him to run off. I helped the girls get ready for bed and tucked them in. Max, Monica, and I sat around the fire a little longer before retiring for the night. Monica wanted to get as much information about Mama and Daddy as possible. We showed her the note and what we did to give them a proper burial. Other than that, there wasn't much to tell. We told her about the National Guard troops and how they were setting up a communication board at the park.

I caught myself nodding off. I got up and excused myself. It had been a long heartbreaking day, and all I wanted to do was crawl in bed and hug my kids.

I didn't remember falling asleep, but I awoke with Max shaking my leg.

"Sissy."

"Huh," I said sleepily.

"Someone is here." Max pointed outside. "There are lights coming up the driveway real slow."

I threw back the quilt and bolted from the sleeping bag bed. "Dallas!" I knew it had to be him. There would be no one else who would be coming here. My heart was racing with excitement. I quickly darted out into the yard.

Max was behind me with his rifle. "Sissy, wait!" He grabbed my arm, holding me back.

"What?" I looked at him with question.

"What if it's not Dallas? What if it's looters? You can't be too careful. Just slow down," he explained rapidly.

I looked at the slow oncoming vehicle. Even though it was dark, I could tell the vehicle indeed didn't belong to Dallas; it was too large. I saw a slim figure climbing out of the back, one too small to be Dallas. I looked toward the driver's window. A voice called out from the darkness, "Is this the Blackwolf place?"

"Yes, it is," I called out. I walked closer to the truck. Whoever it was obviously knew us. A dark slender figure walked toward me. He walked into the headlights of the truck. "Marcus?" I asked. Dallas's son looked shaken and lost.

"I didn't know where else to go. I hope this is okay." Tears began to slide down his face. "I just didn't know where else to go."

I grabbed him and hugged him. "Of course, it's all right. You're safe now." I held on to him for a few minutes, then pulled him back. "Marcus, where is your mom?" I noticed he was shivering; he was dressed in shorts and short-sleeved shirt.

"I don't know." His tears were still coming.

"Tell you what, go warm up by the fire, and I will be there in a minute." I pointed in the direction of our camp. "Max, can you see if he wants something to eat?" Max nodded as he put his arm around Marcus and escorted him to the fire.

I walked up to the truck. An older guy sat behind the wheel. "Good evening, sir."

"Evening, ma'am. The name is Jessup. That young fellow said he belongs here. I hope you don't mind." The gentleman stuck his hand out the window.

I gallantly shook it. "Yes, that is my fiancé's son. Where did you find him?"

"Well, he was wandering around town. He seemed a little lost and a lot scared. I asked him if he needed help. He said he was going to his dad's house and gave me the address. With the lack of landmarks, he was having a hard time finding the place. Not to mention, it was dark. It wasn't too far, and I didn't want him sleeping on the streets. It's not safe for man or beast out there, especially when the sun goes down. I offered him a ride, which he graciously accepted, but only if he could ride in the back. I suppose taking a ride from a stranger seemed safer if he could jump out," Jessup explained with a slight laugh.

"I am very grateful, and his dad will be too. Is there anything I can do to repay you for your kindness?" I asked.

"Oh no, I'm just glad the boy got home. I better get home myself. The wife will be going crazy with worry if I'm too late." Jessup put the truck in gear and started backing out. He stuck his hand out the window and waved. "Y'all take care." And with that, he was gone.

I walked back to the campfire. Marcus was wolfing down some of Monica's soup. He obviously had not eaten in a while. "Monica will be happy that someone likes her cooking." Marcus only nodded as he inhaled another spoonful.

We sat quietly for a little while. Max kept the fire fed. I noticed Marcus didn't have anything with him except a backpack.

"Marcus, can you tell us what happened? Why don't you know where your mom is?"

He finished his plate, sopping up the last little bit with a piece of bread. He swallowed hard and started speaking, "Mom was at work at the hospital. She called and told me to walk up to the hospital. They were going to allow family to stay in the cafeteria. I started walking up there, then everything started coming apart. I followed a group of people into a parking garage. We were pretty lucky there. Only a few walls collapsed, but I lost most of my bags in the process. When it was all over, I got to the hospital, but..." He paused. "It was awful. The building was collapsed one layer on top of another. It was just layer after layer of concrete. I looked around for a while, but I never found her. I expected a work crew to show up. You know, someone to start digging for survivors, but no one ever came. I knew I couldn't wait around forever, so I decided to make my way here. I don't know if Mom made it or not." He spoke with his head now facing the ground. I was sure he was crying, but he wasn't going to let me see it. "Is my dad here?"

"No, he's not. He called and was on his way back from Houston. I don't know how close he got to home." A slow realization came to me. If his mom perished at the hospital and his dad indeed didn't come home, he was basically an orphan. I was the closest thing he would have to a parental figure. I made the decision right then and there to do my part and make sure he was taken care of.

Marcus only nodded. "If it's okay with you, can I stay here until one of them comes to find me?" He realized he couldn't stay by himself. He knew the likelihood of his mom being alive was slim.

"Marcus, you can stay as long as you want to." There was no way I would turn him away.

"Thank you, Ashley." Marcus reached up and hugged my neck. That was the first time Marcus had ever shown me any kind of affection. Like any child of divorce, all he wanted was for his parents to

get back together. He accepted the fact that it wasn't going to happen. However, he never acted hateful or spiteful or showed me any
disrespect, like a lot of kids would have tried to. We had a mutual
understanding and respect.

I patted him on the shoulder. "Tell you what, why don't we get
a good night's sleep? We will see what tomorrow brings."

Marcus laughed a little. "A bath I hope."

"Yeah, I think we all need one. We will figure it out in the
morning though. Let's get some sleep."

We went into the tent. I had to admit, the tent was getting a little crowded. I made do with what I had and made a place for Marcus
to sleep. He lay down and was asleep before his head hit the pillow.

I lay down between Kat and Harley and nestled in for the night.
Taco looked up but never left Kat's arms. I briefly scanned the tent
at my loved ones scattered about. There were seven of us now, nine if
you included the dogs. Our future was unknown, but one thing was
for certain—we were together. Whatever the big bad world had to
throw at us, we would take it on as a family.

CHAPTER 4

I AWOKE WITH AN overbearing feeling of being watched. I slowly opened my eyes only to see a large boxer dog standing over me. "God, Rocky, go away." He leaned his head down and proceeded to lick me in the face until I sat up. "Okay, all right, damn, I'm awake." I patted his head as he backed up. "Jeez, Rocky, I have to find your snooze button." I exited the tent, allowing Rocky to follow me. Immediately smelling the coffee, I inhaled deeply, savoring the aroma.

"Morning," Max called out. "Just in time."

"Don't you ever sleep late?" I questioned.

"Nope. I guess that's one thing I got from Mama." Max snickered as he handed me a cup of coffee.

We sat silently around the fire, enjoying the morning. Monica soon joined with Dannie. Max fixed him a cup of milk and Monica a cup of hot cocoa. "We need to get our tent set up today."

"And we need to figure out a way that we can all get a shower." I sat straight up, stretching my back. "I want to talk to you two about something." Max and Monica both looked at me attentively. "It's been four days since all this started. I need to start thinking about what we are going to do. Dallas told me not to wait for him. He told me as soon as it was safe to head to Montana and he would catch up to me. I think that is what we need to do."

"We don't know if it's safe anywhere else though. What if it's worse?" Monica stammered out in an uncertain voice.

Max put his hand on hers to calm her. "And we won't know until we get on the road, Monica. This is what I suggest: we go to the park today and check out the communications board and see if we can find anything there. We can ask the National Guards about road conditions and such."

I nodded in agreement. "It will do us all some good to get away from here for a little while." I would hold off on talking about leaving till I found out more about conditions farther north. I understood the uncertainty of things was scary; however, it was a fact of life. Every aspect of our lives was uncertain right now.

Marcus and Harley came out of the tent. Kat soon followed, still holding Taco. They took turns going to the toilet.

"We need to call it something else, Mama. It really isn't a bathroom or a toilet," Harley stated.

"Well, just say you are going to use the bucket. We will all understand it and know where you are going," I said through a muffled laugh.

"Hey, Marcus, after you eat, can you help me get a shower fixed up?" Max asked.

"Can I be the first one to try it out?" he asked in a begging tone of voice. His face was smeared with dirt, and his clothes were so dusty he left small dust clouds with every step he took.

Max laughed. "Yeah, you can be first."

Monica fixed scrambled eggs for breakfast. When we had all finished, Harley took our plates and washed them at the only working faucet. I was again impressed by her seemingly unconscious effort to pitch in and help. I hugged her and told her I was proud of her.

Max and Marcus went to work figuring out a way to get a working shower. Kat stayed at the campfire with Taco. Monica went to the truck and found the tent. She and I looked the ground over and found a good level spot to put it up. It wasn't too far from mine but still far enough away to give them a little bit of privacy. I thought to myself, *At least I won't have to wake up to the goofy dog Rocky licking me in the face.* Within an hour, we had the tent up. Monica got all their bedding to make up their beds just the way she wanted them. Rocky went into the tent. He acted happy with his bed, prancing around and making circles around it, but he didn't stay there long. After just a few minutes, he darted out to find Kat still sitting in the same spot, holding Taco. Rocky looked at the little Chihuahua questioningly, turning his head from one side then the other, trying to figure him out.

I decided that Marcus was going to need some clothes. I got a ladder and went to the house. Carefully placing the ladder against it, I climbed to the top. My legs began to shake when I looked down and realized how high off the ground I was. I looked around at what was once my bedroom. It was now a roofless, mangled pile of metal, wood, and Sheetrock. I located the closet door, which was now facing up to me. I knew Dallas had some old clothes in the closet. The floor was all slanted and broken I looked around shaking my head; my heart broke at the sight of it all. I planned my route carefully. I was in the process of swinging my leg over the jagged broken wall when my brother's voice stopped me in my tracks. I gripped the sides of the ladder to steady myself.

"What in the hell do you think you're doing?"

"Well, I'm going to fall and bust my ass if you keep scaring me like that."

"You're going to bust your ass anyway. Get down from there. We can't have the one person with medical knowledge getting a broken neck. Now come on and get down."

I reluctantly climbed down the ladder. "I was going to get Marcus some clothes. He don't have anything else to wear, Max."

"I understand that. He can wear something of mine after his shower, and we can wash his clothes up for tomorrow. We can make do." Max put his arm around me. "You can't take chances like that, sissy. We need you."

"Well, you just brought up another good point. How are we going to wash clothes?"

Max was quiet for a moment. "WWGD."

I looked at him with wrinkled eyebrows. "What?"

"WWGD—what would Granny do?" Max laughed as I punched his arm.

"She would have whipped you for scaring me while I was up on a ladder. That's what she would have done." I had to laugh with him.

"It is a good question. How are we going to wash clothes?" Max asked.

"All we need is a big tub and some soap. A washboard would be nice, but you don't find them anymore. But like you said, we can make do. Tomorrow will be a good day to wash clothes. We will need a clothesline strung up so we can hang them up to dry."

"I will get to work on something to wash clothes in as soon as we finish the shower."

"How's that coming?"

"It's a surprise, so don't go back there and look," Max explained, shaking a finger at me.

"I won't peek, I promise."

"You just don't go and do anything stupid that will get yourself hurt."

"And I'm supposed to come ask you before I do anything?" I had my hands on my hips, looking prissy.

"Nobody likes a smart-ass, sissy." Max laughed as he walked back behind the house. "No peeking. We are almost finished!" he yelled as he was out of sight.

I walked back to the campfire. Monica was taking inventory of groceries, trying to figure out what to cook for lunch. Harley was making up the beds in our tent, and poor little Kat was right where I had left her. There wasn't anything for me to do at the moment. I sat down next to Kat and hugged her close. She laid her head against my arm. "We are going to be fine, honey. You will see." Gently I kissed her forehead. "You have to think of this as a big adventure. We are going to be fine."

I looked around our makeshift homestead. I had to admit, it was scary to think about leaving. We had no idea what we would encounter outside the safety of our confines. At least here, we had our tents set up and groceries. We had enough gas for now. Soon, we would have a shower and somewhere to wash clothes. Once we left, we would lose all that. I had to come up with some ideas.

I went to the van and got my road atlas. I flattened it out on the hood of the van. I studied the roads, flipping to each state all the way to Montana. With the quakes and aftershocks, I didn't want to go through any mountains if necessary. I figured north through Oklahoma, Kansas, Nebraska, South Dakota, then finally crossing into Southeast Montana. It would be mostly flatland. There were several state parks along the way, plenty of rivers and creeks. With any luck, the bridges would still be intact or at least passable.

A series of hoots and cheers broke my chain of thought. I looked up and saw Marcus running around the corner. He had a grin from ear to ear. He started to shout, "We got it! It works! It works!"

I laughed, attempting to match his excitement. "Y'all got the shower going?"

"Yeah, come see." Marcus enthusiastically swung his arms around, motioning for us to follow him.

I got Kat by the hand. She held on to Taco as if he were a lifeline and followed behind me. Monica walked quickly with Dannie in her arms. Harley ran with Marcus, keeping his pace. We went to the back of the house. Max was standing there, proud and smiling big. There was a wooden frame with a shower curtain around it and a piece of plywood on the ground. I recognized the shower curtain from the downstairs bathroom. I looked up and saw the bathtub slopping downward above the newly constructed shower stall. A piece of pipe with a showerhead attached dropped down from the drain of the tub. I small lever was attached to the showerhead that turned the water on and off.

Max started. "It's not the best in the world, but it will work for now. Water is our only shortage. However, when it rains, it will fill up, and we can catch rainwater in buckets and put it in here," he said, pointing to the tub above.

"Can I borrow those clothes now?" Marcus asked with a hopeful voice.

"Good job, honey. We can at least stay clean. And yes, Marcus, I will get you some clothes." Monica turned and went back to the campsite.

I stepped in closer to inspect my brother's handiwork. "Very nice, brother. You got a little creative here. It looks great."

"Well, Marcus helped a lot. I couldn't have done it without him." Max slapped Marcus on the back.

He beamed with pride as he looked up at their construction. Harley came around the corner with a towel, clothes, soap, and shampoo and handed them to Marcus. We excused ourselves to let him have his privacy. As we were walking away, we heard him holler out, "Cold, cold, it's really cold, but it's so great!" He let out a laugh that echoed.

We each took our turn and got cleaned up, refilling the bathtub once with fresh water from our only working spout. We got a turkey and some hamburger meat from the defrosting freezer.

We decided to take the truck to the park. Max, Monica, and Dannie would ride in the front, and the rest of us piled up in the back. I told the kids to sit with their backs to the back glass of the truck. I wanted them to keep their eyes closed so they wouldn't see any of the atrocities that might lie ahead, but I knew they wouldn't. I sat on the side of the truck bed and held on tight. It didn't take long for us to make it to the park. People were scattered all around. Some had their tents set up right there. Some wandered around with backpacks. I was certain those backpacks held the last of their personal possessions. Others were walking around trying to barter for different items. We got out of the truck and got the kids together.

"I want everyone to stay together. No one wanders off. Is that understood?" They all nodded in agreement.

We made our way through the crowd and headed toward the rising smoke of the barbeque pits. I was amazed at their organization. If you brought meat with you and donated to the great cookout, you were allowed to eat. Each of us was given an armband. Without that armband, you weren't allowed to enter the eating area. Once you entered the eating area, they punched a hole in the armband stating you already had your meal. We ate quietly, looking around, trying to get a feel of the place. Even Kat, who was normally a picky eater, ate everything on her plate. When we were all done, we threw away our plates and walked around the park.

The communication board was on the right side of the eating area. Two ten-foot-tall pieces of plywood side by side displayed a map of the new United States. The country was indeed in three pieces. It looked like the first separation occurred along the San Andreas Fault. The greater part of Los Angeles dissolved and slid into the ocean, leaving only a small island in its wake. The second separation started at the southern point of Lake Michigan and ran south through Alabama and emptied into the Gulf of Mexico. The Hoover Dam was currently holding but severely damaged. Areas south of the dam were being evacuated for precautionary measures. Mountains all over the country had been leveled, leaving only rubble behind. Multiple cities had been left in ruins. Several volcanoes not specifically named had begun to vent.

Other news was what we had already heard on the radio. There was no death toll and no advice other than to protect what you have and your family. Gasoline was in short supply. Most of the oil refineries were on or close to the coast and were now underwater or burned to the ground. The government had gas but was holding on to it for military operations.

I backed away from the board, shaking my head. I knew this would dash the spirits of my family and ward them off our impending road trip. The squeal of a loudspeaker broke my personal thoughts. I looked around to see where it was coming from. A stage area had been set up at the north end of the eating area. A very rotund man dressed in a faded denim pair of overalls was standing on it in front of a microphone. People who were allowed inside the eating area began to respectfully take their seats. The less fortunate individuals just sat on the ground outside the eating area. The man began to sing a beautiful rendition of "Amazing Graze." People flocked to the stage area, including us. We took a seat about four rows away from the stage area. There was a laptop computer beside him that was piping music into the speakers. The man's voice rang out loud and clear. My skin protruded with goose bumps as a single tear escaped my left eye. I wiped it away before anyone else could see. When the man finished his solo, he, too, wiped tears from his eyes.

"Folks, my name is Raymond Richardson. I was told that this stage was put up for anyone who wanted to sing or play music. Some folks thought it would do people good around here to hear music and socialize. I lost my wife four days ago when our home collapsed on top of us. That song was for her. I love you, Emma." He paused a moment as if to say a silent prayer. "Now if anyone else can sing, come on up, and we will see what we can do. I have my computer here, and we can just have ourselves a little karaoke party. At least until the battery goes out. We have to get some normalcy back in our lives, so let's have a good time." Everyone clapped in agreement.

A young lady, probably about twenty years old, took the stage with confidence. She went with Raymond to the laptop and picked out a song called "How Will I Live Without You." She sang very well and finished the song with ease. We all clapped for her as she left the stage.

"Is there anyone else who can sing? Anyone else want to give it a try?" Raymond shouted into the microphone.

"My mama can sing."

I smiled and giggled, thinking somebody's kid just nominated them to sing. I looked around and realized it was coming from Harley. She was standing up pointing at me. My smile quickly faded. My kid was the one who nominated me to sing.

"Harley, hush up. What are you doing?" I grabbed her hand and pushed it down.

"Well, you can sing, Mama. Come on, please?" She looked at me with her devilishly innocent eyes.

I shook my head negatively and looked at my brother for help.

"You can sing, Ashley," he said in a matter-of-fact tone of voice.

I looked at Monica. She wasn't much help with her slight hand gesture ushering me toward the stage. I flashed them both a disapproving grimace.

The man on stage battered out his encouragement. "Come on, little lady. Come give it a whirl. We aren't looking for professionals. We only want to have some fun. Come on, folks, let's give her a hand."

I gasped as the crowd starting clapping in a rhythmic tone. With my jaw dropped open, Harley and Marcus pushed me toward the stage, laughing and giggling. I looked back at Monica and Max smiling and clapping right along with the rest of the crowd. Even Kat was smiling. I had no idea what I was doing or how exactly I had just gotten talked into this so fast. Raymond took my hand to help me up. I shook my head in confusion as I got on stage. He escorted me over to his computer and asked me to pick a song. His computer was loaded with almost every song imaginable. I briefly thought to myself, *What do you sing at a time like this?* I didn't know many religious songs and none well enough to entertain a crowd of strangers. If I were going to do this, I wanted to do it for my parents, and there was only one song that came to my mind. I chose the song and asked Raymond to give me a minute. I took the microphone in my hand that was now shaking. I looked across the park area and saw that all eyes were on me. I felt like I was going to hurl as I cocked my head up and raised the microphone to my mouth.

"I also had a great loss four days ago. I lost both my mother and my father, and I haven't heard from my fiancé since all this happened. I don't know if he is alive. We all have had losses, ranging from loved ones to homes to personal belongings. I am fortunate enough to have my brother, his wife and baby, my two little girls, and my stepson with me today. I don't know what our future holds, but I do know that we will face it as a family. This song is for my mama and daddy and everyone one you have lost and to all of us left behind. Now I'm not a professional singer, so please don't throw food at me. It is too much of a precious commodity right now." I attempted to let loose a slight giggle.

"That's okay. We got rocks," a voice from the back boomed loudly. A roar of laughter ran across the crowd.

I looked down at Harley. "Harley, honey, you're grounded." Another roar of laughter came from the crowd. Harley shrugged her shoulders as if saying, "Oh well, it was worth it."

Brad Paisley's song "When I Get Where I'm Going" began to come through the speakers. I closed my eyes, knowing the song by heart. I sang with everything I had to give. I wanted my parents to look down at me and to be proud. I managed to stay in tune, or so I hoped. Opening my eyes on the last chorus, I saw that nothing had been thrown on stage. The crowd was deathly quiet, and all eyes were on me. I closed my eyes again and finished the song as another single tear fell from my eye. I didn't bother to wipe it away. Everyone just sat there staring at me. I started to get scared that I was about to be lynched when one man stood up and began clapping. The rest of the crowd followed suit. I stood there flabbergasted that I was actually getting a standing ovation. Someone hollered out, "Encore!" And the clapping got louder. I looked over at Raymond, who motioned for me to pick another song. I didn't want to do another heartwarming ho-hum song. I wanted something that would be fun and maybe get people up on their feet. I chose Reba McEntire's song "Take It Back." Raymond gave me a second to say something to the crowd.

"Man, you guys are just a glutton for punishment, aren't you? I chose a fun song. It's time to let loose and have a good time. We all deserve it. So come on, get on your feet. I want to see some hands clapping and some feet moving."

I looked to Raymond. He started the music. The saxophone rang out of the speaker. I pranced around a little bit, trying to play out the song. I strained my voice and belted out the song with an attitude that I thought would make Reba proud. I looked over the crowd, who was now dancing all over the park. I smiled and allowed my attitude to grow and finish out the song. My brother let out a cowboy yeehaw that rang over the sound of the speakers A few others followed his lead. It was all going well till the stage began to vibrate beneath my feet. I looked over at Raymond just as the laptop fell off the small table and hit the floor of the stage. The music abruptly stopped as the shaking intensified. It was another aftershock. People began running in every direction, afraid for their lives.

I looked up and saw my family in the midst of all the chaos. I shouted in the microphone, "Get under the tables!" I leaped off the stage onto the nearest table. I used the tables as stepping-stones to get to my family. Just as I was getting under the table with them, I noticed a few of the less fortunate folks outside the eating area. They were running to tables to get the abandoned plates of food and anything else they could get their hands on. The aftershock didn't last long but long enough to put everyone's nerves on edge.

After I consoled Kat, I went back to the stage area to find Raymond. He was leaning up against it, holding his chest. "Raymond!" I ran over to him. "What wrong?"

"I think I'm having a heart attack." Raymond's breaths were quick and labored. He was struggling for each and every breath he took.

"We need some help over here!" I shouted out. "Raymond, I want you to lie down. I'm a nurse. I can help you."

"No," he said, waving and pushing me away.

"What…what do you mean no?"

"I mean no. It's okay. I am ready to see my Emma again. I can almost see her now. She is just on the other side of that light." His voice was fading, and his breathing was growing slower.

I looked up to him. His eyes were now closed, and he looked peaceful. He was ready, and who was I to do anything to keep him from his precious Emma? I had been a nurse long enough to know when someone says no to life-saving measures, that means they have accepted their fate and are ready for whatever awaits them after they take their last breath. I held his hand. "It's okay, Raymond. Go to Emma. I won't stop you."

An elderly woman came up to me and asked if there was anything she could do. I asked her to find out who would be taking care of his burial. She disappeared into the growing crowd.

I sat and watched Raymond take his last breath. When he exhaled, a single word crossed his lips, "Emma." I smiled because I knew wherever he was, they were together. I felt for a pulse and didn't feel anything.

A young man dressed in military attire came over to us. "Is he gone?" the soldier asked.

"Yeah, he's gone. His name is Raymond Richardson." I stood back as the military took over and removed his body from the crowd.

I shook my head and went back to my family. A few people came up to me telling me how well I sang and that they enjoyed it. I smiled and said thank you.

"We better go before it gets too dark," Max said.

I nodded in agreement. I took Kat by the hand, and we walked back to the truck.

The short ride home seemed to take forever. I had not known Raymond Richardson. I shouldn't have any emotional ties to his death, but the fact was, I did. It wasn't so much his death as it was the timing of it. People were having fun; they were letting loose, if only for a few minutes. They were moving their cares and worries aside and having a good time, and then the aftershock came and brought them back to a harsh reality. In this reality, you can never let your guard down. You can never relax, or someone may die. I rested my head on my knees, wanting to cry. I didn't even know when we pulled into the driveway. I felt the truck come to a sudden stop. I caught myself before I slid forward into the back glass.

Max was out of the truck with his shotgun and began quickly walking toward our campsite. Crawling down from the truck, I noticed Monica sliding over into the driver's seat.

"What's going on?" I whispered to her.

"Max saw someone walking around the tents. He is going to walk down there and see who it is. I'm staying here with the kids," Monica explained quickly as she turned off the headlights.

"I'm going with him. If anything happens, get the kids out of here. Go back to the park and get help." I stepped quickly, catching up with Max. I could hear Rocky barking wildly at the campsite. We had tied him up to keep him from following us.

Max shot me a disgruntled look as I caught up to his fast pace. "You should've stayed in the truck."

"There is safety in numbers, remember? What did you see?" I had to admire him. He was always trying to be the protector. He wanted to be the hero, although he would never admit it.

"When we pulled into the drive, someone walked around the van. The fire is still going, so I saw them clearly. I just couldn't tell who it was." Max's eyes never left the campsite. "I haven't seen them again, so I'm not sure where they are."

"Are you sure it was just one person?" I wished I had brought my pistol. I made a mental note to myself to get it out of the van and have it on me at all times from this point on. Silently I was praying that this someone invading our space was Dallas.

"No, I'm not sure of anything at this point." He paused and stopped in his tracks. We were about ten feet away from the van. Max motioned for me to go on one side of the van as he went to the other.

Following his instructions, I took the right side. I carefully took each step, looking around to ensure that I was always aware of my surroundings. No amount of mental preparation could have prepared me for the surprise I felt when the stranger came around the van. Instinctively, I let out a small yell and reached forward. I grabbed ahold of the stranger's shirt and shoved him away from me with everything I had. Max came around like a bolt of lightning. He punched the guy in the jaw. Not wanting to give my brother the satisfaction of having to save me, I charged the stranger, kicking him in the gut. He doubled over with shock. I brought up my knee with force to meet his face.

"Look out!" Max shouted as I was knocked on my ass. I looked up to see another man in position to kick me. I quickly rolled out of the way and was on my feet with a speed that surprised even me. I attempted to kick him, but he caught my leg and began to laugh in a dark, ominous tone. I smiled the most wicked smile I could fathom. He was holding my leg tightly, so I used that as stability. With my free leg, I jumped up and swung it around, landing a strong kick to the side of his head. He let go of my leg and fell to the ground with a blunt thud. I could hear Max fighting with the first stranger. I knew he could take care of himself. I hadn't seen any weapons, so it was a fair skin-on-skin fight.

The second guy was on me too fast. He wrapped his arms around my neck and pulled me up to a standing position, so I couldn't breathe. I tried pulling his arms free, but he was too strong. I only knew of one thing I could do. I made a few grunting sounds, then allowed my body go limp. My plan was working as he loosened his grip, thinking I was unconscious. He let me go completely, allowing my body to fall forward onto the ground. My somewhat controlled fall allowed me to land faceup. Like most dumbass criminals, he leaned over me to check me out. When I knew he was in range, I kicked him in the groin. He fell forward to his knees with pain and yelled accordingly, holding himself. I kicked again, landing it on his nose. A disgusting crunching sound that somewhat resembled an egg being smashed on concrete radiated from his head. The stranger's body was now upright. I watched as his eyes rolled back in his head as his arms went limp at his sides. His nose began pouring blood along with his mouth. His body fell forward and landed on top of me. I felt the warmth of his blood dripping onto my neck. Grunting in disgust, I rolled his body off mine, cursing in protest against him. I had killed him. With my medical knowledge and the sound I heard, I suspected I had broken his nose, forcing the jagged shards of bone into his brain.

I stood up with my body shaking. My shirt, neck, and hair were now soaked in blood. I felt a slight tickle as blood ran down my arm and dripped off my fingers. It was already coagulating in the cool night air and sticking to my skin. My legs were wider apart than normal for my stability. I felt an uncontrollable rage come over me. My breathing quickened as I looked down at the dead stranger, feeling a change come over me. Who was this fool? How dare him come into my homeplace and help himself. How dare him come in and make me have to defend myself.

I looked around and saw Max still fighting with the first guy, and even though he was holding his own, he looked as if he were beginning to wear out. I went over to the campfire and grabbed a butcher's knife Monica had luckily left out. I ran toward the first assailant who now had my brother in a choke hold and jumped on his back. My sudden actions startled the stranger as he released his hold. I briefly saw the alarm in Max's eyes as the stranger tried to shake me off. I held on tight with my legs and one arm. With the knife, I reached around his throat. I felt his warm, sticky blood on my hands as I sliced through his flesh. He fell forward, gasping. In my uncoordinated dismount off the asshole, I felt the knife slice across my left eyebrow. I hollered out, "Son of a bitch!" A stinging sensation was followed by my own blood filling my eye.

Max grabbed me from behind. "Sissy, are you okay?" He began to pull me away from the withering man.

"No! I cut my own eye, dammit!" I cursed, slinging my arm away from Max. Applying pressure to my eye, I felt the blood flow through my fingers. I tried to remind myself that head wounds bled a lot, no matter how bad they were. But at the current moment, that was no consolation. Looking down at the gasping, dying man, I felt pissed off, and killing him wasn't enough; I wanted more. I kicked him over and over, yelling out profanities of every nature. I saw nothing but red, and it had nothing to do with the blood that was in them. I was mad as hell. I felt out of control, and it felt good. When I was too exhausted to stand, Max handed me a rag. I took it from his shaking hand. He didn't speak. I saw fear and concern in his eyes. I applied pressure on my head and took my first look around.

I took stock in what I had just done. I had killed two young men. They looked to be in their early twenties. The thought of murder had never crossed my mind. However, I didn't look at this as murder. It wasn't cold-blooded intentional murder; it was self-defense. These looters were taking our property. Their duffel bags filled with our belongings confirmed that fact. They were the last things we had to our name. These people would have hurt us, possibly even killed us. I did what I had to do to defend myself, my property, and my family.

I took inventory of my current feelings—excitement, exhilaration, fear, and pain. Remorse or regret was not there. I would do it again if the situation arose, although I hoped it never would.

"What was all that? I've never seen you move like that. Where did you learn how to fight?" Max was trying to catch his breath.

I looked at him and knew he needed a little peace. He needed to know that his sister still existed inside this crazy woman who stood before him. "Too many wrestling pay-per-views, I guess." I snickered.

"Well, I'm damn grateful." Max flashed a smile at me. "How are you? Are you all right with this?" He motioned toward the two dead boys.

I nodded. "Yeah, but I don't want the kids to see them. We can pull them behind the house, somewhere they won't see. We can bury them after they go to bed." I looked at Max and noticed he wasn't wearing a shirt. I looked at the rag he gave me and noticed that it was indeed his shirt.

Max let out a slight laugh. "Hell, I wanted to bury them out in the front yard with a sign that said, 'Here lay the last people who tried to loot.'" Max kept his eyes on me at all times. He was almost inspecting me.

I laughed with him as a way to let him know that I was all right. I didn't want my brother thinking he couldn't trust me. "No, I would rather hide this from the kids. I don't know how much they just saw. Let's go ahead and get these guys out of sight so Monica won't be too worried." I paused and looked at Max. "Hey, what the hell happened to the gun? Didn't you have it with you?"

Max hung his head down. "Promise me you won't say anything?"

"I promise."

"I didn't even have it loaded, sissy. I had cleaned it earlier while everyone was showering. I didn't think people at the information center would like it if I brought a loaded gun up there, so I left it unloaded. The whole time we were walking toward the camp, I was hoping it would just work as a fear factor. And honestly, I didn't think I would ever be in a 'kill or be killed' situation." Max looked at the two dead bodies that now littered my lawn. "I guess that's been a dangerous lesson learned."

"Well, I have a pistol in the van that will be with me at all times, loaded." I never wanted to be in a situation where I couldn't defend myself. This time, it had worked out in my favor; next time, I might not be as lucky.

Max and I dragged the bodies behind the garage, ensuring they were out of sight. Even if the kids went to the bathroom, they weren't going to see them. He got the flashlight and flashed it a couple of times, giving Monica a signal that it was safe to come down the drive. We saw the truck moving slowly. I went to the shower and rinsed out Max's shirt with the cold water and pressed it firmly to my eye. Max kicked around the dirt in an attempt to hide the blood. Monica pulled up and got out of the truck with frightful eyes. She retrieved Dannie from the truck and ran forward to hug Max. I heard her mumble something but couldn't make out what it was. Harley and Marcus came sprinting forward with Kat on their heels.

"Mama, did you get in a fight? What happened?" Harley asked.

My ears rang at her high-pitched tone. "Shh, yes, baby, we got in a fight. Some bad people were trying to take our stuff, but Uncle Max and I stopped them." I had one hell of a headache coming on.

"Where are they?" Marcus asked. He had a tone of skepticism in his voice. He had a look on his face that let me know he had seen more than Harley.

"We took care of them, scared them off." I tried to sound happy about it. I didn't want him to worry. Marcus might have been the same age as Harley; however, he had more maturity about him. He lived at home with his mother. After school, he would walk home, do his homework, and cook supper for the both of them. He was acquainted to cooking full meals, not just opening a can. I honestly wouldn't even trust Harley to cook a grilled cheese.

"What happened to your eye?" Harley asked. "You are all bloody."

"I cut my eye, but I'm fine. I just need to look at it when it gets through bleeding." I tried to reassure her. "You need to get ready for bed. You girls go first, then come to the fire and let Marcus get ready." Harley took Kat by the hand and led her into the tent.

Marcus turned to me with knowing eyes. "You killed them, right? You can tell me."

I nodded, still holding the shirt to my eye. "Yes, Marcus, I killed them. They were taking everything we had, and I killed them."

Marcus reached and hugged my neck. "I'm glad you did. I feel safe knowing you can do that."

I patted him on the back. "I'm glad, Marcus. I don't want Harley or Kat knowing about this. Do you understand?"

He nodded and turned back to the fire. He held out his hands as if warming them.

Monica came over to me. "Jesus, Ashley! Are you okay? Let me see." Monica came toward me a bit cautiously. Apparently, Max had already told her about my brief moment of carnal rage.

I pulled the shirt from my eye. "How does it look?"

Monica squinted her eyes and pressed the shirt back to my eye. "I'm not a medical expert, but it don't take a degree to know you need stitches."

"Shit," I hissed in anger. "Well, I'll just have to go in the morning. I have to help Max take care of things here."

"I can help," Marcus stated abruptly.

"Thank you, honey, but I don't think you need to be seeing all that." I felt his mom and dad would never forgive me if I allowed Marcus to do this.

"No, really, Ashley, I can do it. I understand what happened and what you had to do. You need to go to the hospital and get stitched up. I can help Max and let Monica watch the kids. It will be fine." He sounded so grown up and wise beyond his years.

"You know, the longer you wait, the more it's going to swell, and it's going to be harder to sew up. I think you should let Marcus help." Monica nodded to Marcus, and he returned her gesture.

I felt like they were ganging up on me. I knew when to admit defeat and the fact that they were right. I nodded in agreement. I knew it would be a long night waiting at the hospital. However, I also knew they were right. Marcus seemed to have a good understanding about what had just transpired. He seemed man enough to handle things and help Max dispose of the bodies. We talked for a moment, then I kissed my kids goodbye. Taking a deep breath, I sighed as I cranked the truck and headed to the hospital.

Like I imagined, it was a madhouse. A triage area was set up in the parking lot. Cops and ambulances were everywhere. People were on stretchers and cots, and some where even on air mattresses. I signed in and got a yellow tag. Yellow meant you would be treated and released. I took my place in line, holding my registration paper in one hand and still applying pressure on my eye with the other. The line moved fairly quickly, a fact that I was grateful for. Finally, it was my turn. I took a seat as the doctor introduced himself.

"Hi, I'm Dr. Downs. Now what do we have here?" He tenderly inspected my eye. I knew most of the doctors here at the hospital, but I had never met this guy. I suspected he was from the Red Cross or some other organization. "Well, you are going to need a few stitches. What happened?" he asked.

"It was an accident with a butcher's knife, just a stupid accident." I hated to lie, but there was no way I was going to tell the truth. There were people here with more serious injuries than mine, and I was grateful to be in and out as fast as possible. There was no way I was going to get the shit pot stirred and do anything to draw attention to myself. The last thing I wanted was cops asking me questions.

"Well, we will get you fixed up fast enough. Why don't you come back here behind the curtain and lie down on the stretcher?" There was no nurse to assist; he was totally on his own. He went to work, and within ten minutes, I was signing my discharge papers. My eye was thankfully numb.

I was crossing the parking lot when I heard a familiar squeal from behind me.

"Oh my god, girl, I'm so glad you're here! I know just where to put you." Brenda, the head nurse over the emergency department, latched on to my arm and began pulling me in the opposite direction. Brenda was a very large African American woman with an attitude of grandiosity. Nobody liked her and purely hated working for her. We spent most of the days or nights just trying to avoid her.

"Brenda, stop," I pleaded, trying to pull my arm free. My head pounded in retaliation to the tone of my voice.

"We didn't know what happened to you, but I'm so glad that you showed up. We have been super swamped. You have no idea," she was rambling on and on. She wasn't listening to me at all.

"Brenda!" I yelled. "Look at me."

"Oh, don't worry. I don't care if you're not in uniform. We have been wearing whatever we can get." She tightened her grip on my arm.

I twisted and slung my arm free of her grip. "Let go of me now!" I yelled with hatred and contempt in my voice. Feeling that rage building inside again, I flashed a look that told her I meant business. "I'm not in scrubs because I'm not here to work, Brenda. I was here as a patient." I pointed to my eye.

She looked at it quickly and dismissed it, waving her hand. "Oh well, we can put a dressing on it to keep it clean. It shouldn't hinder your work too much. I'm going to put you in the triage area. We are tagging people as they come in according to the seriousness of their injuries. Black tags are the most critical, and believe me, girl, there is enough of them."

"Brenda, you're not listening, as usual. I'm not here to work. I have had a hell of a night, and I'm going back home." I was doing my best to keep my tone of voice as calm as possible. Brenda didn't respond well to anyone who was the least bit assertive.

"Oh yeah, you're going to work. Now you take a chair over there at the triage desk and get to it," she ordered as her hands went to her hips. Her head swayed from one side then the other and bobbed up and down as she spoke. She reminded me of one of those bobblehead dolls.

"No, Brenda, I'm not. I am leaving in a few days to go to Montana. I quit."

Her eyes changed into almost a glowing red color. People were stopping and staring at us. "No, you ain't going to quit on me, little girl. You can get over there and do your job. Things are bad all over, and you are not going to shuck off your responsibility here and abandon us."

I tried to keep my voice calm, but as I spoke, it grew louder. "Or what? You will fire me? Fine, fire me. I don't care. I haven't taken report on anyone, so you can't threaten my license with patient abandonment. I have lost my mother and my father. I have no idea if Dallas is alive or dead. I am going to Montana to be with his family on the reservation. I'm sorry you have your hands full here. I really am. Like you said, things are bad all over, not just in your little corner of the world. I'm leaving, and I'm not coming back. I have my own problems to deal with."

I turned to walk away. I had already killed two men tonight, and I didn't have any remorse over it. I was feeling a rage building inside me that made me afraid. I thought it was best if I just removed myself from the situation. Just then, I felt her grab my arm again. Without missing a beat, I turned around and decked her in the jaw.

"Let go of me, you bitch!" I cupped my hands over my mouth as her big butt bounced on the hard pavement. Immediately an orderly and a cop came over to help her up. I looked at the cop, and he waved me on. I suppose he had been watching the scene we were making and knew she had it coming. That was my hint to take an expedited departure. I almost ran to the truck, fumbling for my keys, when I heard a voice calling from behind me.

"Hey, where did you learn to fight like that?" the voice called out. "You got a nice right hook."

I looked back to see Colby, an EMT from the hospital, coming up behind me. I paused and smiled at him. "Hey, Colby, I'm just trying to get out of here."

"I got something for you. I heard you say you were going to Montana. And if I know you, you will try to help everyone you come across along the way. You are going to need some supplies." Colby held up an EMT bag and placed it in the back of the truck.

I was shocked but pleased. "You're going to get in trouble." I smiled.

"Don't worry about it. Like you said, what are they going to do? Fire me? They need every person they can get. The Red Cross came and dropped off a bunch of stuff. You can use it." Colby was a sweet kid, about twenty-two years old. His slanted blue eyes shone like sapphires. His thick, straight brown hair was worn in a hip tousled style. He was pretty tall and still had a boyish build. He was always clean-shaven, although now he had a bit of stubble protruding from his chin.

"Thank you very much, but I really must go. I have to get home to my kiddos." The truth was, I didn't want Brenda to come after me again. I could see her out of the corner of my eye still rubbing her face.

"I understand. Just be careful, and I hope everything works out for you." He patted the side of the truck and walked away.

I was home before midnight. Max was still up keeping the fire going. I took a seat next to him.

He sat quietly for a few moment. "Montana, huh? You know it's going to be a hard trip, don't you?" He never looked at me.

"Yes, I know that. We may even end up walking because of a gas shortage. I just don't know. All I do know is that it's going to be much harder without you guys. I don't know if I can just drive away, leaving you here and not have any way to talk to you. We should be together. We need each other. Who knows what we are going to encounter out on the road, but we can get through it if we stick together." For the first time, I was scared. I was scared of what might happen on the road. I was even more afraid of facing it alone with three kids.

"Well, one thing is for sure—we are going to build a wagon to pull in case we do have to walk. We can bring our food with us. I think Marcus and I should start on this first thing in the morning," Max explained.

"What changed your mind?" Max and Monica both had been so against this road trip.

"Monica and I talked. If we stay here, things are going to get scarce, and there aren't a lot of options. We are going to have a constant fear of looters. I can't see us staying and living like this. So let's make a move. I just hope we can make it before winter sets in." Max got up without another word and went inside his tent.

I knew he didn't want to go. He felt the need to do something, and there was a lack of options to work with. This was our only other alternative. My eye began to throb as the lidocaine wore off. I took a very cold shower to wash the blood off me, then retired to my tent and hugged Kat. She sighed in her sleep as my arms brought her closer to me. It was the first sound I had heard her make in almost a week. "Things will get better, honey, I promise. It was just a bad day."

The next few days, we spent gathering supplies and building our cart. We used as much wood from my house as possible. We took the tires off an old ATV that Dallas had never gotten repaired and used an old car seat and made a spot for Dannie to ride so we wouldn't have to carry him. I hoped it wouldn't come to us having to walk. Hopefully, this cart was something we were never going to need, but just in case, we were going to be prepared. Monica took inventory of our groceries and carefully planned our meals. Harley and Marcus helped Max, while Kat sat quietly as usual. No amount of coaxing would get that kid to talk. She would sit and stare down the driveway as if she were waiting for someone or something. At night, Max and I sat around the fire and planned out the trip. We looked at all possible routes, knowing we would have to cross a couple of bridges; we also planned alternate routes if the bridges were impassable. We would stop at state parks, creeks, and rivers to replenish our water, wash clothes, and bathe.

The night before we left, Monica fixed a great pot of stew. Harley did the dishes, and Marcus put the last few waterproof containers in the van. We all got a shower, then the kids went to bed. Max went to the park to see if there were any new postings on the communication board. To his surprise, there wasn't. He tried to get information on road conditions but found no one who had been too far outside our area. Some ladies had started a resale shop at the park, so he was able to find Marcus some clothes. Max sweet-talked some people into trade—a fifty-five-gallon drum of gasoline for sugar, flour, and a few rounds of ammunition from a gun that he no longer owned. Gas was the most precious commodity. It would indeed help us get a little further before we had to go on foot.

"The world has pretty much stopped," he said. "They are just dealing with everything on a daily basis."

"That's all any of us can do, Max," I stated. "We better get a good night's sleep. We have a long day ahead of us tomorrow." I got up and went into the tent with the kids.

I had just lain down when Harley spoke up.

"Mama."

"Yes, baby, what is it?" I could tell she was nervous about leaving. "What will happen if we leave, then Daddy D. comes to look for us? Can we leave him a note?"

Marcus sat up and looked at me intently. He wanted an answer to that question as well. He wasn't pleased that we were leaving either. He wanted to stay and tough it out.

"Yes, we can leave a note for Dallas. He knows where we will be going, and he will find us as soon as he can." I tried to sound upbeat.

"If he's alive," Marcus stated as he plopped his head down.

I was shocked. "Marcus, that's a possibility, but I prefer not to dwell on that. I believe with all my heart that your dad is alive.

Things are just so broken apart and the roads are so damaged around the city that he is having a hard time getting home. So we will do what he told me to. He will come find us when he can. You have to think positively."

Marcus never said a word. He only turned over and faced the opposite direction. I thought he might have been crying, and part of me wanted to go to him, but I thought it was best if he had his own time to process us leaving in his own way. After all, he was leaving not knowing what happened to his dad or mom.

I hugged Kat closer. I could tell she was still awake. "I wish you would talk, baby. Do you remember the story Dallas told you? You can't let one bad season affect how you feel about the rest of them. We have had a bad season the past couple of days, and we may have a few more. But you can't let one day define how you are going to spend every other day. You have to live for the now. You have to find joy in each and every day. I just wish you could understand that. It's not just a story, Kat. It's the truth. I want you to find your joy. I've found mine. And guess what? It's right here." I kissed her on the head. "I could find more if you would only speak." I got no response from my daughter. I laid down my head and fell asleep, listening to her deepening breaths that told me she, too, was asleep.

The next morning, I could smell the coffee brewing. The sun wasn't even up, and when I looked, it was only five in the morning.

"How long have you been up?" I asked Max as he handed me a cup of coffee.

"About an hour." We sat silently for a while.

The sun struggled to break through the clouds of debris still left suspended in the air, casting a now familiar amber glow. The fire crackled and danced. It was colder than it should have been for this time of year. We were taking a chance leaving our homeplace. Here, we had everything we needed, for now at least. As time went on, we would run low on supplies with no way to replenish them. We would be at the mercy of others, and that wasn't a place we wanted to be. I looked at the fire and felt its warmth. I wondered if Dallas was warm. Did he have food to eat? Was he injured? Was that why he hadn't come home yet? My heart ached at the uncertainty. I wanted so much to see him coming down the drive at the last minute like a knight in shining armor.

I walked over to the van and got a legal pad of paper. I wrote him a note.

Dearest Dallas,

Honey, I hope this note finds you in good health. We waited for six days and decided to move on. Everyone is fine. No big injuries. I hope you catch up to us soon. I miss you, and I love you, honey. Marcus found his way here, so he is with me. He believes Makayla was trapped inside the hospital when it collapsed. My brother and his family are with us as well. We are leaving today to go to Montana. I hope your mom is expecting us. I'm scared, but I have to be strong.

I love you, Dallas. Please hurry.

Yours truly,
Ash

I put the note in a plastic baggy and nailed it to the porch post. I most likely would have been crying at that very moment if I weren't trying so hard to keep my heart and mind hard and cold. I didn't have the time or luxury to cry right now. I was moving my whole family. I was undertaking a large responsibility. I had to be strong for everyone.

Max was putting the last things into the truck. The cart was strapped down. It was big enough to carry all our necessities. It might take us all to pull it, but we wouldn't have to leave the most important stuff behind.

Marcus and Harley came out of the tent, rubbing the sleep from their eyes. They already had their clothes on and their duffel bags packed. I went into the tent to wake up Kat. I lay beside her and Taco as I brushed the hair out of her eyes. "Kat, honey, it's time to wake up. You can go back to sleep in the van, but I need you to get up."

She sleepily sat up and rubbed her eyes. Harley came in and rolled up her bed. Marcus soon followed and did the same. I helped Kat get dressed and rolled up her bed as well as mine. We got them stored in the van. Monica and Dannie were up soon. I ate dry cereal, allowing the kids to have the last of the milk.

Soon, we had the tents down, and everything was packed. It was time to go. I got the kids in the van as Max and Monica got Dannie in his car seat. Rocky would be in the back of the truck. If someone came up to the truck, they would have to deal with him. I looked around and took one last look at my home—a word that held very little meaning anymore—the place I wanted to raise my kids. I wanted to grow old here. This was the place I pictured my grandkids running up the porch into my open arms; the one place they could always come home to was gone, destroyed. We would never again see this place. I tried to act like I didn't care, but the truth was, I did care. It was killing me inside to drive away. I shook the negative thoughts out of my head. I couldn't bog myself down with negativity. I had a family relying on me to get them to Montana, and I was going to have to be hard and strong to get them there.

I sucked air deep into my lungs and sighed. "All right, are we ready for an adventure?" I clapped my hands and tried to sound excited. Harley let out an excited shout. Marcus joined Kat in the back seat and remained silent with his arms folded. I looked at him. "I'm sorry, Marcus. This is how it has to be. I left your dad a note, and he will catch up to us as soon as he is able." I shut the sliding van door without giving him a chance for rebuttal. I looked over at Max, who was going to take the first lead. He gave me a quick nod indicating that he was ready. I got into the van and pulled my pistol out, placing it in the console between the seats.

"What's that for, Mama?" Harley asked in horror.

"For just in case," I replied. "Just don't touch it. Do you understand me? It is real, and it's loaded, so don't touch it, or you could kill somebody." My tone was harsh, cold, and direct.

"In case of what?" she said inquisitively softly. Max began to drive ahead of me.

I sighed deeply as I pulled the gear shift into drive. "All the above." Harley slid as far away from the gun as possible.

Max pulled out first, and I followed him. We were headed out into the great unknown, an uncertain future with a million possibilities. But at least we were together.

CHAPTER 5

THE ROAD CONDITIONS surprised me. They were, for the most part, cleared. The pavement was cracked, and there was your occasional potholes the size of Volvos. I guessed the military or perhaps remaining survivors had cleared the road. The sides were a different story. Mounds of tattered debris littered what was once people's yards. Home after home was either damaged or completely leveled. Cars were crushed inside garages, the ground uneven with some places rising a good five feet above the rest. It was a bumpy ride, and I hated to think of what the terrain was doing to my tires. I briefly feared a flat; however, I was sure I could get one off the hundreds of abandoned vehicles along the way.

Max slowed ahead. I could see a group of people walking down the road. Most had a single bag holding their last worldly possessions. As we passed them silently, I held my head straight. I didn't want to look into the eyes of the people we passed. I didn't want that image to haunt my dreams. Some were crying; others wailing in complete and total distress. Some were blanked face and in total shock. I wanted to stop and help each and every one of them, but I knew I couldn't. I feared if we stopped, they could easily kick us out and take over the van. Double-checking to make sure the doors were locked, Max stopped ahead of me to allow another truck to pass.

A young Hispanic man looking about twenty-five years old glared at us as he walked toward the van. I reached over and pulled my pistol into my lap. I kept my eyes on him, willing him to keep moving. When he was even with my window, he jumped up on the running boards and began to smile wickedly. "How about a ride, Mommy?"

I felt Harley cringe in the seat beside me as Marcus straightened in his. I rolled down my window halfway. "I'm sorry, sir, but it doesn't seem to be that we are headed in the same direction." I smiled back as sweetly as I could fathom.

"That's okay, Mommy. I'll go anywhere with you. Come on, let me in."

"Back off. I'm just trying to get through, please." I tried to act naive, like his remarks weren't intimidating me.

"I've been walking a long time, Mommy. I need to ride awhile." The man tried to reach his arm through the open space.

I rolled the window down a little further, allowing him to fall in a few inches before he caught himself. He looked at me, confused. I was smiling at him now with my pistol cocked and wedged into his throat. "I said back off, Pedro." His eyes met mine. "You just survived the greatest natural disaster in the history of mankind. Do you really want a mother of three in a minivan to take you out?" That had to have been the most racial thing I had ever said in my entire life, but at that point, I really didn't care if I was being politically correct.

The Hispanic stranger swallowed hard, feeling the cold metal against his throat. "No."

"I didn't think so. Now slowly back the hell up and kindly get off my van, and we can all go about our way."

"Okay, I-I'm sorry," he stuttered, moving slowly as directed, and stepped off the running boards.

I rolled my window back up and looked up at Max and Monica glaring through the back glass. I waved, letting them know I was fine, and we drove on.

It was dark when we reached Alabaster State Park near Freedom, Oklahoma. To our surprise, there wasn't a charge for campsites.

"All of our actual campsites are taken, but you can pull up to the recreation area and pitch a tent there." The helpful park ranger instructed us as to where to go.

We pulled up and found a spot.

"I'll get dinner together real fast." Monica pulled out bread and cans of Spam and went to work preparing plates. We ate quietly, taking in our new surroundings.

Max broke the silence, "I think we should only pitch one tent and sleep in shifts tonight. There are a lot of people around, and I don't want anyone to get the bright idea to break into the van or truck."

I nodded in agreement.

"OH!" Monica exclaimed loudly. "Which reminds me, what did that creep want earlier today? You know, the one who jumped up on your van today."

"He just wanted a ride. Basically, he was being an ass, so I put my pistol in his throat and asked if he wanted to reconsider his actions, and he got off. No biggie."

Max looked at me knowingly. There was no doubt in his mind that I would have dropped that man where he stood if he hadn't backed off.

"Mama, how can I do dishes tonight?" Harley asked, changing the subject.

"I will walk with you down to the lake, and we can do them there." Marcus stood up, offering a hand to Harley to help her up. Max handed Marcus a flashlight. They collected the dishes and disappeared into the darkness.

My heart skipped a few beats seeing them disappear into the darkness. I knew I couldn't be with them every moment, so I sucked in my breath and exhaled long and hard. I fished around and found my cigarettes. I had been trying to cut back so I make them last longer.

"Kat, honey, why don't you take Taco and walk around a minute? Let him use the bathroom, and then you can go put on your night clothes." She silently did as she was told.

"Well, little man, it's past your bedtime. I'm going to see if I can get him to sleep," Monica said as she took Dannie into the tent.

"You okay?" Max gestured my way.

"Yeah, I'm fine. Just tired, I guess, and my back is stiff from driving all day. I hate to wish age on my kids, but I wish at least one of them had a driver's license so we could share the driving." I snickered under my breath.

"No, I mean, are you all right? A lot has happened the last two days, and I just wanted to make sure you are processing everything okay." Max slid beside me and put his arm around me. "I don't want this to come out wrong, so forgive me if it does, but it seems you're teetering on the edge a little bit."

"There is nothing wrong with my processor, little brother. I can handle it. This trip was my idea, and I will do what I have to, to ensure we all make it safely." I smiled and leaned my head on his shoulder.

"Well, if you need to talk, I'm here. You know that, right?"

"Yeah, I know, and thank you for keeping a check on me."

Kat walked back with Taco following her closely. She pointed toward the tent.

"Okay, if you want to go on to bed, you can just be quiet when you go into the tent. Monica is trying to get Dannie to sleep." She walked quietly and went inside the tent.

I began to laugh. I ran my fingers through my hair and rested my head in my hands. I was laughing to fight back the tears that were building up inside me, like a dam that was about to burst.

"What are you laughing at?" Max inquired.

"I told her to be quiet going into the tent. Like the kid makes a sound anyway." I rested my head on my knees. My voice was shaky. "Out of everything, what bugs me the most is the fact that she won't talk."

"She will, sissy. When she is ready, she will. She has to have time to process everything in her own way." Max patted me on the back. "Here come the other two."

Harley and Marcus came back into sight. They put the dishes away, and Marcus went into the tent.

"Mama, can you go with me to the bathroom?" Harley asked.

"Yeah, they have a public restroom right down the road. I'll go with you. Max, if you will, stay here, and when Monica gets Dannie to sleep, you can go with her. That way, there will be one of us here at all times."

"Sounds good to me. You just be careful."

Harley and I walked to the bathroom with a flashlight. I caught myself looking over my shoulder many times. I felt like at any time someone was going to jump out and yell boo. I had my pistol wedged against my back, tucked tightly in my waistband, and out of sight. I didn't want to upset Harley.

"It will be nice to use a regular bathroom again," Harley said cheerfully as she almost seemed to skip down the pebbled pathway to the bathroom.

"Yes, it will, baby." I smiled and did my best to give her a happy face as I took her hand and rounded the corner into the ladies' room.

Harley opened the door to one of the stalls and quickly shut it. She looked at me with a horrified look.

"Harley, what is it, honey? What's wrong?" I quickly went to her and put my hand under her chin, forcing her to look at me.

Harley looked up at me with her innocent blue eyes. "I know I haven't been on this earth as long as some people, and maybe I'm a little late on this recognition, but life really is unfair." Harley opened the bathroom stall door wide so I could see inside.

I cautiously looked into the stall, not knowing what to expect. I immediately saw what she was talking about. Inside the stall rested two five-gallon buckets. The first was labeled Number One, and the second was labeled Number Two. I cupped my hand over my mouth and pinched my lips together. It did little to hold back the burst of laughter that escaped. After a while, I was laughing so hard I was holding my chest. I leaned against the wall and slid down.

Harley stood silently watching me with her forehead all scrunched up. "Mom, seriously, sometimes I think you're really losing it," she said as she disappeared into the stall, shaking her head.

Another howl of laughter escaped my lips. I pulled myself up and entered one of the other stalls. All the forced laughing was making me welcome that Number One bucket. We hurried back to the campsite with me giggling and snickering most of the way.

I took first watch and allowed Max to take the second watch since he seemed to like to wake up early anyway. When he relieved me, the campgrounds were deathly silent. I welcomed the sleeping bag as it seemed to be calling my name. I climbed in between my girls, who never made a sound. Marcus only stirred silently and changed his position. Taco looked up and laid his head back down. Monica was asleep with Dannie in her arms. I watched the glow from the campfire dance against the tent. I listened to the peaceful breathing of my family and drifted off into a dreamless sleep.

It was still dark when Max woke me. The sun was struggling to break through the clouds. It looked like a big orange ball hovering in the bleak sky. We sat quietly and drank coffee, jumping at a mild disturbance. We looked back to see Monica bolting from the tent like a rabid wolf. She never said anything. She had her hand over her mouth, and she was running toward the bathrooms.

"Watch the kids. I'll be right back. I'll make sure she's okay." I took off after Monica. I was scared she had some kind of food poisoning. We had tried to be so careful while cooking. I rounded the corner and found Monica hugging a garbage can, puking. I wet a handful of toilet paper and handed it to her. She finished and slumped against the wall, pressing the toilet paper to her head.

"Feeling better?" I inquired.

"No." Monica gave a sarcastic laugh and continued to press the paper to her head.

"So what's going on?"

"I think I'm living proof." Monica stood up and looked at me directly.

I couldn't get a read on her. Her facial expressions were changing rapidly from scared to worried to an almost happy look. "Monica, what are you talking about? Living proof of what?" I looked at her squarely in the eyes.

"That God has a sense of humor."

"Honey, it's too early for subtlety, and I have had only one cup of coffee. Please forgive me for being slow, but you're going to have to spell it out for me." I scrunched up my face and gave her a goofy, confused look.

Monica hung her head low. "I'm pregnant."

My mouth dropped. I quickly recovered from the shock. "How late are you?"

"Six months."

My mouth once again dropped open in shock. "Jesus, Monica. Why didn't you say something?"

She began to cry. "I was on the pill. When I was finally late, I didn't understand. It's not something we were planning on, you know. It just sorta happened. After a while, I knew I couldn't live in denial. I went to the doctor, and he confirmed that I was pregnant, then he told me how far along I was. I was in shock. I still don't understand it. I knew I had gained some weight, but I didn't put two and two together since I was still on the pill. I just thought I was having a lot of gas. It was actually the baby moving around. I was going to tell Max on the day everything went to shit. And ever since then, I just haven't found the right time." She was looking at me now with tears in her eyes. "What are we going to do, Ashley?"

"Well, it sounds like we are going to have a baby. You are going to have to be careful. Don't be lifting anything heavy, and walk as much as you can. Anytime we stop, you need to get out and walk around. When the time comes, I can deliver the baby. But you are going to have to tell Max soon."

Monica nodded in agreement. "I will tell him tonight after Dannie goes to sleep."

"I will get my girls and Marcus in the tent a little early tonight and give y'all some privacy."

Monica nodded again. "Thanks, Ashley."

I smiled my warmest smile, stood up, and offered her my hand. "Come on, let's get our stuff together and get on the road." I hugged her softly. "We will get through this too. I don't want you worrying about any of this." Monica nodded. I knew I did little to calm her fears, and nothing was going to make her feel better about bringing a child into this world when everything seemed to be falling apart. I had my reservations about it as well, but it was just a setback that we would deal with in three months. The main thing we had to deal with was making sure Monica had adequate nutrition and put as little stress on her as possible.

We made it back to the campsite and found the kids had their hot cocoa and Max had made oatmeal for everyone. I looked over at

Kat, who only held her bowl, looking into it, grimacing. I chuckled to myself. Even as a baby, she hated oatmeal. I went over and sat beside her. "Just pretend it's a steak." Kat looked at me with her little nose wrinkled. "I know you don't like it, but you should be happy you have it. It's cold, and it will help warm you up, so go on, eat it."

"Here's your bowl, sissy." Max handed me a bowl of oatmeal, smiling. "Pretend it's a steak."

I took the bowl hesitantly. I had forgotten that I didn't care for oatmeal either. I looked down at Kat, who was staring at me with a grin on her face and a menacing look in her eyes. She knew I didn't like oatmeal. She was obviously waiting for me to eat mine before she was going to eat hers. Knowing I had to do what I needed to do to make my kid eat, I scooped up a spoonful of the thick, sticky, gooey muck and forced it into my mouth. I tried to chew as little as possible. I looked down at Kat, who was still smiling wide at me. She was smart enough to know what I was doing. It felt so good to see her smile. "It's not so bad. Just take big bites and get it over with. We need to have something in our tummies." I took another large bite and smiled to myself when I saw Kat begin to eat. I swallowed hard and finished my bowl of mushy stuff with three more bites. Harley and Marcus took the dishes and got them washed. Max and I broke camp down while Monica got Dannie dressed.

We got the truck loaded, Rocky tied in, and Dannie in his car seat. I was shutting the doors to the van when my brother came up to me. "Do you want to take the lead today?"

"Yeah, that will be fine. I got the map."

Max nodded and patted the van. "Be careful, and if you need me, just pull over."

And with that, we were on the road again.

We had only been driving for three hours on a lonely, deserted highway when I saw a gas station that seemed to be open for business. I pulled up to the gas pumps. Max took position on the other side of the pumps. He climbed out of the truck and went into the store. Max quickly came out, smiling. "They have gas. It's cash only though."

"If you fill the tanks, I will pay for it. You can get it next time." I wasn't sure how much cash they had, and I didn't want to make things hard on them. "I wanted to get the kids a soda and candy bar."

"Sounds good to me." Max immediately started pumping the gas.

I went inside the store. "I will be paying for a complete fill-up on both vehicles." The small slender lady behind the counter smiled and nodded. She was very short and appeared to be Asian descent. I wasn't sure she could speak English, but at least she seemed to understand me. I went to the coolers in the back of the store to retrieve sodas for everyone. A squeaking door caught my attention. I glanced up to see two small children smiling at me from behind the door. The youngest waved at me. I smiled back and waved. The clerk yelled something in her native tongue, and the door quickly shut. I could still hear children's laughter from behind the door. I guessed the children belonged to the female clerk behind the counter. They obviously lived behind the store.

A jingling bell distracted me away from the hiding children. I looked up expecting to see Max entering the store. Instead, a young man quickly made his way to the counter. "Give me the money!" he screamed at the clerk.

I ducked down behind the aisle of potato chips. The man hadn't seen me, or else, he would be forcing me to the front of the store. I rolled my eyes. *Why does this keep happening to me?* I thought to myself. I knew I had to do something. I couldn't take a chance of Max or any other member of my family walking in on a robbery. I peeked around the corner. The female clerk had her hands up and was now crying.

"No, no, please don't do this," she pleaded with the man.

"Shut up and give me the money and give me a carton of cigarettes too." The man waved a relatively small pocketknife around.

I rolled my eyes again. This stupid guy was trying to rob a gas station with a pocketknife. He didn't look to be starving or emaciated. He was doing this to be stupid. I pulled my gun from my back. Standing up, I closed my eyes and took a deep breath in an attempt to compose myself. Was I really going to do this? Was I really about to attempt to break up a robbery? I started forward. The clerk saw me. I saw the fear in her eyes. I knew she had to be thinking about her own children. She began to poke buttons on the cash register. The robber smiled; he seemed to be happy with himself. He felt a sudden flash of accomplishment by making the clerk do what he wanted.

I stepped silently behind him. I held the pistol tightly in my hands. I raised it and brought the butt end down on the back of his head. I had seen it done in the movies dozens of times. I should have realized nothing works out the way it did in the movies. The robber spun around, cursing, "Son of a bitch." He had turned so that the knife was now pointing toward me. I quickly kicked him in the gut. He doubled over in pain, still clutching the knife. I grabbed his arm and twisted it behind his back and shoved him, forcing him to bend at the waist over the counter. He yelped and whined as I removed the knife from his hand and threw it behind the counter.

"Now what the hell do you think you're doing?" I tightened my grip on his arm, keeping him down. "This nice lady opened her store to the public to help us out, and you're going to pull this on her?" I looked down and noticed a tear coming out of the guy's eye. "How old are you?" There was no response. "Answer me, you little prick." I twisted on his arm a little harder, making him holler out.

"I'm twenty!" he yelled out in pain as another tear fell from his eye.

"Oh no, there's no crying. This lady was crying, and you didn't stop. Why should I?" I looked at the clerk, who was also shaking her head in disgust. "Do you live around here?"

"No."

"No what?"

"No, I don't live around here."

"It's 'No, ma'am,' asshole."

"No ma'am, I don't live around here!"

"So you just saw this place open and thought you would rob it with your little knife?" I laughed. "God, you are stupid." I paused, looking at him. "I'm going to let you stand up, and if you attempt to run, I will drop you where you stand. Do you hear me?"

"Yes." He paused briefly and then corrected himself, "Yes, ma'am."

I loosened my grip and allowed the kid to stand freely before me. He looked young standing there with the tears flowing freely from his eyes. "Why would you want to do something so stupid? You came in here with a knife. What if she had a gun? She could have killed you. What were you thinking?"

"I don't know. I just needed some money. I met up with these guys, and they said I could stay with them, but I had to prove I was tough enough."

I cringed at the thought. Gangs were all over the United States. It should come as no surprise that under the circumstances that new gangs would be forming as people united in an attempt to survive. "Well, you picked the wrong store on the wrong day. You need to learn a lesson, little boy." I raised my gun.

"Don't shoot me, please!" the robber pleaded.

"Relax, asshole. I'm not going to shoot you. That would only give you a lesson in violence. Something tells me you have plenty of that. No, what I think you need is a lesson in humility. You come in here all big and bad, waving your little knife around, and humiliate this woman who has done nothing but open her store to provide people with a service that's desperately needed by so many."

"What are you going to do?" the robber asked me.

"Humiliate you." He looked at me with inquisitive eyes. I felt the eyes of the clerk on me as well. "Strip."

"What?"

"You heard me. Strip. Take off all your clothes."

"I'm not going to—" he began in protest. He stopped short as I cocked the gun, keeping it pointed at him.

"I think you better do what she says," the clerk finally spoke.

The young guy looked around briefly and commenced to undress. He piled his clothes in the floor. He stood before the clerk and me completely nude. His hands cupped together in an attempt to cover himself.

"Now walk out of here and don't come back. If you are smart, you would stay away from that gang you so badly want to be a part of. So far, it hasn't done anything but get you into trouble."

"I can't go out there with my junk hanging."

"You will walk out of here naked and be just as humiliated as you made this lady feel. I have two daughters in the van out there. You will keep yourself covered and keep walking. If you drop your hand or expose yourself in any way, I will take my gun and blow your junk completely off. Do you understand?"

He nodded in compliance. Slowly he backed out of the store, trying his best to keep himself covered. The clerk and I watched him walk away with his head hung down in shame. Max watched in shock as the naked boy walked past him. He looked toward the store in question. I turned to the clerk, who was smiling. "If you will be so kind to ring up my gas and a few sodas and this candy, I'll be on my way."

"I can't thank you enough," the clerk said.

"Well, just remember what he said. There are more of them out there, so this may not be the last you heard from them." I paid for our gas and sodas. "Do you have a gun here?"

"I wouldn't know what to do with one if I had it."

"You may want to get one and learn. You have a family to protect." I motioned to the door where her children had been peeking out of.

On my way out, I stopped and picked up the pile of clothes, then exited the store.

"What was that all about?" Max asked, meeting me halfway.

I laughed and smiled. "Just some dumbass trying to be a punk. I put him in his place. Are we ready to go?" I tried to act happy as if nothing were wrong when in fact my heart was racing.

"Yeah, we got a full tank."

"Great." I gave Max his share of the warm sodas and a juice for Dannie and got into the van without another word.

"Is everything okay?" Marcus asked.

"Yeah, honey, everything is fine. Y'all ready to get back on the road?" No one answered me. I handed Harley the bag of remaining drinks and candy, and she handed them out.

We drove only a short way, and I saw the young man walking still naked down the road. I slowed down and rolled down my window. As soon as we passed him, I chunked his clothes out the window and kept driving. I looked in my rearview mirror and saw the young man scrambling to get his clothes. I couldn't help but smile to myself.

It was a long trip, riding mostly in silence. We couldn't play the license plate game considering there weren't many other cars on the road. We couldn't play the billboard game because most of the billboards were on the ground. Kat napped on and off, as did Marcus. Harley remained awake most of the day, her eyes scanning the destruction as we passed each little town. I was finished trying to protect her innocent eyes. Destruction was everywhere, and there was no way around it.

We pulled into the Lake Mead recreation area about 5:00 p.m. Lake Mead, Kansas, wasn't very crowded. We had to pay a small fee to use a campsite. We chose one close to the lake and not too far away from the bathrooms. We started our routine. Max and I set up the tents, the kids collected firewood, and Monica started supper. We ate quietly around the campfire. I decided that I needed something to lighten the mood. I went to the van and got a small compact disk player. I popped in a CD, and the music began. Max nodded in approval. Since there weren't many campers, I wasn't worried about disturbing the peace, so I cranked up the volume. I placed the CD player on a rock and grabbed Harley's hand, plucking her up from her spot. We danced around the fire like a couple of maniacs. We weren't doing any particular dance. We each did our own thing. Marcus began laughing, as did Kat. Max took Monica's hand, and they began to twirl around the fire. I pointed to Marcus. "Come on, boy!" I yelled. "You and Kat, get up here." They both shook their heads no, but that wasn't good enough for me. I was determined that we were going to have a little fun. I got Kat by the hand, and Harley took Marcus by the hand. And we both pulled them up. We all danced around being silly for the duration of the song. Even little Dannie got into the groove by bumping and stomping around. It wasn't much, but we had a few much-needed laughs. When the song was over, we sat down, still laughing. Monica laid her head down in her lap.

"You okay?" I looked at her inquisitively.

"Yeah, I just got a little dizzy. It's been a long time since I danced like that." She gave a small giggle under her breath. Monica looked positively green.

"Well, you should take it easy." She only nodded in response.

Max broke the silence. "Well, why don't y'all get the dishes done? Then we can start bedding down. I'm going to take Dannie and Rocky for a walk, and we will be back."

"Kat, why don't we get your night clothes and go to the bathroom? Harley, if you and Marcus can handle the dishes, then go get ready for bed." We got our clothes from the van and walked to the bathroom with Taco perpetually by our side. We returned to the campsite and let Harley and Marcus take their turns at the bathroom. I watched Dannie while Monica and Max went to the bathroom.

We reconvened around the campfire for a while. I stared into the dark night sky. I couldn't see any stars even though I knew they were up there. Marcus, Harley, and Kat soon went to the tent and bedded down for the night. Max told me he would take first watch that night, so I soon excused myself, nodding to Monica on my way into the tent. I lay down on top of the sleeping bag and covered myself and Kat with a blanket. I hugged her closely, kissing her on the head. I watched the silhouettes of Max and Monica. I knew she was telling him. It killed the meddling part of me that I couldn't hear what they were saying. They started out sitting close to each other. Eventually, Max had his arms around her. I expected that she was crying. I saw Max when he stood up, bringing his hand to his head. I knew for sure that she had told him. I was prepared to go out there if he got upset. He wasn't standing too long when I saw him kneel beside her and put his arm back around her and hugged her close to him. I knew then they were going to be okay. I closed my eyes and drifted off.

Max woke me up at 2:00 a.m. He had a pot of coffee ready.

"Just in case you're wondering, she told me," Max said with his head hung low.

I could tell he was worried. "It will be fine, Max. I feel confident about delivering the baby when the time comes."

"It's not just that. It's everything, sissy. Is she going to eat right? Is the baby going to be born healthy?"

"Max, those are worries and concerns every parent has no matter what the situation is. That's normal." I went to him and put my arm around him. "Remember how you felt when she told you she was pregnant with Dannie? Were your feelings any different then?"

"Of course not, but at least then we had doctors and prenatal care. It's just different, sissy."

"So we are going to have to treat this like anything else. We will have to make the best of it. We have to watch her close. Don't let her lift anything or do too much. She didn't have any problems with the first pregnancy, and I don't perceive any with this one. We have to be confident and vigilant, and we can get through this like anything else as long as we work together."

Max only nodded. "I'm pretty beat. I think I'm going to turn in. We have another day of driving tomorrow."

"And probably walking too. Have you looked at our gas?" My statement reminded him of our depleting gas supply. His face hung toward the ground. "We will run out tomorrow." We were down to what we had in the reserve tanks. That would get us through tomorrow, and then we would be on foot. We hadn't seen an open gas station since that morning, and there was no reason for me to believe that there was going to be one. We would camp tomorrow night and then set out on foot the next morning. It was something neither of us looked forward to.

Max went into the tent without saying another word. I wondered if he hadn't changed his mind about this whole trip. We really wouldn't have been in better shape as far as the pregnancy if we had stayed. Monica would have ended up delivering on a dirty stretcher in the open air or in a filthy tent with rushed and exhausted nurses. I knew the situation still weighed heavily on my brother's heart, but I still thought we were better off. I hoped, along the way, there would be a Red Cross station or something set up so Monica could be examined properly by a doctor.

I had my worries and concerns as well as anyone else. Random thoughts entered my head sporadically. I looked up at the starless night and wondered if Dallas were somewhere safe, looking up at the same sky, or if he were up there somewhere, looking down on me. I briefly thought of my parents and the sight of their bodies as Max and I covered them with dirt. I was amazed at how much Harley had grown over the last few days. She was pitching in and helping out without complaining. She had a certain maturity about her now that I had never been seen before. I was very proud of her. And poor Kat, she still hadn't spoken, but I truly believed she had the ability to. I had to believe that in time she would choose to speak, and then I wouldn't be able to shut her up. Marcus had been a great asset. He was helping out wherever he could to make himself useful. He was faced with the probable loss of both parents but was handling himself with a maturity that baffled me. I couldn't tell what was going through his mind or how he felt about things, but he at least looked happy with us. Like the rest of us, he was making the best of it. I sat quietly with my private thoughts skipping around in my head, like a flat rock being thrown across a flat body of water. I sipped the strong coffee until the sun began to make its bleak entry into the sky. Another day was upon us.

CHAPTER 6

AFTER A QUICK, repulsive breakfast of oatmeal, we assumed our usual routines. I loaded the last remnants into the van and closed the hatch, taking a deep breath. I was certain that it would be the last time I packed up the van. Our gas was almost gone, and we would be on foot very soon. I had to stay in a positive frame of mind. I had to get my family through this journey.

"I'll take the lead today, sissy," Max called out. "We should get at least a hundred miles before we have to stop."

I nodded in agreement. "I figured when we have to stop, we go ahead and make camp for the night, then pick up on foot in the morning." Max returned with an affirmative nod and got into the truck, where Monica and Dannie were waiting.

As Max predicted, we drove almost a hundred miles before my gas light came on with the annoying ding-dong indicating my gas was low. I honked my horn and flashed my lights to get Max's attention. We pulled off the road. Max got out of the truck and walked back to the van.

"You out of gas?"

"My gas light just came on, so I'm not going to get much farther." I feared that Max totally hated me, even though it was inevitable that we would eventually run out of gas. I couldn't help but feel that it was my fault. I ran out first, and it was my fault for wanting and encouraging Max and Monica to come with me.

"Well," Max sounded off with a hint of enthusiasm in his voice, "I say we siphon what we can out of the tanks and keep it to help start campfires. I'll tell Monica, and we can set up camp over there. It looks like a pretty flat spot." He returned to his truck.

I looked to the van. Marcus was already out opening the hatch. He helped Max get the homemade buggy off the truck. Monica and I set up the tents while Harley watched Dannie, and Kat helped Max gather some firewood. We all had our task and set about getting camp made before it got dark. Monica and I made a pot of soup along with a pan of corn bread. We were lucky enough to have enough daylight left to make some sun tea. It was a nice treat for us. We spent the evening sitting around the campfire making small talk. There was a deep menacing, melancholic feeling that hung heavily in the air around us. We were all dreading the next morning. The best part was sitting in the company of two of the most well-behaved canines. Rocky sat quietly, watching us like a guardian of the night. And poor little Taco was nestled tightly in Kat's arms. His little ears perked up like radars to the slightest of sounds. When we had all the silence we could handle, one by one we retired to bed. Max was kind enough to take first watch.

Sometime around 2:00 a.m., Max woke me with vigorous shaking. "Sissy, wake up."

I sprang from my sleeping bag when I felt the urgency in Max's voice. "What is it?"

"A storm is coming, a bad one." Max helped me out of the tent. I felt the cool wind blowing forcefully. Lightning flashed, illuminating the sky around us. Wiping the sleep from my eyes, I attempted to gain some form of composure. I looked around. The flames of the campfire leaned to one side in the blowing wind. Hot embers danced in the breeze above the flames. Thunder clapped as another bolt of lightning struck. I looked at Max, who was obviously looking to me for suggestions. Seeing the desperation in his eyes, I knew I couldn't let him down.

I started barking orders immediately, "Start getting stuff packed up or tied down. I'll wake everybody up." The wind kicked up another notch. I yelled over it and pointed toward the vehicles, "We will be safer in the truck and van!" Max nodded and went to work.

Luck was on our side as we got the tents down and were safely in the vehicles moments before the rain began pounding the windshield. The van soon seemed to rock from the force of the wind coming from all directions. Marcus had stretched out in the back seat while Harley and Kat lay side by side facing each other on the floor. Harley had her arm around Kat's shoulders. I wasn't sure who she was attempting to comfort, Kat or herself. I kept a vigilant eye on the sky from the driver's seat. I knew we were in what was commonly called tornado alley. It was my biggest fear at the point that nature's fury would be released on us once again.

After several hours, the wind subsided and all was calm, except for a trickle of rain that cascaded down from the sky. I saw Max get out of the truck. I went to meet him.

"We are going to stay in the truck for the night," Max stated.

"Sounds good. Y'all all right?"

"Yeah, we are fine, just tired. Lock your doors, and we should all be able to get a good night's sleep."

We bid each other good night, and I returned to the kids. "Okay, y'all go on to sleep. The storm looks like it's over, but just in case, we are staying in here till morning." They all nodded in agreement. Marcus rolled over and tucked himself in for the night. I smiled when I saw Kat's little hand resting on Harley's shoulder. Her eyes were closed in clear indication that she was already asleep. I eventually dozed off.

My eyes easily fluttered open when Max began tapping on the driver's side window. I looked up to see his big chocolate-brown eyes gazing at me. I got out of the van and stretched my legs. Dawn was approaching, and we had a long hard day upon us. Max and I got everything loaded up on the pull cart. And after a breakfast of dry, cold cereal, we went to the cart to begin our long haul.

"Well, this is an unexpected setback," Max stated as he looked at the cart with the same puzzled look I had.

The rain had softened the ground significantly, and the added weight on the cart had settled the wheels into the softened earth. We were stuck in a mud puddle that looked to be the size of the Grand Canyon.

"I'll pull. You two push," I said, pointing to Max and Marcus with authority. "Let's get this son of a bitch out of here." I was fed up and pissed off. We sloshed around the mud and got into position. Latching onto the cart, I pulled with all my might. Max was joined by Marcus. They pushed with everything they had, our faces turning red with strain. Our feet slipped all over the place. The stubborn cart moved only inches. Repeatedly we tugged and heaved against the stubborn piece of crap. Out of nowhere, a piece of rope fell almost in my face. In our struggle, we hadn't noticed that someone had ridden up on a horse. I looked up to see an elderly thin light-skinned African American man. At first glance, he oddly reminded me of a black eel as his thin body snaked around the saddle. He was bald with muscular upper body and large brown eyes that resembled the puddles of mud we were standing in. His long, lanky legs looked to be as thin as toothpicks. He had nearly nonexistent eyebrows, and his wardrobe consisted of different shades of brown, which was consistent with his Western attire. The horse was a big brown steed with a white patch on its throat.

"Attach this to your cart, and let's see if we can get you folks outta here." His voice was kind but raspy, like he had smoked for too many years.

I did as he asked, tying his rope to our little cart, trusting him to our most treasured belongings without question. Our cart came right out of the excessive mud puddle with great ease.

"Where you folks headed?" he asked as he kept pulling the cart.

"Montana," I said proudly.

The old man looked at me with skepticism in his eyes. "Well, you follow me, and I'll set you up with a good meal. You can get cleaned up and have a place to sleep for the night. With everything that's going on, it's the least I can do to help another citizen." He didn't make any effort to let go of his end of the rope. I didn't feel like I was in a position or attitude to argue with him. With the few words he spoke, he reflected the wisdom and intelligence of years of life experience.

"You really don't have to do that, sir. We have our tents. We just had a bout of bad luck, that's all. We just parked our cart in the wrong spot." I attempted to sound comedic but fell short. Max looked at me, wondering what I was thinking. I shrugged my shoulders. It was much too early in the day for us to even think about stopping for the night.

"My name is Lou Fellows. I have a ranch not too far from here. You folks follow me, and we'll get you sorted out. I won't hear no more about it." His words were pronounced with confidence and firmness. The little voice inside my head suggested that I just go with it.

Max looked at me and held out his arms, suggesting that I should protest. Falling back, I went to my dear brother. "Max, he's an old man. If he wants to rob us, I think we can take him. Just go with it. Something tells me that this is right," I explained.

Max shrugged his shoulders. He probably felt at that point there was no use attempting to argue with any of us. I sympathized with his feeling. He was the leader of his family, and yet he felt useless between me and this persistent old man.

"Why y'all headed to Montana?" Old Man Lou inquired.

"We are going to Browning, Montana," I explained.

"That's Blackfeet Nation," the old man said, showing his geography knowledge.

"Yes, sir. My fiancé is a Blackfoot Indian, if that is the proper way of putting it," I explained briefly, hoping he would not press for more information. I really wasn't in the mood to go explain my relationship with Dallas. It caused me deep emotional pain to think of him too much. I didn't have the ability or patience to go into details at that specific time. I didn't have the luxury of getting emotional just yet. I tried to sound strong, persistent, and determined.

"That is some beautiful country through there, the most beautiful I have ever seen." He nodded with self-assurance and reluctance to go any further with the conversation. We hadn't walked for long when we turned onto a small dirt road. Huge oak trees lined the left side of the dirt road that was becoming nothing more than a wide path. The trees hung over the road, shading the path with a canopy of colorful fall foliage. A beautiful fenced green pasture followed the road on the right side. In that pasture were the biggest cows I had ever seen. The marvelous creatures were a deep reddish-brown color each with their own markings.

"Well, here we are, home sweet home." The old man dismounted his horse. He indeed was as tall as I expected him to be.

We stood in front of a small single-story, with a porch that ran the entire length of the house. The porch sheltered two large rocking chairs and single bench. Wood shavings littered in the porch, dancing in the breeze, was evidence that someone enjoyed whittling, a practice I hadn't seen in a very long time. It was quaint and homey; sun-bleached curtains blew through open windows, showing that this place once had a woman's touch.

There was a large wooden barn in the rear. A tall, lean, muscular man walked out of the barn and made his way toward us. Lou stopped and waited for him. We stood there, not sure where to go or what to do next. The muscleman approached the house and met Lou on the steps. He cocked his head to the side, looking at us intently. Looking away, he shook his head in a negative manner. "You bringing home strays now, old man?" He glared at Lou with a half smile.

His words rang like venom in my brain. I spoke up, "We are not strays. Mr. Lou, if you will, just show us where we can set up our tents and possibly get washed up. We will be out of here at first light."

"Raven, show these folks where they will be sleeping and where to clean up. I'll get the soup on. It will be ready in about twenty minutes. And I ain't gonna hear no more about it." Lou patted Raven on the back as he turned toward the house. "Play nice, Raven."

Raven snickered under his breath. "Whatever you say, old man." He smiled a crooked smile as Lou walked into the house, allowing the old screen door to slam behind him.

I turned to the man called Raven. "Please, sir, if you will just show us where we can set up our tents, we'll be fine. We aren't moochers or anything like that. He just helped us get our cart out of the mud, and he never let go of it."

Raven turned to me. He walked over to me with a slow glide. I had to look to make sure his feet were on the ground. He leaned down to where his face was right in mine. I didn't want to look into his eyes, but I couldn't help myself. They were captivating. "You heard the old man. If you do anything other than what he told you, he will have your ass and mine." Again, he snickered and smiled a crooked smile. Raven was about six feet tall with narrow crystal-blue eyes that were like two windows to the high noon sky. His skin had been kissed by the sun, leaving a beautiful golden tan. His hair was sandy-colored and shaggy, which he kept stuffed under his tattered and worn cowboy hat. With broad shoulders and narrow hips, he had a mysterious lure to him that I found almost seductive. I caught myself staring at him, hardly breathing.

Finally forcing myself to look away, I stammered, "So are you going to show us where he wants us?" I could only imagine what we looked like to him. Here we were, a family of misfits covered in mud seemingly looking for a handout while the world was coming apart from every angle.

He spoke a seductively coarse yet amazingly clear single command, "Follow me."

We did as he asked and followed him behind the single-story homestead to a long building. Once inside, there were metal bunks all along the wall with mattress rolled up on each of them.

"This is the old slave quarters. We use it once a year for harvest season. There are sheets and blankets in the cabinets over there, and the showers are outside in the back. You got about fifteen minutes to wash up. The old man don't like it if you're late, so you'd better hurry."

Turning to express my gratitude, thinking to myself that I was looking for any reason to look into his eyes again, I met an old wooden door being shut in my face. "Well, he is a friendly fellow, isn't he?"

"Sissy, what are we doing? We don't have time to shoot the shit with some old man over dinner. We have to get going." Max had his hands on his hips in frustration.

"Max, I know you're upset, and I know this isn't what we planned, but something just tells me that this is right. I have gone against my gut feelings before and ended up double-dipped in shit as an outcome." I paused and looked at my family. "Please, y'all, just trust me on this. We will be out of here first thing in the morning." Max nodded in a protested agreement.

We gathered our clothes and went to the showers behind the long building. There were four wooden shower stalls open at the bottom for drainage and the top for the plumbing. It was cold as hell but quite refreshing. We washed the mud off and got dressed while Monica and the kids waited. We went around to the front of the house and knocked.

"You ain't gotta knock! Y'all come on in! The soup is hot and ready!" Old man Lou shouted from his kitchen. We walked in and said hello. Raven was there as well, sitting at one end of the table.

"I don't believe I got a chance to properly introduce ourselves. I'm Ashley, and these are my kids, Harley and Kat. This is my fiancé's son, Marcus. This is my brother, Max; his wife, Monica; and their son, Dannie." Everyone gave a nod or a little wave. "I think I speak for all of us when I say thank you for helping us get our cart out of the mud and, of course, for a nice meal." We all took a seat at the table. The soup was already in small stainless steel bowls.

"You are welcome for the assistance. Let's eat, then we can talk," Lou stated in a matter-of-fact voice as he sat and almost immediately brought his spoon to his mouth.

I got the impression that Lou wasn't accustomed to having people disagree or argue with him. He said what he had to say, and that was all there was to the matter. I understood that this was his farm. This was his own little piece of the world, and he was king of his domain. However, we weren't his lifelong faithful servants. I would be nice and play along, but in the morning, we would be gone, even if it meant us picking up in the middle of the night and leaving. What was he going to do, chase us down on horseback? And this farmhand of his, Raven, was the most unfriendly, cocky, and arrogant son of a bitch I had ever had the displeasure of meeting. I couldn't imagine spending too much time around him without absolutely wanting to kill him.

The remainder of the meal was eaten in total silence. The only sound made was the subtle slurping of the soup broth off the spoon until Lou finally said, "Harley, you seem like you're old enough. Do you think you can handle washing up these few dishes while I talk to your mama a little while?" Lou patted her hand gently and smiled.

Harley beamed with the attention. "Yes, sir, I can do that."

"I'll help," Marcus stated as he rose from his chair and helped collect the empty bowls.

I followed Lou onto the porch. He hitched his thumbs into his suspenders and stretched a little. "Little lady, I admire your courage, determination, and conviction, but truth be told, you're not going to make it to Montana with that little cart of yours." He looked at me with intense eyes.

"Do you just enjoy raining on people's parade, or is it just me?" Now this old man wanted to get cocky and superior on me. I was feeling like it was time to leave sooner rather than later.

Lou gave a little chuckle. "Walk with me." He stepped off the porch and began walking toward the barn.

I had no idea why, but I felt compelled to follow him. It could have been the lingering respect for my elders that my mama pounded into me over the years.

"Have you ever heard of the Great Northern Centennial Cattle Drive?"

"No, sir, I haven't."

"Well, that's what I used to do before I settled down here. I worked all the big cattle drives. They made such a big deal about driving cattle from North Dakota over into Montana. But what people didn't realize is that the cattle were actually driven from San Antonio, Texas. It was on that cattle drive that I met Raven. He was just a young buck then. He couldn't tell a steer from a steed." Lou stopped speaking long enough to laugh at his own memory. That didn't slow him down though; he kept right on talking, and for some strange reason, I kept listening. "He was still wet behind the ears and didn't have anywhere to call home. At the age of eighteen, he had lost both of his parents in a bad car wreck. He was too old for the system to put him in foster care. When the powers that be went around asking who wanted to work a cattle drive, he had no idea what he was getting himself into. All he knew is that it was work. So he signed on the dotted line, and the rest is history. He took up with me, I showed him the ropes, and we have been sidekicks ever since." He paused and caught his breath.

We were standing at the barn doors as he opened them wide. There were some large items with a cloth covering inside. I figured some sort of tractor or old car he had stored away. He walked in and continued talking, "That's how I got to see that beautiful countryside you're headed to. And that, my dear, is how I know you're not going to make it with that little cart of yours. You need something a little bit bigger." Lou grabbed ahold of the dusty cloth covering and pulled it off.

My eyes danced in amazement. "A real full-size wagon. Oh my god, they're wonderful." My mouth dropped in awe as I walked around the wagon, taking in this splendid sight. I looked at Lou, who was smiling proudly. "How much do you want for it?"

"It's not for sale." Lou folded his arms over the wagon and faced me from the opposing side with a slight grin.

My mouth fell open with shock. "Forgive me, but why in the hell did you show it to me? You must've known I would want to buy it when you showed it to me."

"I have had these things stored in here for many years." Lou pointed to a second wagon behind me still veiled in secrecy. "You can see how much dust they have collected. I held on to them because I have always wanted to go back to that part of the world. As fate would have it, my time is growing short. Now I'm about to tell you something that I want to stay between you and me. Raven don't even know. Do you think that you can help me keep a secret?"

"Is anyone going to get hurt from this secret?" I asked.

"No, little lady, no one is going to get hurt."

"Then I believe I can help you." I just wanted him to hurry up and make his point.

"Ms. Ashley, I'm a sick man. The good doctors in town have done told me I have cancer and it has spread. It don't matter what kind or where it's at. I have it, and it's not going to get any better. I'm not the kind of man who is going to prolong his death with chemo or radiation treatments. I have made my peace with God and accepted my fate. But I want to see those mountains just one more time before I die." Lou paused again to catch his breath and fixed his gaze on me. "That's where you come in. I believe all things happen for a reason. I came up on you and your family when you needed me, and as it turns out, you are headed in the one direction I want to go. It happened this way for a reason. Do you believe that?"

I contemplated for a moment. "Yes, sir, I do. Sometimes fate just makes more sense."

"Now here's what I have to offer. I can provide two wagons. I have plenty of horses. We'll take chickens so we will have fresh eggs, maybe a cow for fresh milk. All I ask for in return is for you to take me with you. If I get bad, you will need to help Raven take care of me. He's tough, but he will need someone. Then and only then can you tell him what's going on. When I'm gone, the wagons are yours to keep. How does that sound for a deal?" Lou cocked his head to one side, awaiting my decision.

I looked at the grand wagon before me and then to my little pull cart that was pushed up against the house. "Well, sir, to be perfectly honest, I don't think this is something you should keep from Raven, considering how close you two are. That, of course, is your personal decision. As fate would have it, I'm a nurse." I smiled, thinking about fate and how I did agree that all things happen for a reason. It was strange that I met this total stranger and how much we appeared to need each other. "It would be an honor to have you join our journey. I have medical supplies, and you have everything else." I motioned to the wagons.

"It will take a couple of days, but there are plenty of abandoned vehicles on the road. If Max will help out, he and Raven can rig up the wagons with real tires. It will make a smoother ride. These are called shepherd's wagons. It has a real wood-burning stove in it." Lou opened the back of the wagon, allowing me to peer inside the darkened shell. "I figured Max and Monica could stay in that one with the baby. It will keep us warm when the snow starts falling. Monica can cook while we are on the road, and by the time we stop, the soup should be about done." Lou stopped and looked at me with concern. "I have one very important question for you."

My eyes met his. "And what might that be?"

"Can you ride a horse?"

I snickered. "I haven't ridden a horse in a very long time. The last time I took on an adventure like that, the darn thing bucked and bounced me all over the place. Finally, the manager came out and unplugged it." I looked at him as a smile crossed my face. We both busted with a round of laughter that echoed off the barn walls.

"Well, Raven can give you riding lessons." We walked back to the front of the barn, and Lou put his arm around me. "Let me break the news to him about where we are going. He may get a little riled up, but he will warm up to the idea. You just gotta give him a little time, is all," Lou explained.

I smiled the best smile I could fathom. "You mean, he may not be his normal, cheerful, happy-go-lucky self?" I intentionally attempted to sound sarcastic.

Lou laughed and squeezed my arm. "Oh, now give the boy a chance. You may just like him."

"I have someone special, thank you very much." I regretted saying the words as soon as they left my mouth.

"Where is this fellow?" Lou was smiling now. I knew he didn't mean any harm. At this point, we were just making small talk.

"His name is Dallas. He was on his way home from Houston when hell came off the hinges. We got to speak briefly, and we agreed to meet at the reservation. He was going to attempt to let his mother know we were coming. I have no idea if he ever got through to her. My parents are dead. My future stepson has probably lost his mother when a hospital collapsed. I talked my little brother and his family into coming on this journey. Monica just revealed to us that she is pregnant. I feel responsible for each of them. There was nothing for us at home except a future of decreasing supplies and increasing number of people needing them. We've had setback after setback, yet

I'm determined to keep going." I went further into explaining things than I probably needed to. I just couldn't help myself. I opened my mouth, and words just started flowing like verbal vomit.

"I can see that you have already had a long journey. Hopefully, having Raven and me around may take some of the burden off you. It's that determination that's gonna get you through this journey. Don't lose it," Lou said as he patted me on the back.

"Thanks, Lou."

"I'm gonna go find Raven and have a little chat with him. You go let your family know all the details. Breakfast is at six a.m. Don't be late. We have a lot of work to do," Lou explained as he walked ahead of me.

I glanced back at the wagons through the open barn door and smiled. I saw something move out of the corner of my eye. I looked to the edge of the barn, and Raven walked out of the darkness. I jumped a little bit at the sight of him. My mouth gaped open a little. I wondered how much he had heard. He slowly walked toward me. His eyes were fixed on mine. "You scared me."

He waited until he was right in front of me. His crystal-blue eyes reflected the moonlight, which made them appear to glow. "Yeah, I have that effect on people sometimes." He kept on walking to the house without looking back.

I hurried into the old slave quarters where Max and Monica were patiently waiting for me. The kids were already down for the night.

"Well, what did the old man want?" Max said as he stood up.

I wasn't sure how Max was going to take the news at first. "Max, before you say anything, I want you to hear me out." I took a deep breath. "There has been a change of plans."

Max threw his hands up in the air. "What did that crazy old man talk you into, sissy?"

"I asked you to hear me out. He was a cattle driver. He has been to Montana before. He has a couple of wagons, horses, everything we need. All he wants is for us to allow him and Raven to come along and for you to help Raven get the wagons fitted with real tires from the abandoned cars." I tried to get it all out in one breath.

Max looked at me in question. He scratched his head and sat back down on one of the bunks. I finished explaining the story to them. Max couldn't have been happier, just as I expected him to be. He was happy that Dannie and Monica were going to have somewhere warm to sleep. "I will help that guy Raven do anything he needs me to do."

"Well, Lou said that Raven isn't going to be too thrilled with the idea of leaving but that he will warm up to it. So if he is moody, just give him some space."

We talked for a little while and turned in for the night. For the first time in quite a while, I felt truly happy. I felt like we had a better chance of surviving this trip. I felt fortunate to have met Mr. Lou. I still wasn't sure about this Raven character. All we could do was trust in Lou's judgment of him. Since they had evidently been working together for many years, Lou had to know him better than anyone. We would all pitch in and do our part. He might not be happy about Lou's decision, but he sure as hell wasn't going to take it out on me or anyone else in my family.

Perhaps it was my mood or general improved outlook on our future, but the sun seemed to shine a little brighter through the dust clouds that still lingered overhead. With the kids up and dressed, we walked to the main house. Max and Monica soon followed with Dannie. Lou was already up and had breakfast ready. I had never seen such a spread of food—heaping platters of pancakes, sausage, bacon, and eggs.

"Y'all eat hardy. You will be hungry again by lunchtime, I promise." Lou snickered under his breath. "Ms. Monica, this is for you." Lou produced a small wooden box. "Since you'll be doing the majority of the cooking, I reckoned you will need original chuck-wagon recipes. I figured today was a good day to get started. So with that said, lunch is yours."

Monica took the box and began looking through it apprehensively. I smiled at Dannie, who had a sausage link in one hand and a biscuit in the other.

"We will all be busy today. Raven will be back shortly. He will start with the riding lessons today." Lou nodded to me. "I will take

Harley and Marcus riding. Max and Marcus can take turns driving the wagon. They will have to know how to do both."

Harley perked up and stated in an excited tone, "I get to ride a horse?"

Lou sat down beside her and put his arm around her. "I have just the horse picked out for you, but it will be up to you to take care of her. You have to feed and water her and brush her down every night. Can you handle that?"

"Oh yes, sir. Thank you, thank you!" Harley hugged Lou tightly.

"You have a friend for life now, Lou," Max stated.

Just then, the screen door opened, and Raven entered with his gliding strut.

"I beat you, Mama." Harley laughed, drawing my attention back to her.

"I have already thought about that, and yes, you win. But you have to do what Lou says, okay? Listen closely to everything he tells you."

"Yes, Mama."

"What does she win?" Raven spoke up in a dark, ominous tone that told me right away he wasn't a happy camper.

"Harley has always wanted a horse. I told her she could have a horse when I got a Hummer. She swore she would get a horse before that, so she won."

Raven rolled his eyes a little. I didn't care if he understood what that horse meant to Harley or not. He sat down at one end of the table and began to eat. "Walmart will open its doors tomorrow at five a.m. They are allowing ten people in at a time. You get what you want and get out. We are going to need supplies, so we better get there early."

Lou nodded. "Max, would you mind going with Raven in the morning?"

"Of course, anything he needs me to do."

"I can get the supplies. I just need you to stay with the wagon so no one takes off with it or the horses," Raven explained. "We start riding lessons right after breakfast. I'll teach you how to drive the wagon in the morning."

Harley wiggled in her seat. She was so excited. She had wanted a horse for such a long time, but we had never lived in a place that was suitable to have a horse. Even though these weren't ideal circumstances, I was happy that she had something she wanted. Kat scooted closer and looked at me with wonder in her eyes. I knew what she was wondering. Everyone had a role to play except her. "And you will have the most important job of all. You can help Monica cook or help keep Dannie occupied while she cooks. Taco can't ride a horse or walk all that way, so you will have to keep him in the wagon. And every now and then, I'll let you ride with me. How does that sound?" She perked up a little and went on eating.

When we had finished eating, Monica stood up and started gathering the dishes. Raven, Max, Marcus, and Lou went outside to get the horses ready while we helped with the dishes.

"I have no idea what I'm doing," Monica said, holding up the box of recipes. "My idea of home cooking means I open the box at home."

"You will do fine. No one is expecting Holly Homemaker. Just follow the recipe and do your best. Who knows, you may just surprise yourself." I tried to give her a few words of encouragement. I could tell by the look on her face that it was doing no good.

Once outside, Max and Marcus were already mounted on their horses. Harley ran forward to Lou, who scooped her up and planted her firmly on the saddle. His strength surprised me. I wasn't sure if I could pick Harley up if I had to. Lou mounted his horse and led Harley and Marcus down the drive.

"Y'all be careful and listen to what Lou tells you!" I yelled behind them and gave a wave. Harley never looked up. She had a grin from ear to ear. It was the happiest I had seen her in a very long time.

I took a deep breath knowing that it was my turn. I went through the gate leading into the horse pasture. I looked at the giant black horse that was saddled and waiting for me. I looked to Max with insecurity in my eyes as my mouth hung open. "Couldn't you have found a bigger one?"

Max laughed out loud. "Don't look at me. This is your idea, remember?"

I petted the horse gently. My foot couldn't even reach the stirrup. I tried repeatedly, and there was no way I was going to get my leg up that high. I looked to Raven, my supposed teacher. "I could use a little help, please."

"Rule number 1 in horseback riding: you have to be able to mount your own horse." Raven smiled and straightened in his saddle.

I dropped my head and shook it. *Great, this asshole is going to be no help at all,* I thought to myself as I looked around. Taking the reins, I lead the massive creature over to the fence. I climbed onto the fence high enough so that my foot met the stirrup. Wedging my foot securely in it, I swung my other leg across the horse. What happened next, I couldn't really explain. I felt what I could only describe as a blunt thud on my back. I looked up from the ground at the black demon that had just thrown me.

"Ouch, that must have hurt. Are you okay?" Raven said in a mocking tone of voice.

I took a brief assessment of myself. I could move all extremities, so at least nothing was broken. I got up and dusted myself off. Again, I used the fence to give me added height. I swung my leg over and held on tight. Nothing happened; the horse was still. "Okay, maybe it's going to be all right." I pulled the reins ever so slightly to the left to lead him away from the fence. The demon protested and jerked in the opposite direction, crushing my leg into the fence. I held on tight. Maybe he just needed some time to get accustomed to my weight. The black demon bucked and swayed madly. I held on as long as I could, but finally, he knocked me off-balance, and I went down. I landed hard on my left side. I gasped for air, my lungs heaving against my chest.

"That's gonna leave a mark," Raven mocked.

Air flowed more freely as I took in deep breaths. I got up slowly. I didn't know if it was determination or plain stupidity, but I grabbed the reins and tried again. The result was the same. I looked up at the bleak sky and rolled over, pushing myself up from the ground.

"What the hell are you doing to that poor horse?" Raven teased safely from his horse.

I looked at Max. "How did you do it?"

"Honestly, sissy, I don't know." Max shook his head.

"Max, why don't you go ahead and practice riding around the field? I'll stay here with her." Raven dismounted and walked over to me.

Max turned his horse around with great ease and took off riding around the large pasture.

"All right, break's over. Try again," Raven ordered.

I took the horse over to the fence and swung my leg over. He was steady. Raven pulled him away from the fence. I wrapped my legs around him tightly to secure myself. Raven let go and stepped away. I took a few deep breaths to relax myself so the horse didn't sense my insecurity, but still the horse bucked wildly. I tightened my grip, but it was too late. I was already on my way back down to the familiar ground. I didn't stop once my body hit the ground. My foot was still wedged in the stirrup. The damn horse was dragging me. I screamed in protest while trying to reach up and dislodge my foot. My head bounced off the ground. Raven ran over and stopped the horse, and my foot fell free.

"God dammit." I slapped the ground and grabbed the reins. I gripped the saddle horn and pulled myself up with what strength I could muster and sheer willpower. Again, he bucked, but I held on with everything I had, squeezing my legs around him and holding the reins with such force my hands turned white with strain. The saddle horn jammed into my belly, distracting me for the one brief moment the beast needed to buck me off again. Dust flew up around the impact of my body. I got up and went for another depressing round of *throw the rider*. I couldn't understand why it was so difficult for me to do this. I continued for what seemed like hours. Each time ended with the same result. Raven shook his head, never losing that cocky little smile of his. I honestly wanted to slap him, but it wasn't his fault. I couldn't take my frustrations out on him. He was trying to help me. He was at least keeping me from being killed. Max was having no problems with his horse. He looked like a pro riding around the pasture. Again, I bit the dust.

Raven bent over, staring down at my face. "Did poor baby fall down and go boom?"

"Fuck you," I spouted with attitude and contempt. Raven only laughed. I was getting up more slowly now. There wasn't one part of my body that wasn't racked with pain. Grabbing the saddle horn, I pulled myself up. I barely got my balance when my body met the earth again.

"Raven!" Lou yelled at him from the front porch. I had been so preoccupied that I hadn't seen them return. "Get that girl off that stallion. You know you're the only one he'll let ride him."

Turning my head slowly, I fixed my eyes on Raven. He dropped his head but never lost that crooked, cocky smile of his. Max was standing beside his horse, shaking his head with sincere sympathy in his eyes. Raven strutted over to me and offered me his hand. I took it, allowing him to help me up. Raven cocked his head to the side to face me. "Sorry about that. I must have gotten the horses mixed up."

I looked at him, my eyes meeting his. God, I hated to look into those beautiful eyes. This arrogant, cocky son of a bitch had done this to me on purpose. I wasn't about to do anything that showed him that he was getting the best of me. I forced a smile. "That's okay. It was bound to happen."

"What do you mean?" Raven questioned.

"Well, when someone tries to function with a brain as small as yours, they're bound to fuck up something." I stepped forward, looking up, all the while glaring into his eyes. "I know what you're doing. You will not change my mind. I'm going to learn how to ride with or without your help. You have a decision to make. If you are going to join this journey, you can make it easy or hard. But I will be around every day, day in and day out. You can be a hard-ass, cocky bastard and make life miserable for everyone around you, or you can be nice and help out and make things easier on everyone, including Lou. It's your choice." I poked my finger into his chest, turned, and stomped away from him. Pausing at the gate, I shook my leg, allowing a generous amount of dirt to fall out of my pants back to its rightful place.

"Was that really necessary?" Max handed his reins to Raven and followed me.

I passed the main house and saw Lou shaking his head. I made my way into the slave quarters. I wanted to bury my head into a pillow and cry or scream. I wanted to punch something. Instead, I grabbed a clean change of clothes and headed into the showers.

I'm not sure how long I was in the shower when Monica gently knocked at the wooden door. "Ashley, are you okay?"

I shut off the water and began to dry off. Monica pushed the door open and gasped at the splotches of black and blue that now speckled my body. "Oh my god, Ashley," she spouted in horror.

"Yeah, tell me about it. I look like a black-and-blue leopard."

"Lou gave me some ointment. He said it helps with sore muscles. I'll rub it on your back for you." Monica turned her eyes from me out of respect.

"Did he give you a gallon jug of it? Because that's how much it's going to take." I laughed in spite of myself.

"What he did was uncalled for! Lou is pissed."

"I'll handle Raven." I wrapped the towel around my body and headed into the bunkhouse. I stopped and looked at Monica. "No more *Ms. Nice Girl.* And yes, I would appreciate and welcome any ointment that may help."

Monica took her time applying the ointment, attempting to be as gentle as possible. She passed the time telling me about what we were going to have for supper and how she totally botched the first batch of biscuits. I let her talk even though I honestly wasn't paying much attention. I was preoccupied with thoughts about Raven and his mystical eyes and how I could crush him like a bug. I would've been attracted to him if he wasn't such an asshole. The ointment was cool on the skin then warmed up. It was soothing but did little to alleviate the pain.

We walked to the main house and sat down for supper. Harley was so excited while she told me all about her day. When Lou sat down, we all grew silent and ate in peace.

"Monica, you did a fine job. Maybe it's because I know a woman cooked it, but I swear, yours is better than mine," Lou complimented Monica.

"Thank you, Lou. I screwed up the first pan of biscuits, but after that, I think I got it."

"It's better than Lou's. You did a fine job," Raven stated as he snagged another biscuit.

I looked up abruptly. He actually gave someone a compliment. Lou must have taken him out to the woodshed and beat some sense into him. I wished I could have seen it. Hell, I actually would have paid to see it. I smiled at my private thoughts.

Raven continued, "Max, if it's okay with you, we need to get started about four a.m. We can get to the store hopefully before word gets out that it's opened. We can get what we need and head back."

Max nodded in agreement. "I don't have a problem with that. Sounds like a good plan. I'll be up and ready. Just knock at the door when you're ready."

Raven nodded and took his empty bowl to the sink.

"I'll do the dishes tonight." I rose slowly from my chair, my back refusing to straighten all the way up. I walked to the sink looking like a hunchback. My legs felt wobbly under me. I leaned against the wooden cabinets and tried to straighten myself up. Raven strutted toward the door.

Monica and Harley came up to the sink. Harley took the bowl from my hand. "Mama, I'll do the dishes. You need to go lie down." I looked into her sweet, innocent eyes.

"Okay, baby." I didn't want to worry her or Monica.

"Oh, poor baby. Does someone need their boo-boos kissed?" Raven let out a roaring laughter. He stopped and cleared his throat when he realized he was the only one laughing.

I turned my sore, aching body slowly toward Raven, glaring at him maliciously. My eyes beamed with unadulterated detestation. I eased toward him. "Believe me, Raven, I would like nothing more than to have you kiss my ass," I spoke slowly and stressed each word, putting a lot of emphasis on the last one.

"Sissy." Max began to rise to his feet. He saw the look in my eyes as they were focused only on Raven. If only I could get my hands around that thick neck of his.

Raven patted Max on the shoulder. "Don't worry, Max. Some people just like it dirty." He laughed again and bolted for the door and cleared the front porch in a single jump.

I bolted after him. A pain shot through my back and radiated down into my legs. Feeling my knees give out, I caught myself on the sideboard before I hit the floor. I could hear Raven outside teasing, "Run, run, run as fast as you can. You can't catch me. I'm the gingerbread man." More laughing followed, echoing into the darkness.

Max helped me straighten up. I looked at him. "When I can raise my leg higher than a snake's belly, I'm really gonna kick his ass."

"I'll help you to the bunkhouse. You need to get some sleep." Max offered me his arm that I leaned on the entire way. He helped me take off my shoes. I lay down as my brother covered me up.

"Do me a favor, brother. Wake me up when you start to leave in the morning." I looked at him with pleading eyes.

"Okay, I'll wake you up. Just get some rest now." Max shut the door behind him.

I wiggled on the metal bed trying to find a comfortable spot. It was useless. Every part of my body ached, from my toes to my eyebrows. I shut my eyes and drifted off into a deep sleep.

Max woke me at 4:00 a.m. "Sissy, you awake?"

"Are you leaving?" I rubbed my eyes.

"Raven just knocked, so we are about to head out."

"Okay, I need to see him." I got out of bed and stretched. It sounded like every bone in my body popped. I grabbed some money from my purse and went to catch Raven. Max was on my heels, not knowing what kind of thoughts were racing through my mind.

"Hey!" I shouted. Raven turned to face me. "I don't know how much you plan on buying or what it will cost, but here is some money. Lou has already given so much. I don't want him going broke buying supplies for a trip that was my idea. Use what you need."

Raven took the money and put it in his pocket. I trusted him to do the right thing. "Anything you want?"

"Yeah, if there's enough, get a couple cartons of cigarettes."

"What brand?" he inquired.

"At this point, anything with a filter will be fine." I smiled as sweetly as I could. I was going to haunt him with kindness until I could find a way to get back at him. "And if there's anything special you want." The last thing I wanted was to be nice to this bastard; however, even if I liked it or not, he was a part of this journey. He did more than his share of the work. Didn't he deserve something as a human being as a thank you? I didn't think Lou paid him a lot of money as a farmhand. They definitely didn't look like they had much. He raised his eyebrows and nodded. The wagon began pulling away. Max looked back, smiled, and waved.

I turned to the barn and walked inside. "Okay, now let's learn to ride." My voice echoed in the silent barn. I chose the horse Raven was on the day before since that one was obviously the one I was supposed to be on. He was a rusty-brown color with a white patch on his head. I spent a few minutes brushing him and gently talking to him. I saddled him and led him to the pasture. Even though he was considerably smaller, I still couldn't reach the stirrup. Going with my technique from yesterday, I mounted him from the fence. I waited. He didn't buck or sway. I took the reins and led him away from the fence. I trotted the fence line and back again several times. Leading him out into the middle of the land, I got brave and kicked my feet into his belly. Pitching forward, he broke into a run. I held on to the reins and ran him the entire loop of the pasture. As dawn approached, I made my way back toward the house. I saw Lou on the porch with a cup of coffee. I waved, and he returned the gesture, giving me a thumbs-up sign. I made another loop around the pasture. I saw the wagon making its way up the little dirt road. Max stood up and let out a yell, "Woo-hoo! Lookin' good, sissy." Raven shook his head, smiling.

I rode the horse to the barn and took off the saddle. I brushed him down quickly and put some feed and water in his stall, then kissed his head. "Good boy." I went into the main house feeling proud of myself. I was doing it; I was actually riding. And I did it without falling off a hundred times. Max met me with hugs.

Monica came onto the porch. "Y'all hungry?"

"Famished," Raven said as he entered the house. "We can unload the wagon when we are finished eating. We can teach Marcus to drive the other wagon this evening."

"You know, I don't have my driver's license yet, don't you?" Marcus chimed from his seat.

"I don't think that's gonna matter, little man." Raven smiled and patted Marcus on the back.

Marcus looked at me with a scrunched face. He obviously didn't like being addressed as a juvenile. He was much too mature to be addressed in such a manner. Marcus did well to hold his tongue.

Everyone else seemed to be getting along with Raven. Everyone but me, that is. I fantasized about seeing him strung up and horse-whipped. He had a quality about him that made him appear to be superior. Perhaps he was better at farming and roughing it. He knew the horses and wagons. But I wasn't a total idiot. I was capable and eager to learn all I could. He only had to be receptive to having a student. He wasn't better than me. He put his pants on one leg at a time just like me. Of course, his legs were longer, leaner, and more muscular. I shook images of him out of my brain after stealing a glance of him as I took my seat at the table beside Kat. My body was sore and stiff, but I refused to let it slow me down however. I moved slowly but kept a steady pace. I couldn't allow myself to show any signs of weakness. I had to prove to my family that no matter what happened, they could count on me to be strong and reliable.

The day went on without a glitch or argument. Marcus learned quickly how to drive the wagon. Harley rode her horse, which she had now named Shadow, in the field. Monica and Kat fixed supper. I showed off my newfound equine skills with Harley. Lou posed himself on the porch, taking it all in.

Raven waved me over, and reluctantly I went to him. I was scared to look into his eyes.

"I got your cigarettes. I laid them on your bunk, and here's your change. It was enough to cover everything." Raven had a wad of money in his hand, holding it out to me. I didn't want to touch him. I was afraid of what his skin would feel like against mine. I was even more afraid that I might like it.

"Why don't you hold on to it? If we come across another open store, you can see what we can get. Did you get yourself anything?"

"I got the kids some chocolate bars."

"But did you get yourself anything?" I repeated.

"No, but thank you for the offer." Raven looked at me.

Did he ever lose that crooked grin? I thought it had been permanently planted on his face since we first arrived. "The kids will love and appreciate the chocolate. Thank you."

Raven nodded and disappeared into the barn. I rode a while longer with Harley. We put up the horses when Lou rang the dinner bell. I laughed to myself about the fact that he had an actual dinner bell. "Come and get it!" he yelled from the porch.

The next few days went smoothly and productively. Raven and Max got the wagons retrofitted with real tires. Raven even had snow chains for them. We all learned either how to ride and drive the wagons relatively well. Harley loved every moment of being outside. Every day was like a new adventure for her.

Finally, our last night at Lou's homestead had arrived. We occupied ourselves by packing the wagon and finding the perfect spot for everything. The wagons were extremely nice. They were solid wood with a rounded top. It sported a full-size bed and hideaway table slid under the bed when it wasn't in use. Two long benches on each side doubled as a bed. There were plenty of storage areas. A wood-burning stove for cooking would give off plenty of heat to keep everybody warm. Monica, Dannie, and Kat would be staying in one wagon so Monica could do all the cooking. Max and Marcus would alternate driving. Lou would drive the wagon that contained the supplies and tools, and personal belongings went into the other wagon. We had eaten our last meal; dishes were done and packed away safely. Everyone indulged and got a good shower. Monica and I had washed up everyone's clothes. I got the girls bedded down and went outside while Monica got Dannie to sleep.

I went over to the fence and looked up at the endless black night.

"Whatcha lookin' at?" Raven surprised me.

I had done my best to avoid him the majority of the week, but he always seemed to seek me out. "I'm just looking for the stars." I looked over to Raven, who was also looking up. "Do you think they are still up there?"

He smiled and kept his eyes fixated on the sky. "Yeah, they're up there. They are still shining bright, waiting patiently to be seen again." He turned his eyes to me. "I didn't figure you were the type to even notice the stars."

"If you ever took the time to get to know me, I may surprise you." I smiled at him then quickly turned my eyes back to the sky. I figured I would take the opportunity to talk to him. "Look, I know you hate me, and I can't say that I blame you. I mean, here comes this stranger into your lives and changes the course of your future. I can understand how you feel. But please believe me when I tell you that I didn't plan this. I didn't talk Lou into traveling with us or anything."

Raven's mild laughter interrupted me. "I know Lou better than anyone else here, and I know that nobody can talk him into anything. I know this was his idea, so don't go thinking that you know what's going on inside my head. And you're wrong." Raven's eyes caught mine in an intense glare. "I don't hate you." He turned and walked away from me.

I stayed at the fence pondering the blackness above me. I was glad to know that Raven didn't hate or blame me. I couldn't understand why he acted so offensively toward me. I decided that in the best interest of my family and the trip as a whole, it would be favorable to give Raven another chance. Perhaps he wasn't so bad. I went back into the bunkhouse and looked at my family soundly asleep in their beds. I straightened Kat's covering as Taco wiggled under them. Rocky raised his head at my presence disturbing the night's silence. I crawled into my bunk and covered up.

The last few hours were upon us. What lay ahead was a long, hard, and perilous journey. It was unknown what hardships awaited us. We had done all we could do. We had packed everything that we could possibly need. We had plenty of food and feed for the horses. All we could do was hope for the best and be prepared for the worst.

CHAPTER 7

E VEN IF WE were ready or not, dawn approached. Lou knocked at our door. "Time to get a move on. We got a long day ahead."

"Thanks, Lou. Be out in a minute," Max called out as he sat up from his bed. Monica rubbed her eyes. We all got up and got ready for the day. Harley was excited and the first out of the door. Lou handed us each a biscuit and sausage to eat on the dusty road.

I walked out of the bunkhouse. The first thing my eyes found was Raven leaning against the porch post. He had the horses saddled and ready to go. *God, don't these people ever sleep?* I thought to myself. Monica got Dannie and Kat settled in the wagon and listened carefully to Lou's instructions on the wood-burning stove. Max was in the driver's seat, rearing to go.

Harley was already on her brown-and-white horse. "Look what Lou gave me, Mama." Harley showed off a white cowboy hat.

"I see." I smiled at Harley.

Marcus reluctantly mounted on his horse and paraded in front of me. I noticed he had a hat on as well. It didn't suit him well at all. It looked totally out of character on him. "Oh," I exclaimed, "Marcus got one too."

Marcus glared at me with a half smile and half sneer. "Not one word."

"I wouldn't dare." I let out a small giggle as Marcus ignored my comments and went ahead.

Raven turned to me and blurted out, "I'm sorry for the way I have acted toward you. It's a long road ahead, and I wanted to give you something to call a truce, so I got you something. Well, not really got but made you something." He waved his hand in front of the saddle.

My eyes widened. He had carved one word in intricate detailing into the saddle: *Hummer*. "Oh my god, Raven, it's beautiful. You did this?"

"Yeah, Harley may have won, but you still have your Hummer, right, boy?" Raven patted the horse. "Oh, and there's one more thing." Raven produced a box and handed it to me. "I hope they fit. I got your footprint out of the mud, so…" He handed me the box.

"My footprint?" I questioned. I opened the box to reveal a beautiful pair of boots. "Raven, you made these?" My mouth gaped open. They were red and black and had the elegant detailing on them as well.

"Well, repaired them. It's a hobby of mine. They are actually secondhand but totally refurbished, so they are almost like new. Do you like them?"

"I love them. Thank you so much!" I sat down on the porch and took off my old sneakers and put on the new boots that seemed to fit like a glove. "They feel great, Raven. I can't thank you enough, really." I stood up and twisted around, looking at my gift.

Raven beamed with pride. "I'm glad you like them. I'm even more glad they fit. I was kinda worried about that part. Besides, if you're going to ride a horse properly, you have to look the part." Raven cupped his hands together, offering me a boost onto my horse now named Hummer. I looked at him questioningly before he spoke, "You have more than proved you can do the work that's going to be demanded of us out there, and I'm here to lend a hand. So if you need help mounting the horse, I'm here."

"Okay, who are you, and what did you do with Raven?" I snickered.

He returned the laugh. "You want a boost or not?"

I took him up on his offer and mounted the horse. He oddly caressed the boots he had just given me and then looked directly into my eyes. Even though I couldn't feel his skin on mine, I still felt a shiver run up my spine. "Looks good," he said, smiling up to me.

"Y'all through playing footsy?" Lou yelled out with a big smile.

Raven rolled his eyes. "Shut up, old man!" Raven turned and mounted his own horse.

Lou laughed to himself as he pulled the wagon forward. He caught up with Harley. He explained to her that it was best if the adults lead the way. That way, if any danger lay ahead, they could deal with it. She fell back and stayed to the side of the wagon, allowing Raven and me to ride in front. Thankfully, it was mostly flatland, which made an easy ride. The roadway was clear for the most part. Hundreds of cars were abandoned on the side of the road. When the tree line cleared, we could see for miles. We passed a sign that read, "Now leaving North Platte, Nebraska. Come back soon." Not surprisingly, Raven didn't talk much. He sat high on his horse, his back straight as an arrow while his odd eyes constantly scanning the road ahead. If it weren't for his attitude, he would have almost looked majestic sitting up there. Halfway through the day, Max pulled out Harley's little radio and allowed it to play. The music helped to break the monotony. We all sang along with the radio. Raven actually had a nice voice, although I was certain I would never tell him that I thought so.

We rode all day, stopping only briefly to allow Monica safely on and off the wagon. The common and sometimes troublesome inconvenience of being pregnant showed itself. She made sandwiches out of biscuits and handed them out from the back of the wagon along with a bottle of water. The smothered sun kept the temperatures cool. I knew we would need the winter clothes soon. I was certain that winter would come early. With hardly any sun breaking through to help warm things up, it was sure to be unnaturally cold. We stopped before nightfall and made our camp. The kids helped gather plenty of firewood. There were three of us dividing up watch times. I would take first watch with Raven relieving me and Max relieving him. We ate and bedded down. That first day set the pace and routine for what would be many days and nights on the road.

We continued in the same tedious fashion day after day for what might have been weeks. I had lost all track of time. Occasionally, we encountered a cluster of people trudging along the road. Their faces reflected pain, despair, and shock. Most were dirty, their clothes torn and ragged. The extremely lucky ones carried all their worldly possessions in a single bag. Children cried with hunger and fear. Streaking tears left the only clean spots on their tiny faces. Mothers held up their babies, begging us to take them. They looked at our party with envy and malice. We rode through them, trying not to make eye contact.

Once, to my astonishment, a tall, thin man grabbed my leg and attempted to pull me from my horse. I kicked and yelled, attracting Raven's attention. Raven grabbed his rifle and rode to meet me. I continued to kick at the man, who refused to let go. I felt my boots starting to slip over my heel when Raven wedged the rifle into the back of the man's head, freezing him in place.

"You may want to let go, partner. Two things you don't mess with in my world are my horse and my woman. I have killed people for a lot less."

The young man released my leg and glared at me with desperation in his eyes. He hung his head low and continued to walk forward. Raven nodded at me and motioned for me to ride ahead of him. He held the rifle until we cleared the crowd.

All was silent as his words rang in my head. *My horse and my woman.* Surely he wasn't laying some sort of claim to me. I hoped that by me accepting the boots wasn't leading him on. I had no intentions of being with this fool in any shape, form, or fashion. I was going to get to Dallas's mom's and wait for him. I didn't care how long it took. I knew in my heart that he was alive, and he would join me as soon as he could. I thought of Raven as a mangy mongrel dog that had his occasionally weak moments of being civil, and the only reason he was tagging along was because of his friend Lou. The mere thought or mention of Raven repulsed me. Then I thought of his weak moments, the times that he could be pleasantly cordial and his odd mystifying eyes that seemed to lure me in like a bad magical spell. I would be gracious to Raven out of respect for Lou, and that was the end of it. I would only spend time with Raven if I absolutely had to and never alone.

I got a little depressed one night as we pulled over. I had pictured in my mind the farther north we went, the likelier it would be that there would be mountaintops in the horizon. Instead, everything looked the same. There was nothing but forests and flatland, not my splendorous mountains I longed to see. We stopped earlier than usual to make camp. I just thought that perhaps Lou was getting tired. He was a sick man after all.

Raven spoke briefly with Lou and turned to me. "Do you think y'all can handle setting up camp without me today? I'm going hunting. Monica's cooking is good, but we need some fresh meat."

"Yeah, we can handle it," I responded.

Raven grabbed his rifle and disappeared into the woods. After what seemed like forever, a gunshot rang out, piercing the silence. Instinctively I ducked my head and quickly looked around.

Lou laughed and slapped his knee. "Sounds like we are going to eat good tonight." He went directly to the wagon and began rummaging through it, obviously on a great search for something. I could hear what I hoped was Raven stomping through the woods and getting closer. I fixed my eyes on a group of bushes that lay ahead. Raven burst through them with a goofy grin from ear to ear. He was holding up a familiar large dead bird.

"A turkey?" I looked at him with question. I had been so preoccupied with the journey I hadn't realized what day it was. "A turkey!" I repeated with delight. "Good job, Raven!" I patted him on the back as he walked past me.

Everyone had gathered around to see Raven's fresh kill. He walked past everyone and shoved the dead bird into Monica's hands. He kept walking to the fire, plopped down, leaned back, and propped up his feet. My eyes shifted back to Monica, and I couldn't help but laugh. There was poor pregnant Monica standing there with a dirty apron, her hair in total disarray, and a look of shock on her face. She was holding the dead bird away from her body, blood still dripping from its severed head. She had no idea what to do with it.

I strutted over to Raven and slapped his boots. "Get over there and help her. She's pregnant. Are you trying to make her sick?"

Raven laughed. "Oh, all right." He went back to Monica and took the bird from her. "Why don't you take the night off and put your feet up? I'll cook this bird up for us." He politely gave her a quick kiss on the cheek.

Monica nodded vigorously, relieved to be free of the dead bird. "Yeah, you do that. You're good at that."

Lou pulled some black metal bars out of the wagon and placed them over the fire while Raven plucked all the feathers from the turkey. I found some herbs and spices in the wagon, and before we knew it, the turkey was roasting over the fire, filling the air with a sweet aroma. Monica made some tea, and we all sat around the fire, each taking our turn at turning the turkey so it would cook evenly.

"Just so you don't think you're going crazy, it's not actually Thanksgiving yet. We knew this area was well-known for turkeys, and we may not get this lucky on the actual holiday, so I figured Thanksgiving may need to come a little early this year." Raven strung up the turkey and began gutting it. "I'll be doing more hunting. We are going to need more meat to keep our strength up, especially through the winter," he stated as the pale sun began setting.

I only nodded in response as Monica pulled me aside. "I wanted to tell you that I heard Kat today." She continued to explain, "We were in the wagon, and she was playing with Dannie. She laughed, Ashley. It was a full-fledged laugh. It took me by surprise, and I looked at her. And she immediately clammed up and dropped her heard."

"So she is able to speak." I exhaled deeply. At that moment, I was so relieved. "For whatever reason, she is choosing not to. I don't understand it, but I hope she grows out of it soon. Thank you, Monica. You have no idea how much I needed to hear that." I hugged her. "What about you? How are you feeling?"

"Pregnant," she snorted. "He is doing all sorts of somersaults in here." She patted her belly gently.

I paused and looked at her. "Could you be further along than you thought?"

Monica hung her head low. "I'm not sure, Ashley. All the days are running together now. Anything could be possible."

"We will just take it one day at a time, but I need to know how you are feeling. If you feel the least bit of pain, you tell me immediately."

Monica only nodded. "I will. Don't worry."

"Look at our crew over there." I pointed to our family crowding around the campfire. "They look like a bunch of cavemen." We both laughed and joined our primitive family. Max turned on some music as we sat around watching the turkey cook to perfection over the fire.

Around sunset, a booming voice broke our peaceful party, freezing us in place. "Hello at the camp!" Raven's smile quickly faded as he grabbed his rifle and took a guarded stance. I was quickly at his side, along with Max. Monica gathered the kids and got them in the wagon.

"Stay here," he commanded me. "Max, fall back behind the wagon to cover me."

Max nodded.

"Be careful." I pulled my pistol from my back.

Raven walked out to meet a man on a horse. I noticed another man, younger and thinner, on a horse beside him. I strained to hear their conversation.

Raven spoke first, waving his hand, "Good evening. What can I help you with?"

The stranger smiled and dismounted his horse, leaving his own rifle holstered. "Nothing at all. We saw your fire and thought it may be nice to have some company for a while."

Raven lowered his rifle. "We can't feed you."

"We have our own food." The stranger was still smiling. "We aren't looking for handouts, and we don't want any trouble. We can make our own way. We made our own wagon from scraps ourselves." An odd-looking wagon lurched its way over the hill into sight.

"You keep saying we. Who else is in your party?" Raven responded.

"Just my wife, my son, and a good-for-nothing dog." The stranger gave a small laugh.

Raven looked to me. I nodded in approval. He walked closer to the stranger and extended his hand. "The name's Raven."

"Jacob Miller. This is my son, Ricky, and my wife, Rose." Mr. Miller pointed to each of his family.

Raven nodded. "If you want, you can bring the wagon around on the other side to form a circle. We were about to eat. And forget what I said earlier. There is plenty."

Mr. Miller nodded and waved to his wife, Rose, who was driving the wagon. Lou patted the side of the wagon, signaling to Monica it was safe. She and the kids poured out, ready to take on any excitement. When we were all in place, I started with introductions.

"Well, like he said, this is Raven, and that's Lou. I'm Ashley. These are my girls, Harley and Kat, and my stepson, Marcus. Over there is my not-so-little brother, Max; his wife, Monica; and their son, Dannie. The dogs are Rocky and Taco."

"Well, nice to meet you all. I'm Jacob Miller." Jacob went back through his introductions.

I noticed something stir in Harley when her eyes met Ricky's. He was a strapping young man, tall and thin. He looked to be about sixteen, with short spiky blond hair and large blue eyes that looked like pools of water.

"Hi." Ricky's statement was directed to everyone, but his eyes were fixed on Harley.

I looked back and forth between them. It didn't take a genius to see that there was an attraction between them. I smiled.

"Hi," Harley responded in an uncharacteristically shy tone of voice.

"Mrs. Miller, it's a pleasure to meet you." I extended my hand to Rose, who shook it graciously with a big smile. She seemed to be a pleasant woman about my age, appearing very strong-natured with brilliant blue eyes that matched her son's. Her pineapple-blond hair was neck-length and pulled up into a tight ponytail.

"It's very nice to meet you also. It will be nice to have some company for a while." Rose smiled.

"Well, you can sit by the fire. Make yourself at home."

Raven spoke up, "Where are you from?"

"New Orleans. We got out before"—Rose stopped and shook her head—"it got really bad."

"That's where my daddy lived," Harley spoke up but kept her head down. I thought I saw a tear roll from her eye, but she wiped her face before I could be sure.

"I hate to hear that, little lady. It got bad there. We were lucky. I have my pilot's license, and I was able to fly us out. We made it to Kansas City, Missouri, before we had to land. We camped for a while and built our wagon. I bought everything else, and we started making our way west. We have family in Canada." Jacob paused and looked at us. "What about you? Where are you headed?"

"Montana. We have family there," I stated. "It's my fiancé's family. He is going to join us later."

Max broke in, "Turkey is ready. I say we eat."

"Not so fast, Max." Lou stood up. "I'm not extremely religious, but I think if we are going to observe Thanksgiving today, then it's not going to kill us to say a prayer."

Everyone nodded, rose to their feet, and joined hands. I reluctantly joined them. The last thing I wanted to do was give thanks to God for the cold cruelness that was going on in the world that brought us here. We bowed our heads as Lou began to bless our meal. I wasn't paying much attention to what he was saying. I glanced up and caught Raven staring at me. He smiled slightly at me as I lowered my head again. When I looked up again, I saw that Harley and Ricky were conveniently side by side, their hands joined together. Even though I found it a little cute that my daughter was falling in puppy love, I was certainly going to have to watch these two.

"Amen." Lou finished his prayer. Everyone sat down to eat. I glanced around at our growing party when a large dog appeared between Jacob and Rose, licking his chops and staring at the roasting bird.

"Rocky! I thought we had him tied up," I stated.

"We do," Max agreed, pointing to Rocky still tied up at the wagon. Our eyes turned to the duplicate dog.

"That's Baby," Ricky said, calling the large female boxer, which could have been Rocky's twin, to his side.

We all laughed at the coincidence. We allowed Rocky off the rope and allowed the two boxers to get familiar with each other as the rest of us did the same. Soon, nothing was left but the carcass of a large bird and full stomachs.

Monica and I got Dannie and Kat ready for bed and tucked in. I wrapped the blankets around Kat and hugged her tight. "Monica said she heard you laugh. I'm sorry I missed that." I kissed her forehead. "I would love to hear you laugh." I lay down beside Kat and draped my hand over her. "Did you look around tonight? Everyone was having a pretty good time. I think I even saw you smile once or twice." I goosed her as she wiggled beneath her covers and smiled, but no sound escaped her mouth. "I won't pretend to know why you won't talk, baby, but I know you can. And when you're ready, I'll be listening. We've had a rough time. Just consider it a bad day. We can't change it, so no complaining. We just pick up and move on. We can hope that when the sun rises, it will bring a new, better day, but when it doesn't, we got to keep moving. I love you, angel. Sleep tight." I kissed her on the head again. Monica stayed behind to get Dannie to sleep.

I joined the rest of the party at the campfire. "Jacob, I was wondering if you have heard any news along the way about, well, anything."

Jacob picked up his coffee cup. "We stopped at a tent city that the Red Cross had set up back near Topeka, Kansas. They are telling people to go to any military base. They are supposed to be setting up bigger tent cities near the bases. Some are attempting to set up medical facilities, and you can get hot meals." Jacob paused and took a sip of coffee. "As far as everything else, I'm sure you can tell the destruction is everywhere. The quake went from coast to coast. I heard New York is in total ruins, as well as the entire state of California. The tsunami washed as far inland as parts of Ohio and Tennessee. The majority of Louisiana, Florida, and Texas are underwater."

I saw Harley squirm in her seat beside Ricky, who quickly took the opportunity to put his arm around her. It was a heroic attempt to console her. It really would have been an honorable thing to do for anyone except my daughter. I was definitely going to have to keep my eye on this situation. I already had Monica pregnant, and I didn't need a pregnant sixteen-year-old. I scratched the thought out of my head and stopped staring at Harley and Ricky. Marcus sat quietly, petting Rocky, who was preoccupied keeping his big chocolate-brown eyes on Baby. I suppose more than one person was finding puppy love tonight.

"Well, it sounds like things aren't going to get better anytime soon," Max stated. "We're truly on our own."

"Just the way I like it," Raven said as he inhaled deeply on a cigarette. "We are just going to have to be very careful out here."

I had never seen Raven smoke before. I had to think that perhaps my bad habits were rubbing off on him.

He continued, "Jacob, about my behavior earlier, I'm sure you can understand our being cautious of you."

"Yes, of course," he agreed. "I don't blame you one bit. If my calculations are correct, we should pretty much be on the same road for a while, so why not travel together? I believe there is safety in numbers."

Everyone nodded to that statement as we had said it several times before ourselves. If there were indeed scavengers or modern-day pirates, they would surely attack smaller bands of travelers. They would be less likely to be able to defend themselves. One by one, we retired to bed. Soon, only Raven and I were left by the fire. I would take first watch. Raven leaned back on a rock near the fire and covered his face with his hat.

"You can go lie down in the tent. I'm fine." I would have appreciated a few moments of peace.

"I know you can handle yourself. I don't doubt that. You're tough enough. You have more than proved yourself to me, Ashley. Believe it or not, I'm not sleeping out here because of you." He paused and looked at me, then continued, "I just want to sleep under the stars." Raven held up his hands as if embracing the night.

I laughed at him. I didn't know Raven well enough to tell if he was lying, but either way, I was glad he was there as our protector, our dear guardian angel in flannel. I snickered under my breath at the thought. I stayed for my watch without incident. I heard a rustle in the bushes, but it was most likely a small animal, possibly a raccoon. I entertained my own thoughts. I sat in the darkness trying to visualize Lou's mountains that he had told me so much about, the mountains that I dreamed of. I wanted to meet Dallas's mom and aunt and finally be able to say that I was home. That word had lost so much meaning to me.

I stood my watch without incident. Growing sleepier, I kicked Raven's boot to wake him. "Get up. It's my turn to sleep." I threw a sleeping bag in front of the fire and crawled in.

Raven rubbed his eyes sleepily and grabbed a cup of coffee. "What are you doing?"

"If you can enjoy sleeping under the stars, so can I. Besides, it's warmer here. Sometimes I get cold in the tent alone." I realized what I had said as soon as the words left my mouth. I left myself wide open for crude comments from Raven, and he didn't waste the opportunity.

"Well, we can fix that." He softly put his hand on my leg and slowly started moving it up my leg.

"It's going to be hard to hold the reins of that wild horse of yours with only one hand, Raven." The lower part of my face was hidden beneath the sleeping bag, and he couldn't see the smile I had on my face.

Raven only laughed and patted my leg. "Okay, tough girl, get some sleep."

"That will be easier to do now that you're awake. You snore like a boar hog." I snickered again.

"I do not," Raven stated with a phony look of shock.

I popped my head up from the sleeping bag. "Oh yes, you do, mister. I swear I thought a bear was growling in the woods, and it was just you snoring."

"Oh, bullshit. Go to sleep."

I caught Raven smiling at me. It was a little shock to me. "You should do that more often. You have a nice smile." A look of confusion crossed his face. I wasn't sure if he could understand that I had just given him a compliment.

"Yeah? Well, I haven't had much reason to smile in a long time." He stopped, and his smile faded as he looked into the dancing embers of the campfire. "Get some sleep."

I laid my head back down. Raven had to be the most complex and frustrating person I had ever met. It infuriated me to the brink of insanity that he could be so easy to get along with one minute and have a shield of iron up the next. My thoughts drifted into dreams as I slipped away into a peaceful slumber beside the warm fire.

Dawn approached too quickly and interrupted my sweet dreams. I could hear others around me at the campfire. I eased my eyes open and met Raven's face right in mine.

"Morning, honey." He had the same damn goofy, crooked smile. "Get 'er, Rocky."

Rocky replaced Raven and began licking my face and attempting to crawl into my sleeping bag with me.

"Damn, Rocky, I don't need a bath right now. Jeez, at least furnish me a towel." I sat up, and everyone laughed and joked about me. I looked at Raven and just shook my head. Climbing free from the sleeping bag, I pointed at Raven. "You know, payback is a bitch."

"Oh my, I'm scared." Raven flashed that brilliant, genuine smile at me as he offered me a cup of coffee.

I couldn't help but return his smile and take the coffee, still shaking my head. "I'm still gonna getcha."

"I can't wait." Raven snickered and returned to his seat beside Lou and Max. Monica had breakfast ready, oatmeal again.

I excused myself to visit the bucket we carried with us to pose as a toilet. When I returned, everyone was breaking down the campsite and getting ready to get moving.

"Tonight, we are going to be stopping near Valentine, Nebraska. There will be a river we can bathe in. That way, you can get the Rocky smell off you." Raven laughed as he continued to pick up.

"Ha-ha, very funny," I replied.

The rest of the day went along without a single problem. Harley spent all day riding next to Ricky. I could see them talking and laughing with each other. Rose drove the Miller's wagon; she was indeed a strong woman. Rocky and Baby walked side by side for a long time before Rocky got lazy and wanted in, in the wagon. Raven and Mr. Miller took turns in the lead, which left Raven riding beside me for a while. I caught him looking at me several times, but I couldn't figure out why. Once, I caught Lou looking back, smiling at us. I just rolled my eyes. *Shut up, old man,* I thought to myself.

"Mama, what's that?" Harley called out, pointing.

Raven and I rode ahead and saw what she was indicating. A large fenced area was filled with white tents. Row after row of white tents that seemed never-ending surrounded a few larger ones in the center. Military jeeps were there, as well as soldiers on foot, constantly patrolling the area.

"Tent city," Mr. Miller stated. "They may have supplies to hand out or medical care."

We proceeded to ride to the entrance but were stopped abruptly by a large soldier. "Halt! No horses allowed." The soldier held up his hand.

"Sir, I was wondering if there was a medical facility set up. I have a pregnant lady with us whom I would like to get an ultrasound for."

"We don't have that kind of facilities. I'm sorry. We can offer you some supplies, blankets, and one tent per family. You can take it with you or stay here. It's up to you. If you're interested, one member from each family can enter and get the supplies and return."

Rose, Raven, Max, and I entered and got supplies. We were given large boxes that included sugar, flour, canned goods, and some bottled water. In addition, we received one blanket each person in our family. Monica was given baby formula and diapers for her growing bundle of joy.

Upon returning to the wagons, Raven was still talking with a few of the soldiers. We waited patiently for him to return to us. Monica and I stowed away our newly acquired supplies. Raven soon returned and helped me mount my horse. He patted my knee and allowed his hand to lightly rub my leg all the way down to my boots. "It's worse than we thought. I'll explain tonight." He turned and went to his own horse.

My eyes fell to where he touched me. I attempted to shake my head free of the graphic images that were running rampant through my brain. He might as well have poked me with a cattle prod. A tingling sensation worked its way through my leg and up my spine.

Everything about him seemed to be like a bad drug addiction that I desperately needed to avoid. However, knowing I needed to avoid him didn't keep me from wanting more.

We stopped and made camp near a river. Monica and Rose combined a few things and made a large pot of stew for us all to share. Rose also made a pan of corn bread, which was the best I had ever tasted.

"Rose, my dear lady, this is so good it will make you want to slap your mama." Lou laughed.

Rose, being the polite lady that she was, just replied a sweet "Thank you."

Monica and I got fresh clothes for everyone laid out and found a spot at the river for bathing. I sat with my gun and stood watch over the ladies as the men bathed further down. The girls played with Dannie, splashing water on one another. I shook my head when I didn't hear a single giggle escape Kat's mouth. I was sure she was being more diligent at attempting not to make a sound.

When we were all finished, Monica and I bedded Kat and Dannie down. I snuggled Kat in. "I didn't hear you say anything today. I suppose it was just another bad day. Tomorrow will be better. I love you, baby girl." I smiled at her and kissed her on the head.

I exited the wagon and went to look for Harley.

"Raven, have you seen Harley?"

Raven looked up from the campfire and pointed to the top of the hill without a sound. I looked. Harley and Ricky were standing at the center of the hilltop. A full moon shadowed by the dust that still lingered in the sky hung over them. It was as if the moon were there specifically for them. They were holding hands and looking deeply into each other's eyes. Ricky raised his hand and stroked her face, and Harley fell into his arms. He closed them around her as she looked up at his face as I witnessed my oldest daughter's first kiss.

"You want me to get my rifle and break them up?" Raven whispered as he sneaked up behind me.

I laughed at the thought. Harley would never forgive me if I did that to her, and for some reason, I didn't want to. This moment was hers, and I didn't want to take that away.

"No, but thanks for the offer. I'm just going to have to watch them more closely."

"I'll help with that. I can find so much work for that little booger to do. He will be too tired to put his lips on anything but food." Raven leaned onto the wagon and hitched his thumbs into his pockets.

"Thank you, Raven. That's sweet of you. I don't think it will go too far. His parents and I are always around, but an extra set of eyes won't hurt." I walked past him and took a seat by the fire. He soon joined me. Lou had already turned in for the night, as well as Max, Monica, and Marcus. Jacob and Rose were by the fire, chatting. "So what did you find out today at the tent city."

Raven shook his head. "This whole country, if that's even what you want to call it, is in total trouble. The guard units haven't heard from the president. They don't even know if he were still alive or not. No one knows who is making decisions. They are all going on instinct and trying to help as many as they can for as long as they can."

"It sounds like they are doing about as good as the rest of us," Jacob commented.

"They know that the volcanoes are being watched closely, as are the nuclear power plants. Aftershocks are still being felt. New York is in ruins, as well as Houston, Chicago, all the major cities. There isn't a part of this country that hasn't been affected in some way. There are still fires burning out of control." Raven flung his arms around in frustration.

Harley and Ricky came around the wagons. Ricky opened the door for her, and Harley went inside. I shook my head with a slight grin.

"We are going to have to watch those two," Rose said with a smile.

"Well, they don't need to be getting too attached. We are going separate ways, and they probably won't see each other again," Jacob stated with Rose poking him in the ribs. "Well, it's the truth."

"I couldn't agree more." I nodded to Raven about our previous conversation.

After a little small talk, we said our good nights and took turns staying watch. It seemed like the days were getting shorter. Just another sign that winter was around the corner. After my watch, I snuggled into my sleeping bag and nestled against the earth. I suppose I had always been strange, but I loved the smell of dirt. Not the nastiness that was on your clothes but the actual rich loose dirt. I lay there quietly, pretending I was asleep while watching Raven as he watched over the rest of my sleeping brood. He was indeed a good-looking guy once you got past his stubborn, jackass side.

My eyes drifted away to a safe place where everyone was happy and healthy, a place where rainbows danced down from the clouds. I was on a mountaintop looking down into a valley of roaming cattle. Snowcapped mountains jutted out of the horizon. Birds peacefully soared over a lake, their reflection like a mirror in the calm water below. I was imagining my idea of Montana. Only one thing was missing—Dallas. Why was he not in this dream?

I searched the entire mountain. Was this dream trying to tell me something? Was I going all this way for nothing? Was Dallas dead? I didn't like this dream anymore. I wanted to wake up, but I couldn't seem to force my eyes open. I kept climbing that mountain. Finally, I saw him sitting on the ground, leaning back on the rocks. I went over to him and put my hand on his shoulder. "Dallas!" I called. He lifted his head and looked at me with those strange eyes. It wasn't Dallas though. Upon seeing that cocky smile of Raven's, I slowly began to back away. "No, this isn't right. It's not you. Where's Dallas? You're not the one I'm looking for!"

He only grinned at me with that little crooked, cocky grin of his and replied, "Are you sure?"

A slight vibration of the ground awoke me from my nightmare. The thought of aftershocks rang in my mind as I sat up, rubbing my eyes. I got up and noticed Raven standing on the hill looking down into the valley below us. I walked to him. When he saw me, he raised his hand and motioned for me to approach quietly. I stepped softly and finally reached him.

"What are you staring at?"

Raven pointed to the valley and uttered one simple word, "Amazing."

I looked down and noticed what he had been watching. A family of elephants and giraffes were making their way through the valley. My mouth gaped open in awe. I shook my head in utter disbelief at what I was seeing, quickly searching my mental vocabulary to describe what I was feeling. "Oh my god" was the only thing I could say.

"I think it's safe to say that a couple of zoos got damaged beyond repair." Raven had a smile from ear to ear. I couldn't decide what was more beautiful, seeing his smile or watching the amazing sight before us. "Can you imagine what this will do to the ecosystem around here?"

"They are moving south. Their caged animal instinct has kicked in. They know it's going to get colder," I responded.

We continued to watch as they passed through quickly. I looked at Raven intently. "I wonder if all the animals escaped."

"We have to consider the possibility. We are liable to cross things none of us has ever seen before except in a zoo." Raven quickly pointed and almost yelled out, "Look there!" Monkeys gracefully jumped from tree to tree. They were too far away to determine what kind they were, but they were there all the same. It was a beautiful moment, and before I knew what had happened, Raven was holding my hand. I looked down in realization. He quickly let go. "Sorry," he said and turned toward camp.

"It's okay." Raven stopped and stared at me in question. "I mean, I understand. Never mind."

We walked silently back to camp and let the others know what we had seen. Everyone walked to the hill to get a glimpse of the oddity we had witnessed. They all shared in our awe and wonder.

After the excitement was over, we started picking up camp and getting the horses ready. As I threw the saddle over my horse, Raven yelled out, "Wait!"

I stopped and watched as he came over to me. He lifted the saddle and removed a large brown ball with long thorns on it. "It won't permanently hurt the horse, but they will buck like a bronco when you sit on this." He held the thorny ball up for me to see. "I reckon you have been thrown enough." He smiled and threw the thorny ball off to the side.

"Thank you."

"Welcome." Raven nodded, giving a little wink of his eye as he went about his business.

He could be extremely nice when he wanted to be. I felt myself beginning to like him, but I couldn't afford to get too close. I didn't know if he planned on staying around once Lou died. But when Dallas caught up to us, I wouldn't need Raven anymore. He would be free to leave at any time. He was handy to have around though. I was getting acclimated to his sense of humor and demeanor; I honestly couldn't imagine not having him around. These feelings could prove to be a dangerous threat, and I needed to keep them in check. Raven still had payback coming from the whole "horse-riding incident." I would focus my energy toward finding ways to pay him back. I looked at the thorny ball he had just discarded. I picked it up and safely put it away. "I may need this later." I laughed in spite of myself. Oh yes, Mr. Raven was going to get payback one way or the other.

CHAPTER 8

I N THE DAYS that followed, we made it well into South Dakota, traveling through the Rosebud Indian Reservation. They were very welcoming and grateful at the news we had shared with them. They shared some shattering information with us as well. Our planned route was demolished. Native Americans from the Spirit Lake Reservation and Fort Berthold Reservation in North Dakota had traveled to Rosebud for sanctuary. Mountains had crumbled; bridges collapsed. Destruction to most, if not all, roads left travel almost impossible. Our spirits were dashed. There was no word from Montana; I was now more determined than ever to get there. I had to see for myself that Dallas's family was safe. I felt that it was my duty.

At Monica's request, we camped near White River. We had to do laundry even if we wanted to or not. We were all getting a little ring around the collar. Monica, Rose, and I washed laundry by hauling water from the lake and boiling it over a fire. Lou had given us two large washtubs, one for washing and one for rinsing, along with a washboard and soap. Marcus and Lou hung up a clothesline between the wagons. We made a whole day of it and washed everything, including sheets from the wagon beds. Max, Jacob, Raven, and Ricky went hunting, while Harley and Kat kept Dannie occupied.

We planned to stay for two nights. That would give the clothes time to dry and Lou to catch his breath. He was looking thin and pale, although he was adamant that he felt fine. I wasn't sure how much longer he could go on. I could tell that he was frail and getting weaker by the day, but the impression he gave off was that he wasn't going to slow down or stop until he absolutely dropped. I would have to be the one to tell Raven about his friend and the secret he shared with me. That was one confrontation I wasn't looking forward to.

Soon, our strapping, mighty hunters returned with their kill. They had bagged a couple of rabbits and other small game, nothing big that would take too long to cook. Rose made more of her special corn bread, and we sopped it up with broth from the soup. We called it an early night and turned in. The guys were tired from walking the woods, and we ladies were spent from a fun-filled day of laundry.

I tucked Kat in and kissed her forehead. "I didn't hear you laugh today. It was just another bad day. Tomorrow will be better."

Harley said good night to Ricky and went into the wagon. I smiled when I saw how happy she was. Ricky joined his parents in their wagon and was soon snoring as loud as Raven. Lou and Marcus were already snug in their wagon. Max and Monica were hugged up to Dannie.

I stepped out of the wagon and grabbed an extra blanket on my way out. It was colder tonight than it had been. I draped the blanket over my shoulders and stopped quickly. I heard music playing, a guitar, that wasn't coming from any radio. I walked around to the campfire and found Raven picking away at a guitar. I stared at him in surprise. He was playing beautifully. I recognized the song as Metallica's "Nothing Else Matters." I slowly walked to the fire as he looked and stopped.

"No, please don't stop. It sounds great." I took a seat next to the fire.

Raven picked up where he left off and continued to play. I went over the words in my head.

"I'm surprised you know this song. I didn't think it would be in your genre." I snickered as I poured myself a cup of coffee and lit a cigarette.

Raven laughed and kept playing. "There's a lot you don't know about me," he said, flashing his mysterious smile. "I'm surprised *you* know this song. I can't imagine they play this at the country club."

Was this fool insulting me again? I put down my cup. "I'll have you know, I was quite the headbanger back in the day," I said proudly. "And I have never been a member of a country club, thank you very much, so I wouldn't know what they would or would not play there."

Raven laughed at my comments. "Seems like we have a lot to learn about each other then."

"It would appear so," I agreed.

Raven looked at me, his hopeful, glowing eyes dancing in the fiery embers. "Does that mean you want to learn about me?"

Oh god, I left myself open for that one. How can I turn this around? I squirmed in my seat as I thought to myself. "We are traveling together, Raven. I'm sure there are going to be things that we learn about each other, as well as from each other. For instance, I have to get Rose's recipe for corn bread." I laughed, trying to brush off the current conversation.

"Nice one." Raven continued to play. He wasn't stupid; he knew what I was doing, but he was a gentleman and didn't press the issue further. He placed his guitar to the side, put his hat over his head, and drifted off.

I walked around quietly, standing my watch, entertaining my own private thoughts. When it was time, I woke up Raven by kicking his boot. I got snuggled into my sleeping bag as he gallantly placed the extra blanket over me. "Thank you," I said.

"I don't know why you insist on sleeping out here." He took a seat beside me and draped his arm over my shoulders.

I was scared for him to be so close, but he was warm. I decided that no matter how tempting it might be, I wouldn't look into his eyes. I feared I would get lost in them and lose myself in the moment. I liked to think I was stronger than that, but there was something about Raven that made me want to lower my inhibitions. "I just don't want to be alone. I have nightmares when I'm alone. When I'm around you, I don't." I wasn't trying to flirt or lead him on; I was just being honest. I nestled my head in his lap and quickly fell asleep without thinking how it might look for us to be this close.

I was in a peaceful slumber, dreaming of my sweet Montana sky, when a gunshot pierced the silence of the night. Raven and I jumped up in a single swift motion. He had his rifle in hand before I could even locate the pistol on my hip.

"What the hell?" I shouted, holding one hand over my ringing ear, looking around in total confusion.

Jacob was standing near us with his rifle pointed toward the forest. "Wolf. He has been out there for a while watching us, prowling around the camp."

"Why didn't you wake us up?" Raven asked demandingly.

Jacob laughed and smiled at Raven. "Well, y'all looked so cozy. I didn't want to disturb you. But that critter came into the camp, and I had to scare him off. I apologize if I scared the two of you." Jacob was attempting to be sarcastic.

I flashed Raven a look of concern. It had felt good to lie close to him. I missed lying next to someone. I felt safe and truly had a good night's rest. I was only glad it was Jacob who found us instead of Kat or Harley. I didn't want to confuse them.

Raven went to collect a little extra firewood. The morning was colder than usual. The clouds were a deep gray color.

"It's gonna snow soon," Lou said, exiting the wagon. "I can feel it in my bones." He stood up and stretched, taking a seat by the fire.

"I suppose years of life experiences have made you a human barometer?" I looked at Lou, smiling, as I took a seat beside him and wrapped myself in a blanket.

Lou chuckled at me. "I suppose it has."

"How are you feeling?"

"Oh, I'm all right. I have good days and bad days. I have been tired a lot though. I think I will take today and just rest up since it's going to snow." He looked at me smiling, his years of wisdom showing in the saggy lines around his eyes. "You and Raven seem to be getting along better."

"He's not so bad once you get past the stubborn, pigheaded, arrogant, cocky attitude he has." We laughed together.

"He's a good man with a big heart. He don't show it to a lot of people," Lou explained.

"He's a hard man to figure out, that's for sure." I fixed Lou and myself a cup of coffee.

"Ain't we all?" Lou said, taking the cup of coffee.

"Some more than others." I got up to retrieve my sleeping bag. "You keep me posted on how you are feeling. I don't want you hurting. Do you understand?"

Lou held his cup up to me as if raising a toast. "Yes, ma'am."

As the sun attempted to rise, I thought the temperature would go up. However, it seemed to be dropping rapidly. The kids wrapped up in blankets and kept warm by the fire. Harley, of course, sat next to Ricky and nestled closely to him as he put his arm around her. Rose and I looked at each other, shaking our heads. Max and Raven had collected enough wood to keep the fire going strong all night.

By noon, our clothes were crisp on the line, and the wind was blowing with an animalistic power I had never before seen. It seemed to slice through you. It felt as if tiny needles were being poked into your skin. Monica told the kids to get into the wagons out of the cold. Harley chose to stay behind; I guess she'd rather spend time with Ricky out in the cold rather than have no time at all. We kept the coffee going to warm us up.

Soon, the temperature proved to be too much for Rose and Lou, who retreated to the safety of their respective wagons, leaving only Max, Raven, Jacob, and myself at the fire. I huddled into my sleeping bag, shivering. Raven made loops around the camp, checking things out.

"Max, I have to tell you something. Please don't be mad at me," I said, feeling a familiar sensation stirring inside me.

"What?" Max looked at me in question.

"I gotta pee." I busted out laughing. I had been holding it for some time, and I hated the thought of sitting on that cold five-gallon bucket.

Max laughed as well as he helped me up and walked me to the edge of the woods and stood watch while I disappeared behind a large bush where the bucket was hidden.

Raven saw Max leaning by the tree and hurried over to him. "I'm going to leave the horses near the woods tonight. It means we will have to watch for predators a lot closer, but at least they will have the shelter of the trees."

"Sounds like a plan," Max agreed.

Raven tucked his head down and kicked the dirt. Peering up at Max in a shy way, he said, "I think I'm doing a little better with your sister." He paused.

Max was twitching his head and eyes, attempting to warn Raven that I was behind the bush.

"I think she is actually starting to like me." Raven allowed his cocky little smile to slide out from the sides of his lips. Then he noticed me as I stood up from the refuge of the bush that concealed me.

I buttoned my pants and walked over to him. Max rolled his eyes and shook his head. I strutted over to Raven, and reaching up, I flirtatiously fixed his collar. Max stiffened his shoulders behind me. I knew he was getting ready to pull me off Raven if I went nuts on him. I slowly traced the side of his profile with one of my fingernails, watching the chill bumps develop on his neck. I knew it had nothing to do with the dropping temperatures. It made him apprehensive to have me this close to him. He looked into my eyes with hopefulness. I smiled at him seductively, stepping closer into him. I spoke in a whisper, "I'm afraid you have mistaken my unnaturally friendly behavior toward you, Raven."

"Oh, have I now?" he replied in a low tone.

"Yes, you have, because you see, I've seen corpses that didn't repulse me as much as you do." I playfully slapped the side of his face and turned to walked away.

Raven shuffled his feet and turned to Max. "You couldn't give me a heads-up that she was back there?"

Max laughed. "Dude, what do you think all this was for?" He reproduced his head and eye actions from a few moments before.

Raven watched me walked away. I could feel the heat from his eyes on me as if they were hot coals on my skin. I laughed to myself. *So it made him uncomfortable for me to be close to him. I think he could be beginning to really like me.* I didn't want to seem conceited, but I did find it a little amusing that he could be falling for me. I had no intention of leading him on or making him think that I wanted to be with him. However, perhaps I could use this to my advantage somehow in my plans of retribution for him for him being such an ass before.

The next morning, we awoke to a thick blanket of snow covering the ground. It was still hammering down as I exited the tent and went straight to the fire.

"When did this start?" I asked, holding out my arms in amazement.

It was Lou who answered. "About three a.m., I reckon. I told you it would snow soon."

I just laughed at Lou. "Know it all," I teased and took a seat beside him.

He returned the laughed and offered me a cup of coffee. "Travel will be a little slower, but at least we have roads."

Raven was busy packing things up with Max's help. Monica and Rose were making breakfast. I was certain it would be oatmeal again. I got my long underwear and went to the bucket. I put on extra socks and long-sleeved shirt with a sweatshirt on top of that and then a jacket. I felt warm and snug. Kat handed me a scarf and toboggan when I returned to the camp. "Thank you, baby." I put the garments on. I helped finish packing while Harley fed the horses. Kat and I were both delighted when we saw eggs for breakfast. Max and Monica were talking while they wedged Dannie between them. I saw her hand go to Dannie's head as he coughed. I hurried over to them.

"What's wrong?"

"I think he just has a cold, just a slight fever and a cough, that's all."

Without hesitating, I went to my medical bag and got my stethoscope. Listening to Dannie's chest, I found it to be clear. I sighed in relief. *At least it's not pneumonia.* "Okay, here is some Motrin. Give it to him every four hours until the fever is gone. And if you will, keep a watch on the others and monitor them for fever. Y'all are in tight quarters, and something simple can spread real fast."

"I will. Thanks, Ash."

"If it gets any worse, I do have some antibiotics I can give him, but it's best if he can fight it off himself." Monica carried Dannie to the wagon and told him to go play with Kat. My daughter waved to me and shut the door, securing Dannie and herself in the warm wagon.

"I wish we could all ride in the wagon. I worry about y'all out here." Monica put her hand in mine.

"I know, but it will be too much for the horses," I explained. "I just appreciate you taking care of the kids and doing the cooking."

"Well, we all do our part." Monica hugged me and retracted suddenly. "Ouch, what is that?"

I pulled the thorny ball I had tucked away and smiled at it.

"What is that?" Monica persisted.

"Payback, and right now is as good a time as any." I looked at Monica and flashed a sinister smile. "Keep watching. What comes around goes around."

I saddled my horse and then went to Raven's. I carefully placed the thorn under the blanket and put the saddle on top of it. I smiled to myself and went on my business. I caught a glimpse of Raven, who just nodded sweetly. When everything was ready to go, I mounted my horse. I motioned for Monica to watch Raven. He gallantly mounted his horse. The beast let out a whinny and threw itself back on its two hind legs. Raven held on with all his might but lost his battle with gravity. He let out a yell as his body landed with a sickening thud on the ground. I swiftly rode over and looked down at him withering on the ground. He was shocked and dumbfounded as to what had just happened.

"Ahhh, poor baby fell down and went boom," I said, laughing, as I rode back to Monica, who was covering her mouth with her hand. I gave her a wink as I went by.

Raven picked himself up and went to his horse. He lifted the blanket and found my little thorny treasure. Holding it, he glanced at me with a hint of the devil in his eyes. Raven looked mad, and there was no doubt in his mind that I was behind this prank.

I raised my eyebrows and flashed him a "What are you going to do about it?" smile. "I told you payback is a bitch."

Raven threw the thorn into the fire, mounted his horse again, and rode over to me.

"So you think you can play with the big boys?" Raven cracked an evil smile.

For the life of me, I couldn't wipe the sheepish smile off my face. "Well, when I find one, I'll ask him if I can play."

Raven dipped his head and nodded. "Okay, I see how you want to be. I just hope you can take it as good as you give it because, baby, it's on."

"Ooooh, I'm so scared. Bring it on," I repeated his statement from the night before, giving him a taste of his own medicine.

Raven only nodded and continued to ride ahead.

Soon, we were on our way once more. Lou was correct; the travel was slower. You could barely see the ice that was forming on the blacktop. The snow was still coming down but didn't feel as cold. I was warm and snug in my thermals and layers of clothing. The horses knew it too. They were stepping more carefully. The last thing we needed was to have one of our horses slip on ice. I wasn't completely sure that was even possible, but I knew enough to understand it wouldn't be a good thing.

Around noon, we stopped to eat lunch. Raven and Max took a few minutes to go hunting. They bagged a couple of rabbits, then skinned, gutted, and cut them up.

Monica took the cleaned animals to make stew. "Thanks for doing the dirty work, guys. Soup should be ready by the time we stop for the night."

During the day, I kept one eye on Raven and the other on Harley, who was still riding beside Ricky. I was unsure what Raven would do to me as payback for the thorn. However, I wanted to be on my toes, and I almost welcomed his attention. I surprisingly smiled to myself. Poor Harley was falling head over heels for Ricky. He seemed to genuinely like her as well. He looked at her with something that went beyond love. It was as if he were her protector. She'd had boyfriends in the past, but it was just the normal "teenage guy of the week" scenario. I had always said I wouldn't allow her to date until she was sixteen, and this trip had turned into one very long date for her. She was spending almost every moment with Ricky. I knew I was going to have one brokenhearted little girl when we parted ways.

All I could do was try to prepare her and be there for her when she needed me.

We stopped a little earlier than usual; the sun was setting faster in the winter sky. We would need its shaded rays to set up camp. The wagons and one tent were set up in a circle, with our fire in the middle. The kids collected firewood, and Harley placed the bucket in a safe private spot. We sat around the fire and ate. I noticed that Jacob's family didn't have as much to eat as ours.

Pulling Monica to the side, I inquired, "They don't have much to eat."

"I noticed that too," Monica agreed. "I know they have supplies. I have seen them. I just don't think Rose can drive the wagon and still have time to cook."

I nodded, breaking the silence of the night. "Jacob, I don't mean to intrude, but I notice y'all don't have much to eat tonight."

"We are just rationing what we have." Jacob flashed a smile at Rose and continued to eat.

"Well, I was thinking, Monica cooks for us anyway. What if she and Rose get together and plan out some meals and we combine supplies and we all eat the same thing?"

Jacob popped his head up from his plate. His eyes showed concern. "Are y'all running low on supplies?"

"No, I just want us all to have plenty to eat, and Rose doesn't have much time to cook if she's driving the wagon all day," I explained. "Y'all can't survive for long on gravy and bread."

Rose nodded in agreement, indicating she understood.

I continued, "And since Monica is pregnant, maybe Marcus can drive your wagon a day or two. That would allow Monica time to rest and Rose time to cook for all of us. I'm sure we would all love to have more of her delicious corn bread."

"Well, if Monica needs time to rest up, I don't see a problem with that." He turned to Rose. "Would you be willing?"

"Yes, I think that is a very good idea." Rose smiled. She looked at me with gratitude and nodded.

Raven stood up. "Well, some of you may have noticed that we changed direction. We are going more west now. Lou and I looked at the map and figured the farther north we go, the slower the travel it's going to be. So with that in mind, if we go west through Pine Ridge Indian Reservation over to Hot Springs, we can then go north to Rapid City. We can cut through the eastern tip of Wyoming and then finally into Montana."

"I noticed the change. Our family is just over the Saskatchewan border. I figure if we stay with your party till about Great Falls, we can go our separate ways there. And I appreciate the offer to combine supplies and let Monica and my Rose come up with some meals. I think we better do as much hunting as possible. It's colder now, snowing. We should be able to pack meat in a cooler and pile snow on it. It should keep at least a day or two," Jacob explained, taking a sip from his coffee cup.

"That sounds great, Jacob." I raised my own cup. "However, I say as soon as we find an open store, we get more supplies. We need more potatoes, and extra sugar, flour, and cornmeal wouldn't hurt."

"There will most likely be something around Rapid City. It's a big area, so our chances are better there." Raven took a seat beside Lou, who was wrapped in a blanket.

It was quiet then, too quiet.

I looked to Raven. "Play something."

"And what would you have me play?" he asked, pulling his guitar around in front of him.

"I don't know anything."

"Kum-ba-ya," Max started out, then busted out in laughter. The rest of us joined him.

"Are you going to sing, Mama?" Harley asked with a twinkle in her eyes.

"No."

"Wait, you sing?" Raven inquired, smiling.

"No, I don't."

"Yeah, she does," Marcus stated, sitting up from Rocky's side.

"No, I don't. Y'all hush. Ain't it y'all bedtime yet?" I argued with them.

"Come on, Ashley, just one song," Monica cheered.

"You ain't helping." I stood up and started to walk off.

"Come on, sissy. You can sing, so give us one song." Max grabbed my hand.

"Yeah, come on, Ashley. If you know Metallica, then I'm sure you know this one." Raven began playing his guitar. I noticed the familiar tune. It was Kid Rock and Sheryl Crow's "Picture." Raven began singing the male part. I knew I was supposed to pick up and sing the female's part.

Of all the songs, why this one? It was a song about not being able to be with one person because of commitments to another. What was he trying to do? Was this some sort of hidden message here? *Fine, if what he wants is to humiliate me by having me sing, then that's not too bad. I'll give them a good show.*

I picked up the female's part and turned to face Raven. We sang our respective parts. I walked around the campfire until the song joined parts. I found myself standing next to Raven. He was staring deeply into my eyes. I felt that shiver run up my spine. It felt as if he were singing directly to me. Thank God he had to keep both hands on the guitar, or I would've probably lost it right then if he touched me. We finished the song in unison and total harmony.

Everyone clapped, hooted, and cheered for us. I just rolled my eyes. "You know I hate you for that, right?" I was inches away from him.

"You haven't seen anything yet." He smiled at me. "Besides, you're good. Give yourself some credit." Raven began playing us another song.

Monica and I tucked Kat and Dannie into bed. The wagon was nice and warm. I was a little jealous of their accommodations. *But if I slept in here, I wouldn't be close to him. Why does that matter? You don't like him, remember? Maybe, maybe not. He can be nice when he wants to. He's an asshole. Not all the time. Oh my god, I'm sitting here arguing with myself. I must really be going crazy.*

I exited the wagon and walked around to the fire. Almost everyone had dispersed for the night—Lou in his wagon, Jacob and Rose in theirs. Ricky and Harley were saying their wet, slobbery good nights.

Max kissed me on the cheek as he went to the wagon. "Good job tonight, sissy. You sounded great."

I just shook my head and rolled my eyes. "I think you all need your hearing checked."

Max just laughed. "I don't know. I think we all enjoyed it." He motioned his head toward Raven, who was at the fire, still playing.

"What does that mean?" I asked Max.

"Nothing. It just seems like he has feelings for you, even if he won't admit it. It doesn't take a genius to see that."

"Well, that's not a good thing, Max. I'm engaged."

Max held his head down. "Sissy, it's been a long time. If Dallas was going to catch up to us, don't you think he would've by now?"

"Maybe not."

"I'm just saying if worse comes to worst, Raven's actually a good guy. I wouldn't think less of you if—"

"If what?" I interrupted. "If I just threw my feelings for Dallas into that fire over there? I'm not giving up on him, Max." I was trying not to yell. "Raven's a nice guy at times, but I'm not going to jump in the sack with a farmhand just because I'm lonely. Dallas is alive. I would feel it if he wasn't. I'm not giving up on him. He will come. He will."

"Thing is, sissy, are you trying to convince me or yourself?" Max nodded to me and went into the wagon and shut the door behind him.

I stood outside the wagon with my mouth gaping open. *He has a point. No, he don't. It's just easier to say Dallas is dead and move on. It takes love and commitment to believe he's alive.* My internal voices were fighting again. I walked back to the fire to finish my coffee.

"I'll take first watch tonight. Jacob and Max are going to take second and third, so you can sleep tonight."

"Oh, so now you're trying to get rid of me?" I snapped.

Raven gawked at me in confusion. "Um, no, it's just that you watch every single night. Jacob was thankful for the offer of combining supplies and working together on meals, so he offered to take your watch tonight. By your tone, it seems like you could use some extra sleep."

I exhaled deeply. I had just snapped and bitten his head off for a simple, nice gesture. "I'm sorry. I suppose I do sound like a bitch. I don't know. Maybe I do need sleep."

"What's going on?"

"Just a bunch of shit in my head. I think I'm going crazy some-times." I could feel tears welling in my eyes. "Max just basically told me to give up on Dallas ever coming. Am I just supposed to give him up for dead?" I looked at Raven. "I don't think I can do that."

"You shouldn't have to. You will know within yourself when it's time if you need to do that. That's not something you need to be rushed into."

I looked at him in surprise. "Are you serious?" I was shocked. Maybe I was wrong. If Raven really was falling for me, he would encourage me to forget about Dallas.

"Yeah, I'm serious. We all need something to believe in." He began strumming the guitar again and then sang. I recognized the song as "Something to Believe In" by Poison.

Before I realized it, I was singing along with him. I felt a single tear escape my left eye. I looked at Raven playing and singing to me. The campfire illuminated his facial features, making him look like a golden prince. *A prince in flannel,* I thought to myself.

He finished solo, then looked at me. "It's a long journey, Ashley. We have to hold on to whatever we can to get us through this. If thinking Dallas is alive and eventually going to meet you gets you through from one day to the next, then believe it. But there will be a point when you have to be honest with yourself. Don't get so lost in your illusion that you can't reel yourself back into reality." He looked at me and smiled his beautiful smile. "But don't think for a second that it means I can't mess with you in the meantime."

I smiled and dropped my eyes to the ground, easing my way over to him. Leaning down, I kissed him softly on the cheek. "Thank you. It seems like you're the only one who knows what I'm going through." I walked to the tent, stopping short of going in, and turned back to him. "What keeps you going, Raven? What do you hold on to?"

He rose to his feet and looked at me with his arms folded across his chest. "The fact that one day you will reel yourself back into real-ity, and when you do, I'll be there."

I stared at him in shock, unable to speak. I only nodded and went into the tent. He was falling for me. I entertained my own thoughts, tossing and turning in my sleeping bag. *You could do a lot worse. He is awfully cute, and he has an ass on him that fills out his pants just right.* I lay there, unable to fall asleep. I sent Dallas messages in my mind, telling him to hurry. I prayed for his safety and hoped he knew how much I needed him. Eventually, I did fall asleep as silent tears flooded from my eyes.

I woke to a cold, wet feeling on my head. *Great, now the tent must be leaking.* I opened my eyes and found a large nasty bullfrog on my head. I screamed and sat up, knocking the frog into my lap. One thought crossed my mind—*Raven*. I screamed again, kicking myself free of the sleeping bag. "Raven, you asshole!" I stood up, and the frog jumped toward me. "I can't stand these nasty-ass things!" As I looked around, there were several other frogs in the tent blocking my exit. "Oh god, Raven, get in here."

Raven showed up just as I drew my pistol. "Whoa, don't shoot 'em. You will waste bullets, not to mention put holes in the tent. Just walk over here. Come this way." He was laughing hysterically as he motioned for me to come to his extending hand.

Reaching out for his hand, I gently took a step toward him. One of the nastiest creatures God ever created leaped toward me. I squealed like a schoolgirl and jumped back. "You did this. Now get me out of here, or I'm going to start shooting, and when I do, I'm not going to stop with the frogs."

Raven laughed. "Okay, hold on." He came back and tossed a tennis racket into the tent.

I quickly picked it up. "Why do we even have a tennis racket?" Another slimy bastard jumped at me, and I whacked it with the racket, knocking it out of the tent. I sent another flying right over Raven's head. I continued until they were all gone, cursing as I hit each one. I had to admit, knocking the crap out of those things felt good, and by the time I clocked the last one, I was almost laughing.

Raven looked at me. He must have seen my eyes radiating through him. He ran ahead of me as I bolted from the tent, still holding the tennis racket. I chased him, cursing and waving the racket around like a madwoman. We slipped and slid over a fresh blanket of snow that had fallen. Raven fell down a hill, and I followed. We were both laughing by the time we landed at the bottom.

"You're an ass. You know that, right?"

"Yeah, I know. But you know what the weird part is?"

"What's that?"

"You wouldn't have me any other way." Raven rolled on top of me, supporting his weight on his hands. I gasped; I couldn't believe he was ballsy enough to do that. It made a part of me extremely uncomfortable having him hover over me in that manner. However, another part of me just wanted him to kiss me. Instead, he flashed me that devilish smile of his. Without a moment's hesitation, he popped a fast kiss on my forehead and scampered up the hill.

"You mean I wouldn't know you any other way."

He stopped at the top of the hill and looked down at me. "Whatever gets you through the day, sunshine."

I wrinkled my forehead and began my climb up the icy hill. *Did he just call me sunshine?* Reaching the hilltop, I now watched him walking away from me. *He does fill those jeans rather nicely.* I was now staring at his ass.

Raven looked back and caught me staring at him. His teeth gleamed in the sun as he reached Max and placed his hand on his shoulders. "Tell me something, brother."

"What's that?" Max questioned.

"Is your sister checking out my ass?"

I wasn't sure if he knew or cared if I could hear him. I stood straight up in an insulted tone. "I most certainly am not."

Max snickered. "I think you were, sissy."

"Oh, you men will take sides no matter what. I think you all need your heads examined." I stormed past them, making an extra effort to childishly stomp my feet.

"We need our heads examined, all right. Just not for the same reasons you think we do!" Raven shouted from behind me.

I spun around with attitude, beaming toward him. "You know, I would sleep with one eye open from now on if I were you. Frogs, why on earth would you infest the tent with frogs? I hate those slimy, godless, nasty things. And another thing, where did you get that many frogs? It's winter, for God's sake."

He walked forward. "The frogs don't know it's winter. The seasons are all screwed up. And if I were going to pay you back for making my horse throw me, you don't think I would treat you to ice cream, do you?"

"And what is the sunshine crap?"

Raven smiled and repeated the childhood song as he walked away, "You are my sunshine, my only sunshine. You make me happy when skies are gray."

I folded my arms over my chest. "Yeah, we'll see how happy I make you. You put frogs in my tent!" I stated, stomping off to check on the kids.

I found them playing in the snow. Harley and Ricky were having a snowball fight, yelling and laughing at each other. Kat was showing Dannie how to make a snowball and then throwing it at Monica. All of a sudden, something cold smacked me on the side of the head. I looked in the direction it came from and found Raven laughing.

"Oh no, I think I made her mad," he teased, placing his hand to his cheek childishly.

"I'll show you mad, you heathen." I picked up a handful of snow and chunked it at him. He ducked as the snowball went past him.

"You couldn't hit the broad side of the barn." Raven threw another snowball that again hit me in the head.

I couldn't help but smile and laugh as I returned the icy mixture, landing it on his throat. Raven stopped as his hands went to his throat. One hand reached out to me. His eyes grew larger. It looked as if he were having difficult time breathing.

Running over to him, I gently lowered him to the ground. "Raven, what's wrong? Can you breathe? Talk to me, dammit."

He looked at me with pleading eyes. Taking a long, deep gasping breath, he finally spoke, "I was just wondering if you would be upset if something happened to me, sunshine."

"You asshole! Jesus Christ, I thought something was really wrong with you!" I pushed him away and got up. "I should take one of those snowballs and shove it where the sun don't shine."

"Hey, are we going to stay another day, or are we going to pack it up?" Jacob called from the camp.

I was glad he was breaking up our icy party. I was ready to get moving. The longer we stayed here, the more likely it was that I would kill or kiss Raven. I just didn't know which one would come first. We broke camp and got things ready to move out. I saw Raven check under his saddle blanket and look at me. I uncontrollably laughed and shook my head.

We made it through the Pine Ridge Indian Reservation within three days. On the fourth, we made camp in Hot Springs, South Dakota. Raven and Jacob scouted and found us a private area with an area of hot water. It would be more suitable for bathing.

"We will be able to bathe and actually feel clean!" Jacob shouted with pride.

We all cheered, being very happy with their find. We started out in the usual way. Harley placed the bucket in a private area, then helped the rest of the kids gather firewood. Rose got a fire going, and Monica placed the supper pot over the fire to keep it hot while Rose fixed her infamous corn bread. They were becoming good friends. We gathered clothes together, and I stood watch as the women bathed and washed their hair. I helped Dannie get dried off and dressed, followed by Kat. Harley and Monica spent a little extra time in the water, enjoying the heat. Finally, we were all back at the camp. The men wasted no time in eating.

"Monica, can you watch the kids? I'm going back to bathe," I stated.

"Sure, but you don't want to eat first?"

"No, I want to wash off the grit and grime and get my hair clean. Just keep the kids in the wagon till their hair dries so they don't get sick."

Monica nodded, and I went back to the hot springs. I welcomed some time alone. I bathed thoroughly and washed my hair until it squeaked. I swam around and enjoyed the heated water. It wasn't until I started to get out that I realized I was being watched. Raven stood at the water's edge, his eyes fixed on me.

"Raven," I said, shocked, and attempted to cover myself. "What the hell are you doing?"

Raven kept his eyes on me while munching on a piece of rabbit. He leaned against the tree where my towel was hanging behind him. "Dinner and a show." He motioned toward me.

"I thought I was alone. Is it too much to ask to get a little alone time? I mean, we are out in the middle of nowhere."

"Exactly, there's no one around for miles except bears, mountain lions, wolves—"

"Okay, fine, you've made your point. Now will you go so I can get out?"

"Nope."

"Raven, come on, at least turn around."

"Nah, I don't think so," he stated teasingly.

"Raven, please," I begged.

He smiled at me. "No."

"Fine." I dropped my hands and began to make my way out of the water. I exited the water the same way I entered, totally nude. I let my hands fall to my side, revealing myself to him. The moonlight danced off my body. I could feel my nipples hardening in the cold air. He obviously wanted to see me, or he would've turn away. He stood there gawking at me with his lips parted slightly. The rabbit bone he held dropped to the ground. I walked to him and placed my right hand on his shoulder. He touched my left cheek and allowed his hand to trace the side of my face and down my arm. I shivered at his touch.

I had to end this quickly, or I would find myself in trouble. We were face-to-face and only inches away from each other. "You know what?"

"What?"

"Just when I think you're going to be a nice guy, you show me how much of a pig you can be." I plucked my towel from the tree behind him and quickly wrapped it around me. I gathered my dirty clothes and turned to walk away.

Raven grabbed my arm, spun me around, and pulled me into his arms. "I think you need to be kissed. You've had too much frustration in your life, and you need to let go before you explode. You're too much of a lady to let your temper flare at someone you truly love, so why not me? Let me be your release. Take your frustrations out on me."

I looked into his eyes. It would've been so easy. At that very moment, I wanted nothing less than to be taken into his embrace and kissed. I wanted him to make love to me until I was too sore to move. I wanted to feel his bare skin on mine. I had to remind myself to breathe. "I can't."

"Can't or won't?" he asked.

"Does it matter?"

"You can't deny that there is something between us." Raven looked at me. His eyes seemed to be screaming at me.

Releasing his hold on me, I remained in place. "I'm trying to be strong, Raven, and you're not making it very easy. It would be so easy for me to let go of everything right now, but I can't. It wouldn't be fair to you or me. I can't be with you, and when Dallas comes back… It just wouldn't be right. I would feel like I betrayed him and used you. You want me to be honest with myself. Then here is honesty for you. I can't be with you until I know within my heart that Dallas isn't coming back."

"I suppose I understand what you're saying, but I'm here if you change your mind." He turned and walked away just as quietly as he came.

I exhaled deeply and gathered myself. I sat on the bank of the springs and stared up at the pale moon. "Dallas, if you're out there, please hurry." I closed my eyes. I had never been a very religious person, but I felt the urge to pray. "God, if you can hear me, I need your help. I need Dallas to find me, or I need to feel it inside if he's dead. I think I'm falling in love with Raven, and I can't seem to stop it, or at least it's getting harder to stop it. I need your help, because I feel lost and I don't know which way to turn." I wiped the tears from my face and stood up. I couldn't afford to break down over something this trivial. I solemnly walked back to camp.

Everyone was saying their good nights. I tucked Kat in and made sure Harley went into the wagon. I went and sat quietly by the fire. It wasn't long after everyone else went to bed that Raven made his way over to me.

"I'm sorry."

I looked up to him. "What for?"

"You're not going to make this easy, are you?" He laughed as he sat across from me. "I'm sorry for the way I acted by the water. You don't deserve me putting you on the spot like that."

"Don't worry about it. I'm sorry I can't give you what you want."

"What I want is for you to want me around. It's been a very long time since I have found someone that I actually want to spend time with, Ashley. And I don't want to ruin it by acting a fool," Raven explained.

I could sense the sincerity in his voice. "I hate to hear that. You acting a fool is one thing that attracts me to you." I smiled and laughed under my breath.

He returned my laugh. "You're a glutton for punishment."

We shared a laugh. "So are you going to play the guitar tonight or not?"

"Okay, I'll play. It's too cold for any critters to be out tonight anyway."

Raven played for a while, then I went into the tent. He stayed up and watched over all of us as the great protector in flannel.

CHAPTER 9

OVER THE NEXT few days, several feet of fresh snow blanketed the ground. I wished we had another hot spring to bathe in. Without one, we had resorted to heating up water over the fire and bathing between the two wagons with only a blanket to protect us from the wind. Perhaps it was fine for Dannie to bathe in this manner, but I never felt fully clean. My hair was nasty and felt as if it were slickly glued to my head. I kept my hair in a ponytail when I didn't have my hat on. My face was reddened and dry; my lips cracked and sometimes bled when I tried to open my mouth too wide. I was grateful that the sun wasn't shining brightly, or it probably would have blinded us by reflecting off the snow. All you could see was white, no matter where you looked or what you looked at. We all had on layers of clothing and wrapped ourselves in a blanket for the day's dreary ride. We would ride until sunset, then stop and make camp. Everyone had their chores to do and went about them accordingly. Amazingly, no one complained, and I enjoyed the team-work. There were no arguments about who was going to do what. I laughed, remembering how only a short time ago my girls would fight over who would do the dishes.

We were about a day's ride away from Rapid City and about to stop for the night when a haggard-looking man came over a hilltop, yelling and waving his arms erratically.

"Wait here," Raven commanded as he rode ahead to meet the man. I saw him grab Raven's boot, pleading and pointing to the direction that he came from. Raven patted him on the shoulder and motioned for me. "Bring your bag!" he yelled.

I slapped the side of the wagon. "Monica, hand me my bag, please."

Monica quickly opened the door to the wagon and handed the large red duffel bag to me. "What's going on?" she asked.

"I'm not sure. Some guy is in trouble." I came around the wagon and saw Raven talking to Lou and Max.

"Follow me," he said again in a commanding tone.

"What's happening, Raven?"

"His wife is in labor. They are camped at the bottom of the hill down there."

"Oh," I said, trying not to make a big deal about it. I had a sinking feeling in the pit of my stomach.

Raven looked at me with question. "Can you do this?"

"Yeah, sure, I can deliver a baby." I felt confident enough in my skills that I could do the task at hand. I had no question about delivering Monica's baby when it was time. I rode behind Raven and reached the small camp. I could hear a woman groaning in the government-issued tent.

The frazzled, terror-stricken man was beside himself as he extended his hand. He almost vibrated while trying to explain their ordeal. "My name is Charley. My wife is Kim. I told her we should have stayed in the tent city till she delivered, but she wouldn't have it. We are at least a day's ride to the nearest hospital. I don't know what to do. Can you help us, please?" he pleaded with me.

I placed my hand on his shoulder, speaking in quick plain sentences, "Charley, remaining calm is the best thing you can do for her. I'm a nurse. I will examine her and see what we have and go from there. I will help you in any way I can." I smiled to give him that reassurance he desperately needed. "If you will be so kind as to help my party set up. We will have food, and if you can get some water heating up, that would be very helpful." Charley nodded and hurried about his assigned task.

Raven looked at me; he seemed puzzled. "Do you really need boiling water?"

I laughed. "Well, normally, no, but since we are out in the middle of nowhere, I will need warm water for the baby when it's born to clean it off, and it gives a frantic father something to do."

Raven laughed with me. "I suppose so. Do you need any help in there?"

"Not right now. I'm going to introduce myself and examine her. I'm sure the fewer people in there, the better it will be for her. If it were me, I wouldn't want a bunch of strangers standing around," I explained. "Just keep an eye on dear ole dad over there."

I went into the tent and looked at the panic-stricken woman. "Hi, Kim. I'm Ashley. Your husband, Charley, flagged us down. I'm a nurse, and I may be able to help you." I sat my bag down and opened it, retrieving a pair of exam gloves. "Are you okay with me examining you?"

Kim nodded and leaned back against a pillow.

"Has your water already broken?"

"Yes," she said in a whisper.

"How long have you been in labor?" I put on the gloves.

"I have been uncomfortable all day, but it got really bad about four or five hours ago."

"Is this your first baby?" I probed for some kind of medical history.

"Yes, we tried for years to get pregnant. Finally, it happens, and the whole world goes to shit."

"Well, I'm pretty sure one didn't have anything to do with the other." I placed a hand on her leg in an attempt to comfort and relax her. "Okay, Kim, I'm going to insert my fingers and feel to see how far your cervix is dilated. I need you to relax and take a deep breath and exhale slowly when you feel my fingers. Do you understand?"

Kim nodded and did as she was told. I inserted my fingers into her vaginal cavity. She released her breath, and her muscles began to relax. I went slowly so I wouldn't frighten her. I felt her cervix, and she was a solid 8 percent dilated. Just as I was about to withdraw my fingers, I felt something else, something strange. I slowly moved my fingers around and found it again. It was something foreign that didn't belong there. I clasped my fingers around the oddity as it withdrew back within the cervix. I gasped as my eyes widened. "Okay, give me just a few minutes. You just try to relax. If you feel a contraction, breathe through it. Don't push, okay?" I explained, attempting to maintain my composure.

I exited the tent and immediately found Raven and motioned for him to come to me.

He saw the horror on my face and wasted no time in coming to me. "What's up?"

"My blood pressure—" I pulled him away from everyone so we wouldn't be heard. "I can't do this, Raven."

"What do you mean? I thought you have done this before."

"I have, but not like this. Something is wrong, and I mean really wrong." I wasn't sure how to explain things.

"What is it?" Raven pressed for more information.

"While I was examining her, I felt something. When I probed a little more, I felt it again, and then I was certain." He looked at me inquisitively. "I felt the baby's foot, Raven. This baby is breech. She can't have this baby normally. She needs a cesarean."

Raven looked at me. His eyes showed me he understood. "Is there any way she can make it till we can get her to Rapid City? We can ride through the night if we have to."

"No, she's already dilated eight centimeters. The more riding and bumping around is only going to make her labor go faster." I rubbed my forehead in frustration. I had no easy answers.

Raven gripped my shoulders and forced me to look at him. "Okay, go into medical mode, Doc. Think about this like you would any other patient. What would you do?"

"Rush her into a sterile operating room and perform an emergency cesarean."

"What would happen if you didn't do that?" he asked calmly.

"The baby would die, perhaps even the mother."

Raven let go of me. "Well then, you have your answer. It's not the one you were hoping for, but it's an answer."

Charley saw us talking and started over to us. He removed his hat and held it tightly in his hand. "I see it in your face. Something's wrong, isn't there?"

"Yes, Charley, there is." I sighed slowly. I didn't want to explain to this man that the baby they had tried so hard for was about to die.

"Just tell me," Charley pleaded.

There was no sense putting it off. Kim was in the tent moaning and groaning, doing her best to take deep breaths. Rose had gone in to do her best to comfort her. I took a deep breath and began, "The baby is breech, meaning it's trying to come out feet first. There is no way that baby can be born that way and survive. It will strangle before it's born. Your wife needs a cesarean for the baby to be born alive. There is no safe way to do that out here." I took a deep breath and exhaled slowly in a feeble attempt to steady myself. It was then that I felt Raven's hand on my shoulders. To a small extent, it was a comfort to me.

Charley looked at me. You could tell the moment it sunk in as to what was happening. His knees went weak, and Raven helped him sit down. Charley buried his face in his hands, attempting to hold himself together. Finally, he looked at me. "Can you do a cesarean?"

I looked at him, horrified. "No, there's no way I can do that out here. I have no experience in this, no anesthesia. She will need blood, and I don't have any to give her. Even if she somehow survived the surgery, there is a major risk of infection."

"But if you don't, then the baby will die, and she may die anyway. Am I right?"

"Yeah, that's right," I agreed. I didn't like the way this conversation was going.

"Then there's a decision that needs to be made." Charley got up and went into the tent. He talked with Kim in hushed tones. We could make out their shadows on the sides of the tents. I could hear them crying together. My heart went out to them. I couldn't imagine losing my child. Soon, they called for me to come into the tent.

I went inside to meet reddened eyes.

"Ashley, I want to thank you. You didn't ask for any of this, and I want you to know how much we appreciate all your help."

"You're very welcome. I just wish I could help you more." I tried to smile to them.

"You can," Kim said, sitting up. "If you did the cesarean, could you get the baby out safely?"

My eyes widened. This was the option they were considering. "I, um," I stuttered. I looked into their desperate eyes and understood. They had tried so hard for a baby they were willing to risk anything to bring it into the world. I struggled to gather my composure. "I feel like I can get the baby out, yes. But I can't make any promises about you. There are just too many unknowns."

They looked at each other and nodded. "It's a chance we are willing to take. I want my boy to have a chance. I have lived my life, and I feel like I owe it to my son to give him every chance at life, even if it means giving up mine." Kim's eyes never left Charley.

"You know it's a boy?"

"We had an ultrasound a few months ago, and they told us. It will be hard on Charley, but he can raise a boy," Kim spoke with soft, gentle words.

"I don't have any anesthesia. It's going to be the most horrible pain you can imagine," I explained, even though nothing I said could prepare her for having her body cut open while she was fully awake.

Charley looked at me. "No, the worst pain is losing the son that you have waited so long for."

"Give me just a few minutes to get my stuff together." I exited the tent, rubbing my forehead, trying to get my head in the game. I couldn't believe I was about to do this.

Raven came around to me. "I can see it in your expression. I know what they decided. Are you okay with this?"

"I don't have a choice."

"Sure you do. We can pick up camp right now and keep going. Just say the word."

"And let them both die? I can't do that, Raven. I have to try. At least if I do this, I can save one of them," I explained. "It just isn't going to be pleasant."

I found Monica and told her what was about to happen. She would tend to the kids and try her best to keep them from hearing too much.

"Make them put on headphones or something, especially Kat."
I was concerned about what this turn of events would do to Kat's
well-being.

"Mom, we are going to take a walk if that's okay," Harley stated,
holding Ricky's hand.

"Mind if I tag along?" Marcus stood up.

It was Ricky who answered. "Sure. Come on, Marcus." Ricky
turned to me. "We won't go far, Ms. Reese, and I have my gun."

"Thank you, Ricky."

I quickly found Rose. "Do you think you can help me out?"

"Oh, I'm not sure if I could handle being in there." Rose looked
at me with a horrified look in her eyes.

"I just need you to take the baby from me and get him cleaned
off and clear his mouth and nose and get him to cry," I explained.

A look of relief crossed over her. "Oh yeah, I can do that."

"Raven!" I called out.

"I'm right here." He never seemed to be too far away, ready and
eager to help.

"I need you."

"You don't know how long I have waited to hear you say that."
He laughed slightly and flashed that crooked smile.

"Shut up. I need you to help hold her steady while I cut her
open," I spoke bluntly. "It's going to be bloody and gruesome, and
she is going to be yelling. Now I need to know. Can you handle it?"

Raven dropped his head and thought for a moment. "If it will
help you, then yes, I can handle it."

"I mean it, Raven. I can't have you in there passing out. I need
you to be strong. Once I'm in there, that baby is my only concern.
I'll hand him off to Rose, and then I'll be trying to keep Kim alive. I
need you to be sure that you can handle this."

"I'll be fine," he said, doing his best to reassure me. "Besides, it
can't be much different from gutting deer, right?" Raven walked away
from me and went by the tent.

I took off my coat and rolled up my sleeves. I took a good long,
deep, cleansing breath; however, it didn't do any good. My stomach
was doing somersaults as I entered the tent. Charley was holding

Kim's hand. Raven came in behind me and placed his hand on my back.

"You can sit down over there on her left side." I pointed, telling Raven where to go. Kim looked at me, a bit confused, as Raven took his place. "Kim, this is my friend Raven. He is here to help hold you."

I opened my bag, retrieving another pair of gloves, a scalpel, and the materials I needed to do stitches. Kim was still having contractions, and they were getting closer together. We were running out of time. I was going to have to work fast before the baby slipped further down the birth canal. I handed Kim a bite stick that would normally be used for a patient having a seizure. It would serve the same purpose in this situation. I had everything laid out and within easy reach.

"I'm starting an IV, then give you some morphine to relax you." I completed the first task at hand. I sighed a breath of relief when I saw Kim's muscles beginning to loosen. "Rose, are you set up outside?" I called out.

She poked her head inside the tent. "I'm right here. I have a blanket ready. We are good to go here."

I took another deep breath. "Okay, Kim, like I said, this is going to be very painful. I wish I could do more. The only thing you can do is try to remain as still as you can."

Kim nodded. "Let's just get this done."

"Charley, Raven, hold her as still as possible."

"We got it. Just do it," Charley almost commanded.

I picked up the scalpel with my shaking hand. I steadied my breathing as I placed the scalpel against Kim's stomach. With one final deep breath, I started to cut, inserting the scalpel just below her belly button, and pulled down to just above her pubic area. Bright red blood oozed from the incision. Pulling apart the skin, I began the second cut. Kim was screaming now. Her eyes rolled back as she twisted her head from side to side. Once the incision was deep enough, I could make out the baby's body from inside the uterus. My incision on the uterus had to be precise. I couldn't risk cutting the baby. I could see the outline of his little body wedged into the small space. Kim's body went limp.

"She passed out," Raven stated as he eased his grip on her.

"That's probably for the best." I made the final incision, and I could see the baby's skin. Reaching my hand into Kim's body, I got a firm grasp onto the baby and pulled him free. I quickly tied off the umbilical cord and cut it. "Rose!"

Rose reached her hands in and took the baby.

I quickly went to work on Kim. Removing the placenta left me free to start sewing her up. Blood had pooled up into her body cavity. "Rose, I need a few towels, something I can use as a sponge." A towel immediately appeared through the opening of the tent, and Raven took it.

"Put on some gloves." I nodded to where they were in the bag. He did as he was told. "Now I need you to hold back the skin and keep the blood wiped away so I can see to sew her up." Raven didn't hesitate as he donned the gloves instantaneously and shoved the towel into Kim's belly, soaking up the blood. With him holding back the skin, I was able to see more clearly how to stitch her up.

My ears perked up, and I felt a huge relief as soon as I heard the baby crying behind me. I smiled big. "You hear that, Kim? That's your baby crying for you."

Charley shook her a little. Kim opened her eyes, smiling slightly as she heard the baby crying.

"Almost done, guys. Hang in there a little longer." Raven looked pale and weak. "Don't you dare pass out on me, you wimp," I said, looking over at Raven, who was white as a ghost.

"I'm fine."

I continued to stitch layer by layer. From the first cut to the last stitch, it took me almost an hour. I wiped her belly clean and removed the trash and bloody towels, placing them right outside the tent.

"Rose, hand me the baby. Help her sit up a little."

Rose opened the tent flap and handed me a perfect little baby. He was cleaned up and wrapped in a blanket. His eyes were open and ready to face the world. "It's a girl!"

I looked at her, shocked. "A girl?"

Rose nodded positively. I handed the baby to Charley, who in return handed it off to Kim. She took the baby girl with tears in her eyes. "A girl," she said in a solemn whisper.

Charley adjusted the blanket around the baby to get a better view of her. "She is beautiful, just like her mama."

Raven excused himself and left the tent. I felt a big relief come over me. I had done well. Feeling an enormous sense of accomplishment, I patted Kim's thigh. "I will give you a few minutes." My hand felt wet. I looked down and noticed Kim was soaked in blood. I lifted the sheet. "No, it's too much." My accomplishment was rapidly replaced with dread.

"What's wrong?" Charley asked.

My voice was shaky. "She's hemorrhaging. She's losing too much blood too fast." I looked at them grimly. "I can't stop it. I'm sorry." I knew she only had minutes to live and at the very least deserved some privacy.

I pulled myself from the tent. Holding my bloodied hands out in front of me, I walked away from the tent like a zombie. My breath was quick and uneven. I was on the verge of breaking down. Raven followed me. I found the warm water to wash my hands. I splashed the water on my face. The cool breeze felt refreshing but did little to calm my nerves. I could feel Raven's presence behind me.

"Did things take a turn for the worse?"

"It'll be over soon." I turned to face him. "Everything was fine, and then she just started bleeding."

"Is there anything we can do?"

I shook my head and folded my arms across my chest. "She's losing too much blood, and I can't stop it. If I only had…"

Raven grabbed me and pulled me into an embrace. He took me by surprise, but I welcomed it. I was on the verge of tears, but I fought them back. I couldn't afford the luxury of breaking down, not yet.

"Kim! Kim! No, don't leave me. Don't go, Kimberly." The agony in Charley's voice was all I needed to hear to know she was gone. I buried my face into Raven's bulky arms.

"I need to go to him." Pushing Raven away, I went back into the tent. Kim's pale body lay limply on the ground, the baby still in her arms. "I'm so sorry, Charley."

"It's not your fault. You did all you could. I don't blame you." Charley looked at me with desperation in his eyes. "Can you tell me what the hell I'm supposed to do with a girl? It wasn't supposed to be a girl."

"You will do what's best for her, Charley. That's all any of us can do as a parent." He just stared at Kim and the baby. "I'll get some help. We'll take care of the burial." I left the tent again, unable to stay in there any longer. I couldn't take the pain in his eyes.

Max found me and hugged me. "It's gonna be all right, sissy."

"We need the shovels," I stated, wasting no time. I didn't want to linger on this for too long. I wanted it to be over and done with. I didn't ask to be dragged into this. Tomorrow would be a better day. It had to be.

"We can handle it. I'll get the guys together. Go warm up by the fire." Max handed me my coat.

I hadn't realized how cold I was until then. It was bitterly freezing. The wind whipped all around. Lou was by the fire, finishing his soup. I silently took a seat beside him.

"Damn, it's cold," I said, rubbing my arms.

"Scary thing is, it's going to get colder." Lou put down his empty soup bowl and looked at me. "I don't care about what's bouncing around in that brain of yours. You did good in there. And it won't do you any good to be thinking anything different." Rising from his seat, he patted me on the back and went into his wagon without another word.

Ricky appeared from the darkness and went into his wagon. Max soon came into sight, as well as Jacob.

"We have a problem," Max stated as he sat beside me.

Standing up, I twirled around to face Max. "What now?" I said, throwing up my arms. Part of me wanted to scream at them to take care of it and stop coming to me. I didn't have all the answers.

"The ground is frozen," Raven hesitated. "We can't dig a proper grave."

"Well, there is only one other thing we can do." I looked at them and waited for the answer to sink in. Raven nodded understanding to what I meant.

Max just shook his head. "What? I don't get it."

"We have to burn the body." Raven jumped in to explain, saving me from sharing the horrible details with my brother. He patted Max on the arm. "We will have to wait until morning when we leave. If we do it now, none of us will be able to stay around here. The stench of burning flesh and hair, not to mention all the internal organs, will knock us over."

"Thank you, Raven, for the morbidly graphic description," I said sarcastically, folding my arms as I buried my face. A feeling of sadness and despair flooded over me as I overheard Charley softly sobbing while the baby began to cry. I felt like my body was unraveling at the seams. I was coming apart. I wanted to hit, kick, or punch something, and I needed a good stiff drink. Knowing I wasn't going to do either one, I spoke up, "I don't want to be rude, but can I have a few minutes alone?"

"I was about to go to bed anyway." Max walked over to me and hugged me. "I'm proud of you, sissy."

I looked up at him, dumbfounded. "What?"

"I'm proud of you," he repeated. "You didn't have to do anything, but because of you, that baby is alive. Mama would be proud of you too." He paused, looking down at me. "Good night."

Raven followed Max to the wagon. I could only imagine their conversation. I suppose they were commenting on my quick actions, possibly expressing concerns for my mental state after this debacle. I didn't want to even imagine it. I just wanted to be left alone to wallow in my own emotions for a while. I felt a single tear escape my left eye.

"Are you crying?" Raven asked, startling me.

I quickly wiped my face. I didn't want him to see me. "No," I snapped. "It's cold, and my nose is running," I lied.

"I was going to save this for a special occasion, but it looks like you could use it now. Plus, I wanted to call a truce in our payback battles." I looked up and noticed Raven was holding out a bottle of Jack Daniel's whiskey.

I took the bottle, a sight for sore eyes. I felt a wide smile begin to grow as I marveled at this pure excellence. Gallantly Raven draped a blanket over me, then wrapped up in one of his own and took a seat beside me.

I flashed him a playfully cold stare. "You've been holding out on me." I cracked the seal on the bottle and opened it. I took a good long smell. *Oh god, that smells good.* I put the bottle to my lips.

Raven wiggled against me, making himself comfortable. "I don't have a glass or anything—" He stopped midsentence and watched as I drank straight from the bottle.

I swallowed four mouthfuls before I felt that familiar but welcoming burn in my throat and chest. I noticed him watching me. "What?" I said, noticing him watching me. *Great, now he's going to think I'm an alcoholic.*

He snickered. "I think maybe your brother was right."

"What do you mean? What did he say?" I inquired as I offered him the bottle.

"I bought this the day Max and I went into town for supplies. I asked him if he thought you would be upset that I bought it. He told me you wouldn't be upset and, in fact, you would probably take it away from me." He took a drink from the bottle. "He also said you could drink me under the table."

I laughed out loud. "Well, he was right, on both accounts."

It's good to see you smile. I wasn't sure if I would see that again for a while. You did really good in there. I can't imagine a real doctor doing any better under the circumstances."

"Thank you. You didn't do so bad yourself."

"Well, it wasn't my first rodeo."

I looked at him in confusion. "Huh?" I questioned.

"I have been in a similar situation before."

"With what, a horse?" I stated sarcastically and took the bottle from him.

Raven stopped and looked dead at me. "No," he stammered as he lowered his head, "with my wife."

I froze in my tracks and glared at him. "What?"

"My wife." He fidgeted with his hands.

I could tell he was having a hard time. "I didn't know you were married."

Raven took a deep breath and stared into the fire. "I was, for about two years."

"What happened? I mean, you don't have to tell me if you don't want to." I was hoping he wanted to. I wanted more information.

"No, it's okay. It's about time I told you. I met a young lady named Tabitha during a cattle drive. She was the most beautiful thing I had ever seen. She was so soft-spoken and easy to talk to, just one of these people that you meet and automatically fall in love with. When you talked to her, you felt like she was listening and that she cared about what you had to say. We fell in love and got married, and then we got pregnant. We were young, and like any first-time parents, we didn't know what we were getting ourselves into. It was the next logical step in our lives. She did everything by the book, then…" He paused. "One day, when she was about six or seven months along, she started hurting really bad. We went to the hospital, and they did all sorts of tests. They said the placenta was tearing away, and it was clear that the baby wouldn't survive. It was just too early. They induced labor, and she delivered a very small baby girl. They immediately took her away and cleaned her up. Tabby was crying, wanting to hold her. I'm not sure what all happened next because it was all so fast. Tabby's heart rate went sky-high. Her blood pressure bottomed out. She passed out and never woke up. The baby actually lived longer after birth than Tabby did. Lou said that the baby meant everything to her, and knowing it wouldn't survive, he was sure she just gave up to go be with her baby."

"You worked for Lou back then too?"

"Yeah, Tabitha was his daughter."

My mouth dropped open. "Oh, Raven, I'm so sorry." I wanted to cry again. My mind reeled with the story he had just told me.

"It's okay. Everything happens for a reason, and I'm sure one day I'll figure out what the reason was. Or at least that's what Lou keeps telling me." I watched as he smiled his genuine smile. "And that's how I know that what you did tonight was a good thing. You have nothing to blame yourself over. You saved that baby. That baby will have a chance at life. She will grow up and live on. Who knows, maybe she may do something great one day. And you are the one who gave her the opportunity." He placed his arm around me and pulled me closer. "It's cold."

I allowed myself to nestle against him, taking another drink. "I'm actually starting to warm up." Part of me felt like I was betraying Tabitha. I was sitting here with her husband. I would be furious if someone was sitting wrapped up with Dallas right now, but there I was, snuggled up to Raven and enjoying every moment of it.

He playfully snuggled closer and made a sound in his throat. I poked him in the ribs when I realized he thought I meant it was him being so close that was warming me up. "It's the whiskey that's warming me up, you dope."

"Damn," he stated, snapping his fingers.

"Jackass."

I rolled my eyes at his childish gesture, then we sat silently for a long time. We listened to the wind howl harmoniously with the wolves. Charley never came out of the tent, and the baby had stopped crying. I didn't want to think about what was going through his mind. My head swam as the effects of the Jack Daniel's kicked in. Leaning my head back onto Raven's shoulder, I shut my eyes. I was already slipping into peaceful slumber when I felt Raven lean down and kiss my forehead gently.

I awoke to Max kicking my boots. I opened my eyes and looked at him. "Max?"

"We have a problem."

"Seriously, Max, you have to find a new way to start a conversation with me," I said, rubbing the sleep from my eyes. Sitting up, I disturbed Raven, who now began to stir beside me.

"Okay, how about Charley is gone and he left the baby for you?" Max glared down at me, smiling wickedly.

"You're kidding," Raven said as he sat up with wide eyes.

I heard the baby girl crying from within the tent. "Oh my god, you're not kidding." I uncoordinatedly bolted toward the tent just as Monica came out holding the baby.

"He left a note for you." Monica handed me a piece of paper.

My hands were shaking as I cautiously opened it, as if I were expecting it to explode.

Ms. Ashley,

Thank you so much for all your help. I have thought all night about my situation. I don't feel I'm in any mental state to be raising a child. I don't know what to do with an infant, much less a girl infant. It wouldn't be fair for the child to suffer from my lack of knowledge. Please take her and raise her as your own. I left some money and what supplies I could spare. I'm sorry for not being able to do more. Please take care of her and let her know how much we loved her.

Sincerely,
Charley

There was a photo of Kim and Charley posing with her exposed pregnant belly. They looked so happy.

"I can't believe this," I said, shaking my head, reading over the letter once more to see if I missed anything. "Son of a bitch."

"He left a good bit of money." Max came out holding a second envelope full of money. "It's mostly twenties and hundreds."

Raven spoke up, "We'll get to Rapid City today and hopefully find a store. We will have to get some baby supplies." He made a gesture with his hands as if sizing the baby.

Monica walked over and handed the baby to me.

"What?" I said in a shocked tone.

"She belongs to you now."

"What am I supposed to do, strap her down inside the saddle-bag?" I looked at the little girl. *She is pretty.*

"Rose and I will help you, Ashley. We know you can't hold her all day while you ride, but at night, she's yours." Monica put the baby in my arms and walked away smiling without batting an eye.

I shook my head in disbelief. *What the hell am I going to do with a baby?* She looked up at me with the biggest bluest eyes I had ever seen. She had a head full of shiny black hair that matched her mother's. Looking at me, she smiled a genuine smile, and immediately my heart melted. I shook my head and hugged her close as I kissed the top of her head. "Okay, kid, it's you and me, at least for a while." I noticed Raven watching me. He was biting on his thumb and smiling at me. I mouthed the words "Shut up."

I fed and changed her and gave her back to Monica so we could leave. Max and Raven stayed behind to burn Kim's body. I didn't want to stick around for that sight or smell. They allowed us to get a decent distance ahead before they started the fire.

We rode for several hours and finally reached Rapid City. It reminded me of a boomtown in a bad Western movie. There were several stores open, and they all wanted cash. Some would consider equal trades if you had something of quality to offer.

Raven briefly talked to an American Red Cross worker and turned to ride over to me. "The Walmart isn't far away. They are giving food and stuff like that. However, if you're wanting to get the kid some clothes, we are going to have to buy it here. There is a resale shop about two blocks this way. I think we should hit that first. I know Marcus could use some more clothes as well."

Raven dismounted and went to tell the others. Lou, Ricky, and Jacob would stay with the wagons and horses while the rest of us shopped. I gave Marcus some money and told him to find himself some warm clothes. Kat and Harley went with Monica and Rose to help carry items that were purchased.

I dismounted and made my way over to the wagon. Monica handed the kid to me. I took her gently and began to walk toward the resale shop Raven had told me about. A group of kids ran screaming out of a building. They played in the dusty, debris-strewn street for a few minutes before a nice-looking young woman came out and yelled at them.

"You kids get out of the street! If you want to play, you can go out back." She ran after the kids, rounding them up and quickly ushering them back into the building. She stopped beside me, rubbed her forehead, and sighed heavily.

I looked at her inquisitively. "Is school back in session already?"

She looked at me and smiled. "Oh no, not yet. This is an orphanage." She ran back into the building after the kids, smiling.

I stood looking at the building and read a white sheet with spray-painted words that hung from the wooden frame that read Rapid City Children's Center. I looked to the peacefully sleeping kid in my arms. Thoughts raced through my mind. *Would she be better off here? They could find her a proper home.*

"Whatcha doing?" Raven came up behind me.

"Just thinking," I stated solemnly.

"Well, don't. I can see it in your eyes, and the answer is no. She wouldn't be better off." I looked up to him as he continued, "You saved her life, Ashley. Look at all those kids. Most of them will never find a home. They will never know or remember the feeling of having a mother to love them. Think about it. Now is not the time when people are going to be looking to take in an extra mouth to feed. Don't throw her away. She deserves better than that."

"What the hell am I supposed to do with her, Raven? I'm not prepared to raise another baby."

"You will have help, Ashley. Monica and Max—"

I cut him off, "Monica and Max are going to have one of their own. They aren't going to have the resources, time, or energy to help me."

"Then I will…" He stopped and looked at me. "If you let me."

"You don't know what you're saying."

Raven hitched his thumbs in his pockets. "Yes, I do." He looked at me with his sparkling eyes. "I will help you, Ashley. I know we aren't together, but we can raise her. I will help in any way if you let me. I never got to have a kid. This may be the closest I ever get.

Please don't take that away from me or her." His eyes seemed to be begging me.

I must have been out of my mind. I had the perfect opportunity to get rid of the kid and be done with it. I should have been running up the steps of that orphanage, and yet I found myself hesitating. The only reason I came up with why I wasn't was because I wasn't sure I wanted to. She was a beautiful baby. If things happened for a reason like I had always believed, then I had to go with my gut intuition. I had saved this baby's life for a *reason*. Her mother died for a *reason*. The father dumped her on me for a *reason*. I had to believe there was a *reason* I had been given this kid. I looked at her peaceful, angelic face and knew I had to keep her. No matter what hardships lay ahead, she was now a part of our family. I looked at Raven in his childishly hopeful eyes. "You promise?" I smiled as I saw his eyes grow big.

"Yes, I promise. I will even change dirty diapers."

"Well, call me a softy then, because I'm keeping her. But I'm holding you to your promise. You're not going to get out of it."

Raven grabbed me and hugged me. "Thank you. Thank you." He acted like a kid in a candy store. "You won't regret this, Ash, I promise." Raven smiled down at the kid. "Can I hold her?"

I handed him the baby. "Hold her like you would a football." He had a smile from ear to ear. "I hope you know what you're getting yourself into."

"Let's get to the resale shop. Daddy's got to buy his girl some clothes."

I rolled my eyes and walked in the direction he had previously pointed. We came upon a large tent that was decorated with hanging clothes.

"Good morning," an older lady greeted us as we entered the tent. "Can I help you find something?

Raven motioned toward me.

"I need to get baby clothes and supplies."

"How old is the baby?" she inquired.

"She's a newborn."

"Oh my, and you're getting around so well."

"I got lucky with an easy delivery." I looked at Raven as I lied to the woman. He was still playing goochy-goochy-goo with the kid, paying me absolutely no attention. I could have told the woman that aliens had flown down from the sky and given me the kid, and he wouldn't have noticed.

She showed me where she had the newborn clothes. They were in big plastic totes. I got all the thick blanket sleepers she had, as well as thermals. I found a few pacifiers and a few extra bottles. I felt like I hit the jackpot when I found a whole bag full of cloth diapers.

I was paying the lady when she spoke up, "Now if you tell Walmart what you need, they may let you in the store to buy some things. I heard if you show them you have cash, they will let you in."

"What is Walmart giving out as far as supplies?" I inquired.

"I know they are giving food and water. I think they will give you diapers and formula for the baby as well."

I nodded and finished paying for the items I had chosen. We walked back out into the busy street of carts and buggies. This time, I noticed men walking around with guns. They all had on badges. Upon closer inspection, there were also men on the roofs of some buildings all with guns.

"They are most likely deputies," Raven explained. He must have looked up long enough to notice I was looking around. I felt uneasy about the whole situation and wanted to leave quickly.

We made our way back to the wagons. Marcus soon found us with his new treasures. Monica and her group weren't far behind. They were being very secretive with what they had purchased, but Kat had a big smile on her face as she attempted to hide a small bag behind her back. Max helped her climb into the wagon, and Monica gave him a quick kiss as she entered. Her belly was growing larger. She looked like she should be miserable; however, she looked like she couldn't be happier.

Raven took the kid to the wagon and passed her off, along with the new clothes.

"Do you think we have room for these in here?" I asked Monica.

"I will make room for her clothes." Monica smiled at me. "You look good with her."

"Yeah, well, Raven said he would help out too, so I suppose she is a member of the family now." I fathomed a smile, still a little unsure about my decision to keep her.

Monica nodded as she and the kids took their places, and soon we were on our way again.

We found the Walmart easily. There was a long line of people mostly on foot. We waited in line, and finally, it was our turn. A tall, thin man greeted us. He looked like one of those pencil-pushing nerds who should be working behind a desk crunching numbers. "Afternoon, folks. How many in your party?" he asked Lou.

Lou spoke up, "There are two for this wagon." He continued as Raven rode up beside him.

The man wrote on his clipboard and disappeared. Soon, there were three young men walking toward the wagon with bottled water and boxes of food. They handed the boxes to Raven, who had dismounted and began placing them in the wagon.

The pencil pusher came to our wagon next. "How many are in your party?"

I spoke up, "We have eight, but one is an infant. If possible, I would like to get some formula and diapers." I looked at him with hopeful eyes.

"Is the infant on any special formula?"

"No, sir."

Again, he disappeared, and men came with boxes. They had their own little system going. I dismounted and began putting boxes into the wagon. Harley was taking them and putting them on the beds. We could reorganize when we stopped for the night. I saw the pencil pusher and got his attention.

"Ma'am, I know it's not a lot, but it's what we have to offer."

"Oh no, it's not that. This is wonderful. I was just wondering. Is the store allowing anyone in to buy anything? I had a baby, and I really need a few things for her. You see, we lost everything. I don't even have clothes for her. I have money."

He put his hand up. "Say no more. Here is a number. Go to the front entrance of the store. They are letting five people in at a time. You will have ten minutes to get what you need."

"Can someone go in with me? I'm not getting around too fast."
I was getting good with this lying stuff.

"I will give you one extra number. One other person can go in
with you. Have a good day."

"I will, and thank you so much." I smiled and gave the other
number to Raven.

"Okay, what do we need?" I asked.

"Tell you what, I'll handle food if you handle the baby stuff. I
will try to get potatoes, things like that, for soups."

"That sounds great. Do you need some money?"

"No, I got it covered. Just get my girl whatever she needs."

I punched his arm. "I'll take care of it. I want to look for something else really quick if I have time."

"What?"

"It will be Christmas soon, and I want the kids to have
something."

"I hadn't even thought about Christmas."

We patiently awaited our turn and were finally allowed into the
store. Raven ran to the produce, grabbing and snatching. I laughed as
I hurried to the baby section. I began taking things off the shelves—
pacifiers, bottles, thermometer, clippers, blankets, sleepers, gowns,
anything I thought we might need. I got several different sizes also. I
didn't know when we would find another open store. Sprinting over
to the jewelry, I selected two different necklaces. They weren't expen-
sive but something for my girls on Christmas morning. I didn't want
my kids to think Santa forgot about them. Running back through the
men's wear, I grabbed a baseball cap for Marcus. I thought he might
like it better than a cowboy hat. I picked him out a long-sleeved shirt
with a decorative skull on it. That was more to his taste. I made my
way to the checkout. On impulse, I grabbed several chocolate bars
and began placing things on the checkout counter. I could see Raven
at the door waiting patiently for me. I couldn't understand how he
got done so quickly. I was out of breath, like I was in one of those bad
game shows they show on late-night television. I paid for my stuff
and met Raven and put everything into one wagon. We could sort it

out later. I retrieved the chocolate bars and handed them out to the kids, who were very excited to get them.

We traveled in silence, except for the distinctive clopping of horse hooves. We went through several small towns that were in total ruins. However, kids were still running around. They were happy to see someone new coming through. We would make small talk till their moms instinctively called them back home. We traveled through the Black Hills area. It looked like large odd-shaped rocks jutting up from the ground. Nothing like my mountains I so longed to see.

Just before dark, we came to a clearing. Large oak trees towered overhead. You could still see the hints of green grass through the fallen snow. There was a large star-shaped monument. It had to be at least twenty feet across. I dismounted and went over to the large hunk of granite.

"Belle Fourche," I tried to pronounce the odd word.

"It's *Bell Foosh*. It's French for *pretty fork*," Lou said as he walked up behind me. "It's the Geographic Center of the Nation." I flashed him a look of confusion, and Lou chuckled as he continued with his history lesson. "If you hung the United States from a rope, the balance point is about twenty miles north of Belle Fourche. The actual spot is in a cow pasture a few miles from here. I guess some of the bigwigs wanted to make a big deal of it, so they made this granite monument, put up a bunch of hotels and museums to make a buck. At one time, there were a lot of rodeos here. I guess they don't do that so much anymore." Lou walked back to the wagon and began handing things to Raven. Max and Marcus soon appeared to help out. They were attempting to reorganize our newly acquired possessions.

"Hey, guys, Ricky and I are going hunting to see if we can get anything for supper! We won't be long!" Jacob shouted out as he and Ricky rode off.

I went to Monica, who was holding the kid out for me.

"I have her bottle ready. She is ready for it too. Kat fed her once today. I think she enjoyed it," Monica said, smiling, as she handed the kid to me.

"Yeah, she probably can't wait till she gets older so she has someone to boss around," I stated, securing the kid in my arms.

"We are going to gather firewood and get the fire going before it gets dark. If you want, sit in the wagon where it's warm and feed her." Monica stepped to the side and walked off with my girls and Dannie.

I sat in the wagon feeding the kid. I found myself peacefully humming to her as she sucked greedily at the bottle. After burping and changing her, I rocked back and forth. She nestled her little head against my neck. At that moment, I felt that everything that had gone wrong in the world and everything I had done wrong was right again. This little accidentally acquired bundle of joy was silently and unknowing making it right. Just looking into her little eyes, watching her tiny fingers intertwining with my own gave me a sense of security. I held her close till I knew she was asleep, then eased her down onto the bed and gently placed a blanket over her. The wagon door came open. I looked up and saw Raven standing there. I placed my fingers to my mouth, indicating to him to be quiet. "Shhh." I stepped out of the wagon. "I have her down for a while."

"I missed it?" he asked.

"Don't worry. She will be up again in a few hours wanting more. There will be plenty of times to feed and *change* her," I added and emphasized the word *change*, letting him know he wasn't going to get out of the dirty part.

"You're really good with her." Raven placed his hand on my shoulder.

I gazed at his hand. It felt like a hot coal on my skin. He was always so warm. "Well, Raven, if I didn't know you any better, I would say that was a compliment." I took him by the hand and led him to the campfire. He immediately picked up his guitar and began strumming an unfamiliar tune.

Lou looked at me with tired eyes. "What are you going to call her?"

"Who?" I questioned.

Lou rolled his eyes and responded, "The baby, of course." He laughed to himself. "You can't call her the kid all of her life."

"Oh, um, I don't know. I haven't really given it a lot of thought."

I hadn't thought a lot about anything, really. I suppose we would have to come up with a name for her. It couldn't be just anything. It had to be something special. It had to be something that represented her and something that would make her parents proud. I noticed Raven looking at me, smiling, as he strummed the guitar.

The temperature dropped quickly once the sun went down. It was soon too cold to be outside. Ricky said good night to Harley. Jacob, Rose, Max, Monica, Marcus, and my girls decided to call it a night and went into their respective wagons. I was taking first watch. When the kid woke up, Raven could feed and change her and give her back to me in the tent. He would take second watch, then Jacob would take over for the third watch. Max would take the fourth. They had decided if we divided our watches four ways that no one would be outside for more than a few hours. It would decrease our chances of illness. We would keep the fire and coffee going as usual.

Soon, it was only Raven and me at the fire. He put away his guitar and took a seat beside me. I didn't refuse when he put his arm around me and pulled me close. "I have an idea of what to name her."

"Tell me." I looked at him.

"It may sound a little stupid. I don't know."

"Well, are you going to tell me?"

He took a deep breath and said the most beautiful name for a child I had ever heard, "I want to call her Night Sky. But spell it N-Y-T-E S-K-Y."

"How did you come up with that?"

"Her hair is as dark as the night, and her eyes are as blue as the sky."

I looked up at him. In that moment, he looked so sincere. Visions of that little girl danced in his eyes. I understood at that very moment that no matter what was done, she was his daughter. I knew he would never leave her. He would always be there to protect and provide for her. I couldn't deny him the honor of naming her.

"I think…" He looked at me with childishly hopeful eyes. "I think it's beautiful. I can't think of a name that would fit her better. Good job, Raven."

"So it's settled. That's what we will call her?" Raven seemed uncertain.

"Well yeah, it sounds great. Why?" I wasn't sure what he was thinking at this point.

"I don't know. I guess I thought that you may think it was stupid. I had this whole argument worked up."

I began to laugh. "I think you just want to argue with me." I snuggled closer to him, trying to internally convince myself that it was only for the heat. "I think the name is great. I have no problem at all with naming her Nyte Sky."

He leaned down and kissed the top of my toboggan. "Thank you, Ashley."

"Yeah, well, like I said, I think this whole trip is making me soft or something."

"I think it's just the opposite," Raven mumbled under his breath.

"What do you mean?" I wasn't sure if I was supposed to hear his statement.

"Forget it." He sat quietly for a few moments. "I suppose I'm going to turn in for a little while. Will you wake me up when Nyte wakes up?" He smiled big at the sound of himself using her name.

"I will change her and get the bottle ready, then wake you up. I will stay up till you have fed her. She can sleep the rest of the night with me in the tent." His eyes dropped and smile quickly faded. "What is it?"

"I hadn't thought about sleeping yet. I suppose I'll stay in the wagon with Lou."

I could tell just by the look on his face that he wanted to sleep with her too. He felt like he was going to miss out on something while she slept. "Tell you what, when Jacob takes over for you, come in the tent and bed down. We can put her between us, and it will keep her warm."

"Are you sure? It would mean people knew we slept together."

"It's not like we had sex, Raven. You just want to spend time with the kid." I stopped, then corrected myself, "I mean with Nyte."

A slight smile crept across his face. "Thanks, Ashley. You're all right."

I sat quietly, keeping myself warm by the fire. I knew Raven was hopelessly devoted to this little girl. This was something he had wanted for a long time. He was cheated out of fatherhood. It was ripped out from under him like a dirty rug. For so many years, he'd lost himself on that farm. I got lost in my thoughts. A distant sound snapped me back to reality. I rose from my warm spot, feeling the cold breeze around me. I scanned the tree line as one of the horses let out a whinny. Then I saw them—two glowing eyes low to the ground. A dark figure hid deep within the shadows. A low growl carried across the soundless night. I knew without a doubt that it was a wolf. I grabbed my pistol and aimed at the dark figure while inching closer to the horses. There was no way I was going to allow it to attack our only means of transportation. I checked the ropes to make sure they were securely tied. I knew when I fired my pistol, it would spook them, and the last thing we needed was to have to track our horses through the snow. The eyes lowered to the ground even further. I knew it was getting ready to pounce on the horse or perhaps even me. I held my gun steady. The wolf leaped from the bushes right at me. I fired and closed my eyes, expecting him to be on top of me in an instant. I opened my eyes and saw the large gray creature lying on the ground before me. I had dropped him with one shot.

Raven bolted from the tent just as Jacob and Ricky jumped out of their wagon.

"Damn, good shot." Jacob inspected the dead wolf.

"Lucky shot," I said. I was now shaking, and I wasn't sure if it was the cold or frazzled nerves. I turned quietly and went back to the fire.

"Are you okay?" Ricky asked.

"I'm fine. Just cold."

"Ashley, you just killed a wolf. He could've attacked you!" Raven exclaimed with a high-pitched tone.

"Yes, but he didn't." I rubbed my hands together in an attempt to warm them up. "Besides, that's not the first thing I've killed."

"What do you mean?"

I looked at him with intensity. "I mean, I have killed before."

Max exited the wagon, holding Nyte. "Everything okay?"

I went to him and took the baby as he handed me a bottle. "Everything is fine. I killed a wolf that was around the horses. No big deal."

Max only nodded at me. "Tell Jacob to wake me for my watch."

I returned his nod. "I will keep her with me for the rest of the night. Get some sleep." I turned away and went back to the fire. I had a pot of hot water hanging over the fire. I put the bottle in the hot water for a little while to get it warm. Nyte was ready for it. Raven appeared and took her from me. I watched as he fed her. His eyes never left hers. When he began to burp her, I went into the tent and bedded down. He soon followed. She was already back to sleep.

"I changed her too." He laid her down beside me, placing her back to my chest. Raven leaned in close and looked at me. He was inches from my face. He quickly changed directions and kissed Nyte on top of the head. "Daddy is going to have to build his girl a cradle so she can get off the ground."

"Be careful on your watch. There is at least one more wolf," I said in a dismissing tone.

"Okay, I'm going. Keep her warm."

I only nodded.

"See you in a few hours."

I nestled with Nyte. I had forgotten how humbling it was to bond with an infant. I hugged her close and covered us up. I eased off to sleep. At some point, Raven eased into the tent and went to sleep. He stared at his two sleeping girls. He straightened their blankets, ensuring that Nyte was covered and warm. He laid his head down and drifted away.

I woke up just as the sun was making its bleak entrance into the sky. Raven and Nyte were gone. I knew he had taken her to the fire. I rolled up our bedding and went to join them.

Everyone else was already awake. Monica and Rose were cooking breakfast. I was happy to see scrambled eggs in the skillet. Everyone was laughing and joking around, huddling together for warmth. Raven had Nyte, feeding her again. He boasted about naming her. Everyone seemed to love the name and found it to be very fitting. He beamed with pride as he looked into her crystal-blue eyes. If I had never seen love before, I knew I saw it in Raven every time he looked at Nyte.

I looked around at our growing family. Either by blood or friendship, that was what we were. I smiled and felt my moment of realization.

CHAPTER 10

B Y NIGHTFALL, WE had reached what we thought was the Powder River. We had just started getting camp set up when two young men bounded out of the woods, laughing and punching each other in the arm. They stopped in their tracks at the sight of us. They seemed just as surprised to see us as we were to see them. Seconds later, two older men dressed in camouflage joined them. They stood staring at us as we stood around staring at them. The men had guns draped over their shoulders. They talked among themselves for a brief moment.

I walked over to Raven. "Do you think we are on private property?"

"I don't think so." Raven looked down at me. "Don't take it out. I just want to make sure you have your gun."

"Yeah, I got it."

"I'm going to talk to them." Raven walked toward the men.

Monica got the kids into the wagon until we knew what was going to happen. However, the rest of us stood around the wagons as Raven approached the strangers. We watched him extend his hand. Even though we couldn't hear what was being said, we breathed a little easier when each of the strangers shook Raven's hand in return. There were smiles and laughter going on, which was a good sign. Raven pointed in our direction a few times. One of the younger men took off running through the woods as one of the older ones yelled out, "And tell them we are hungry!" Raven turned toward us with the remaining men following him. They approached us eagerly.

"Guys, I would like you to meet John and Randal Streeter."

Both men extended their hands and shook ours. John was a large burly man with a full beard and bad teeth that he showed proudly through his smile. Randal was thinner and cleaner-shaven and had much better dental hygiene.

"Call me Randy, please. It's nice to meet you all," Randy Streeter said as he shook my hand.

"We haven't seen too many people coming through this way. Where are you headed?" John stated, and he pulled up his pants.

"Browning, Montana," I stated proudly.

"Ah, Blackfeet Nation. You got family there?"

"My fiancé's family. We are supposed to meet him there."

"Randy and I are brothers," John stated proudly. "And the younger one is his son, Josh. My son, Matt, ran ahead to tell the others that we are bringing guests for supper."

Jacob spoke up. "So you have a homestead around here?" he inquired.

"It's more than a homestead. We are members of the Montana Preppers Militia. We have a compound not far from here."

"Militia?" I questioned, looking at Raven, wondering what he had brought into our midst.

"We are a group of people who for years have believed that basic techniques of survival will save us. We have lived off the grid for a long time now. We aren't necessarily an anti-government organization like some groups. We are simply a group of people who have come together to ensure that life goes on," John continued. "I would like to invite you and your party to our compound for supper. You can see for yourself what we are doing and what goes on."

"We will welcome a good meal." Jacob put his arm around Rose.

We loaded up what we had already dragged out and followed the three men who were on foot. Raven stayed near them and talked back and forth. I stayed back between Harley and our wagon. We approached the large compound. It looked like a medieval fortress. A ten-foot fence surrounded the complex. Large wooden buildings lined the inside of the compound. Clothing dangled on lines outside. Smoke billowed from chimneys. One large building located in the center seemed to be the center point of activity. We parked the wagons outside the fence. The horses were left tied up, and we all walked into the compound toward the center building. Monica handed Nyte to me, along with a warmed bottle. I felt reluctant to leave everything we had unattended. People were coming out of the wooden buildings and showering us with attention. The people didn't appear to be haggard and worn like everyone else we had come in contact with.

We entered the large center building. Tables lined up in rows in the center and a large buffet table full of food. The smell was overpowering. My stomach growled immediately. Randy showed us where we could sit. "You can help yourselves to the food."

Jacob and Ricky wasted no time in getting to the food.

Raven made sure I was fine before he helped himself. "I'm fine. I'm going to feed Nyte, and then I'll get something to eat. He nodded and graciously took Kat by the hand and helped her fix a plate.

When everyone was seated with a plate of food, Randy and John came over to us and began talking.

"So what do you think about our setup here?" Randy started.

"Well, it all seems very nice. You seem to have all the necessities here," Rose stated politely.

"I'm more interested in your group in general. The word *militia* sorta throws me off. Are you a religious group, or what do you believe in? How did you come to live here?" I asked while feeding Nyte.

Randy began explaining their way of life. "My wife, Sandra, and I lived in Seattle for a long time. I was a lawyer, and she was a nurse. Every day we witnessed all the wrongs that were going on in the world. I was seeing criminals getting off on technicalities and good people dying because of senseless crimes. We grew tired of the world in general. Sandra told me one day that she was pregnant. We talked for a long time and came to the conclusion that we didn't want to raise a child in the current world we lived in. My brother John already lived here in the compound and invited us to join him. So we made the leap and moved. I have to say, it's the best thing we've ever done. We grow our own food, put it up for the winter. Our kids go to school and get an education. Some have gone onto college. We have our own teachers. We build our own homes. It's usually a couple of families in one unit, but we all have our own space. We are strictly self-contained and self-reliant, and we work together."

John broke in, "The word *militia* came from years ago when the group was first formed. It was about the same time as the whole Y2K controversy. Everyone was scared to death that the world was going to crumble overnight. The New World Oder would use the chaos created and the fall of Western civilization to declare martial law and tighten its hold on everyday hardworking people. Our founders preached sovereign citizenship. Some went as far as surrendering driver's licenses and Social Security cards. During those years, we were associated with the Aryan Brotherhood and a few other organizations. They spent more time getting arrested than contributing to the group. Our original founder left the group because his wife became ill, and he took a job to better afford her health care. Since then, we have pulled away from all other groups. We spend our time providing for ourselves. We believe all people have equality of life. We believe in being good to all people regardless of race or religion. We do have church here for those who want to go, but you're also allowed to worship in your own home if you wish. We have doctors here for basic health care. We have our own laws and punishments, which are more strict and stiffer than anywhere else. Now we are just simply a group of people who want a simpler way of life, then we can't get outside those gates."

It seemed like good ideology. Wasn't it the same thing we were doing? I put Nyte up on my shoulder and burped her. Raven and Jacob talked in detail with John and Randy. Max and Monica played with Dannie. Harley chatted with Ricky, while Marcus and Lou paid close attention to the conversation. Two young men standing by the door caught my eye. They were staring intently on Harley. It was making me extremely uncomfortable. I noticed Kat sat quietly as usual. She seemed out of place or even confused. She was a little jumpy, and I decided she didn't feel comfortable in here.

"Kat, are you ready to go back to the wagons?" I asked.

Her little face perked up as she nodded yes.

Almost everyone was through eating. I rose from my chair with Nyte and took Kat by the hand. "We are going back outside. Ricky, will you and Max walk Harley back to the wagons? We will see you in a little while." I turned to Randy and John. "Thank you so much for your hospitality."

John and Randy rose from their seats. "Well, it's our pleasure. We hate to see you go so quickly."

"It's getting late, and I got to get these kiddos to sleep. But if you want to join us by a campfire, perhaps Raven could play the guitar for a while."

"Yeah, that sounds fine." Randy sounded excited. "I'll round up some guys, and we can pick and grin till the cows come home."

Lou laughed out loud. "Well, you will have to do it without me. It's past my bedtime too."

"And it's past Dannie's bedtime as well." Monica took Dannie by the hand and followed behind us, expressing her gratitude. Max followed behind her.

Raven smiled his evil little smile at me. I couldn't help but return a smile. I had just volunteered him to play for all these people.

Harley and Ricky followed suit. "We will get some firewood, Mama."

"That sounds great. Thank you."

I couldn't wait to be back outside in the open air, even if it was freezing. Maybe I had spent too much time outside. Inside that building was momentarily nice, but it didn't take long before the walls started closing in on me. We moved our wagons closer to the tree line. Harley picked out a place for our bucket that was a little deeper in the woods than usual, but we never went alone, so it should be fine. Everyone began showing up. We had lots of help setting up the tent and collecting firewood. Soon, we had a raging fire going, and the kids bedded down. Kat seemed happier back in her familiar surroundings as she snuggled into her covers.

"I didn't hear you talk today. I guess it was just another bad day." I kissed her on her head. "I love you, baby. I want you to know I would give anything to hear you talk again." Kat just shrugged her shoulders. "Whenever you're ready, I'll listen."

I came out of the wagon and went to the campfire and joined the growing crowd. Raven met me with his guitar in hand. "You know I hate you for this, right?"

I looked at him directly. "Hmm…that sounds familiar. I told you payback's a bitch." I shrugged my shoulders and gave him an "I told you so" look.

"I thought we called a truce," Raven said, placing his hand on the wagon, preventing me from going around.

I looked down and sighed heavily. "Honestly, I was just looking for a way to hurry up and get out of there. I wasn't expecting all these people to come out here on such a cold night. I'm sorry." I was almost ashamed of myself. He had been nice and civil for a while now. I had to volunteer him to perform for an audience we hadn't counted on.

"It's all right. I don't mind playing. I was a little uncomfortable in there."

I looked at him with wide eyes. "Really? God, I thought it was just me."

"No, it was me too. I couldn't wait to get back out here." He inhaled deeply.

"Maybe I'm becoming antisocial or something."

"No, I think we are just becoming one with nature." He laughed.

Harley walked up to us. "Mama, I need to visit the bucket. Can you take me?"

"Doody calls." I walked around him, laughing.

"Don't be gone long. I need a singing partner," he said with a smile.

"Ha! Don't count on it," I said, still laughing.

Using a flashlight to illuminate the darkness, we found the bucket. It seemed to be deeper in the woods than I had originally thought, but I could still hear the activity at the campfire. I closed my eyes and smiled as I heard Raven singing. Harley hurried to the bucket. I turned my back to give her some privacy. Closing my eyes, I focused so attentively on Raven's voice that I didn't hear the bushes rustle behind us.

"Mama, look out!" I heard Harley scream.

Out of the blue, something hard smacked me in the head. My eyes went black as I fell to the ground, landing on my back. Something heavy on my chest was making it difficult to breathe. I could hear Harley's muffled screams not far away from me. As my eyes regained focus, I could tell that there was someone on top of me, holding me down. Harley was struggling against a separate assailant. He had her pinned against a large tree. I felt proud as she stomped his foot and began elbowing him in the gut. If she'd only been a little stronger, it might have helped the situation. She tried to bite the rough hand that covered her mouth, preventing her from screaming.

"Get the little bitch down. Don't let her run off."

I heard a massive smack, then a blunt thud. I knew someone had hit my baby girl, knocking her to the ground. I tried to gather myself. I could see clearly now. Our attackers were the same two hooligans who had been watching Harley inside the compound. They had probably moved the bucket that led us deeper into the woods. I could still feel my pistol wedged into my waistband. I heard another smack as the bastard hit my daughter again. I heard her beginning to cry. Raising my head, I found her on the ground only six feet away from me with the young punk on top of her. She never had a chance to pull up her pants. He was touching her in ways that made me want to vomit.

"Please don't," I heard her say through her trembling tears. Her pleas were met with another slap.

I paused long enough to take a quick account of my own body, ensuring that I could feel and move everything. The punk holding me was strong but stupid and not paying any attention to me. Obviously, I wasn't the target of this attack. His job was merely to incapacitate me, to keep me from interfering with their horrible plans for Harley. I was being held down at the base of a large oak tree with its trunk at my head. I only had one chance to do this right. I had to put a stop to this and get help out here. Harley's cries were getting more distressed. The punk holding me was watching and laughing while urging his friend on.

I thrust my hips forcefully forward, knocking his body off-balance. His head thudded into the tree. I quickly rolled onto my side and slid out of his hold. I instantly grabbed my pistol and fired once, hitting him in the back. His eyes widened in instant shock and pain.

"Raven, help!" I screamed at the top of my lungs.

Hearing another gunshot, I looked down at Harley. She was looking at me through horror-struck eyes. I hadn't taken into account that the punks themselves were armed. I raised my gun and held it steady on the punk-ass kid who had just shot me. He seemed shocked and disturbed at his actions. Somehow managing to keep my aim on him, I fired off one round, hitting him directly in the throat. Blood splattered onto Harley. She screamed, covering her face in defense. The boy fell onto his side, freeing her from his monstrous hold. My left arm went numb, and I instantly felt tremendously weak. My head spun with dizziness, and my legs went limp as I crumpled to the ground. I saw Harley scrambling to pull up her pants. The forest seemed to spin around me as I lay staring through blurred eyes at the bleak night sky.

Next, incredible waves of pain, combined with a powerful burning sensation, strongly pulsed through my body. My arm felt like it was being jackhammered with a fire torch. Harley hurried to my side, crying uncontrollably and shaking violently. My field of vision began to fill with a warm, inviting white light. I thought to myself, *So this is what it feels like to die.* If I indeed was about to die, I at least wanted to tell my daughter that I loved her before I sank into whatever oblivion that awaited me. Opening my mouth in an attempt to speak, my words were replaced by a ghastly gurgling sound. Raising my right hand, I stroked my daughter's beautiful face. The last thing I saw was the ribbon of blood my fingers left on her flushed cheek.

Raven

I watched her walk Harley into the woods. I knew it wouldn't take much to get her to sing with me. I thought she enjoyed it whether she admitted it or not. Getting my guitar, I joined the growing crowd by the fire and began playing. A few others joined in with their instruments. I sang the slow love song as if I were singing it to her. I closed my eyes and envisioned her on a grassy hilltop, snowcapped mountains dotting the background. Her long hair wrapped around her, blowing ever so slightly in a gentle breeze, and a smile beaming brighter than the sunshine itself. I completed the first song and looked up, expecting to see her standing at the edge of the fire smiling at me with her arms folded. Looking the crowd over, she was nowhere to be seen. I couldn't imagine what was taking so long. A second song started, and I joined in. I saw Max scanning the tree line. He was looking for them as well. I got a feeling in the pit of my stomach that something was wrong.

A gunshot rang out, piercing the darkness. I stood up, dropping the guitar at my feet. All eyes fell on the forest. Max was already running toward the trees. I joined him and kept his stride. I had never seen such a big boy move so fast. I momentarily froze as I hear the sound of Ashley screaming my name, puncturing my heart, filling it with fear and dread. My pulse quickened, as did my feet. I passed up Max in my run. Just as I made it to the trees, we heard a second shot. I ducked my head in an automatic response but kept going. I couldn't imagine what was happening. I would never forget the fear and desperation I heard in Ashley's voice as she called out my name. We entered the woods, stomping through the dense brush. Briars and low branches seemed to reach out and grab at me as I attempted to keep them out of my face. Max had his rifle. In my fortitude to get to her, I had left mine behind. A third shot rang out. Only thirty seconds had passed since I left my warm spot by the fire. Time, however, seemed to be moving at a much slower pace. Then Harley's cries came clear.

"Harley, where are you?" Max shouted.

"Uncle Max, here, I'm here! Hurry!" Her voice was shaky.

"Keep talking, baby, so we know where you are!" I shrieked as I scanned the dense, dark forest for some sign of them.

"Here, here, we're here! Hurry, please. It's Mama. Please hurry!"

Breaking through the trees with a fury, we found Harley kneeling beside her mother, crying hysterically. They were both covered in blood. The bodies of two dead boys littered the ground. Harley's face was swollen; her left eye was quickly turning black and her lip bleeding. Her pants were unbuttoned and scantly covering her backside. Her shirt had been halfway ripped from her body, leaving her breast exposed. Tearing off my coat, I threw it over her shoulders. Quickly I pulled her to a standing position, then pushed her into her uncle's arms. Harley fell into a fit of tears on his shoulder. I turned my attention to Ashley, who lay in a puddle of blood. I tried to console myself with the fact that she was still breathing.

"Don't you die. Not now," I whispered to her.

Ricky came into the clearing with John and Randy on his heels.

Max cupped Harley's face in his hands, fixing her eyes to his. "Harley, what happened?" He gave her a gentle shake.

Through broken tears and snot, she described the ordeal, "Mama brought me here to use the bucket. These two came out of the woods and hit Mama over the head. One got on top of me. He was going to rape me. The other one held Mama down so she couldn't help me. But she was too strong for him. She shot him. The one holding me down shot Mama, then she shot him too." Harley busted into tears again, unable to speak further.

Max held her close and tried to console her. "Can you walk?" She only nodded in response. "Ricky, will you take her to Monica, please?" Max asked as his voice started trembling.

"Yeah, I can do that." Ricky put his arm around her and held her close.

She stopped and turned back. "Raven, please don't let my mama die." Ricky pulled her away from the grisly sight.

I rolled Ashley over and saw that she had been shot in the shoulder.

Max's face turned red with rage. "Is this what your group stands for? Is this how you act here in the wild, like a bunch of savages?" He pointed at his sister's body on the ground.

"No, it's not. This is a surprise to us as well. Please, we have a complete infirmary inside the compound," Randy said as John checked the two young boys, who were obviously dead.

"Do you really think any of us would set even one foot back in that place?" Max shouted.

I looked up to Max. "I know you're upset, but Ashley needs a doctor now. We're at least a full day's ride to any big town. We need their help."

"How can we trust them, Raven? Look at this mess. How can we trust anything they say or do?" Max was visibly shaken, his body vibrating with anger.

Scooping up her limp, bloody body from the ground, I turned to Max, holding his sister in my arms. "How can we not? Stay with our group. I'll go with Ashley and send word to you as soon as we know something." Turning, I redirected my attention to Randy. "Show me the way."

Taking charge, I walked past Max, leaving him in the darkness feeling helpless and powerless. My main focus was getting her medical treatment. She was the only one of us who had extensive medical knowledge. However, she was in no condition to treat her own self, so we were at the mercy of these people.

As we came out of the woods, I could see everyone at the camp making over Harley, who was now crying in Monica's arms. They solemnly watched in silence from a distance as I carried Ashley into the compound. There was no music, no laughter, no singing. The night was completely quiet. I held my head high and followed Randy to the infirmary.

When we entered the medical facility, several people sprang into action. I placed Ashley on an exam table as gently as possible, turning away quickly as they ripped her shirt open, revealing the wound. Maybe it was all the blood, but it looked like a huge hole in her arm. I felt sick to my stomach seeing her this way, so vulnerable and frail. Her skin was so pale it appeared transparent. My legs went weak under me. Finding a seat in the corner, I stayed out of the way, allowing the professionals to do their thing. They ran here and there, starting an IV, and hung a bag of blood. I was impressed with their speed and available equipment. Running my fingers through my hair, I then rested my head in my hands, keeping my face hidden. It was hard to watch someone so strong in such a fragile state. Leaning back against the wall, the steady, fast rhythm of the heart monitor lulled me into an uneasy slumber.

A kind, soft-spoken nurse tapped me on the shoulder. "Excuse me, sir."

"What?" I jumped and quickly looked around.

"The doctor can talk to you now." She pointed to the table where Ashley was now covered with a blanket. Her wound was cleaned and neatly dressed as a tall, thin man towered over her.

Upon standing, my legs and back felt rigid from sitting in the uncomfortable straight-backed chair for so long. I got up and went to her. "How is she?"

"I think she will do just fine. It was a clean shot. No broken bones from what our x-rays showed. She lost a lot of blood, but she's getting it back." He pointed to the bag of blood hanging above her. "Really, we have done all we can. The rest is up to her."

"Why hasn't she woken up yet?"

"We gave her a medication called Halcion. It will make her extremely sleepy for a while. She won't remember a whole lot that happened, which may be a good thing. I know you are anxious to get back to your party, but she needs to remain here for a little while longer. I will give you some time with her," the doctor explained.

"Will you send word to her daughters that she is okay?"

The thin man nodded affirmatively and left the room, closing the door behind him.

Pulling my chair to the edge of the exam table, I took a seat beside her and looked her over. She looked a lot better now that she was cleaned up. A large bulky bandage was on her shoulder, and her arm was cradled by a sling. Her skin was still pale, but the color was returning to her cheeks, so maybe the blood was doing the job. I took her cold, limp hand and held it up to my face.

"All right, you crazy, stubborn female. It's time to get up and get it in gear." My voice echoed in the room. "You have no idea how bad you scared me. When I saw Harley crying over you and you were covered in blood, I thought…" I couldn't even finish the statement. I couldn't say those words. "Well, I naturally thought the worst. Harley is fine by the way. I haven't seen Kat or Nyte, but I'm sure Monica has them safe and sound. You should have seen your brother running. Man, that wasn't a pretty sight." I laughed as a tear escaped my eyes. I wiped it away with one finger. I was surprised to see it. I hadn't cried since I lost Tabitha and the baby. It felt odd that I was again crying over a woman in a hospital.

"You got to be okay, Ash. I don't think I could handle it if something happened to you. It's just not fair, you know. Out of the blue, you walked into my life and changed everything. I know that wasn't your plan, but you did. You changed it all. And you know what? It was for the better. I'm glad you came into my life. You and your girls have brought something to us that we haven't had in a long time, something *I* haven't had in a long time. You have given me a reason, a purpose. Every day, without even realizing it, you give me a reason to get up. You're my motive to keep going. I can't lose you, not now. I will get you to Browning if I have to carry you on my back the entire way. You just have to be strong a little longer. You can make it. I have never met anyone like you before. No matter what's thrown at you, you take it with a grain of salt and keep going. I know because I have thrown a lot at you." I laughed when I thought about her first attempt to ride a horse and how deliberately mean I had been to her.

"At first, I tried to run you off. I saw you as an unwanted parasite that had invaded my territory, but somehow, that changed very quickly. You're so strong, and you don't give up. That's part of why I love you." I tenderly kissed her hand and placed it under the warm covers. "I can't believe I just said that out loud, but it's the truth, and I understand that now. I love you." I hoped she couldn't hear me. I didn't want to make a total fool of myself. But at that moment in the woods, when I realized she could die, I knew I loved her. I couldn't deny it any longer. I would give her the time she needed to accept that Dallas was dead and not coming back. I would give her time to mourn or whatever she needed, but I couldn't deny the fact that I loved her.

I laid my head on the exam table beside her. I must have dozed off again. The next thing I felt was her moving.

Ashley

My eyes fluttered open. I immediately squinted against the especially bright light. I felt extremely cold. My body began to shake with the chilly air. My first thought was of Harley.

"Harley!" I tried to scream, but it came out more of a whisper. I tried to sit up. My arm throbbed with pain, forcing me back down. Then he was right there over me.

"Hey, it's okay," Raven stated as he put his arm over me. "Harley is fine. She is with Max and Monica. The bastard didn't rape her."

I looked around, confused. My head felt heavy and thick. My thoughts were fuzzy. "What happened? Where am I?" I rubbed my head.

"Calm down. We're in the infirmary inside the compound. You were shot. Do you remember anything?" If he were any closer, I would have to share his hairstyle. I pushed him back a little to focus easier on him.

I tried to think. "We were in the woods. There were two guys, one holding me down and the other trying to rape Harley. I shot them." I closed my eyes, realizing that I had done it again. "I killed them, didn't I?"

"You don't need to worry about that now." He could tell the regret in my voice. "You did what you had to do to protect your daughter. No one thinks less of you for that."

"I got to get up." My first attempt to sit up failed. Raven put one arm around me and the other under my legs. He swung my legs over the side and pulled me to a sitting position. My head swam, and my eyes rolled as the room spun in circles around me. I grabbed onto Raven to steady myself.

"I gotcha. I'm not going to let you fall."

"I got it! I got it!" I yelled, pushing Raven away, and steadied myself by holding on to the sides of the table. I was pissed at myself for killing those kids. I was even more pissed for allowing myself to get shot. Now I was growing downright angry because I was so weak. We didn't have time for this inconvenient turn of events. Nor could I afford to be hurt. I had to stay strong and keep going. First and foremost, I needed to see my daughter. I needed to see for myself that she was safe. "I got to go. I need to see Harley." I slid off the table. The moment my feet hit the floor, the rest of my body followed. My legs felt like gelatin, unable to support my own weight. The blanket that had covered my naked body was no longer doing its job.

Raven joined me on the floor, sitting cross-legged in front of me, and placed his chin on his laced fingers. He stared at me with a goofy face.

"What the hell are you doing?" He was acting stupid. I tried to push myself up with no luck. My body was racked with pain. I had absolutely no strength, and I was as naked as the day I was born. I wanted to see my daughters, and I knew there was no way I could get back to the wagons on my own. Hell, I couldn't even support my own weight. I was going to have to suck it up and do the one thing I didn't want to do. Raven's goofy face had been replaced with one of worry. "I need to ask you something," I stated half out of breath.

"I'm listening."

I took a deep breath. "Will you help me? Can you help me get to my babies?"

"Will you do whatever I say for the next few days, no questions asked?" Raven childishly put a finger up to his chin.

"Huh?"

"Well, if I'm going to help you, you're going to have to do something for me. I think it's only fair that you do what I say for the next few days."

"You want me to be your personal servant for the next few days with my arm in a sling?" I exhaled deeply. "Okay, fine, whatever. Just help me get to my kids."

Raven popped up from the floor and extended his hand to me. I took it with my good hand and allowed him to pull me up. I sat in an old straight-backed chair that was beside the exam table. He produced my clothes that had obviously been delivered while I was in la-la land and helped me get dressed. I was surprised at his gallantry. He never made a move that was questionable to me. It was almost sweet the way he seemed to be taking care of me. I put my arm around him and allowed him to help me stagger out of the infirmary. People got out of our way or held doors open for us. We exited the building rather uncoordinatedly and hobbled down the steps as best we could. It felt good to be back outside. The sun was trying to rise in the bleak winter sky as we crossed the compound courtyard. Once outside the gates, I could see the welcome sight of our camp not far away. Lou and Max were already awake and by the fire.

Max was on his feet in an instant and headed toward us. "Sissy, are you okay? How do you feel?"

I laughed in spite of myself. "Like I've been shot." I was a little short of breath, so I forgot to protest when Max began helping get me to the fire, or so I thought. They began directing me toward the tent. "Wait, where are we going?"

"You're going into the tent and going to bed," Raven declared proudly.

"I most certainly am not. I'm going to sit here by this fire and see my kids." I struggled to break free of Max and Raven, showing my objection.

"All right, that's it." Raven spun me around and threw me over his shoulder.

"Ouch, Raven, what the hell are you doing?" I used my good arm to beat on his back. "Let me go, Raven, dammit. You told me you would help me. You promised."

We entered the tent, and he planted me firmly on the bedroll. I looked at him with fury-filled eyes. He looked and pointed his finger at me as his voice rang out with authority. "First off, I never promised you anything. Secondly, the deal was that I would help you get to your kids, and then you are supposed to do what I say for the next few days. So you are here. The kids will be here in a minute. And here you will stay for the next few days. We will bring you food and water and anything else you need. One of us will help you to the bucket, or we will bring one in here for you. When you can stand and walk on your own, you can come outside. End of story. That's the way it is. It's not open for debate, so get accustomed to it." He turned to leave but quickly turned back. "And if I so much as see you stick your head outside this tent before I say you can, there's going to be hell to pay. Do you understand me?"

It had been a long time since anyone, especially a man, had spoken to me in that tone. I found myself unable to speak, unable to do anything except nod.

"Good. Now stay!" he commanded, still shaking his finger at me as he walked out of the tent.

I wasn't sure what else to do. I could hear the pitter-patter of feet approaching. The flap came back on the tent, and Harley and Kat came pouring in. They stopped and looked at me for just a moment.

"I'm fine. Come here and give me a hug." Harley was the first to me. She held me tightly and cried on my shoulder. Kat fell into my lap and wrapped her arms around my waist. I held them both. "Shh, it's okay. I'm fine."

"Mama, I was so scared," Harley mumbled through her tears.

"I know, baby, but it's over now."

Harley pulled back and allowed Kat to hug me properly. She, too, was crying. This bit of trauma was probably the last thing she needed right now. Here I was trying to get her to talk again, and now this got dumped on us.

I pulled Kat's little face up so I could meet her eyes. "I'm fine, honey. I know you were scared, but it's over, and I'm fine. It was just another bad day. Today will be much better. The sun came up today, and it will come up tomorrow." Kat nodded and hugged me again. "I tell you what, I'm a little hungry. Do you think you can find me something to eat, something besides oatmeal?" She nodded with a big smile and left the tent in a hurry.

I turned to Harley. "Are you really all right?" I touched her face. Her right eye was black, and her lip was busted and swollen, but otherwise, she appeared fine.

Harley nodded. "Yes, I'm fine. Aunt Monica helped me get cleaned up last night, and that guy never..." She stopped short of finishing her statement. "Well, he didn't rape me. You saved me, Mama." She hugged me again. "Thank you, Mama."

"I did what any mama would do. I protected my baby." I patted her leg. "Why don't you help Kat find me something to eat?"

Harley flashed me a smile and was gone in an instant. I sat quietly for a moment but then realized I couldn't stand it anymore. I decided it was safe if I inched closer to the front of the tent and cautiously pulled back the flap.

"Aaaannnkkkk! What did I tell you?" Raven startled me by yelling at me like you would a dog that got on the porch. I quickly let go of the flap. He evidently meant what he said. He was going to keep me in here like a prisoner. I would go absolutely stark raving mad within a day. There was nothing to do but sleep, which was exactly what he wanted me to do.

Raven entered the tent and placed a plate of steak and eggs complete with a pitcher of orange juice in front of me. "Here you go, compliments of our new neighbors."

It smelled delectable. My mouth watered as my stomach growled. "Is it safe to eat? Hell, they already shot me once. Who's to say they didn't poison the food?"

"They're also the ones who saved your life. You wouldn't be here if it weren't for them," Raven explained as he took a seat in front of me.

I looked at him as he slid the plate closer in my direction. "You're wrong. I wouldn't be here if it weren't for you." His liquid crystal eyes were fixed on me. "You came when I needed you, Raven. If you hadn't shown up, I would've died."

His forehead wrinkled and eyes scrunched up. "Did you have any doubt in your mind whether or not I would show up?"

I thought for a moment. "The fact is, I didn't think about anything. I could've called for Max, Lou, or Jacob, but I called for you. You were the first person I thought of. You were the one I wanted to show up. What do you think that means?"

He couldn't help but smile. He tried to hide it, but I saw him. "I think it means you didn't have any doubt that I would come to your aid. It also means that you need to eat, so eat it all. You need the protein to get your strength back, especially if you want to see the outside of this tent again." He stood up and flashed me an evil smile and left me alone to my meal.

I was a good girl and did as I was told. I ate the whole plateful of food. It wasn't hard considering how hungry I was, and it was actually very tasty. As I finished off the orange juice, I found myself getting sleepy. My eyes began to droop, my arm felt like it weighed a hundred pounds, and my head was foggy. My eyes drifted and rolled. Everything went blurry. "Raven!" I yelled out.

He came through the tent with a smile that quickly faded. "Ash?" He came over to me. "What's wrong?" He wrapped me up in his strong arms.

My breaths were coming quick. I didn't want to go to sleep. I was scared. "I can't see straight. Something's wrong."

He let out a small giggle. "Nothing's wrong, honey. It's pain medication. I knew you would never take it on your own, so I put it in your orange juice. You're fine. Just lie back."

My whole body felt like a bowl of wobbly gelatin. Raven leaned me back and gently lowered my head down onto the pillow. Somehow, I managed to get my arm around his neck as I latched onto his shaggy hair. I looked into those mystical eyes of his and said softly, "I hate you."

"Yeah, tell me something I don't know." He was still smiling.

The mixture of his eyes, his smile, and the drugs lowered my inhibitions. My words came out slurred but still audible. "I don't want you to let go of me." My eyes closed softly. My hearing was fading but still intact.

"I'll always be with you any way you will have me." His tender voice seemed to be reaching out for me from a distance. I felt his warm lips on my forehead as he kissed me good night.

When I awoke again, everything was dark, minus the glow from the campfire outside. "Raven?" I said sleepily.

"Shhh, Nyte is asleep finally." His voice came from my right side.

I looked over and found him curled up with Nyte. "How is she?" I said, sitting up.

"She's fine. How do you feel?"

"Rested." I snickered. "You're right. I never would have taken the pill on my own. But now I have a big problem."

"What's that?"

"I gotta use the bucket. My eyeballs are floating here. I don't think I've peed in like forever."

"I'll help you. Max is on watch, so he can keep an eye on Nyte."

I laughed. "It's not like she's going to run off anywhere, Raven. She'll be fine."

He made a dumb face at me and helped me up. Max smiled stupidly when he saw me coming out of the tent. "Ah, look who gets to rejoin civilization."

"Not for long. She just needs to visit the bucket," Raven corrected him, letting him know that I wouldn't be staying.

I rubbed my shoulder. It was freezing outside, maybe even a few degrees under. A fresh blanket of snow had fallen. Raven directed me to the new closer, safer bucket location. He politely turned around, allowing me a little bit of privacy. I soon realized I had a big problem. With my arm being so tender and in a sling, I couldn't unbutton my own pants. "Raven, I need some help."

He turned to me and quickly realized my dilemma. He positioned himself behind me without saying a word. Wrapping his bold arms around me, he gently unbuttoned my pants. His breath was hot on my neck as he released me and turned away, giving me some privacy. It was so cold. I hurried as fast as I could. I would welcome the warmth of the tent again. I couldn't be getting spoiled by all this. I couldn't allow this special treatment to soften me. Raven helped me back to the camp and into the tent.

"What time is it?" I asked.

"I know it's after midnight. That's what time Max relieved me, and he's been out there awhile now. Are you hungry?"

"No, not now. I think I'll go back to sleep. And in the morning, I would like to join everyone for breakfast."

He nodded as he lay down next to Nyte. "That sounds good. You did walk better just now. I suppose I can give you that since you did behave and eat."

"Jackass," I said as I slapped him with my good hand.

"We've all talked. We know you are going to need help doing certain things. We can all pitch in if you let us," he explained.

I lay back and watched him nestle with Nyte, our child. I gave him a nod. "When is it going to stop, Raven?"

"What do you mean?"

I felt like I wanted to cry. "I don't know. It just seems like when things are going good, something happens to knock us down. I feel like there is always something in my way, and I spend half my life pushing and shoving to break through. And when I do get through, the road is good, until something jumps up and pushes me back down. I'm just so tired of continuously pushing."

He moved from our daughter's side and joined mine. I allowed his brawny secure arms to wrap around me. It felt good to have him close. "It's a little thing called life, Ash. That's what it's all about. Only the strong survive. Why do you think you're still here? You're strong, and you will make it. You will see those majestic mountains Lou keeps going on about. That I promise you."

"And then what, Raven?"

"Then we take it day by day, together, if you let me stay with you."

I honestly couldn't imagine going through the rest of my life without Raven in it. I wasn't sure what was happening to me. I was so confused inside. My head was messed up in ways I couldn't begin to explain. And even though I could blame him, it had nothing to do with the pain medication he gave me. "Can you do me a favor?" I looked up at him with hopeful eyes.

"Anything. You name it."

"Don't call me Ash. Dallas calls me that, and every time you say it, I think of him." I didn't want to hurt his feelings, but if I were going to move on one day, he couldn't call me the same nickname that Dallas did.

I felt him nod. "I suppose I can understand that. I will have to come up with my own pet name for you. How about Fluffy or Mitzie?"

"Don't get corny," I instructed him as I pushed away. We placed Nyte between us and bedded down. When I could hear him slightly snoring, I opened my eyes and watched him sleep. I watched how he protectively held our daughter close. I knew my brother was right. I could do a lot worse, but I wasn't ready to give up on Dallas. I knew he had to be alive. And if he came back, what was I supposed to do about Raven and our daughter? Would Dallas understand and allow Raven to stick around? Would Raven even want to stay around? I was so confused. My head as well as my heart was in total turmoil, and only time would sort it all out.

CHAPTER 11

MORNING CAME MUCH too early. I sensed Raven wake up when Nyte began to cry. He took her out to sit by the fire and fed her. I sat up and attempted to rub my eyes. My arm throbbed with pain at the movement. It pissed me off that I was so weak. I couldn't afford a single solitary weak moment. My family was depending on me. My girls had barely seen me, and they had their own worries, concerns, and fears. They had to see that I was able to handle anything. It was me who needed to give them that sense of security. I had to suck it up and get moving. Raven wouldn't like it, but he was going to have to deal with it. I refused to sit on my ass anymore, stowed away in this tent like I was dying.

Looking around the tent, I collected my jacket and went outside. The wind howled around me. Raven was by the gate of the compound talking to someone. I couldn't have cared less if he saw me or not. Rose was feeding Nyte. Everyone else was sitting around eating quietly.

"Good morning, everybody."

"Well, she's mobile again." Jacob slapped his knee.

"Yes, I am." I looked toward Raven, who was looking at me, shaking his head. "Some people may not like it, but I can't stay in there anymore." I looked at Jacob and his family. "I would like to thank you for sticking around and helping out."

"We wouldn't have left with you hurt, Ms. Ashley."

I smiled at his kind comments. "I appreciate that." I found Harley wrapped up in Ricky's arms. "Harley, can you help Mama get this coat on, baby?" She instantly came to me with smiles and took the coat. I took off the sling that held my arm securely to my chest. The pain was horrible. I winced as my arm slid down. "Let's put in the bad arm first." Harley held the jacket and allowed me to put my arm in at my own speed. As soon as it was on, Harley adjusted the sling, and I put it back on. There was no denying that it helped. Kat brought me a pair of gloves and hugged me tightly.

"Hey, where's Taco? I haven't seen him."

Kat unzipped her coat, and a small nose stuck out and immediately retreated to its warm sanctuary. I laughed. She had the damn dog in her coat.

"Oh well, I guess it keeps you both warm. Have you already eaten?" She nodded and pulled my good hand by the fire and fixed me a plate of oatmeal and eggs.

"Pretend it's a steak, sissy." Max laughed as the rest of us joined in.

Raven soon joined us. He stood beside me with his hands on his hips. I tried to pretend that I didn't see him. "What do you think you're doing?"

"You said last night that I could eat breakfast with everyone."

"Oh, all right, fine, but when you get finished, it's back in the tent," he instructed in a demanding tone.

"Nope."

"Excuse me?" He moved to stand in front of me, hands still on his hips, trying to make himself look more intimidating.

I looked up at him with determination all over my face. "I said no."

"The deal was—"

I held my hand up, interrupting him rudely, "The deal is off, Raven." I put my plate down and stood to face him. "You want to do this now before I've had my breakfast? Fine. I appreciate everything you've done. I couldn't have made it without you. I've done everything you asked without too much argument. I will continue to go slow and accept any and all help I can get, but I refuse to stay in that tent like a damn dirty secret. I got shot, I'm hurt, but I'm not dead, nor am I dying. We still have a long way to go. I'm sure everyone else is ready to get back on the road. I can ride a horse if someone can help me mount it. Now are you going to help me or waste my time and yours by making an argument you're not going to win?" The authority in my voice was matched by my finger pointed and poking into his chest.

He dropped his head and shook it. "Okay, everybody, she's back and feeling better. We move out after breakfast." Raven leaned forward and kissed my cheek lightly. "Good to have you back." He handed me my pistol.

I took it, smiling, and put it in the inside pocket of my coat. "Good to be back."

Cheers busted from around the fire. Lou slapped his knee and got up and began packing stuff up with Kat on his heels. Harley went to help Monica while Ricky helped his parents. Marcus started collecting and stowing things away as well. Raven took our daughter from Rose. I was prepared for more of a fight. I sat and finished my breakfast that was quickly getting cold. I couldn't help but smile in spite of myself.

Max came up and hugged me. "I'm glad you're feeling better, sissy. Just don't overdo it. If you need to stop, you let us know."

"I will, Max."

I washed my plate and took it to the wagon. Opening the door, I saw Monica. I was so happy to see her. Climbing up into the wagon, I hugged her and kissed her on the cheek. "I missed you. How are you feeling?"

"Not bad. Just bigger and better." She laughed and rubbed her growing belly. "He's active, doing all kinds of flips. Kat finds it amazing." She laughed out loud.

I joined her. "Have you heard her talk anymore?"

Monica only shook her head. "Not one sound. I don't know, Ashley. It's like she is waiting for something. I don't understand it. I know she can speak. She just won't."

"She will when she's ready. Whatever she's waiting for, I wish it would hurry up."

Monica just shrugged her shoulders. "Y'all 'bout ready out there?"

"Yeah, they won't let me help, of course, but they are all working together."

She peeked outside. "We have a good family."

"Yes, we do," I agreed.

"Ant Ashe!" Dannie shouted from the bed. My mouth dropped in amazement. He called my name. He climbed down from the bed and came to me and hugged me. "Ant Ashe got a boo-boo." He gently touched my shoulder.

"Yes, I do, but it's much better."

That was all he needed to hear. He was distracted and climbed back up into the bed to play.

"Wow, I wasn't expecting that," I stated proudly.

"Yeah, he's talking more. Now if I can just get him to tie his own shoes." We laughed together.

We were packed up and began to move out within an hour. The quickness and teamwork amazed me.

Raven helped me mount Hummer. "I got a surprise for you later."

"What?"

"You'll find out. Don't worry. You will like it. If you need some help, just call for me."

I laughed. "Don't worry. I have you on speed dial."

He flashed me a smile. "I like that." He nodded and went to his horse.

We were on the road again, awaiting the next adventure.

As the sky was beginning to darken, Raven rode back to the wagons. He gave directions to Jacob and then Lou. "Monica, I need a bag of sugar!" he hollered out, slapping the side of the wagon.

Monica opened the door and handed him a full bag of sugar. He rode off in a hurry. I wasn't sure what was going on. I wanted to ride a little faster to see for myself; however, the long day of riding and jostling of my arm was taking its toll. My wounded arm ached and burned with intensity. I would break down tonight and take a pain pill willingly without it being hidden in my food or drink.

We came over a large hill and turned onto a private driveway. Raven was holding the gate open for everyone. I was the last through the gate before he closed it.

"What's going on, Raven? Are we on private property? For God's sake, don't you dare get us shot. I've had all I can handle," I stammered in frustration.

"You're not going to get shot at. Just shut up and follow me."

My eyes widened with shock at his sharp statement. "Jackass." I knew he heard me because he began smiling under his hat.

Passing an old farmhouse and continuing to the rear of the property, my eyes widen as I saw what he was talking about. A huge pond of water lay before us. Steam rose from the water, filling the air above it with a heavy fog. It was a natural hot spring. The north side was protected by a large hill. Our wagons were parking on the south side in a line, allowing privacy for when we took a bath.

Raven walked up to me, smiling proudly. "So what do you think?" He helped me dismount, then held me in his arms.

"This is my surprise?" I tried to sound unimpressed.

"Yeah, a guy at the compound told me about it. It's on private property, but the owner will trade for the use of the springs," he went on to explain. "I rode ahead, informed him of our situation, and all he wanted was some sugar, so I gave him a whole bag. We can stay the night and use the springs. I figured the hot water would feel good to you." He turned his head to get a second look at the splendorous sight.

The inability to hold myself back took over. "You're wrong. It won't feel good. It will feel great. Thank you, Raven!" In my excitement, I leaned in to kiss his cheek at the same time he inadvertently turned his smiling face toward me. My lips landed directly on his. I pulled back quickly, realizing my mistake. I looked at him as the shock crossed over my face. Lowering my head, I felt half embarrassed and half ashamed. "Please play nice, Raven," I stated in a soft whisper. I realized my statement made it appear that I blamed him for the incident.

"I'm sorry. I didn't mean it. I mean, I just turned my head." He sighed heavily in frustration. "Never mind." He set me down.

"Don't worry about it." I started walking off.

"Ashley, I am sorry. When I do kiss you, I guarantee you will know I mean it. It won't be an accidental passing of the lips."

I swear if I ever came close to blushing in my life, it was right then. I smiled and looked at him. "Don't get cocky, Raven."

He flashed me a smile and set right to work preparing the camp. It was getting dark, so Kat and I picked up firewood. She made no effort to speak at all, but she was full of smiles. She seemed happy and content. By the time we made it back, Monica had soup ready. Ricky and Jacob returned from hunting with a few rabbits. They happily gave one to the property owner as an added token of thanks to sweeten the deal for him. We sat around the fire and ate. We gathered our clothes and met by the water. My bandage needed changing, so I wasn't worried about getting it wet. The hot water felt so good against my skin. After the bath, everyone was busy doing one thing or another except Raven, who was alone by the fire holding our daughter.

"I need some help." I had my first aid bag in hand. He looked up at me. His eyes seemed to be glowing against the flickering firelight. "Is she asleep?"

He nodded and went into the tent. "Whatcha need?" he asked as he laid Nyte down.

"I need to redress my shoulder. I can't do it with one hand, and everyone else seems to be busy. Do you mind?"

"No, I don't mind." He took the bag from me and began digging through it, finding what he needed.

I began taking off my shirt slowly so I wouldn't hurt my arm more than it already was.

"Um, what are you doing?" Raven asked sharply. He seemed shocked and startled.

I flashed him a look of confusion. "I have to take off my shirt. The dressing won't do any good if it's on the shirt and not the shoulder."

He looked really uncomfortable. "I'll go get Monica. She can help you." He dashed out of the tent like a scalded dog. I looked around, befuddled by his actions. I remembered when he sat on the floor of the infirmary and I was nude. Why did this bother him?

It wasn't long before Monica came in. "Raven said you needed some help."

"Is that all he said?"

Monica looked at me. Now she was the one who was confused. "Yeah, why?"

"Well, everyone was busy, so I asked him to help with the bandage. We get in here, I start to take off my shirt, and he freaks out. He left out of here like his ass was on fire."

Monica started laughing slightly. "Ashley, it made him nervous. Haven't you noticed how he's been around you?"

"You mean overpowering, stubborn, bullheaded, and cocky? Sounds like the same ole Raven to me."

"No, I mean overprotecting, cautious, watchful, and alert to your needs. He's the one who's been taking care of you. He pretty much ordered the rest of us to leave you alone. Max actually thought it was sorta sweet the way he stood over you. He likes you, Ashley. I mean really likes you."

"That's going to be a problem."

"You like him too." She looked at me with knowing eyes.

"I do not!" I knew there was no use lying to her. She was a very insightful young woman. I plopped down on the floor of the tent. "Shit, does it show?"

She laughed and sat beside me. "No, you do a pretty good job at covering it up with sarcasm, but I can tell. I see the way you watch him when you think he's not looking. He's a good guy. A little rough around the edges, but overall a good guy."

I rested my head in my hands. "Monica, I'm so screwed up in the head. I don't know what to think or to feel. I have agreed to raise Nyte with him, but what if Dallas shows up? What's he going to think? How's he going to feel about me having a baby with Raven?"

"Do you realize what you just said? You said *if* Dallas shows up. It used to be *when* he shows up." Monica began to tenderly apply the bandage to my arm.

I exhaled deeply in frustration. "Am I holding on to a dream, and if so, how long am I going to hold on to it?"

"Honey, you're asking me questions I don't have an answer for. All I can do is offer advice."

"Well, offer away, please, because I'm grasping at straws here," I begged in frustration.

"Okay, go with the flow. Don't always try to swim against the current of things. Take it day by day and see what develops. You have no control over anything except your attitude and your reaction to things. Once you realize that, I think your life will get a lot easier." Monica quickly finished the bandage.

"How did you get so smart?" I asked.

"I watched a lot of daytime soaps on TV." She chuckled. "You'll be fine. You got a really good support system. If you need to talk, just let me know."

"Thanks for the bandage. You did a good job."

"You're welcome. That part I learned from you." Monica got up and assisted me with getting my shirt and coat on. We joined everyone who was gathering by the fire. Max turned on the radio for a little while but got only static. I quickly retired to bed. We were all exhausted. Raven took it upon himself to get up through the night to feed Nyte, allowing me to sleep. I hadn't had a lot of time with her recently. During the day, she was in the wagon with Monica, and during the night, Raven was doing daddy detail. If I were going to be any kind of mother, I had to find a way to spend more time with her. As we bedded down, I took my pain pill and fell fast asleep. No dreams polluted my rest.

I woke up before Raven and left the tent. The baby was still asleep, and I felt no need to wake her until she was ready. I exited the tent and found Max by the fire. I inhaled the deep, rich aroma of coffee.

Max smiled up at me and poured me a cup. "Well, howdy, stranger."

I laughed at his words. "Hey."

"How are you feeling?"

"I'm stiff and sore, but otherwise fine." I shook the sugar into my cup and then a smidgen of milk.

"There is another hot spring near Lewiston. It will be about a three days' ride," Max said.

I was glad to hear that. I welcomed any hot water after a long day's ride. I wished we could have one every night. If I were able to get to a computer with internet, I would find every hot spring and stop at them all. There was something to be said about bathing in the cool open air and the warmth of the water caressing your skin. It was a place where you can let your guard down and relax.

One by one, we awoke and joined the fire circle and took part in our breakfast, cleanup, and the tedious packing details. We had gotten efficient in our endeavors. Even without me helping, it didn't take long before we were on the road again.

The snow began falling again around noon when the wind kicked up. We made our turn west onto Highway 200. We stopped at a roadside park near a small ramshackle town called Jordan. There were no open stores, no water source, nothing we hadn't seen before.

Raven helped me dismount, and we didn't hesitate to get a fire going. It was so cold Monica decided to serve the soup from the wagon. We just got our bowls and went inside our own respectable wagon or tent. I swallowed a pain pill as Harley came around collecting dirty bowls. Raven had the baby in the tent, feeding her. I heated up some water and took it in. We bathed her and rubbed her down with sweet-smelling baby lotion. She was dressed in a pretty pink-footed sleeper and was asleep before I had finished. Raven sat and watched me. His eyes focused on every detail. It was as if he didn't want to miss anything. I placed a small amount of baby oil on her head and put a toboggan on her, carefully ensuring it covered her little ears, then wrapped her in a blanket. Raven disposed of the bathwater for me as I bedded down with Nyte. He came back in and stood watching us from the entry of the tent.

"Are you coming in or out?" I asked him, wishing he would close the flap.

"Out. I have first watch tonight." He turned his head from side to side. "Are you feeling okay?"

"I'm still sore, but better. I imagine it will get a little better every day." I reached up, rubbing my injured arm.

"You have everything you need?"

"Yeah." I looked at Nyte, who was sleeping soundly. "I have everything I need right here." I lay back and relaxed, keeping Nyte tucked in close to me. Allowing the pain pill to do its job, I slipped into a peaceful sleep.

The next two days, we traveled in almost total silence. Freezing north wind whipped all around us, stirring the snow on the ground. I had never been in a blizzard, but that was what it felt like. Snow pelted our faces like small needles piercing the skin. I wrapped a scarf around my face, leaving only my eyes exposed to the elements. I had lost all track of time. It was getting near whiteout conditions. We could only see a few feet ahead when Raven stopped and directed the wagons to the side of the road, explaining that we would take shelter from the winter storm in the trees. We found a place to pull the wagons and set up the tent. We made the kids stay in the wagons as the adults set up camp. Again, Monica served supper from the wagon. Jacob got a fire going. It was hard to find wood that wasn't frozen or too wet to light.

Raven found me in the tent with Nyte, feeding her. "You're going to stay in the wagon with Lou and Marcus tonight. It's too cold for you and Nyte out here," he stated in a commanding tone, letting me know he wasn't going to argue about it.

"I love the way you asked me. Normally, I would argue with you till the cows came home, but"—I looked down at Nyte, who was finishing her bottle—"I have to think about her. I don't want her getting sick because I was stubborn. So yes, Raven, I would love to go sleep in the warm wagon with Lou." I stood with her and exited the tent, making my way to Lou's wagon.

Raven caught up to me and opened the door. "Lou, y'all gonna have company tonight." Raven allowed me inside and closed the door behind me. I looked around and took a place opposite of Lou.

"Well, Ms. Ashley, come on in. Make yourself at home," Lou stated. "How's that little girl doing?"

"She's just fine, sound asleep. She's a pretty good baby, so I don't think she will keep you up tonight."

"Oh, she is fine. You just keep her warm and dry, and she will sleep."

Lou never got up from his sleeping spot. I covered Nyte and myself up and settled in. I had no idea what time it was, but it didn't matter. I was exhausted. I had wanted to tuck Kat in, but I knew if I stuck my head out the door, Raven would bite it off. Marcus was already asleep or doing a good job at faking it. I could hear his deep, relaxing breaths in almost a snore. I felt out of place but welcomed. I fell asleep keeping my hopes up that tomorrow would be a better day.

I awoke with Raven opening the door to the wagon, letting in a gust of cold air. "Morning, sunshine."

I looked at him through sleepy eyes. "What's with the sunshine crap?"

"Well, I see someone has had their bowl full of grumpy with two scoops of bitchy this morning." He sat beside me and offered me a cup of coffee. I sat up, greedily accepting the caffeine. He took the baby and began changing her and then fed her, allowing me time to wake up fully.

I sipped the hot coffee and looked at him with a halfway smile. "Bite me," I joked.

"Mommy doesn't do mornings very well," he jested, making faces at Nyte.

I noticed he looked rested and wide awake. I had always been jealous of those people who could wake up in a good frame of mind. As soon as their feet hit the floor, they were ready to go tackle the day. It took me time to get oriented to my surroundings and to know where I was and who I was. Normally, by the time I finished my third cup of coffee, I was functional. Raven seemed to be one of those annoying morning people whom I envied. When the baby was finished eating and burped, we came out of the wagon.

My mouth immediately fell open. It was nothing short of a winter wonderland. The trees were heavy with snow. It seemed to cling to every protruding branch. There was hardly any actual tree visible. It looked like we were in a Christmas tree farm, and all the tree had been heavily flocked, but this was real snow. The wind wasn't blowing like it had been the night before, and there was a strong fire going.

"I cut down a few trees during the night and got us some firewood," Raven stated proudly. "I had to do something to conduct body heat." He looked down at me, almost blushing at his comment.

Harley was running around laughing with Ricky chasing after her with a snowball. Kat and Dannie were playing by the fire. We went to join the rest of our family. We had our breakfast and began packing. I even helped a little before Raven gave me a look that told me I had better stop.

We only rode for about half a day when we pulled into Lewistown, Montana. It was a cute small town. Amazingly, most of their redbrick buildings were still intact. Once we were on Main Street, I gasped in awe. I stopped Hummer in his tracks and stared into the horizon. I could just see the mountains jutting out of the horizon. I released a breath of relief. I felt for the first time we were getting close. I knew in my heart we would make it. I just had to keep everyone going for a little while longer. I smiled in relief as Raven got directions from an old man. He supported his weight on a cane and wore tattered clothing. We continued on for at least an hour more before pulling onto a small single snow-covered lane. The horses strained to pull the wagons. We didn't push them too far. We kept the wagons inside the trees for cover against the elements as we hurried to set up camp. Without the wind blowing, I would be able to sleep in the tent next to the fire. Raven and Jacob gathered the firewood, while Monica and Rose got supper together. Soon, we had a roaring fire; good, hot food; and good company to keep us warm.

Raven and Jacob went to find the hot spring that was hidden within the frozen forest. Raven and Jacob returned full of smiles. Max, Marcus, Jacob, Ricky, and Lou followed Jacob back. They happily trotted off into the woods; they were as excited as the rest of us to get a good, hot bath. Raven stayed behind to be our protector. Upon the men's return, Raven showed me where the hot springs were. The plan was that I would bathe, then go get the other women and allow them to bathe. That way, there would be someone to stand watch at all times.

I looked at my surroundings. The large hot spring was in a wide clearing in the forest. There was a small pier extending over the water. A large rock seemingly stood guard at the base of the pier. Steam rose from the water like a fog.

I gazed at Raven. "I've got it from here."

He returned my looked and only smiled and dusted the snow off the rock and took a seat.

"Raven, really, I'm fine!" I exclaimed. "I don't need a babysitter."

"I hear you. I'm just not paying you any attention. You go on, get your bath, swim around, and relax. I'll be right here." He held up his hand, covering his eyes. "I won't even watch." He parted his fingers slightly, allowing himself to peek through them.

I crossed my arms and growled in frustration. Sneering at him, I made my way down the small wooden pier. Looking back, I could tell he wasn't going to leave. I began attempting to unbutton my shirt. It should've been a simple task. I'd managed to get it on, but somehow, now the buttons seemed smaller. My hands were dry and cracked, and I was having an extremely hard time. I struggled for a few more minutes and seriously considered just ripping it off.

"Here, let me help."

I jumped. "Jeez, Raven!"

He started unbuttoning my shirt. I shouldn't have felt uneasy or intimidated considering I had on two layers of clothes, but there was something erotic about Raven no matter how much flannel or thermal underwear was involved. I decided since he was being a gentleman to accept his help. He helped me with the arm sling too. I winced as my arm extended down.

"Want me to get your pain pills?" he asked, showing his concern.

"No, I'm fine." He was glaring at me with those beautiful eyes. I couldn't help but smile at him. "Really, I'm fine. I got shot. It's going to be sore. I'll take a pill tonight to help me sleep." I looked up at him and stated firmly, "Now turn around and let me undress."

He snickered under his breath and readjusted his hat. "Now who's not playing fair?" He turned away from me, playfully looking over his shoulder several times, making me jump. I could feel his smile and couldn't help but secretly return it.

I sat on the pier and carefully slid into the hot water. Raven sat on the pier with his legs crossed, keeping his eyes on me. I kept my back to him and bathed. I washed my hair as best as I could with one hand. I could feel his eyes on me. Perhaps I should've been repulsed that he was watching me like some kind of pervert, but I wasn't. I felt comfortable with Raven. I felt we had an unspoken understanding. He respected me, my wishes, and my feelings, and I felt truly safe. As much as I looked out for my family, he looked out for me. I couldn't imagine my life without him. We'd inherited a child and agreed to raise her together. He was a permanent fixture in my life now, just like Nyte. And if Dallas came back, he would have to deal with it.

I was so wrapped up in my own rambling thoughts I hadn't noticed Raven enter the water. He eased up behind me. Sensing a presence, I spun around and found him standing before me wearing only a cowboy hat and a smile.

"What are you doing?" I asked, feebly attempting to cover myself.

His grin grew wider. "I have to bathe too."

"Are…are you like totally naked?" I stuttered.

"That's usually how you take a bath, sunshine."

"No one likes a smart-ass, Raven." I let a smile slip. "You just stay over there. I'm almost through."

He laughed, holding out his arms. "What, you don't trust me now?"

I peered at him through squinted eyes. "Who said I ever did?"

"Ouch, that hurts." Raven put his hand over his heart.

I couldn't help but smile at his idiocy. "You're such a nerd."

Raven childishly put his hand on his nude hips. "I know you are, but what am I?"

I only rolled my eyes in protest.

"You know what I think?" He inched his naked body even closer.

I couldn't help but stare at him. His muscles were well-defined. The little bit of facial hair he had seemed to be naturally well-groomed. I had never seen him with a razor before. Even the masculine underarm hair was miniscule. His chest also hosted no hair. That could explain his childish behavior. The poor boy had never hit puberty, I thought to myself. He was now standing inches away.

"No, Raven, I couldn't possibly know what you think. I couldn't think that slow even if I tried."

He smiled down at me. "I think you trust me, but I don't think you trust yourself around me."

Steam rose from the water, only adding to the sensual atmosphere. His body seemed to be illuminating under the soft glow of the dim moon. I felt so torn. Part of me wanted to jump into his arms, wrap my legs around him, and throw all caution to the wind. I could so easily forget everything and everyone else in my life. I could get lost in this moment, and to hell with the consequences. The other more dominant and sensible part of my subconscious reeled me back in from the extreme fantasy I was silently entertaining. I looked at him, wanting so much for him to take charge. If he would only grab me and kiss me, taking me by surprise, I would lose all control of myself. I knew him too well. Even though he was arrogant and cocky, he was also honorable and trustworthy. He would never pressure me into something in fear I would send him away forever.

I was breathing as fast as my heart was racing. I raised my good arm and gently pushed him back. My eyes watched as my fingers lightly trailed down his abdomen. He inhaled deeply and slowly released it. I looked at him, my desires building every second. His eyes were closed and head tilted back ever so slightly in reaction to my touch.

"Maybe you're right. Maybe I don't trust myself. So I'm going to put my faith in you to have enough patience for the both of us."

"But no pressure, right?" Raven joked. "Perhaps you have too much faith in me, sunshine, because when it's all said and done, I'm still a warm-blooded man. I have needs and desires like everyone else." He was smiling now, trying to make light of a rather tense situation.

I figured if I were going to end this situation with my dignity intact, then this was a good time to make my exit. I turned and made my way out of the water. I wrapped my wet, shivering body in a blanket and gathered my clothes. I turned back to Raven, who was watching me in waist-deep water. I stuffed my feet into my boots and turned back to him. "And when the time's right, that's what I'm counting on." I flashed him a gentle, sweet smile. "I'll meet you back at camp." I sloshed back down the snow-covered path, smiling while indulging in my mental fantasy.

CHAPTER 12

THE NEXT MORNING, we woke early as usual. I sat and drank my coffee as Raven fed Nyte. He looked great with her. You couldn't tell by looking at him, but he was a natural father. I sat watching him with her, and I knew she would be so spoiled that she would absolutely stink. The kids played in the snow, laughing as they threw snowballs back and forth. I watched them and enjoyed the twinkle in their eyes as a fresh blanket of snow began falling. Kat caught my eye. She had stopped playing and was drawing away from the others. Standing in almost ankle-deep snow, she was staring intently on the tree line. I quickly scanned it for whatever she might have seen. I rose from my seat and continued to watch her. She turned her head from one side then the other. Quickly Kat scanned around at all of us then back to the trees. Slowly she began walking toward the tree line. She stepped cautiously, like a creeping tiger stalking its prey.

"What is she doing?" I said.

"Who?" Lou asked.

"Kat, she is acting weird. It's like she hears something." I walked toward my daughter, who was now close to the tree line. My steps quickened as I made sure I had my pistol with me.

Kat reached a tall tree that awkwardly forked in two directions, staring curiously, twisting her head from side to side. Reaching up, Kat dug her little fingers into the tree. I reached her just as something fell out of the tree and hit the ground. Kat bent over and picked up a small black stone.

"What is that, baby?" I stated as I placed my hand on her shoulder and peeked over to get a look. It looked like a fossilized shell and oddly resembled a bear.

She shrugged her shoulders and looked confused as she showed me the black stone.

"It just looks like an odd rock, baby." I hated to disappoint her.

Kat shook her head adamantly, indicating that I was indeed wrong. She turned and walked back to camp with determination in her steps. She stomped straight over to Lou and showed him the stone.

Lou took the stone from her hand. He stared at it for a long time from several different angles. He looked to Kat eagerly waiting before him. "You heard the song, didn't you?"

Kat's little mouth dropped open in shock. She nodded with a steady rhythm.

"What song, Lou? What's going on? I didn't hear anything," I stated in confusion.

"No, you wouldn't have." A gentle smile crossed Lou's wrinkly cheeks. "This is called a buffalo stone. It's a major object used in medicine in many Native American cultures. In the old days, it was used to magically call the buffalo back to the prairie. It usually draws attention to itself by singing a song only the chosen one can hear. Today it's considered a good luck charm. If you find one, it's supposed to bring you good luck for the rest of your life. So always keep it with you, and good luck will follow you around. You can't give it away. It won't work for anyone else. And if it's stolen, it will strike down the thief with a strain of bad luck. You're a very lucky, little lady." Lou carefully placed the stone back into Kat's hand, then closed her hands around the stone, securing it. "Take good care of it." Kat gleefully nodded and shoved the stone into her pocket, then took a place at the fire.

We packed up and rode to Utica. After pulling into a secluded section of forest, we made camp for the night. The mountains lingered in the distance, growing closer every day. I was getting excited, and my hopes were high. My family had gathered around the fire to stay warm. Monica and Dannie were missing. Max was there refilling everyone's cup with coffee, laughing and joking around.

"Hey, where's Monica?" In the instant the last syllable left my lips, a bloodcurdling scream pierced the night like a bullet. Every hair on my body stood on end. I felt my blood pressure rising from my toes. It was Monica screaming.

We dropped everything and ran in the direction of the dreadful screams. Monica bolted from the forest wagging, Dannie on her hip. Her face was pale white in the dim moonlight. The look in her eyes was one of sheer terror.

"What is it?" Max shouted. "Are you hurt?"

Monica staggered in the deep snow and held her stomach. She gasped for air as she put Dannie down and managed to stammer out a few words, "Wolf." She pointed to the trees, stammering out of breath. "Rocky!" Seeing that Monica was safe, Max bolted through the trees.

"Rose, will you help Monica back to camp?" Jacob ordered as the rest of us were already stomping through the forest behind Max.

The horrid sounds of growling and barking, mixed with snarling, echoed all around us. We broke through the trees and found Rocky entangled with a large gray wolf. Any other time, I would have thought it was a beautiful creature. However, right then, it was a menacing monster invading our peaceful lives.

Raven had his rifle aimed at the tangled mess of fur. "I can't get a clear shot."

Max wasted no time as he fired a shot in the air. "Rocky, get out of there!" he shouted. Neither animal made an attempt to stop.

With their lips pulled back, exposing their teeth, the two canines wrestled and roared against each other. They bit each other, tearing out patches of fur and flesh. Twisted mounds of fur flipped and flopped over the ground. Only brief intermittent whimpers interrupted the horrific sounds that seemed to be radiating from the two angry animals before us. The wolf had made it a personal fight by invading our temporary territory and threatening Rocky's family. I knew the animal instincts wouldn't stop until one of them was dead.

I had to do something. I gripped and cocked my pistol firmly and ran toward the fighting animals.

"Ashley," Raven yelled at me, "no!"

Totally disregarding his unwavering words of caution, I continued running to Rocky's aid. I got within a few feet and, with every ounce of strength, leaped forward, landing on the wolf's back, momentarily knocking Rocky free, and pinning the creature to the ground. Wedging my pistol into his throat, I quickly pulled the trigger. The blast echoed in my head as the creature's blood sprayed onto my face.

Raven was on me in an instant, pulling me back by the collar of my coat. "What the hell are you doing? Have you gone completely crazy? You could have been killed."

I was out of breath and holding my bad arm. I looked up at him with pleading eyes. I didn't want him to be mad at me. "I had to stop it. He was killing Rocky." I looked at Max. "I had to."

Raven flung his arms around erratically. "You damn crazy, stubborn, foolish, deranged female." He stomped off, constantly mumbling to himself.

Max crouched down beside his beloved dog. Rocky winced as Max got his first look at his friend. I crawled over to Max and took a quick assessment of Rocky's wounds. "Oh, Max," I said in a whisper. Rocky had a long deep gash along his belly. A portion of his intestines spilled out of the gaping wound. Another section of intestine had been sparsely ripped open; their gooey contents soiled Rocky's fur mixed with the blood. Large chunks of flesh were missing from his throat, giving him the appearance of being partially decapitated. He was bleeding profusely. The growing puddle of blood saturating the snow-covered ground beneath his mutilated body was evidence of exactly how much blood he was losing and how quickly.

"Can you save him, sissy?" Max looked at me. His eyes seemed to be begging with me. Hot tears streamed down his cheeks.

I shook my head. "I wouldn't know where to start." My voice was shaking, my chest heaving. The one time Max needed me and I felt unable to help him. I knew my brother needed my strength and encouragement.

"What do I do, sissy?" Max asked me through his tears.

"Just hold him, Max. Just let him know you're here." Rocky had been a vital part of Max's family for three years. He was more than a dog; he was a friend.

I sat with my brother quietly. I had one hand on Rocky and the other on Max. Rocky's breathing became shallow, and his heartbeat slowed. He was bleeding to death.

"Good boy, Rocky. I love you, buddy."

Rocky looked at Max with his big chocolate-brown eyes. The initial warmth of the free-flowing blood was melting a little bit of the snow beneath the bloodied dog. Rocky whimpered as he raised his head and licked Max in the face, then allowed his head to fall back into the snow. Max patted his head as Rocky closed his eyes. I held my brother's hand as he said goodbye to his best friend for the last time. Rocky gave his life to protect Monica and Dannie. He died being the hero we always knew he was.

Max took a deep breath and pulled himself together. "I need to go to Monica."

Raven and Jacob stepped forward. "Go on, Max. Jacob and I will take care of things here."

Max didn't say a single word. He patted Raven's shoulder and walked away without looking back.

Raven walked over and put his arm around me. "How are you doing?"

I kept my eyes on my brokenhearted little brother. "I'm fine. He's the one who's hurting."

"Max is tough. He will pull through."

I knew Raven was attempting to make me feel better.

"He was more than just a dog. Max has always wanted a boxer. When he and Monica got married, she took a part-time job. She saved her money and bought Rocky for Max's birthday," I explained. "He was like their first baby, and he was special."

"And he always will be," Raven stated.

I briefly leaned my head on Raven's shoulder. "I better go check on Monica." I couldn't allow myself to stay there much longer. I was afraid I would break down.

I made my way back to the camp. Max was consoling Monica by the fire. Dannie was clinging to his daddy, crying. He saw me and squirmed free and ran to me. "Ant Ashy, Wocky gone bye-bye."

I scooped him up, hugging him tightly, thanking the elusive stars above that he was safe. "Yeah, buddy, Rocky went bye-bye. But I'm so happy that you're okay." I kissed his forehead and walked over to Monica. "How are you doing?"

Monica nodded. "I'm fine." Her eyes were red from crying. "That wolf came out of nowhere. He lunged at us, and before I knew what was happening, Rocky jumped in front of us, and the fight was on. All I could do was grab Dannie and run." She was crying again as she buried her face into Max's arms.

Dannie wiggled in my arms, and I put him down. He went to his mama and patted her leg. "It's okay, Mama."

My heart was breaking seeing my brother and his family hurt. Leaving them to their privacy, I found Rose and collected Nyte. I held my baby daughter tightly. Harley and Kat gave a round of hugs and sat beside me at the fire. Marcus soon joined us as well. One by one, we retired for the night.

That night, I bedded my kids down to sleep and counted each of them a blessing. My body racked with emotion. All I wanted to do was sit and cry, but instead, I got myself in a stronger frame of mind. Rocky's death just confirmed the fact that we had to keep moving. I had to stay strong. I was more determined than ever to get my family to safety.

The next day's ride was hard. The air hung heavily around us, affecting everyone's heart and spirits. The looks on my family's faces were ones of despair, agony, and hopelessness.

Raven caught my attention as he came over a hill with a huge smile on his face. He rode up to me, grinning like a rat in a cheese factory. "Just up ahead, there is an old abandoned barn. It will be a great place to stay the night." He wasted no time in telling the others, who only solemnly nodded in response.

I rode over the hill and saw the huge barn right off. I looked around at its surroundings. It was beautiful. The barn sat in the shadow of a large snow-covered hill. The crisscrossed wooden fencing was lined in snow. Leafless red bushes sparsely jutted up from the ground. The red bushes looked amazing against the white ground. We drove the wagons straight into the barn and set up a tent. We used some wooden planks that had fallen away from the frame of the barn for firewood. The horses munched on old leftover hay that still looked eatable. Raven put a tarp over the large opening in the loft of the barn to block out a lot of wind. Within the hour, we had the barn nice and cozy.

Marcus found me leaning against the barn door, staring out into the open field of snow. "Ashley?"

"Hey, kiddo, how are you doing?" I looped my arm in his and pulled him closer.

Marcus nodded. "I'm good, but I think Lou is sick. I have driven the wagon for the past two days. I don't think he has hardly been out of bed. I know he hasn't eaten or drank anything since breakfast yesterday."

I knew in my heart Lou's time was growing short. I had to play it off though until he was ready to let the rest of the world in on his secret. "Well, it's been pretty cold. It probably makes his bones hurt. You know how old people are." I didn't know what else to say. I looked back to Lou's wagon. He was in there right now possibly dying, and I was harboring his secret. I knew it was a matter of time before it would be exposed. "I think I'll go check on him."

I padded my way to Lou's wagon. I entered and saw him lying in his bed. "Hey, old man, how you doing?" Lou had himself wrapped in a blanket that barely revealed his face.

"Good evening, Ms. Ashley," Lou mumbled, barely lifting his head.

I sat on the edge of the bed. "Marcus said you hadn't been feeling well. I thought I would poke my head in and check on you."

"I'm fine for now. I don't think I'll be doing much of anything from now on." He peered over his covers, looking at me.

"Level with me, Lou."

He took a deep, exasperating breath. "I'm weak with no appetite. Every little thing I do seems to wipe me out. I hate feeling like this."

"It's only the beginning."

He shook his head. "Ms. Ashley, you are only half right. This is the end for me. I know my fate, and I'm okay with that. I made my peace with God a long time ago."

I looked into his tired eyes peeking at me from the warmth of his covers. "Do I need to go have a talk with Raven?"

"Not yet. I'll let you know when it comes time for that. Right now, I just want to sleep. If that boy of yours wouldn't mind driving the wagon from now on, maybe I can prolong the inevitable." Lou gave a slight giggle and quietly fell back to sleep.

I eased out of the wagon as to not disturb him. I talked with Marcus, who didn't mind driving the wagon at all. Being the smart kid that he was, he could tell there was something going on even if I wouldn't admit it.

Night fell, and we took turns standing watch as usual. It had been a while since we had seen anyone on the road. I woke up and fed Nyte, then took my watch. I watched as Raven balanced her tiny body on his bold chest. Wrapping myself in a blanket, I went to stand in the open barn door. Glaring out across the field, I listened to my family's peaceful slumber. I could almost tell who was taking a breath by the sound they made. A sound stirred from behind me. Spinning around, I found my brother holding a cup of coffee.

"Hey, brother," I said as I turned back to my snowy field.

"Hey, sissy, I wanted to talk to you if you had a minute." Max leaned against the wooden door.

"All I have is time, Max." I smiled.

"I wanted you to know that I don't blame you, for Rocky, I mean." He shuffled his feet in the loose dirt. "Monica and I felt it was important for you to know that."

Looking at my little brother, in that moment, I found the man he had grown into. "Thanks, Max. I needed to hear that. It killed me knowing I couldn't do anything to save him."

"I thought so. It was hard, still is, but I wanted you to know that." He took a drink of coffee and adjusted his coat with his free hand. "It's been harder at times than I ever could've imagined.

However, if you consider everything that has happened, we have had a fairly easy trip so far."

I abruptly looked at my brother. "What?" I shook my head. "Max, we have all lost our homes, my daughter still won't speak, I still haven't heard from Dallas, I got shot, Monica and Dannie were almost attacked by a wolf, Rocky died, Lou is sick. In my mind, what else could go wrong?"

"But, sissy, that's just it. It could've been a lot worse. We could've died."

"Well, we aren't there yet. There's still time, so don't lose hope yet."

"That's a horrible thing to say. Why would you say that?"

"I don't want you getting your hopes up, Max. There is still time for things to go horribly wrong." I didn't want Max letting his guard down. He had to understand where I was coming from. I wanted not only him but also everyone to be prepared for the worst to happen. "One thing I have learned in life is, just when things seem to be going good, something jumps up and bites you in the ass. I want you on your guard at all times."

"I understand that, sissy, but you can't forget the good things in life either. Otherwise, living isn't going to be much fun," Max explained.

I turned to my brother sternly, my hands now resting on my hips. "I'm not forgetting anything, Max. I just can't afford to dwell on the hope of good things for very long. It's the good things that make you soft, vulnerable, and weak." I poked myself in the chest. "I intend to remain strong. I'm trying to get us to Browning alive and in one piece. So forgive me if I'm not too worried about having fun right now."

Max looked at me with the same eyes he had the night by the fire when I had taken the lives of those two young boys. "I'm not sure if I know who you are right now."

"That tells me that I'm in the right frame of mind. When we get to the reservation safely, then I can let my guard down. Until then, this is what you got, so find a way to deal with it. I refuse to allow anyone or anything else I love to die on this journey that I started." I turned and went to the tent. I fell onto my pallet of covers. I wanted to bury my head and cry. Instead, I watched Raven asleep with Nyte on his chest. I fell asleep watching them, jealous of their restless slumber. My sleep was diseased with nightmares that kept me tossing and turning for the rest of the night.

Dawn came too early. Raven woke me with a light kick to the boot.

"I'm awake!" I yelled at him.

"Your brother wanted me to make sure you were okay. Did you two have a disagreement last night?"

"No, I just refuse to allow myself to be distracted or get softened. I have to stay hard and stern to ensure we all make it alive," I tried to explain. If anyone could understand, surely it was Raven.

"Lou wants to see you. He's in the wagon."

I peered up at Raven. I knew what that meant. Bolting from the tent, I ran to Lou's wagon, jerked open the door, and found him lying in the bed.

"Lou, I'm here."

"Good morning, Ms. Ashley." His words were soft and frail.

Sitting beside him, I gently pulled back the blanket to see his face. His eyes looked as if they had sunken into his head. His cheeks were so thin you could almost see his bones through the skin. Somehow, he had managed to hide how thin he had become. "Lou."

"It's okay now, Ms. Ashley. I believe it's time you had a talk with Raven. I'm not going any further. Y'all can go on. I don't want to hold you up."

"We aren't going anywhere without you. I'll get my bag and see what I have."

Lou grabbed my arm with what little force he could muster. "You don't have a cure for cancer in that little bag of yours, kid, and you're not going to waste good medicine on me. Now I expect you to hold up to your end of the bargain. You go have that talk with Raven, and when you're finished, he can come see me."

I nodded and patted Lou's hand, tucking him back under the covers. I left the wagon.

Jacob was packing up a few things. I looked at him and said, "I wouldn't bother with that just yet, Jacob." His eyes locked on mine and then to Lou's wagon. I think he immediately understood what was happening. "Where's Raven?"

"He's outside." Jacob nodded in the general direction.

I nodded to him and somehow found the strength to propel myself forward. I found Raven sitting on a wooden crate outside, shuffling his feet in the snow.

"Raven, I need to talk to you. It's about Lou." I was so ashamed; I couldn't even look at him. We had come so far in our friendship, if that was what you wanted to call it. Now he was about to find out that I had kept this big secret from him the entire time. I knelt down in the snow beside him. "I have to tell you something, and it's not easy to say."

Raven interrupted me, "Let me guess. This is the part where you tell me that Lou is dying. He made you swear not to tell me, and then he conned you into bringing him up here with you?" He cocked his head to the side. "Does that about cover it?"

I look at him with shock. My mouth hung open like a little flytrap. "He didn't con me, but wait, you knew about this?"

"Oh yes, he conned you. That man has been after me for years to ride with him up here. I just kept putting him off. Lou has been an honest, straightforward man his whole life. Then you and your brood show up pulling that crappy little cart headed to the great land of Montana. That gave him the only excuse he needed." Raven smiled at me. "Girl, he played you like a fiddle. He knew he couldn't make it on his own. He knew I would never agree to take him. Why do you think I protested so much about this trip?"

I only shook my head in total confusion.

"It was because if he were going to die, I wanted him to die at home, where I could properly bury him next to Tabitha. He offered you the wagons in exchange for letting him come with you. He knew if he told me that he was leaving with you, I would follow." Raven stopped and shook his head before continuing, "I've known for a long time that he was sick. We live in a very small town, and news travels fast. I had enough respect for the old man not to say anything and allow him to have his little secret. I figured he would tell me when he was ready." He put his hand on my shoulder. "So tell me, how long does he have, Doc?"

I stood up, shocked and shaken. Raven wasn't upset at all. He knew the entire time and never let on. I didn't know if I should feel pissed or relieved. "Um, I'm not sure. No more than a few days. He's extremely weak. He wants to see you."

Raven stood and patted my shoulder. "Well, I better not keep him waiting." Raven went to Lou's wagon and entered. I shared the news with everyone else. Jacob and Rose decided to stay with us no matter how long they had to wait. I appreciated their friendship. I was dreadfully going to miss them when we parted ways.

Max, Jacob, and Ricky left to go hunting. Dannie and Kat played in the snow, while Harley and Marcus brushed down the horses. Monica and Rose fretted over Nyte as I patiently waited by the fire for Raven to return. It seemed like forever before the door to Lou's wagon finally opened. Raven came out carrying Lou. I hurried toward them and helped get Lou into the tent. He laid Lou down on the sleeping bag and covered him up. Lou's eyes were closed, and he looked peaceful. Raven put his finger up to his lips, indicating that I should be quiet, and then motioned for me to follow him out.

Once outside, Raven finally spoke, "He has been going in and out of it. When he wakes up again, he wants to talk to both of us."

Raven went back inside the tent and stayed with Lou. I remained by the fire with Nyte. Our mighty hunters returned with a large deer. We would have plenty to eat for the next few days. By nightfall, the deer was roasting over the fire. Harley was back in Ricky's warm arms by the fire, listening to Max and Jacob exchange hunting stories.

After we ate, I tucked Kat and Taco in for the night. I hugged her closely. "Today was another bad day, baby. Tomorrow may not be much better, but new, brighter, and better days are on the horizon. We are so close now." I looked into her innocent blue eyes, then buried my head in her neck. "I would give anything to hear you say 'I love you, Mama.' You could always make me smile when you said that." I pulled away, not wanting her to feel guilty.

She raised her hands and did sign language for "I love you."

I smiled at her and let out a small breath of relief. "I love you too, angel, so much. Good night." I backed out of the wagon as she turned over, smiling herself.

I rejoined my family by the fire as I rocked Nyte back and forth. Soon, even she was asleep. I jumped to my feet when Raven came out of the tent and called for me.

"Here, Ashley, I'll take Nyte." Rose took my baby without hesitation as I went to Raven's side.

"He's awake and wants to talk to both of us." Raven held the tent flap open for me as I went inside.

Lou extended his emaciated hand and called out to me, "Ms. Ashley." I sat on one side of him as Raven sat on the other. Lou took my hand, then Raven's. He laced our fingers together and rested our hands on top of his chest with his hand resting on top of ours. Through tired eyes, he looked at me. "Now I'm sorry I tricked you, Ms. Ashley. I hope you don't think bad of me for it, but I'm not sorry for making this trip. I have had the time of my life out here. My only regret is that I'm not going to see my beautiful mountains again." Lou paused and took a long deep breath.

"Now, Raven, son, you have had a hard life, but you need to be good to Ms. Ashley. And, Ashley, you need to give the boy a chance." Before I could interrupt, he continued, "Raven's a good man. It doesn't matter if you'll admit it to yourselves or not. He loves you. I can see in your eyes that you love him too. You both need to let go of the ghosts in your past and move on to a bright future together."

I hung my head down, unable to meet Raven's gaze. I was embarrassed, because in my heart, I knew it could possibly be true, and I wasn't going to argue with a dying man.

"I have never met two people who belonged together as much as y'all do. You're a good team, and you work well together. If you give each other a chance, you will play good together too." Lou gave a small chuckle and began coughing. He slowly recovered himself, declining the need of water. His breathing was labored, but still, he continued, "Now if you two decide to go back to the ranch, go see Sadie Campbell. I left her the deed to the ranch. I told her she could work the farm till one of you came for it. She's a good woman and will honor the deal. As far as that little girl of yours, Nyte, I want to leave her Tabitha's wedding ring. She is the nearest thing to a granddaughter I'll ever have, and I want her to have it. If it's okay with Ms. Ashley, you know where it is, Raven."

Raven only nodded. He looked as if he were about to cry. He had never looked so vulnerable, and it hurt to see him in this state.

"I'm pretty tired now. I think I'll sleep for a while." The old man closed his eyes.

Raven and I eased out of the tent. We only looked at each other, as if speaking with our eyes. He broke contact first and went outside the barn. Going the opposite direction, I reached into my pocket and found my cigarettes. My hands were shaking with cold. After attempting several times to light the cigarette, I threw the lighter in anger and frustration. I wanted to kick, scream, and punch something, but I stood firm, breathing hard, my feet placed in a wide stance and my shoulders squared. Taking a deep breath, sucking my feelings deep within myself, I closed my eyes. I waited for the rage to pass. I couldn't afford to lose it now. I could express my emotions later when we were safely on the reservation.

Looking up, I saw him staring at me from the doorway. "You're going to blow up one day if you keep doing that."

"When this trip is over, I'll find time to have a nervous breakdown, but for right now, I'm a little busy trying to keep the rest of us alive."

"Oh, don't go blaming yourself for Lou. If you're pulling that crap, you can go blow it up someone else's ass, because I'm not buying into it." Raven scoffed at me. "Hell, he's a sick old man. He's more than paid his dues to this earth and is ready to give it up and go be with his daughter. That isn't your fault. It's not anyone's fault. It's just a fact of life. He was dying long before you came along."

His words rang in my head. He was right. I knew all along that Lou was dying. True enough, I figured he would make it all the way to Browning. However, that was not what fate had in mind for him. "You're right."

"What?" Raven looked at me with a goofy, crooked grin.

"You heard me. Don't make me say it again." I returned his smile as I leaned against the barn door. "Like he says, everything happens for a reason, right?"

Raven smiled and nodded. "Yeah, that's what he says. I never thought too much about it, but I'm beginning to understand it more every day."

"Me too." I smiled at him. "I just really thought he would make it all the way. It just seems so unfair after everything that he's not going to." My words quivered, and my eyes began to water. I couldn't finish.

Raven looked at me with those beautiful eyes, leaned closer, and kissed me lightly on the head. "Thanks for being here." Quickly he pulled away and left me standing there with my mouth half open, hardly breathing and wanting more, much more. I watched him go back into the tent with Lou.

"Where else am I going to go?" I whispered.

Claiming a spot by the fire, I lit my cigarette with a burning piece of wood. Rose had taken Nyte to bed with her and Jacob to stay warm. Harley and Ricky were saying their wet, slobbery good nights, and Monica was asleep with Dannie.

Max sat across from me, staring at me. I knew I had to say something to him. "I'm sorry I yelled at you."

"I understand what you're doing, sissy. I just don't want you to lose yourself in the process," Max stated. "I have lost a lot. I don't want to lose my sister too."

"You won't. I'm still me in here." I pointed to my heart. "And I still love you, brother."

"I love you too, sissy. I'm going to get some sleep. Wake me for my watch, all right?"

I nodded as he passed me by and went into his wagon. I was alone again. The night was literally dead silent with the exception of the wood in the fire crackling, popping, and whistling. From far away, a wolf's howl echoed in the night. I knew I had my pistol, but I checked anyway if for no other reason than to give myself something to do. The sound of my clothes moving seemed to ricochet in the stillness. Pouring myself a cup of coffee, I went and stood by the barn door. Staring up into the sky, I didn't find a single star. I longed to see at least one star shining bright. That would mean the dust cloud was starting to settle and maybe things would get a little better. I looked around and found my purse and fished out my old cell phone and wasted some time trying to see if I could get a signal. It was useless; there was no signal, nor any evidence that there had ever been a signal. This also meant no voice mail and no text message. I was hoping that Dallas had found a way to leave me some sign that he was alive. I shoved the useless piece of machinery into my pocket and tried to forget about it.

Jacob relieved me around midnight. I checked on Raven and took him some coffee. He was still awake and at Lou's side. I stayed long enough to count Lou's breaths. He was breathing very slowly and shallow. I knew it was just a matter of time. I got a blanket and curled up by the fire, not wanting to disturb anyone else by entering a wagon, and it was warm enough in the barn. I quickly fell asleep listening to Jacob read aloud from some dumb book that held no interest to me.

It was Max who woke me up around five that morning. "Sissy, Raven is calling for you."

I jumped up and hurried to the tent. I pulled back the flap. Raven had his hand over Lou's eyes. It took me a moment to figure out that he was closing them. "Is he…" I couldn't finish it.

"He's gone." Raven stood and held his head down.

"I'm sorry, Raven. I'm so sorry." I went to his side, and he put his arm around me.

"He told me he loved me like a son and for me to be good to you. He simply exhaled one last breath, and that was it. It was just that fast."

"I'm not sure what to say." For the first time in a long time, I was at a loss for words. I felt bad for Raven. Lou had been like a father to him for many years.

"It's okay. He's not hurting anymore, and he's at peace." Raven wiped a stray tear from his face. "That's the way it should be, and I'm okay with that." He paused for a moment. "The ground is too frozen to bury him." He looked around at the barn, nodded, and let out a small chuckle and shook his head. "There's a reason for everything."

"What are you talking about?" I had no idea what was running through his head.

"We found this barn, then Lou dies. The ground is too frozen to bury him, so when we get ready to leave, I will set fire to the barn. The old man can go out in a blaze of glory." Raven walked off and started packing up a few loose items.

Max found me. "Is he okay?"

I smiled knowing in my heart that somehow he was. "Yeah, he's fine. Tell the others when we leave, Raven is setting fire to the barn, so we want to make sure everyone and everything is out." Max immediately understood what I meant.

Once everyone was up and gathered around the fire, Raven made the announcement that Lou was gone. He had died peacefully in his sleep without any pain. Kat silently cried on my shoulder. She'd found a friend in Lou. He appreciated her vow of silence, and they had their ways of communicating without words. Lou seemed to know what Kat meant just by the look she had in her eyes. Harley leaned on Ricky's shoulder. Max and Monica, along with Jacob and Rose, gave Raven their polite condolences. It went well but still seemed to be a heavy cloud of dread hanging over all of us.

With a long way to go, we ate and packed up and set out for another day's ride. When we were a safe distance away and everyone was accounted for, Raven lit a fire inside the barn and left. It didn't take long before the old rotten wood was consumed. We watched until the roof collapsed, then went on our way. I found myself saying a little prayer for Lou. Praying wasn't something I gave much thought to or had much faith in, but just in case there was some celestial being up there beyond the stars listening, I wanted it to know that Lou was a good man and was loved by many.

We traveled for several hours. Jacob came riding toward us, smiling like a fox in a henhouse. "Malmstrom Air Force Base is right over that hill. It's beautiful, Ashley. You're going to love it."

I politely smiled at Jacob and gave him a nod. I didn't understand why I would love a military base. It held no particular interest to me. We topped the hill, then my eyes found what he was talking about. I saw my mountains in the horizon. We were getting closer. Correction, we were almost there. The large snowy mounds of ice and rock were beautiful. I had something in my field of vision, a motive to keep us going. I knew we were going to make it. Age-old voices rang in my head. *Are we there yet? Not much further now.* I smiled to myself.

"Are you crying?" Raven asked me with a smile.

"Not yet." I returned his smile.

"Looks like they have a tent city, but it's pretty small. We should be able to pick up a few more supplies in Great Falls."

I nodded; it would be nice to see another functioning town again. "That sounds wonderful." I would like to get the girls and Marcus something new to wear and maybe pick up some larger clothes for Nyte before she grew out of what she had.

We pulled up to the base, and Raven dismounted his horse. "Evening, sir."

The soldier met Raven and shook his hand. "Good evening. Where are you folks from?"

Raven looked to me then back to the soldier. "Well, parts of us are all the way from Texas. We are headed to Browning. Do you have any news out of that area?"

The soldier shook his head. "No, don't think we have heard anything from Browning. That's the Indian Reservation, right?"

Raven nodded. "Yes, sir, the Blackfoot Reservation."

"No, we haven't heard anything, but that's not a bad thing. We rarely hear anything from them. There is over a million acres with very little population. They take care of their own. We have a tent city set up. You are more than welcome to come on in and take a spot. There is firewood for you, and we have a mess tent set up for meals. So come on in and help yourself."

We started pulling the wagons through when the soldier hollered out behind us, "Hey, we lock the gates up at ten p.m., so if you go into town, make sure you are back by then!"

Raven turned back to speak with him. I knew he was asking about open stores. We found a good spot to park and claimed it.

There were very few people in this camp. This could be a good or bad thing. Either there was so much destruction that no one survived, or there was so little that people were still in their own homes. I personally was hoping for the second choice.

We had already started setting up camp when Raven found us. "Almost the whole damn town of Great Falls is open."

Harley looked up quickly at the mention of Great Falls. She looked at Ricky, horrified. She knew that was where Jacob and his family would be parting ways. The realization sunk in that this might be her last night with Ricky. I would have a heartbroken little girl come tomorrow night.

Raven continued, "Let's get camp set up, then a few of us can go into town and see what we can find." Raven beamed like a schoolboy.

Everyone pitched in, and camp was quickly set up. We had a fire going and were ready for the night. It was decided that the men and myself would go into town. We would take only our horses and get only what we could carry. We had plenty of bottled water, so that wasn't a concern. We could probably refill our empty containers before we left the base. Once we were satisfied that everything and everyone were secure, I left my kids in the care of Rose and Monica and left with the men to go into town.

We arrived in Great Falls and found a store. There were no cars on the road. Gas had ran out a long time before we got there. Everyone was on foot or horseback, even bicycles. Max gave me his list and stayed with the horses while the rest of us went into the store.

It was beautiful inside. Christmas decorations were hung everywhere. A large decorated tree was in the center of the store. It was nice to see civility in the cold, new world we were growing accustomed to. We separated, and I shopped by the list and got everything on it. I bought some candy for the stockings. I found each of the kids a small gift. Christmas was definitely going to be different this year. I had always gone all out for the holidays. I would decorate everything visible. I bought so many gifts by Christmas morning you could barely see the tree itself.

I went outside and stayed with the horses, allowing Max to go inside. He wanted to look for something special for Monica and

Dannie. Jacob and Ricky came out laughing and joking. They were obviously proud of their purchases. Raven came out and mounted his horse. I packed my bags in the saddlebags and locked them up. I wasn't taking any chances. The town looked civilized, but you could never tell when some desperate soul would get an itch and try to take your stuff.

"I'm going down here. Y'all go ahead, and I'll catch up," Raven instructed.

I waited for Max. When he returned, we were ready to go. Raven still hadn't returned. It was beginning to get dark. "I tell you what, I'll find Raven and ride back with him. You guys go on, and we'll catch up."

Everyone agreed, and they were on their way. Max helped me mount Hummer. I started down the street but didn't see him anywhere. All I saw were different stores and a bar. I stopped in my tracks. It didn't take much convincing to come to the conclusion that Raven was in the bar. I tied Hummer up outside the bar. An armed security guard was outside, so I felt safe leaving my stuff behind for a few moments.

I smiled to the guard. "Excuse me. I'm going in here to get a friend of mine."

"No one will mess with your stuff, little lady." He gave me a polite nod and tipped his hat.

"Thank you. I won't be long." I entered the bar and found Raven sitting at the bar. I took a seat beside him without saying a word.

The bartender spoke up, "What will you have, miss?"

"Jack Daniel's."

The bartender poured me a jigger of Jack and placed it on a napkin. I smiled at the novelty of the napkin. Here I was, nasty, in dire need of a bath and head washing, and my drink was served on a napkin. I never acknowledged Raven sitting beside me.

"Did it hurt?" Raven asked, turning to face me.

I was confused by his question. "Excuse me, did what hurt?"

"Did it hurt when you fell from heaven, because you must be an angel?" Raven looked at me and grinned with that crooked little smile of his.

I laughed at him. "Does that line ever work?"

"Don't know. First time I ever used it. Ask me again in the morning, and I'll let you know."

I laughed again. "You are so full of it."

The bartender was trying hard not to laugh. He kept drying the same glass while Raven and I talked.

"Tell you what," Raven started, "dance with me and then tell me if you don't want to leave with me."

I looked at him in question. "Did you say a dance?"

"Yeah, a dance, just a dance."

"Just one."

"Just one," he repeated.

I couldn't help but smile. No one in this place knew that Raven and I already knew each other. "All right, cowboy, I'll give you the length of one dance to prove yourself to me."

That was all the encouragement Raven needed. He spun around and took me by the hand, leading me out to the dance floor. A slow country song, of course, began to play. Secretly, it was fine with me. It gave me an excuse to be close to Raven and allow him to hold me securely in his big muscular arms. He was careful of my bad arm. We swayed back and forth. It was obvious that neither of us were much of the dancing type.

I laid my head on his chest momentarily. Pulling back just as quickly, I looked at him. "I have a question for you. Why did you freak out and run away the night I asked you to help me with my bandage? You had already seen me naked twice. What was the big deal with me taking off my shirt?"

Raven snickered. "Well, the first time I saw you naked, you took me completely off guard. I never expected you to do that. I expected you to yell and scream until someone else came around. The second time, when you fell off the exam table there at the compound, you were…" He stopped, looking in his mental vocabulary for the right word. "Vulnerable. You weren't in a condition for any horseplay. And then that night you asked me for help, you weren't so vulnerable. I wasn't about to do anything that you weren't ready for, and I didn't think I could be around you that way and not make a move. So I removed myself from the situation before I ruined everything with you."

I nodded. "You had respect for me?"

"Yeah, I suppose I did, or do," Raven breathed deeply and stated proudly, holding his head a little higher.

I laid my head back down on his chest and concentrated on his heartbeat. I think we stopped dancing before the song was over, but neither of us noticed. When the song ended, I looked up into his crystal eyes. God, I loved those eyes.

"Do you think you will ever be ready for me to make that move?" Raven asked me, concerned.

"Perhaps one day." I playfully punched him in the arm. "Just not today." I smiled at him and made my way back to the bar. I finished my jigger and paid the bartender. Raven wasn't far behind.

"You ready?" he asked, smiling, as he readjusted his hat.

I laughed and spun around. "Yes, I'm ready. Take me home, cowboy." I slid free from the barstool and headed to the door.

The bartender dropped the glass he had been drying. It crashed to the floor into a million tiny pieces as his eyes darted back and forth between Raven and me. Raven began laughing, then spoke quietly to the bartender, "Looks like that line works after all." Raven tipped his hat to the bartender and smiled childishly.

We rode back to the base and found our family with ease. They had a large fire going, and several other people had joined them. They were all recounting their stories and where they had come from and so on. I looked around and noticed Harley and Ricky alone by the wagon. I could tell Harley had been crying. This was going to be hard on her.

"You want me to break them up?" Raven said as he walked up behind me, placing one hand on my waist.

"No, leave them alone. Let them have this night. This is going to be hard enough on her without me making it any worse. Just help me keep an eye on them."

Raven laughed and pulled me back toward the campfire. After about an hour, people started departing to their own tents, leaving just our family.

Ricky nodded to Jacob, stood up, and knelt down on one knee in front of Harley. I felt Raven's hand on my back. Ricky took out a small box and opened it in front of Harley. Her little mouth gaped open. I looked to Max and Monica, whose mouths hung open as well. My eyes landed back on Harley and Ricky as I slowly rose to my feet. Raven was there with his hand on me, ready to pull me back. "Easy, Mama. Remember what you said? Let them have this night."

"Now I want to say this quickly since I know your mama is watching right now, and I don't want to give her a heart attack. This isn't an engagement ring." He peered over his shoulder at me and smiled.

I sat back down. "Thank you, Ricky. You're back on Santa's nice list." We all laughed briefly, then grew silent, allowing the kids to have their moment.

Ricky started again, "This is, however, a promise ring." Ricky took out the ring and dropped the box. He placed the shiny circular piece of metal around my daughter's finger. "I have already talked it over with my dad. As soon as I'm able, I will come find you at the reservation. We will be together. Harley, you are the sweetest, most honest person I have ever met. From the first time I laid eyes on you, I knew you were something special. I have treasured every moment with you from the start, and I will treasure every moment of the future. And if you accept my promise, I will come back and find you, and we will make a life together. As Lou said, everything happens for a reason. We found each other when the time was right, and it was for a reason. Please accept this ring as a token of my promise to you and as a token of my love for you."

It was the sweetest thing I had ever seen. This young boy loved my daughter so much that he was willing to leave his family and come back to live with us.

Harley looked at me with tears in her eyes. "Mama?"

I laughed. "Don't look at me, baby. This is your choice. Do you want him coming back for you or not?"

"Yes!" Harley uttered and nodded.

"Then accept that boy's promise. Don't leave him hanging." A single tear escaped my eye as Harley accepted Ricky's promise. He pulled her up, and they kissed in front of us without a care in the world. Everyone clapped and cheered for them.

Harley was all smiles and tears. She made her way over to me and showed me her ring. "He loves me, Mama!"

"Yes, baby, I believe he does." I hugged her tightly.

Harley nodded. "Can I stay up awhile tonight, Mama?"

"That will be fine, Harley. Just make good choices."

Harley looked at me, confused. "What do you mean?"

Bless her heart. Harley was the type who had to have things spelled out for her at times. She didn't understand subtlety well.

Ricky came up behind her and wrapped his arms around her. "She's trying to tell you not to have sex and get knocked up tonight."

"Oh." Harley blushed and hung her head down.

"Thank you, Ricky. Yes, that's exactly what I meant." I couldn't help but smile.

"Don't worry, Ms. Ashley. I ain't ready to be no daddy just yet. I just want to enjoy what time we have left together." Ricky smiled and stuck out his hand.

I shook his hand sweetly. "You just stay in that frame of mind, and we will get along just fine."

"You got it." Ricky flashed me a smile, and the two went back and sat quietly by the fire.

Raven put his arm around me and laid his chin on my shoulder. "You handled that pretty well."

"Well, it's only a promise ring. They aren't engaged, and she's not pregnant, so I'm fine with a promise being made."

"Really?"

"Yeah, why?" I turned to look at him. Even for Raven, he was acting funny.

"Because today while we were in town, I got this for you." Raven held up a silver necklace. A pale-yellow pendant hung from it. "It's called citrine. It's November's birthstone, Nyte's birthstone."

I looked at him in question. "And why did you get it for me?"

"Citrine is a form of quartz. Giving someone a gift of citrine is symbolic of hope and strength." He looked at me with those eyes. He went around behind me and placed the necklace around my neck. I noticed Max and Monica watching us but trying to pretend they weren't. "I got this for you for three reasons. One, because it's our daughter's birthstone; two, we can all use a little extra hope and strength; and three, because I'm making a promise to you as well."

I looked at him, wanting only to throw myself at him. I did well to hold my composure. "And what might that be?"

"Ashley Reese"—Raven put the necklace around my neck and closed the clasp—"I promise that you can count on me. I will be there for you when times are hard and tough. I will be there to help lift you up and remind you of everything good in the world. I will be there when times are happy and easy, and with your permission, I'll enjoy them by your side. I promise to be there for our daughter and for your daughters as well. Will you accept my promise?"

"What are we, teenagers?" I tried to laugh off my embarrassment.

"I feel like one when I'm with you." Raven looked at me intently. His eyes danced in the pale moonlight. "Do you accept my promise?" he repeated.

I looked at the necklace hanging around my neck. I knew Raven was going to be someone I could count on. I honestly couldn't imagine my life without him. And we were sharing a daughter. I hoped he would stay around to make sure she grew up with a father. I looked up at him directly in his eyes. "I don't want to send you the wrong signals, Raven. I do accept your promise only because of Nyte. I want you to be a part of her life always. I want you to be a part of our lives. I'm just not certain about anything else at this point in my life, and since you are such a good, honest, sincere man, I know you can understand why."

"I will take that as a positive thing." He wrapped his arms around me and hugged me tightly. "I just don't want you to send me away."

Reaching my own arms around him for the first time, I embraced Raven as tenderly as I could. I kissed the side of his neck. "Thank you, Raven."

He pulled me back and looked at me. "For what?"

"For just being yourself, for being here with us"—I held up the citrine pendant—"and for being the hope and strength that keeps me going."

"I can't think of anywhere else I would rather be."

I just smiled, and then we joined the rest of the family by the fire. One by one, we retired. I tucked Kat in and did our bedtime routine. She finished with her sign language for "I love you," and I went to my tent. I changed and fed Nyte and bedded her down. Raven joined us and fell asleep almost immediately. We weren't afraid of thieves in the night since it was a military base and the small population of the camp. Harley and Ricky had stayed up most of the night and kept the fire going strong. I watched their silhouettes against the tent. I was nervous about leaving her up unsupervised, but she was almost sixteen. I had to trust her at some point. Ricky seemed to have a good head on his shoulders. I had to have faith in him as well. I fell into a peaceful sleep.

Come morning, we ate and packed up our camp. Raven had spent the greater part of the morning talking with the soldiers. When we were ready, we gathered back around the fire at his request. He walked to us with the soldier at his side. "I asked this young man to come over and talk with us. His name is Sgt. William Andrews. He has some information I think you would all like to hear." Raven nodded to the sergeant.

Sergeant Andrews stood with his hands locked behind his back. "Thank you. I'm under the impression that you may have gotten some bad information. I can tell you what we have been told. The destruction of the comets was horrible, don't get me wrong. However, the information that we have received doesn't say that the country isn't in three parts. California had a large amount of destruction. A portion did separate from the mainland, making the greater part of Los Angeles pretty much an island. The true number of dead and missing may never been known. A lot of our troops are there helping sort things out and establish some working order. To our knowledge, there is not a second separation like you were told. There is a new canyon a lot similar to the Grand Canyon. It covers a great deal of Arkansas, the eastern part of Missouri, as well as Western Kentucky.

The Mississippi River expanded by more than fifty miles across. It swallowed everything in its path, and there remains extensive flooding in the areas along the river.

"Not only did we have the damage from the initial impact of the asteroids but it also did trigger earthquakes, as I'm sure you have felt. Some of these quakes went over a 10 on the Richter scale. New York, Philadelphia, Houston, the Dallas / Fort Worth area, Savannah, Chicago—all the major cities are in ruins. Florida and most of Louisiana and Texas around the coast are underwater. In some places, the ground level rose by more than twenty feet, while in others, it sank more than thirty. We have new canyons and valleys and new wetlands. The Hoover Dam is still being monitored. The areas below the dam have been evacuated. They are trying to save it. If it breaks…" He stopped and paused. "Well, that'll be a whole new level of catastrophe for us to deal with. Volcanoes all over the United States are venting. There simply aren't enough troops to be everywhere at once. They are advising people to leave now while there is time.

"Most of the oil refineries are still underwater, so don't count on getting gasoline anytime soon. The government has seized it and is using it for military operations only. The president has spoken on the radio. I heard him myself. They are first working on getting communications working. That has been our hardest thing to deal with. There are no cell phones at all. Some landlines work, but they are few and far between. It's the old-fashioned phones that will still work. There is no electricity anywhere. If you have satellite internet, you're lucky, but with no electricity and no gasoline for generators, the common man is out of luck on that one too. The next order of business is to work on public services. Hospitals and emergency services are strained. They are using cruise ships as hospitals near the shore. A couple of other countries have made airdrops of supplies, which have been a great help. I'm not sure what else I can tell you. You seem to have done well for yourselves. You're lucky. Don't give up. You will make it to where you're headed."

Raven shook the soldier's hand and turned back to us. "I just thought you may want to hear it from a good source."

Jacob slapped his knee as dust floated up in the air. "Damn good to hear it, Raven. That's the best news we have heard yet."

Spirits were a little lighter now. There were smiles and laughter being passed around.

"I have something to say if I could have a moment of everyone's time," Rose spoke up. She motioned to Jacob, who retrieved a small box out of the wagon. "I was scared to death when we started out, but when we met you and joined your group, well, it was like a breath of fresh air. I didn't worry so much, and I made friends that I hope will last a lifetime." Rose smiled to Monica. "I have something for Monica." Rose removed a card from the box. "Now I know I showed you a few times, but I wrote down the recipe for my corn bread, and I'm giving it to you. Now you can continue to cook it for your family."

"Thank you, Rose. I will treasure it always," Monica said as she hugged Rose tightly.

"Now," Rose clapped her hands and continued, "Raven, Ashley, Harley, Marcus, Max, these are for you." Rose dragged out knitted scarves and gloves. We spent just a moment matching the colors. She presented Dannie, Kat, and Nyte a crocheted blanket. We all hugged Rose and thanked her accordingly.

Raven spoke up next, "Well, since we're in a mushy mood, I have something I would like to give to your family, Jacob." Raven produced a compass. "Fate allowed us to find each other the first time, but I don't want to rely on fate to bring us together again. I want you to have Lou's compass, and I want you to use it *when* and *if* you decide to find us again."

Jacob stepped forward and took the compass. "I can't take this from you, Raven. It's too special."

"No, Jacob, it's just a hunk of metal. However, if you use it to find your way back to us, then it will be something special." Raven smiled at Jacob, and the two hugged a brief man hug, then finished with patting each other on the back.

"Well, I figured we will ride with you till our cutoff, then go our separate ways," Jacob stated as he rejoined his family and placed his arm around Rose.

No one, including myself, wanted to see Jacob and his family drive away. They had been a major part of this journey, and I desperately hated to see them leave. I felt like we were losing a part of the family.

We made it to the cutoff faster than I thought any of us expected to. Harley was already crying.

I rode up to Jacob's wagon. "I will be thinking of you guys. Take care of each other, and I hope to see you soon."

"I hope all goes well for you, Ms. Ashley. I hope you find everything you're looking for," Rose stated as she patted my hand.

I smiled sweetly to her and looked around. "Rose, I have everything I need with me already."

"Take care of that baby. I want to see her walking next time I see you!" Rose shouted as Jacob started pulling away.

I waved frantically as if it would make them go slower. I noticed Harley had dismounted her horse and was standing with Ricky at the crossroads. I rode on to give them their last few moments of privacy. Catching up with Raven, I had at least one tear in my eye. It dried in the frigid air quickly before he could see.

"We are going to have one depressed little girl tonight," Raven stated, motioning toward Harley.

"Yes, we are, but she will be okay." I glanced back toward Harley. Ricky had helped her mount her horse.

"If she is anything like her mama, she will be." Raven smiled at me with that crooked grin.

Ricky kissed my daughter for the last time and slapped the horse, making it drive forward. She waved continuously, shouting "I love you" several times.

I waited for Harley and rode beside her. She cried quietly for a while.

"It'll be fine, Harley, I promise. Ricky is young, but I expect him to be a man of his word."

She was quiet for a while, then finally spoke, "Mama, do you love Raven?"

Her comment stopped me in my tracks. "What?"

"Do you love Raven?"

I wasn't sure where it was coming from. I wanted her to feel like she could talk to me, so I felt it was important to keep her talking. "I'm not sure, Harley. I haven't given up hope on Dallas yet. Raven is definitely a part of our lives now, and I don't want him to leave." I looked at my daughter. "Why are you asking all these questions?"

Harley shrugged her shoulders. "I don't know. I guess I just wanted to make sure you were happy. If you want to be with Raven, I just wanted you to know that I was okay with it. He's a good guy, Mama."

I snickered. "Yeah. He's turned out to be a pretty good guy. And I appreciate you letting me know that, Harley. I am happy, and I think I'm pretty lucky."

"Even though you got shot?" Harley questioned.

"Yes, even though I got shot, I still consider myself lucky." I rubbed my sore arm. It was healing but remained stiff. However, the cold temperatures weren't helping the mobility, and even though Raven protested, I was using it more every day. At least I had the ability to hold Nyte with both arms again. I was able to hug my daughters without withering in pain. As long as I kept it clean and free from infection, it would be fine. I looked at my daughter, who was still visibly upset but had stopped crying, at least for the moment. "Are you going to be okay?"

"Yeah, I'll be fine. Ricky told me whenever I got to missing him, just look at my ring and remember his promise." She smiled thoughtfully as she gazed down at her promise ring. "I have a question for Raven."

Harley quickly rode ahead and caught up to Raven. I had no idea what she was asking, but I wanted to give her some space. She needed time to herself. I tried to keep my mountains in my field of vision.

Raven's laughter snapped my attention back to reality. He stopped the wagon Marcus was driving, and they talked for a few minutes. Marcus jumped down and retrieved his horse that was following the wagon. Harley dismounted and joined Raven in the driver's seat of the wagon. Marcus collected their horses and tied them up behind the wagon. I quickly rode forward to find out what was going on.

"Harley?" I called out in question.

"Mama, I'm going to learn how to drive the wagon. I can relieve Marcus. Now that Lou is gone, we need an extra driver. You may not like it, but I'm going to do it," Harley stated with determination and security.

I looked at Raven, who was staring at me, glowering. "She's your daughter."

I shook my head and rolled my eyes. "Fine, just be careful." I dropped back and rode beside Marcus.

We rode in silence for a while. Then it was Marcus who broke the silence. "Ashley, do you think my dad is still alive?"

He also took me by surprise. I guess this solemn day of good-byes had stirred up many lingering emotions and questions. I had known this conversation was going to happen sooner or later. "I don't know, Marcus. I hope so."

"Don't you think he would have caught up to us by now?"

"That all depends. We don't know what he was facing. He could've been hurt and had to get better before heading this way. There are just too many what-ifs in the picture."

"How long are you going to wait for him before you move on?" Marcus asked.

I didn't have to look up to know that his eyes were on me. I knew he was talking about Raven and our growing relationship together. "I'm not sure. I think instead of me putting a time limit on it, I should let the time choose me. If it's meant to be, it will just happen." I looked at him. For as long as I had known Marcus, he had never been so young and vulnerable. "I'm only sure of one thing. You're not my son, and I'm not your mother, but I love you like a son, and I'm glad you're with us. I don't want you being upset if things"—I paused in attempt to find the right word to describe whatever it was happening between Raven and myself—"develop between Raven and I or anyone else. It doesn't mean I didn't love your dad. Do you understand what I'm saying, or am I just rambling?"

"I understand." Marcus nodded. "And even though it's hard, I'm glad that I'm here with you too." He was quiet for a few moments. "It's the not knowing that's the hard part."

I only nodded. "I know exactly what you mean, Marcus."

The rest of the day was quiet. The sky was beginning to turn dark when we pulled over to a roadside park somewhere north of Conrad, Montana. According to the map, we had less than sixty miles until we reached Browning. We were almost there, and I wanted to push forward, but I had to consider the rest of my family.

We made camp and got a fire going. We had split the leftover venison with Jacob's family. Monica made a hearty pot of stew out of it. She had it ready by the time we had camp set up. Even though I was grateful to Monica for doing all the cooking, I had to admit that I was getting tired of stews and soups. It was always good, and I knew that I couldn't have done any better. She was doing the best she could with what she had. It couldn't be easy to plan and make a meal big enough to feed all of us with what supplies we had, but Monica always found a way. But when we finally got settled, I hoped I could find a way to cook something other than a damn soup. We sat around for a short time and listened to music and ate. It seemed a lot lonelier without Rose and Jacob igniting stimulating conversations. We all agreed that Nyte and I would stay in the wagon with Marcus. Max, Raven, and I would still take turns standing watch. Marcus and Harley were going to take turns driving the wagon during the day. With a little luck, we would make it to Browning by the following night.

Nyte fell asleep in my arms. I reluctantly handed her off to Raven so I would take first watch, Raven would take the second, and Max would take the last watch. The night went by pretty fast. The wind had begun to blow, and it was lightly snowing again. I finished my watch, fed and changed Nyte, and put her back to sleep. I sighed as I bedded down warmly in the wagon. I had to admit, it was a nice change from the cold ground in a drafty tent. Raven kissed his daughter good night and turned to head out when I called out to him, "The wind is picking up. Make sure you bundle up."

"Yes, ma'am." He adjusted his jacket and quickly went out the door, shutting it securely behind him.

Marcus peered over the loft and looked down at me. "I suppose he really is a good guy. I didn't like him at first."

I laughed. "I didn't either, Marcus." I exhaled deeply and bundled Nyte tightly. "But he does grow on you."

"Yeah, just like a fungus," Marcus added as he rolled back over.

I could tell that he hadn't completely warmed up to the idea of Raven and I being together, but in his own small way, Marcus was letting me know that he wasn't totally ruling out the idea. It wasn't long before I heard Marcus's breathing relax and deepen. I knew he was asleep. I looked down at Nyte, her little supple lips suckling as she slept. I heard the distinct distant sounds of Raven chopping wood. He had been using his time at night to chop wood to keep the fire going strong. Whatever was left, he gave to Monica to use to cook with and keep the wagon warm for her and the little ones. I slowly drifted off into a slumber.

I felt like I had just closed my eyes when Raven woke me up. "It's time to rise and shine, sunshine."

I opened my eyes as he shook my boot. I flashed him a look of detestation. I hated the nickname he had obviously chosen for me; however, it was better than calling me Ash, which was a constant reminder of Dallas. It didn't bother me to be reminded of him. I thought about him a lot actually, a lot more than I wanted to admit. Marcus was correct; it was the not knowing that was the worst part. If I just knew without a doubt that he was alive, then I would be fine. It was the uncertainty that drove me crazy. Was he alive? Was he dead? If he was, had his body been found, or was he still covered up with some sort of debris? I shook the thoughts out of my head. I couldn't afford to dwell on things. I didn't mind the reminders, but I couldn't dawdle on them for too long, or it would drive me insane.

I forced myself up and got ready to start a new day. Today was the day we would make it. I felt so strongly about it. It was going to be a long day, and I was going to have to push my family hard, but we were going to make it. We just had to.

I fed and burped Nyte. She soon fell right back to sleep. I tucked her in my bed and went to join my family by the fire. Monica handed out breakfast. I took it, expressing my gratitude. I looked down into the bowl—oatmeal. My nose wrinkled as I swallowed hard. Oatmeal, soups, and stews—three things I would never eat again if I could help it. I noticed Kat looking up at me. She knew I didn't like oatmeal any more than she did. Taking a big bite of the nasty shit, I made a face at her. She smiled and continued to eat her own bowl. I was showing her I would suck it up and eat it even though I didn't like it. She followed my lead and ate her whole bowl.

Harley did the dishes and got ready to drive the wagon. Raven showed her a few things and gave her reminders while I helped Max and Monica get things packed up. I was attempting to get my saddle on Hummer when Raven found me and finished the job. He looked at me with scolding eyes for lifting it.

"We got a storm coming. It's going to be a bad one too."

I could see the concern in his eyes. I looked up at the sky. The clouds were rolling angrily. "How bad exactly?" I asked.

"Lots of snow, wind, possibly blizzard conditions, I'm not sure." He looked at me. "I can't help but think that we should stay here another day at least."

"No, no, no!" I demanded. "We are so close. If we just push forward, we can make it. If it gets too hard, we can stop, but we have to keep going while we can."

A smile escaped the corner of his mouth. "Okay then, we move on. Are you sure you can handle it?"

"Yes, I'm sure."

"Then take these." Raven handed me a pair of sunglasses.

"What the hell are these for? Is there a beach down the road I don't know about?"

Raven laughed. "They are for the snow, smart-ass. Have you ever heard of snow blindness?"

I hadn't heard about it. In fact, I had no idea what he was talking about. "I'm from Texas, Raven. We hardly ever have snow."

"It happens when you stare at the snow for too long. Usually, when the sun shines on the snow, it reflects back. If you stare at it for too long, your eyes burn like fire and you can't open them. It's very painful, and I don't want to take any chances. We have been through enough for something else to go wrong." Raven patted Hummer and walked away.

"I'm really beginning to hate Mother Nature." I tucked the sunglasses into my jacket, noticing Raven giving a pair to Max and Harley as well. I had no idea where he got them, nor did I care. He was again stepping up and looking out for our best interest. He was being my great protector in flannel once more.

CHAPTER 13

WE GOT ON the road and started out on what I hoped would be our last day of traveling. Max strapped the radio to the wagon, and music busted from it, helping to break the monotony. He played one song after another till the batteries got weak. It was at that time that I detected the snow falling harder and faster as the wind kicked up. I put on the idiotic sunglasses Raven had given me and saw him nodding in approval toward me. He turned and stayed a little ahead of Harley so he could direct her.

Harley was doing a good job at driving the wagon. Even in the deep snow, she was holding her own. She had really matured over the last few months. I hardly recognized her. I pictured her in my mind the way she was before all this started, spending the greater part of an hour every morning applying her makeup. Concentrating on her eyes, she would apply black eyeliner with perfection. Harley always wore her hair down, with long wavy blond curls crawling down her back. As a perfectly normal teenage girl, she was always on a great search for her next miniskirt or black leather boots. She would spend the greater part of Saturdays at the mall with her friends shopping and complaining that she only got a measly fifty-dollar allowance. She was so consumed with friends, boys, cell phones, MP3 players, and the material things in life. She had her daily routine of school, followed by volleyball practice and dance classes in hopes of making the drill team next year. She led a typical teen life full of promise and hope. I looked at her now sitting in the driver's seat of a wagon dressed in thermal underwear, flannel, and a thick coat, sporting a cowboy hat. She also had the biggest smile on her face; she looked like she had never been happier.

My poor Kat, however, had been a vivacious little girl. She was smart and got excellent grades. Even though she was in a new school, she had no problems fitting in, and her teachers loved her. She always had something to talk about; it seemed that I could never shut her up. At the time of the disaster, she had almost memorized every world record that had ever been recorded and took great pleasure in telling me every single one. I remember growing so tired of hearing all those worthless facts. Now I would give anything just to hear her speak.

I don't know how long I was lost in my thoughts when the piercing wind ripped through me. The sky was darkening quickly. The clouds that were visible seemed to be rolling with anger.

Raven rode back to me. "Maybe we need to stop for the night. This looks like it's going to get bad."

"No! We are almost there. We can make it!" I shouted over the howling wind.

"Sunshine, I don't want—"

"Stop with the sunshine shit! We are this close. Just shut up and keep going!" I shouted, riding ahead, leaving him alone in the snow. I couldn't see any reason we couldn't make it to the reservation as long as we kept going. We just had to be tough. I knocked on the wagon. "Marcus, relieve Harley. She needs a break."

Harley stopped and allowed Marcus to take over. She got into the wagon to warm up, flashing me a look of concern.

"Max, you doing okay?" I looked at my brother with a harsh tone.

"Yeah, I'm fine for now, but—"

"Good, then let's get a move on," I interrupted. I didn't want to give anyone a chance to argue with me. We had to keep moving. I saw Harley handing out blankets to Raven. He passed them out to Marcus, Max, and me and keeping one for himself. I took it with gratitude and lay it over my legs since that seemed to be the coldest part of my body. I rode beside Marcus, allowing Raven to take the lead once more.

The wind was a viscous monster. I let my hair down and wrapped my scarf around my head and neck. I thought the hair would work as little added insulation. However, it did little against the ferocious wind. My eyes were the only thing visible, and they were covered by funky sunglasses. I flipped the collar of my coat up and tucked the blanket under my butt. I patted Hummer, hoping she would get me through this storm. I glanced at the other horses that were struggling against the wagon.

I looked up at Marcus. He, too, had changed so much over the last few months. Before all this started, he had this image that he kept up. I called it gothic. I snickered to myself as I remembered he politely informed me that it wasn't gothic; it was called emo. He never went as far as to hurt himself, but he liked that style of clothing. Almost everything in his wardrobe was black. He didn't own a pair of pants that didn't have buckles or chains on them. He wore tight T-shirts that showed his mini six-pack when he wasn't covering it with a black leather jacket with zippered sleeves and pockets, which was hardly ever. It could be a hundred degrees, and that kid would have that jacket on. All his friends dressed in the same manner, but oddly enough, they were a great bunch of kids. They were all straight A students who held positions in the band or other academic clubs. It was the strangest thing I had ever seen. Marcus himself was an accomplished piano and saxophone player. Now he could add wagon driver to his list of accomplishments.

I fell back to ride beside Max's wagon. I knew Raven would take care of Marcus if he needed help. I wanted someone beside Max. My brother looked at me as I joined his side.

"You okay, sissy?" he asked.

"I'm fine. I'm just not letting us slack off. We are this close. There's no reason why we can't make it. I understand it's cold. Just suck it up and keep moving." I knew I sounded cold and heartless. I never allowed my eyes to meet his.

Max nodded and kept his shaded eyes forward. We had all lost so much. I could still see my beautiful house sitting there. I remembered how I felt when Dallas showed me it for the first time. He had made the girls and I wear a blindfold. He was so happy and thrilled to get it for us. I could see it playing out like a movie in my head as he took the blindfolds off our eyes and told us to look. We stood in front of the house, this grand piece of construction. Everything I had ever wanted in a home sat before me, just waiting. The girls ran excitedly into the house to pick out their rooms as Dallas carried me over the threshold. I remember crying on his shoulder, telling him that it was beautiful and how much I loved it.

Max and Monica had worked so hard on their home too. It was an older home, but still a sturdy one. They had replaced all the floors, had vinyl siding, storm windows and doors installed. Max had put in new cabinets, and after months of Monica begging and voicing multiple requests, he surprised her by putting in a dishwasher. Something so trivial to us now meant so much then. When they found out they were going to have a baby, they were both so excited. They had spent weeks painting a mural on the baby's wall. I threw them a baby shower, and they got almost everything they needed. I was there when Dannie was born. I remember standing there at the nursery glass looking at him. He was Max made over. Max had put his arm around me. I remember telling him, "You're a daddy now." A tear escaped his eyes, and he only nodded. He couldn't take his eyes off his son lying in that plastic basinet, sleeping peacefully.

My parents were also there. They looked at their new grandson with pride. Mama got upset that she couldn't get a decent photograph. I remembered her cussing the glare from the nursery window. She eventually threw a big enough fit that the nurses allowed her to go in long enough to take a good picture. My heart ached when I thought of my parents. I shook the thoughts of them out of my head.

I thought of Raven and how he had acted toward me when we first met at Lou's. He had been intentionally malicious toward me. I thought about how silly I must have looked repeatedly trying to ride that horse of his. His intentions were to run me off. He knew Lou was sick and wanted him to die at home. Lou was too smart for that, though he saw us and his opportunity. I learned a lot from that old man. He was a friend I desperately hated to lose. I just had to see his mountains.

I looked up and noticed I could barely see anything. The wind whipped all around me. Snow swirled, looking like a tornado of white dust. The sky was dark, and I had no idea where we were or how long we had been on the road. I had been so lost in my thoughts that I had lost all track of time. I rode ahead and found Raven. He was drifting off to the side. I quickly rode to him and grabbed his reins.

"Where do you think you are going?" I asked, trying to assess him quickly.

"I think I fell asleep." He looked bad; his face was red and cracked. His eyes were weak and droopy, and his whole body was shaking.

"Okay, we have to stop. Do you think you can help Marcus and pull up over there?"

"There aren't many trees. There won't be any cover."

"We will have to build a fire and keep the horses on the one side of the wagon to block the wind off them. We will do the best we can."

Raven nodded. "You better get your brother. I don't think he's doing so good."

I saw Max's wagon drifting off the road. Max swayed in the driver's seat like a drunk. I quickly got to him. "Max!"

His head perked up. "Huh?"

"You okay?"

Max bobbed his head from side to side. "I can't open my eyes!"

I dismounted Hummer and climbed up on the wagon beside my brother. I easily removed his glasses. I gasped at the sight. His eyelids were red and frozen together. "You were crying?"

"I got to thinking about Mama and Daddy," he stuttered through half-frozen lips.

"I know. Me too. I'm parking the wagon." I directed the horses close to the other wagon and jammed the brake into place. Raven immediately went to work with the horses. I helped Max down and led him to the rear of the wagon.

Monica opened the door. "What happened?" she said in horror.

"His eyes are frozen shut. Lay him down and put a warm rag over his eyes and face, not hot, just warm." She nodded, indicating that she understood, and helped Max into the wagon. I shut the door securely behind me. I got the axe and began cutting on a small tree for firewood. I had to keep the horses warm. We wouldn't get anywhere without them. Raven grabbed another axe and started to help me. I could tell by the way he was swinging that he was getting to the point of exhaustion. I chopped at the tree with aggression. I'd be damned if we came this far to lose a horse, or worse. I finished with the tree I was working on and helped Raven finish his. I didn't know how I was still going. My arm was throbbing with extreme pain. I had to be pushing forward with sheer will. He helped me get the wood closer to the horses.

"Get in the wagon!" I commanded. He looked at me in confusion. "I don't need you getting sick or passing out on me. You won't be of any use. Now get in there and warm up." I knew he must be past exhaustion because he didn't even argue. I got a raging fire going and kept the blankets over the horses, thinking maybe it would help keep them warm. When I felt like I had done everything I could, I went back to Max's wagon and went inside.

"How are we doing?"

Monica was replacing the warm rag. Max was snoring. He, too, was exhausted.

"We are okay. He can open his eyes, and he can see. Are you hungry?"

I hadn't even thought about food until she mentioned it. As soon as I did, my gut growled. "Yeah, if it's okay, I'll just take a small pot and everything and serve it up in our wagon."

Monica looked a little disappointed but gathered everything I needed. I picked up Nyte, and Monica helped me to our wagon with everything. Harley was sitting with her arm around Marcus, trying to help keep him warm. Raven sat quietly with his head leaning back.

"I have food. Harley, if you will help me, we will get these men fed." I laid Nyte down, and being the quite little angel that she was, she never made a whimper.

Marcus and Raven ate quietly and slowly. They cleaned their bowls, and by the time they were finished, they seemed to be revived a little.

Raven looked at his watch. "It's almost four."

"A.m. or p.m.?" Marcus asked. He, too, had lost all sense of time.

"P.m., buddy." Raven smiled. "We did well."

"We didn't make it to the reservation though," I added.

"We're close." He looked at me. "How are the horses?"

"I think they will be fine. I got the fire going and left their blanket on them," I explained.

Raven nodded. "As long as we can keep that fire going, they should be fine."

"I'll take first watch. You try to get a little sleep." I stood up and started putting on my coat. "I'm going to check on Max again and then the horses. I'll wake you up later. Keep Nyte warm."

I quickly left the wagon before giving him a chance to argue. Max was fine and still asleep. I went to Kat and tucked her in. I tenderly kissed her forehead. "I love you, angel. Did you talk today?" She looked at me with a disgruntled face. "Well, it was just another bad day. Tomorrow will be better."

Kat pointed to the side of the wagon. I looked up and noticed that she was pointing to her stocking that Monica had hung up for her. I had been so wrapped up that I hadn't even realized that it was Christmas Eve. I saw the look in my daughter's eyes. She wanted to know if Santa was going to find her. "You know, he won't come till you are, asleep. It works the same way, even out here. He will find you. I will stand out there and flag him down if I have to." I playfully pinched her nose. "You will have something special in that stocking when you wake up, but you must go to sleep first." I tucked her in tightly and kissed her again. "Maybe tomorrow will be a better day, baby."

On my way out, I told Monica to let me know when she was asleep so we could fill the stocking. She agreed, and I left to tend the horses and feed the fire. It was imperative that I kept it going. It wasn't long before Monica found me. I retrieved the Christmas items from our wagon and filled Kat's stocking.

I caught myself nodding off around midnight. The wind was an evil demon, howling all around. If there had been a wolf close, I wouldn't know it till it was right on top of me. I went to the wagon and woke Raven up. He eased Nyte down onto the bed. He was more than eager to stand his watch. He seemed reenergized and willing to take on whatever I had to throw at him.

"Are you okay?" he asked as he took my hand in his.

"Yeah, I'm just disappointed that we didn't make it. I know we could've if it hadn't been for this damn storm."

"We will make it. Have faith." He sweetly kissed my hand, then left me in the wagon. Why couldn't I just tell him how I felt? He was the hardest person to talk to that I had ever met. I filled and placed Harley's and Marcus's stocking at their head. I knew they were older and probably didn't care about a stocking, but I wanted them to get something. Nyte was too little this year, but next year would be fun. It had been a long time since I had one this little to enjoy Christmas with. I took off my coat and snuggled close to her. I fell asleep quickly.

It was Harley who woke me up early by shaking me. "Mama."

"Huh? What is it? What's wrong?"

"Nothing. I just really gotta pee. I had to go last night, but it was just too cold."

I put on my coat and helped her get the bucket ready.

"Mama, do you think we will ever have a real toilet again?" Harley asked.

"Yes, baby, one day we will." I hoped I wasn't lying to her.

She finished and quickly went back inside. "If Nyte wakes up, let me know." I found Raven sitting on the snow by the fire. It looked as if he had carved out an ice chair. "What are you doing?"

He smiled. "It's my throne."

"Your throne? What, are you the king now?"

"Sure, I'm the king of the North American continent. Didn't you know that?" Raven chuckled.

"Now I know all this snow has affected your brain." I laughed as I sat beside him and looked up. He was so beautiful, from his skin tone to his eyes; he was simply just a beautiful person. "Merry Christmas, Raven."

"Merry Christmas, sunshine."

I rolled my eyes as he leaned forward, producing a bottle of Jack Daniel's, and handed it to me.

"I got it when we stopped in Great Falls. I've had it sitting in the snow, so it's nice and chilled."

"Thank you, Raven. Will you share it with me?"

He smiled boyishly. "I thought you would never ask." He opened the bottle and allowed me to take the first drink. I felt that welcoming burn in my throat and instantly began to warm up.

"At least the storm is dying down. What time is it?"

"It's about four in the morning."

We sat quietly for a little while, passing the bottle back and forth. I had a nice buzz going when Raven leaned back on his ice chair.

"Ouch! What is that?" He leaped forward to his feet.

"What, did the snow bite you?" I laughed, trying not to sound stupid.

"Yeah, I guess so." Raven lifted his shirt, exposing a bleeding scratch about two inches long.

"Jesus, Raven, what happened?" I tried to get a closer look at the small puncture wound that was now beginning to seep a thin trail of blood.

"I have no idea!" He began to remove some of the snow. "It's some sort of metal arrowhead or something."

"What?" I questioned. I began dusting off some of the snow to see what he meant. I saw the hunk of protruding metal. It was a dark rusty color, and indeed, it looked like a metal arrowhead. A thought snapped in my brain. All the times I had looked at Browning on the internet, I remembered there was a large metal statue at the entrance to the reservation.

"Oh my god!" I said in a quick breath.

"What?"

"Help me!" I screamed as I began climbing up on the snow, knocking off as much as possible. "I gotta see it. Help me!" I shouted again. I rubbed my gloved hands across the snow until more of the metal was exposed. "This is it!" I quickly looked around at my scant surroundings. Going by what I had seen on the internet, there was a sign with the town name on it somewhere close by. I searched around trying to match some landmark with something I recognized from the internet. "Where is it? Where would it be?" I yelled out in frustration, swinging my arms around.

"What the hell are you talking about?" Raven had stopped uncovering the statue and stood confused and somewhat scared.

I never paid him any attention. I knew the sign was around here. I went to the wagon and grabbed a hammer from the toolbox. I began slashing the hammer through the mounds of snow.

Max heard the commotion and came out of the wagon. He saw me wielding the hammer like a madwoman. "What's going on?" he asked Raven.

"Hell, I don't know. I think she's lost her damn mind. She won't give me a straight answer."

I had to find the sign. It would tell me for sure. I didn't want to think I was seeing a mirage, like someone who had been in the desert for too long. I kept swinging the hammer through the snow mounds, until finally, it hit solid metal. I stopped abruptly and dropped the hammer, my chest heaving against every breath I took. I put my shaking hand up to where the hammer had struck the metal and forcefully pushed the snow off the frozen sign. My eyes widened at the now exposed bright green sign that gloriously read, "Browning one mile." It could have read "Welcome to heaven," and I wouldn't have been more elated.

I began smiling and breathing faster. "We're here," I said in a whisper. "We're here." I got a little louder. "WE'RE HERE!" I shouted, looking back at Raven. I nodded.

Raven threw his hat in the air and let out a true cowboy "YEEHAW!"

I laughed in spite of myself. Being half drunk with Jack Daniel's and half on exhilaration, I stumbled through the snow, falling into Raven's awaiting arms. He hugged me and held me tightly.

Max couldn't help himself. He latched onto me as well. "You did it, sissy. You got us here." He let go and did a little happy dance.

I looked at Raven. I wanted to kiss him right there, but that could wait. "Do you think the horses can make it?"

Raven squeezed my shoulder. "They will or die trying. I'll hitch the team."

"I'll get Harley." I practically skipped to the wagon and opened the door. "Harley, get dressed and ready." She jumped straight up as I called her name. "Do you think you can drive this big bitch one more mile?"

A large smile materialized across her pale face. "Yes, ma'am." She catapulted into a scramble to get her coat and boots on.

"Marcus, keep an eye on Nyte for me, please." Without giving him time to answer, I hurried around the wagon.

Max and Raven busied themselves with hitching up the team. I saddled our horses and began throwing snow on the fire to extinguish it. Within minutes, we were on our way. It was still dark and hard to see without the moonlight, but we knew the general direction to go. The wind was still blowing, but not as bad as before.

Raven and I bundled up and mounted the horses. "Harley, do your best to follow me!" he called out.

Harley nodded as the horses lurched forward. We moved at a snail's pace for a while, and then the road began to clear. It looked as if it had been plowed recently, perhaps as recently as last night. No matter when it was, we were able to travel a little faster.

We pulled into the small town of Browning around six in the morning. The sounds of our wagons rolling, clacking, and clanging seemed to wake up every dog in the county. Before I knew it, there were several dozens of dogs of all sizes following us. They began barking and howling at our presence.

"Why are there some many dogs? Look at them all," Raven said, pointing.

I looked around, and every building seemed to have at least four or five dogs around it. The heavily coated canines were waking up and responding to the others that were barking their heads off. "Back before they had horses, they used dogs to help. They used them to haul and pull things that were too heavy. So now, even years later, they refuse to get rid of the dogs or dispose of them in any way out of respect for their ancestors."

"I bet they have one hell of a Kibbles bill." Raven laughed. "So where is this lodge?"

"I have no idea," I stated, looking around the town.

It was good to see buildings still standing. People's homes and businesses were still in working order. Life here seemed to be unaffected by the catastrophe that was taking place all around them.

"It looks like we're starting to wake people up." I noticed that lights in the buildings lining the streets were coming on. People were beginning to wake up and hear the commotion going on. I knew it was only a matter of time before someone looked out their window and saw our strange wagons.

I didn't have to wait long before someone opened their front door. A slender female figure wrapped in a blanket hollered to someone else in the house.

Raven and I stopped. Harley and Max stopped the wagons too, and we waited. A tall, brawny man entered the doorway and stood beside the woman. They looked at us with interest and intrigue.

I looked at Raven. "I suppose I need to go ask for directions or something." I dismounted and walked toward the man and woman. More doors began to open with people peering out at the spectacle that was happening on their streets. They didn't seem to mind the cold or the wind. Our arriving party seemed more interesting than any cold wind stirring in the air. I tightened up my coat and kept walking. Stopping at their doorstep, the man looked bigger up close, if that were possible. He looked at me with hard eyes of uncertainty.

I wasn't sure what to say. I knew I had to find the lodge. "Excuse me, I'm sorry to wake y'all up this time of the morning. My name is Ashley Reese, and I was wondering if we could get directions to the White Pine Lodge."

I allowed my eyes to meet the large man's. The woman let out a small gasp. The man gave her shoulder a slight squeeze. He looked at me with a different expression. He smiled a smile that seemed more radiant than the sun could ever be. "Ms. Reese, we had just about given up hope. We've been expecting you."

I looked at him. My eyebrows went up, and my breath began to quicken. "You've been expecting me?" I asked in question.

"Yes, we have. I'm Pete Bearclaw, Dallas's cousin. This is my wife, Anna. Please, won't you and your family come in and get warm? I'll have some men take care of your horses, and then we'll get you up to the lodge."

I laughed a little under my breath. "We finally made it," I said in a whisper.

"What's that?" Pete questioned and leaned a little to hear me.

"Nothing. I'll go get my family. You sure it won't be a problem with the horses?"

"Not a problem at all," Pete assured me with a happy smile.

I ran back to Raven, sliding on the icy roads, almost losing my balance. His beefy arms immediately clutched me. "This guy is Dallas's cousin, Pete. He said they will take care of the horses and for us to come in and get warm."

He smiled. "Then this is it. We're here." Raven tenderly squeezed me in his arms.

"We're here." I smiled back.

Pete walked into the middle of the ice-covered street. "It's okay, everyone. This is Ashley Reese. We need a few volunteers to take care of the horses and someone to help me get them up to the lodge." His booming voice grabbed my attention as I snapped my head around to see him.

Everyone started nodding and going back in their homes. A few men came out in heavy jackets. Anna came out and helped Monica and the kids out of the wagon. Pete helped Harley down from the wagon.

We filed into the small house. Anna came in and shut the door quickly. Even though the door had been open, the roaring fire quickly had the place warm and toasty. We stood in the living area. I looked around the cabin. There was a large Christmas tree in the corner decorated with handmade ornaments. Popcorn was strung on strings and draped around it like garland. The mantel was decorated in fresh pine greenery spotted with cranberries. The fire heated the mantel decoration and filled the air with a rich pine aroma.

"Well, you must be half starved. Please take a seat and have something to eat," Anna politely stated.

"Oh, thank you, but we did eat last night," I began.

"Well, that was last night, and I'm sure these little ones wouldn't pass up sausage, eggs, and pancakes." She smiled as she tweaked Kat's chin.

Kat smiled and looked up to me. Her little eyes almost begging.

"I guess we could eat something. I suppose introductions are in order. As I said, I'm Ashley. These are my daughters, Kat and Harley. This is my brother, Max; his wife, Monica; and their son, Dannie. This is my friend Raven and our daughter, Nyte. And this is Marcus." I touched each member of my family proudly as I called their name.

"Marcus, the last time I saw you, you were only knee-high to a grasshopper." Pete reached forward and grasped Marcus's hand and began shaking it firmly. "Please, everyone take a seat. There's plenty of room." Pete motioned toward the table as Anna began placing big plates of food around it.

My stomach growled at the rich aroma. It had been so long since any of us had a full breakfast like this. I could only imagine what we looked like standing before Anna and Pete. Our clothes and hair were dirty and tattered. Our faces were dirty, and no one's hair was fixed. However, none of that seemed to matter to them. They seemed happy that we were there and safe. We all took our seats and sat quietly.

Pete looked us over. "You must have had a long journey."

"Yes, sir, long and hard. We made a couple of good friends along the way and lost a few."

Anna put the last platter on the table. "Please help yourselves."

Harley took a platter and began passing it around. Kat placed two pancakes on her plate and stared at it as if it were two round bars of gold. I was grateful for the food, but even I had to admit that I was happy it wasn't oatmeal.

When our plates were full, Pete began, "So I have to ask, where is that cousin of mine?"

I knew the question was coming, although I wasn't totally prepared for it. I hung my head and took a deep breath. "I haven't heard from Dallas since the day this all started."

"Is it bad out there?" Anna questioned, trying to change the subject.

It was Raven who rescued me. "Yes, ma'am, it's bad. But it seemed the further north we got, the better it was."

I looked up and, for the first time, noticed something amazing. I swallowed hard and almost choked. "Can I ask you something?"

Pete looked at me and nodded silently.

"How do you have electricity?" Everyone stopped and looked around. They obviously hadn't noticed it either.

Pete laughed. "Well"—he leaned forward, cupping his hands together over the table—"Browning is a leader in wind power. We have a wastewater system and a power plant that's run on wind power. We only use the electrical system at night. During the day, we just open the curtains."

I only nodded and watched as my family enjoyed their meal. I graciously took Nyte from Raven and began to feed her.

"Can I ask you a question, Ashley?"

"Yes, of course."

"You said that the baby belongs to you and your friend Raven?" Anna inquired.

I smiled. "Yeah, I knew that would raise some eyebrows. To make a long story short, we met Raven in Nebraska. Along the way, we came across a couple in trouble. The wife was in labor. I delivered the baby, and the mother died. The father didn't think he could raise a girl, so he skipped out in the middle of the night, leaving her behind. So basically, I more or less inherited her."

Raven interrupted, "Ashley had an opportunity to give her up back in Rapid City. There was an orphanage there. I pretty much begged her not to. I lost my wife and child a long time ago, and it would have killed me to see her give away this child. I promised her that I would do everything I could for as long as I could to help her with the baby."

Both Anna and Pete nodded in understanding. We were almost done with our meal when we heard a roar coming from outside. Pete slapped the table and stood up. "Sounds like your ride is here."

We headed to the door. My eyes opened wide when I saw our ride.

Pete spoke up, "Have any of you ever driven a snowmobile before?"

"Oh, hell yeah!" Raven had a wicked grin from ear to ear.

"I'm from Texas, Pete. We never have snow," I said, smiling, holding Nyte tightly.

"It's not too different from a four-wheeler. Why don't you ride with Raven? He seems to know what to do with one of these babies. That way, you can hold the little one there."

We paired up and mounted the snowmobiles. Once everyone was secure, the engines roared to life. I smiled at the sound that was almost foreign to me and wrapped one arm securely around Raven's waist. He looked back at me with a flirtatious grin.

"Shut up and don't get any ideas. I have your child back here, so be careful." I couldn't help but smile back at him. Raven gave a slight nod but never lost his smile. The snowmobiles took off, and I held on tighter and tucked my head down behind Raven. The lodge didn't seem to be too far. We were there in no time. We parked the snowmobiles and began to get off. Raven graciously took Nyte from me.

I looked up at the large lodge that stood before us. The sun was struggling to break through the sky, casting an orange and pink glow on the snow-covered roof. I looked around. The lodge consisted of a large main building and then an elongated building with many rooms. It sat on a steep slope. A cliff on the north side revealed an inescapable view of the glacier peaks. Lou's mountains were now in front of me. I inhaled deeply and took it all in. They were more beautiful than I could have imagined.

A short, stocky woman came out onto the porch. "Pete, is that you?"

"Yes, ma'am. I brought you a Christmas gift." Pete put his arm around me and ushered me toward the porch. The woman clutched an old patchwork quilt tightly around her shoulders and watched with wise eyes. "Aunt Greta, this is Ashley Reese. She has faced great hardships and has come a long way to get here."

Greta's shaking hand went directly to her mouth. "Oh my!" she whispered. She began waving her hands, motioning me to come forward.

Stepping up, I stood before her, nervous and not knowing what to say. I had come all this way and never gave much thought as to what I would actually say to Dallas's mother. She placed her hands on either side of my face. "I was beginning to think that you wouldn't make it." In one swift motion, she grabbed me and hugged me tightly.

I wrapped my own arms around the woman. The only words that could describe it was a mother's embrace. It was one of love and relief. I could feel tears welling up in my eyes. I did all I could to fight them back. "I haven't heard from Dallas at all since that day."

"It's okay, honey. It's going to be all right." She forced me back and cupped my face in her hands again. "You're safe now."

"I have imagined the moment of us arriving here and Dallas walking out of the door to greet us." I couldn't help but look toward the door.

"You can look all day, angel, but he's not here. I'm sure wherever he is, he's glad that you're here." The old lady took my hand. "Now you come inside." She motioned to the rest of my family. "Everyone, please come inside. Get warm."

We entered the lodge that was filled with taxidermy bears and other native wildlife. Deer horns lined the walls, giving off a rustic atmosphere. I introduced everyone and explained again about Raven and I sharing the responsibilities of raising Nyte. I was a little concerned about Greta's reaction. She surprised me and seemed to be content with the idea. I was reeling from the excitement of finally arriving at the lodge. Everything was happening so fast. We met Greta's sister Frances, and the two ladies retrieved several keys and showed us to our rooms. Max and Monica, of course, got their own room with Dannie. Harley and Kat shared a room. Marcus got his own room inside the lodge, which turned out to be Dallas's old bedroom when he was a kid. Raven had his own room, and I had mine that I would share with Nyte. I sat on the bed in total peace and quiet for a moment. I wasn't sure how to act with all of us split up. For months, we had all been together without much privacy. The ticking of the clock, the dripping of a leaky faucet, the sounds echoed in the quiet room. I was relieved when Pete and some other men delivered our wagons and put the horses up in the barn.

I hurried outside to escape the deafening silence, leaving Nyte asleep on the bed with a pillow on either side of her. Feeling confident about leaving her for a few minutes, we retrieved our personal belongings from the wagons and began putting them up in our rooms. It felt good to have a little normalcy back. I took the kids' stockings to their room and watched them open them. They all loved their trinkets and candy. Kat still remained silent as she looked around at everything in awe.

"Mom!" Harley yelled from the bathroom. "Come here, hurry!"

I bolted toward the bathroom door. "What is it? What's wrong?" I couldn't imagine what would be so threatening here. For months, I had been on edge and ready to jump at a moment's notice.

"Nothing. Everything is great now." Harley began pointing. "Look, they have an actual shower and a working toilet." She couldn't help herself as she reached down and flushed the toilet, letting out a small sound of relief. "That has to be the most beautiful sound in the world."

I looked intently at her. She had a smile from ear to ear. I couldn't help but laugh. "Can I take a shower and put on some good clothes, Mama?"

"I'm sure Greta would appreciate all of us getting a shower and getting cleaned up before lunch. Go ahead. You stink."

Harley's mouth dropped open, then changed her expression in realization. "Yeah, you're right. I do. But so do you." She pushed me out of the bathroom and shut the door behind me.

"You get a shower and wash your hair when your sister gets out. I'll check back with you in a little while. Kat only nodded. She seemed happy but still wouldn't utter a word.

I went back to my room and found Raven sitting in a chair next to a portable crib. "Where did this come from?"

"Pete brought it in for you." He covered Nyte up and sat quietly for a moment, looking at me. "You know our rooms are joined together, right?"

"No, I hadn't noticed. I must admit, I'm a little relieved."

Raven looked at me a little confused. "Why's that?"

"Well, we have all spent so much time in close quarters I'm not sure how to act with everyone being so scattered now. I like the fact that someone is close by, even if it is you." I kicked his boot and smiled. "Besides, it will be easier for you to help with Nyte if you're close," I said, reminding him of his promise.

"I know exactly what you mean. I'm sitting here and can't help but wonder, What do I do next?"

I sat on the side of the bed for a moment, and like Harley, there was only one thing I wanted to do. "Are you going to sit in here awhile?"

"If it's okay with you, I will. Why?" he asked.

"I'm going to take a shower." I got up and got a set of clothes and disappeared into the bathroom. I had to admit, Harley was right. It was nice to have indoor plumbing again, something so simple that we had taken for granted. I started the shower and watched as steam filled the small room. I stripped and climbed into the shower, taking my time and scrubbing myself. I washed my hair as good as possible, then just stood under the hot water. My shoulder still ached and throbbed. Removing the bandage, I cleaned the wound properly. I would get Monica to apply another bandage soon to keep it covered, but allowing some air to get to it would help the healing process since I was going to be able to stay properly clean now.

I got out of the shower and dried off. The towel felt so soft and smelled fresh. I stood naked in front of the mirror, looking at the reflection of a stranger. I had changed. I had slimmed down and somehow acquired some muscle tone. My one bad arm was still a little scrawny, but my other was defined with strong yet still feminine muscles. Even my breast seemed perkier, and you could actually see the different muscles in my stomach. I turned from side to side, examining my new physique. My body had never been in this shape before. My butt was even firmer. Combing out my wet hair and putting on my clothes, I examined myself one final time and laughed to myself. My pants were too big without thermals on under them. I would definitely have to get more pants. The shirt, I thought, would be okay. I opened the door to the bathroom, the steam flowing into the room. Raven was on his feet in an instant.

"Feel better?" he said, smiling.

"Yes, I do. Thank you. It's your turn. Go get cleaned up."

"Yes, ma'am." He quickly ran into the bathroom and closed the door behind him.

Sitting in the silence hearing nothing but the soft sounds of Nyte breathing, I decided that I had to do something, so I began putting clothes into the dresser. I heard the shower turn off, and Raven came out in a towel. He hadn't bothered to dry off. His body was still glistening with beads of water. I looked at him through bulging eyes. He was gorgeous. My mouth gaped open a little, and he noticed I was staring.

"Is this where I'm supposed to accidentally drop my towel?" He laughed.

"Don't you dare. You just go"—I motioned toward his room— "go get dressed. I'm sure lunch will be ready in a few minutes."

"Lunch can be ready right now if—"

"Raven, go!"

"All right. Goodness, just trying to have a little fun," he whined, trying to act like I had hurt his feelings. It might have worked if he hadn't had a smile on his face the whole time.

"Be good," I told him.

He quickly turned back to me with his hands on the towel, like he was about to rip it off. "Oh, but I am good."

"Go, RAVEN!" I laughed and threw a pillow at him just as he shut the door to his room.

He opened it briefly and stated, "I like pillow fights too." Then he quickly shut the door before I could voice a rebuttal.

"Jackass," I said softly, laughing at his behavior.

I sighed in relief as he returned a few minutes later fully dressed. He was still breathtaking, but it was easier to control myself when he was dressed. "Will you stay with Nyte? I'm going to get Monica to dress my arm, and I'll meet you in the dining room."

"Yeah, how's the arm looking anyway?" he inquired.

"It's okay, a little red in one spot, but otherwise, it's just stiff and sore. Sometimes it throbs, but I will live."

I walked to Monica's room, and she dressed my arm. We then collected the kids and went to the dining room.

The large rustic dining room was buzzing with people who wanted to meet us and hear our stories. There was a large Christmas tree in the center of the room. It was decorated with years of treasured ornaments. I found one ornament that had Dallas's name on it; the date on it was worn and illegible. A roaring fire in the massive stone fireplace filled the room with a warm, welcoming glow. The long dining table was set with beautiful red dishes trimmed in gold, matching napkins sat beside each plate that held a place card with our names indicating where we were to sit, and polished silverware sparkled. It seemed like a dream. Most of the ladies made over Nyte, taking turns holding her and feeding her. Marcus sat and talked with one of his cousins who were about his own age. Max stood beside Monica, holding Dannie on his hip, conversing with someone about Rocky and Lou. Harley looked especially good with her hair fixed and makeup on. I know she had been looking forward to wearing it again. Kat sat quietly across from an old man. They didn't say a word but stared at each other. They could have been having a telepathic conversation or something. Everyone seemed fine and happy. I couldn't help but feel that I had been rendered useless. Everything seemed to be going on around me without me. It all seemed so surreal, and there was nothing for me to do. Greta and Frances had already run me out of the kitchen, and no one needed my help to do anything. I sat quietly with a fake smile and tried to enjoy my foreign surroundings.

Soon, Greta lightly clanked her knife against a glass and got everyone's attention. Frances was by her side in an instant. "Could I have your attention, please?" She paused for a moment. "I just wanted to say welcome to our new friends who have come such a long way. It's a pleasure and an honor to have you here to share this special day. I hope we make you feel welcomed and that we have many more days as special as this one. So I raise my glass to friends and new family." Everyone who held a glass held it up. "Now let's eat."

She looked as if she wanted to cry. I couldn't help but look to the door again. I so much wanted to see Dallas just blow through it and take me in his arms. It would be a perfect ending to the grim fairy tale I had been living. Instead, I just smiled to Greta and thanked her and everyone for their hospitality. We had been met with accepting arms of love. Everyone seemed to understand about the Raven and Nyte situation. I was commended time after time for not giving her away. Raven just stood back proudly watching me. Harley had no problem fitting in with the other teens. They all seemed interested in her. I was sure she had told them all about Ricky and showed off her ring. They seemed to be enthralled about an up-and-coming New Year's Eve talent show powwow.

We soon gathered around the table, and the old man who had been staring at Kat said a prayer in the native tongue. I wasn't able to understand him, but just going by the tone, it was heartfelt and sincere. We all ate till we were rudely stuffed. The kids cleared the table and did the dishes as the adults gathered for dessert and coffee. Raven was never too far away from me. I had great appreciation for that. Even though everyone was nice, they were still strangers. I thought of Jacob and Rose several times throughout the day. I hoped they were warm and safe. They had become an extended part of the family. Perhaps it was just the Christmas spirit, but I missed them so much at the moment and longed for their company. I could only hope and pray that I would get to see them again one day.

It had turned dark outside. Marcus was asleep on the couch, and Kat had fallen asleep beside the old man, her little head resting on his arm. I noticed Harley had grown quiet and looked as if she were about ready to drop. Raven was holding Nyte, who was growing fussy. I went and took her and looked at Raven. "I think it is bedtime. Can you fix a bottle for her? I'll get the others." I woke up Marcus and Kat and told them to go to their rooms; neither of them argued.

Kat nodded and started to walk away, then stopped. She turned to the old man and ran back and hugged him tightly. His arms went around her as well. I wasn't sure what their connection was, but they had definitely made one. I thanked Greta and said good night to everyone. I got Kat tucked in as Harley was changing into actual night clothes. I adjusted their heater and left the room. Raven was waiting for me with a bottle and took Nyte from me. I had planned on feeding her, but if he wanted to, I wasn't going to deny him. Excusing myself, I went to the bathroom and put on a pair of jogging pants and sweatshirt. I thought it would be appropriate bed attire if Raven was going to be coming in and out of my room. I lay on my bed and watched Raven as he fed Nyte and rocked her to sleep. Feeling my body relaxing for the first time in many months, I had the security of knowing my family was safe and that Raven was here if I needed him. I never knew when my eyes shut.

* * * * *

Kat woke up early the next morning, got dressed, and left the room without waking Harley. She walked to her mother's room and peeked in. Seeing Raven asleep in a chair and her mother asleep in the bed, she eased the door closed.

Ms. Greta was in the kitchen cooking breakfast. She wasn't ready to go in just yet, so she took the opportunity to look around her surroundings. She saw a large boulder overlooking a steep cliff. She quietly walked out and sat on the boulder. Sitting and staring at Lou's mountains as the sun struggled to break through, a tear came to her eye, and she thought about Lou. She missed him so much. He always seemed to understand her. She wished he was here to see the sight before her. She was so lost in her thoughts that she didn't notice the old Indian man sitting beside her. She liked him too. They had stared at each other for a long time the night before. It was like without speaking a word, his soul talked to hers. Until this moment, neither of them had actually spoken a word. He reminded her a lot of Lou. Perhaps that was why she felt a connection with him.

It was the old man who broke the silence first. "I have much respect for a child who doesn't make a sound. Much can be said about silence. Sometimes it allows you to see things in a whole new light."

Kat never wavered and kept her eyes forward on the glacier peaks.

The old man continued, "A lot has happened. You have seen and heard things that shouldn't have fallen on a child's eyes or ears.

You handled things as best as you could, I suppose, but your mama is a different story. She feels like she has failed you in some way. She blames herself for your silence."

This statement captured Kat's attention as she turned her little blond head to face the old man. She flashed him a look of concern.

"Oh yes, she blames herself, or at least that's what her soul tells me. Your mama held it together and got her family here safely, but the number of hardships and heartbreak she has faced has taken a toll on her. When I look at her, I see the soul of a shaken, fragile woman on the verge of a breakdown, and I believe you are the only one who can save her. You can let her know it was all worth it. I know it's a lot to put on your shoulders, but after everything your mama has done to get you here, I think you can handle it. The thing about silence is, if you never make a sound, you will never be heard."

Kat nodded. She opened her mouth and, for the first time in many months, spoke. Her words came out quivering but still clear. "Will you help me help my mama?" She smiled at the sound of her own voice. "I know what I want to do, but it will take some planning." Kat exhaled deeply.

The old man smiled, revealing his yellowing teeth. "Little one, I will help you in any way I can. What do you have in mind?"

Kat jumped from the boulder, smiling devilishly, and took the old man's hand in hers. "Can you keep a secret?"

* * * * *

It was dawn when Raven woke me up with a cup of coffee. "Morning, sunshine."

I growled at him, taking the cup of coffee.

He laughed under his breath. "You'd think someone who's slept so long would be in a better mood." He nestled Nyte in his arms.

"It did feel good to sleep the whole night through."

"The whole night, honey. You slept all night, all day, and all night last night," Raven explained.

"What?" I stated with a startled tone of voice. "Why did you let me sleep that long?"

"Because you needed it. Don't go getting your panties in a bunch. Everything has been handled. The kids are fine. Everyone is fine. You needed to sleep. If you weren't physically exhausted, you were mentally. I know this has been hard on you, and I wanted you rested."

I thought for a moment. "Thank you, Raven, for allowing me to sleep. That should've been my response."

Raven nodded. "You're very welcome."

"So where is everyone?" I asked, sipping the coffee.

"Harley and Kat are at the auditorium in town with some of the other kids. They are working on the talent show thing for New Year's Eve. They asked me to sing."

I laughed. "Are you going to?"

"I don't know yet. They want you to sing too. Harley made me promise that I would ask you." He looked at me inquisitively.

My eyes dropped from his as I shook my head. "I don't think so. I'm not much in the singing mood these days."

"They're worried about you."

"Who is?" I asked sharply.

"Everyone," he replied. "Harley, Marcus, Max, and Monica, even Ms. Greta."

"Oh, for shit's sake, I'm fine." I got up from the bed. "I wish everyone would stop walking around me like they are waiting for me to bust into a million pieces." I put my hair back in a ponytail out of habit. "I'm tough, and I'm fine," I stated firmly, placing my hands on my hips.

Raven came over and placed his hands on my shoulders and kissed my forehead. His lips almost seemed to sizzle on my skin. "I know you're tough, but the thing is, you don't have to be anymore." He left me standing in the room alone with Nyte, closing the door behind him.

"Yes, I do," I whispered. I felt tears welling up. An internal storm was brewing, and it was only a matter of time before lightning struck. I had so many confusing feelings swirling around inside like a tornado. I wasn't ready for my emotional vomit to surface; I could deal with it later. I sucked them back and took a deep breath and finished my coffee.

CHAPTER 14

I T WAS MY first real look at the territory, and it was truly breathtaking. Lou was right when he said there was no other place like it on Earth. Feeling that Nyte was safe, I wandered out a little farther to a large boulder resting on a cliff overlooking a glacier peak. The peak itself was covered in a fresh blanket of snow with very little stone showing. It looked like an enormous white pillow among the darkness that shrouded me inside. Below the cliff was a vast forest separating the cliff from the peak. Looking over the edge of the cliff, which was a sharp drop off, I saw nothing below me but rocks and treetops. I heard a piercing screech from above. Jerking my head toward the sky, a bald eagle was gliding above me. It only added to the beauty that surrounded me. I had never felt the power that I felt from this place. This sacred place had stood resilient to the disaster that covered the rest of the United States with panic and dread.

For a long time, I only sat and enjoyed the splendor surrounding me. I liked it here, and my thoughts seemed clear. Eventually, I got pulled back to reality by Harley calling for me.

"Mom," she called.

"I'm here." I inhaled crisp, pure mountain air, breathed out, and went back to being mama. I would definitely have to visit this boulder again. This would be my secret spot, a place I could lose myself, but not far enough away that I would make everyone worry.

Hurrying inside, I listened to Harley ramble about the talent show. She and some of the other teens were going to do a traditional

Indian dance. Excitement radiated from her as she happily bounced from one thing to another. She was happy.

Turning my attention to Kat, I asked, "And what about you? What are you going to do for the talent show? I heard you were helping." Her little face quickly turned to her sister as if asking for help.

"Oh, she's helping painting props and stuff," Harley quickly stated, giving her sister a gentle pat on the back. "And it's a very big help." Kat started nodding quickly in agreement.

"Well, that's good. I'm glad to see you two smiling and happy. Why don't you get ready for dinner?" They hurried off to their room. Nyte was awake but content in her crib.

Raven soon came back and hugged me, smiling. "I got a job."

"You did what?" I bellowed and playfully slapped his arm.

"I got a job. I'm helping feed the buffalo and keeping them rounded up. It's not cattle, but it's close."

"Well, I'm proud of you!" I sat on the bed as he played goo-goo gaga with Nyte. "Raven, are you happy?"

Looking at me quickly, he slowly made his way over to me and kneeled in front of me. "I am as long as I'm with you and this family, no matter where we are. It doesn't matter if we are crammed in a tiny wagon, here, or anywhere else. As long as I'm with you, I'm happy." He lightly kissed my hand. "What about you? Are you happy?"

My answer was hesitant. "Yeah, I'm happy. I'm just feeling a little lost since we got here. There isn't much for me to do or—"

"Go get a job," he interrupted. "There's a hospital in town, and I'm sure they would love to have you. Ms. Greta has said she would help with Nyte."

"I'm not sure that's the answer, Raven."

"Then what is?"

I shook my head. "I'm not sure. Maybe that would make me feel better, like I had a purpose or that I was making a difference."

"Hey"—he took my chin in his fingers and tilted my head up to meet his eyes—"you make a difference every day. And don't you ever think that you don't have a purpose. You have the most important purpose of all."

"Oh yeah? Please enlighten me oh ye of so much knowledge. What's my purpose?" I asked sarcastically.

"Well, someone has to keep me in line." He chuckled and squeezed me in a bear hug. "Don't worry, sunshine. It will get better." He kissed my head. I leaned into him, actually hugging back. It felt so good to hold him and have him hold me. I could hear his heart beating. I closed my eyes and began to sway with the beat his heart was keeping. I pulled back and looked into those crystalline blue eyes. Just as he was leaning down and his lips were within millimeters of mine, there was a knock at the open door.

I jerked my head around to see the old man standing in the doorway. "Time to eat."

"Yes, sir, thank you very much," I said politely as he turned quickly and left. "I'll go get the girls."

Freezing in place, I lowered my head, unable to meet his eyes again, and Raven held on to my hand. "We can finish this later."

"The moment's passed, Raven. It is finished." His hand fell from mine, allowing me to leave him in the room.

"There will be other moments. I'll make sure of it!" he yelled out.

I shook my finger, scolding him, as I crossed in front of the window. He had a grin from ear to ear. I couldn't understand how or why he was so tolerant and patient with me. I couldn't decide if I was lucky or if he was just stupid.

Gathering the rest of the family, we went to the dining room and enjoyed another meal with Dallas's family. I was secretly holding out for the time when we all got a bath and bedded down for the night. I welcomed the sanctity of my little room. It was not that I didn't like Ms. Greta or her everlasting hospitality, but something wasn't right. This wasn't home. I had spent the last few months trying to get here, and now that I was, it didn't feel right. I felt out of place. I was trying desperately to fit into a world I wasn't sure I belonged in.

The next four days were long and boring. The kids were busy preparing for the talent show. Raven went to work with the buffalo every morning. Max had joined him on the job, while Monica came and dressed my shoulder every morning. All signs of infection had disappeared. On the fourth day, I talked her through removing the stitches. Her belly was large and round-looking, as if she could pop at the slightest touch. She admitted having false labor pains but assured me she would notify someone in plenty of time to get her to the hospital. Max had taken her into town and saw a doctor. He said she could deliver at any time. This surprised Monica because she had it figured that she wasn't due till sometime in January.

Taking Raven's advice, I saddled Hummer and rode into town. The hospital was easy enough to find. Reluctantly, I applied for a job. The interviewer consisted of the nursing manager looking over my application and two words, "You're hired."

I left the hospital with a depressing sense of accomplishment. I wanted to wait till the kids were back in school and talk it over with Raven and see what he thought. The nurse manager understood when I said I would get back to her on a start date. On the ride back to the lodge, I couldn't help but think that maybe Raven was right. Maybe this job was what I needed to continue bringing back the normalcy into my life. I found myself riding faster to hurry home to him. That word struck me hard—*home*. This place, even though beautiful, wasn't home, or at least it didn't feel like it. I had lost my home, my hometown, my home state. That word held very little yet so much meaning to me. I found my way back to the lodge without any problems. The town of Browning wasn't very big, so if I had gotten lost, it would just prove that I was an idiot.

Raven was there waiting for me, waving like a big goof with a grin to match. Filling him in on the job, we talked it over and felt the day after school started would be a good day to go back to work. The thought of Kat going to school frightened me considering she still hadn't spoken. Her silence gnawed on my heart like a bad disease. I felt for sure once we were here and got settled that she would come out of it and start speaking.

That night, I sat on Harley's bed watching her going through her clothes, attempting to pick out the perfect outfit for the talent show. "Mama, Raven was supposed to ask you. Will you sing at the show? I just wanted to let you know that it wasn't too late."

"I don't think so, Harley."

"Oh, but, Mama, please, you got to!"

"No, I don't, Harley. Listen, honey, you don't need me to sing. You do your thing, and I will be there watching you." I tried to explain without going into too much detail.

"I don't need you to sing. I want you to sing. I want to see my mama on that stage in all her glory, doing what she does best. I want to see you happy, Mama." Harley looked at me with her pleading eyes.

"Harley, baby, I'm happy. We are here, and we are safe" I pulled her down on the bed beside me. I placed one arm around her and the other around Kat. "I'm happy as long as my girls are happy. You two make me happy. Seeing you enjoy yourselves and seeing you smile, that makes me happy."

Harley got up and looked at me with her hands on her hips. "No offense, Mama, but that's a cop-out. You looked happier when we were on the road than you do now. I think you need to sing. You obviously can't talk about your feelings, so maybe you can sing them. You tuck all your emotions in that shell of a body and won't let anything show. You say you want us happy. Well, maybe we would be happier if you set the example and found happiness yourself."

Pushing herself free of my embrace, Kat stood beside her sister as if in agreement.

"I don't know where this tone and attitude is coming from, Harley, but I don't like it."

"Tough shit," Harley stated bluntly, crossing her arms over her chest. "I call things as I see them. That much I learned from you."

I stood dumbfounded for a moment. Kat nodded in firm agreement as Harley stormed out of the room. Turning to follow her sister, she met the wood of a slamming door. Quickly changing directions, she climbed into bed, pulled her covers over herself, and rolled over without so much as a grunt or growl. She wouldn't even look at me. Feeling beaten, I left the room and pulled the door closed.

Passing my brother's room, I peered in on them. Dannie was sound asleep in one bed, while Monica sat on the edge of the other bed, laughing softly. Max had his hand on Monica's belly, feeling the baby kick. Smiling, I moved on so my presence wouldn't intrude on their private moment.

Moving forward, I was soon standing outside my own window, watching Raven swoon over Nyte. I couldn't, for the life of me, understand how everyone else could be so happy while I was so miserable. What was wrong with me? I was going to have to do better at faking it. I couldn't bring down the rest of my family. I didn't want them spending their time worrying about me or my state of mind. I entered my room smiling my fake smile. Raven greeted me with a hug, which I welcomed. In that moment, I realized when I was around him, my smile was actually genuine. We sat and talked for a little while before I nodded off. I awoke in the middle of the night and found Raven asleep in the chair beside Nyte's crib. I shook my head at him. I knew he wasn't going to leave unless I told him to, and I could see no reason he should have to. She was his daughter too. I got up and tapped him on the shoulder. He jumped at my touch. I pressed my finger to my lips. "Shh, come to bed. You can't sleep in this chair forever." I climbed back into bed and patted the empty spot beside me.

"Are you sure?" he asked.

"Keep your clothes on and keep your hands to yourself. In other words, behave."

"Yes, ma'am," he said, sliding in bed beside me.

I wasn't sure how I would feel once he was there lying next to me. I found myself inching close to the edge to give him plenty of room. I knew we were both fully clothed, and he said he would behave, but it was me I was worried about. I put the thoughts of him beside me out of my mind and soon drifted off to sleep.

As usual, he was up before I was the next morning. I found him feeding Nyte. There was cup of hot coffee on my bedside table waiting for me.

"Morning, sunshine. Guess who slept all night long and woke up starving?"

"She did sleep all night. Wow," I stated, taking a sip of the coffee that was kindly left for me.

"You want to take over? I'm going to work and then into town to help out with final details for the talent show tonight."

I held my arms up, ready to receive Nyte. "That's right. It's tonight, isn't it?"

"Yep. Have you decided what you're going to sing?" he asked.

"I'm not singing, Raven," I vowed firmly, taking Nyte.

"I hate to hear that." He rubbed his chin. "I know two little girls who are really counting on it."

"I know. Harley and I had a minor confrontation about it last night," I stated, remembering Harley's hurtful words the night before.

"Really? What did she say?"

I shook my head. "It doesn't even matter. I'm not singing. I want to go and watch the show like any other spectator without being the spectacle. I know my kids think I can sing, but I'm just not comfortable with it."

Raven leaned down and kissed my head. "You sing very well, and if you don't want to, that's fine. No one is going to pressure you into it. I think since you sang at home and you sang on the road with me, it would give them some normalcy if you sing for them here. I think they're reaching out to you. They want you to show them that everything is okay with you, with them being here, the whole shebang."

I nodded in understanding. "But no pressure."

"No pressure. If you can't give them the reassurance they need through a song, then I'm sure you'll find another way." He walked to the door. "Thanks for allowing me in the bed last night. I slept really well. It was almost like I was supposed to be there." He left and shut the door quickly behind him.

Looking down at Nyte, who was greedily finishing her bottle, I spoke to her, "But no pressure."

After the feeding, burping, and changing routine, I took a shower. Harley came in gruffly to inform me that she and Kat were riding to the auditorium with Ms. Frances and that they would see me tonight. She left abruptly, closing the door behind her in the same manner. I understood I had hurt her deeply, or at least she felt like I let her down. Was it selfish of me not to sing? Should I do it even if my heart wasn't in it? I felt everything spinning out of control. Now even my kids hated me.

I lay back down on the bed. Reaching over, I pulled Raven's pillow closer. His scent was still captured within the tiny fibers. I inhaled deeply, taking in his essence. I wished I could just scream what I was feeling. I wished I could put into words the confusion, pain, anger, and resentment that was being mashed into the relief, friendship, affection, admiration, and love. My mind snapped at the word *love. No, I can't love him. It's just not right. But why isn't it? Why can't I love him? We are sharing a child. He obviously cares for me.* My thoughts ran wild as I fell asleep.

I awoke and checked on Nyte, who was awake and keeping herself occupied and content. The talent show was in just a few hours. Laying out my clothes, I looked at my wardrobe in disgust, wishing I had something decent to wear. I wanted to look good when I showed up to support my daughters, and I wanted to look nice for Raven. I fed Nyte again, burped and changed her, and laid her back down. I went to the main kitchen and refilled my cup of coffee, then sat on the porch, enjoying the serenity that only the mountains offered me. I could think clearly out here. There seemed to be more room outside under the huge open sky for me and all my rambling thoughts. It was those same thoughts that kept me so enthralled that I didn't hear the old man sit on the porch beside me.

"To answer your question, the answer is yes, you can," he stated bluntly out of the blue.

I looked over at him. "Excuse me, what did you say?"

"The answer is yes, you can love more than one person. You can't be unfaithful to a memory. I'm sure Dallas would want you to be happy in this life as well as the next. Wouldn't you want the same thing for him?"

My thoughts swam. "Who the hell are you, old man? And why do you continuously pop up out of nowhere? Are you a mind reader or some old native soul-searcher?" I got up from the porch swing with a slight furious tone in my movements. "Are you going to have me smoke a peace pipe and go on some spirit journey next? No, thank you. I've had all the journeys I can handle for this lifetime. I'm home here with my family, and we are here to stay."

I stopped in my tracks. The old man looked at me with a knowing smile as I began to ramble sporadically.

"I'm home…my family…Raven is a part of my family… unfaithful to a memory." My breath quickened, and my hands began shaking. That internal storm that had been brewing for so long was about to break loose. The tears began to well in my eyes, and I knew this time, there was no force on earth that would hold them back. My coffee sloshed out of the cup, burning my hand. I dropped the cup and watched it fall to the porch with a crash. I was shaking my head as the realization of my own words sunk in. "This is home, and he's here with me and my kids. Dallas isn't coming back." I looked at the old man. "Is he?"

The old man gently shook his head.

I looked down at my left hand. My engagement ring sparkled even in the pale sunlight. "I can't move forward if I don't let go, can I?" I didn't have to look at the old man to know that he was shaking his head again. My entire body quivered, and tears began flowing freely. I felt like I was going to implode if I didn't do something. It seemed that everything and everyone around me was stopped in time.

Bolting from the porch, I ran to my boulder overlooking the cliff, stopping at the very edge. Without hesitation, I threw my engagement ring with all my might off the cliff to land somewhere in the wooded oblivion below. Just then, something hit me, knocking me off my feet. Looking up from the ground, Raven was on top of me, looking at me, breathing heavily. He had tackled me.

"Raven, what the hell are you doing?"

"Really, I was going to ask you the same thing. You think throwing yourself off the cliff is really going to help our kids? Killing yourself isn't going to solve anything."

I looked at him, shocked. "What? I wasn't trying to kill myself, Raven. Why did you think that?"

"When I saw you upset and you took off running toward the cliff, what was I supposed to think?" Raven paused long enough to catch his breath. "If you weren't going to jump, then do you mind telling me what the hell you were doing?"

I looked down at my hands. "I was trying to say goodbye." I held up my naked left hand to show him.

"Your ring...you threw your ring off the cliff! Why?" Raven exclaimed with shock and politely helped me to stand.

Leaning against the boulder for added support, I began crying again. "I can't stand looking at it every day. It's only a reminder. I can't move forward if I'm constantly dwelling on what I've lost."

"So you accepted that he's gone and not coming back?" Raven was trying his best to follow my aimless rambling.

I shook my head. "No, don't say that." It hurt too much to hear those words out loud.

Raven threw his hands up in confusion, not knowing what else to say. He began to walk away, then stopped, turned back, and flashed me with a cold, hard stare. Determination filled his eyes as they slanted, and his forehead wrinkled. He had come to the conclusion that this was worth fighting for no matter what the outcome might be. "No, we do this here and now. He's gone, Ashley."

I pointed my finger at him. "No, don't you dare." My voice quivered through streaming tears.

Grabbing my arms, preventing me from turning away, he began to yell, "He's gone and not coming back!"

"No!" I continued to shake my head and sob.

"He's dead and—"

"No!" I screamed as I jerked my arms free and threw a forceful punch that landed on his chin. I watched as his head snapped back as if in slow motion. My hands immediately cupped over my mouth. "Oh my god, Raven! I'm so sorry."

Surprisingly, he smiled back at me. "What, you didn't think I expected that?" he said, rubbing his jaw. "I truthfully didn't expect it to hurt that much. Damn, girl, you can throw a punch."

I started crying again and collapsed to the ground in front of the boulder. "I don't know what the hell I'm doing anymore. I'm so confused. I don't know how to act or how to think." I buried my face in my hands and cried.

Raven sat cross-legged in front of me and stared at me for a while with his head resting on his hands. When he felt it was safe, he scooted closer and placed his arm around me. He gave me a gentle squeeze. "It's going to be fine."

I jerked my head up. "How can you say that? I'm a freaking basket case. I have one daughter who won't speak and another who hates me. I'm raising a child with a man I'm not married to while holding on to a dead man. There's an old man up there whom I think can read minds. I just threw a two-thousand-dollar diamond ring off a cliff, not to mention that I punched the only other man in the entire world who could possibly love my psychotic ass. Now please explain to me how everything can possibly be fine!"

Raven raised his eyebrows and sighed. "Well, since you put it that way, forget it. You're screwed."

I couldn't help but giggle through my snotty tears. "Asshole."

"Are you willing to listen to me for a minute, without throwing any punches?"

I only nodded without looking up at him.

"All right, fair enough." Raven took a deep breath. "Look, you have been strong for all of us for so long. You have been the glue that's held this whole trip together. You lost your home and your parents. You convinced what was left of your family to set out on a journey where you didn't know what was going to happen. You ran out of gas, then met Lou and myself. You know, I thought you would lose it when Nyte's mother died, but you didn't. I thought you would lose it when Harley was almost raped and you were shot, but you didn't. I thought you would lose it when Rocky died, but you didn't. I knew for sure you would lose it when Lou died, and you almost did. But you pulled it together and got through it. You have denied yourself the whole grieving process for so long. All those emotions have been sitting there building up, and yes, sooner or later, they are going to boil over. Honey, I'm sorry this is hard on you, and I wish anything in the world that I could make it better. You've had a huge loss." He stopped and looked into my eyes. "However, with loss comes opportunity."

317

"What are you talking about? What opportunity?" I questioned firmly.

"I'm talking about the opportunity in front of you." He paused and sat up. "I'm talking about me."

I looked up at Raven's beautifully tanned face. His voice rang of sincerity.

"I'm going to tell you something that I should've said a long time ago. I love you, Ashley."

"No, don't say that." My tears were still flowing freely.

"It's the truth. Lou was right. He knew it all along. We belong together. I'm here for your girls, for Marcus, for Nyte, and I'm here for you. I'll be here by your side till you tell me to leave."

He was being honest and sincere. I wasn't sure if I was ready for this conversation. However, I could tell he wasn't going to let me avoid it. "This is really unfair to you. You've laid your feelings on the line. I respect that, and I suppose it's only fair that I do the same. The fact is, I don't want you to go anywhere, Raven. At this point, I can't imagine my life without you." I wiped my face on my sleeve. "I would be lying not only to you but also to myself if I said that I didn't feel something for you, Raven. Every time you look at me, smile at me, or even touch me, I feel something. But I'm so screwed up I'm not sure what it is. You've told me that you love me, but I'm not in a place where I can repeat those three little words to you, not till I'm sure. I don't want them to be empty words. I want to mean it. Right now, there's only one thing that I'm certain of. You're my best friend. And I know that I don't want to lose you." He was staring at the ground now. "You're right. I have denied myself the luxury of dealing with all my emotions, especially the grief of losing Dallas. Maybe, just maybe, if you give me some time, I can start." I took a deep, shaking breath. "So now it's your turn. Can you stick around and give me some time?"

"Your best friend?" He began nodding, keeping it down where I couldn't see his eyes. He obviously didn't like the friend remark. I suppose most men do hate that phrase. He rose to an upright position. I was preparing myself to see him walk away, never to return. Raven shocked me as he extended his hand, which I gratefully took as he pulled me up beside him. He opened his hands toward the mountains. "All I got is time, baby. Where else am I going to go?" He was smiling at me now as my heart began to melt. "I do have a request…well, two actually."

"What's that?" I asked. At this point, I would do almost anything.

He eased closer and placed his arms around my shoulders, pulling me into his chest. "I'll give you anything you want if one, with your permission, you allow me to sleep in your bed, because that chair is really killing my back. I promise I'll behave." He gave a little chuckle as he rubbed my back. "And I want to stay by your side and help you deal with any emotions you have."

Attempting to stop myself from crying, I looked up into those beautiful eyes. "Permission granted." I buried my head into his shoulder. "Unfortunately, you can't give me what I want."

"Maybe you underestimate me. It wouldn't be the first time. What is it that you want?" Raven pulled me back and brushed away a tear that was streaming down my cheek.

"Three things actually. I want Monica's baby to be born happy and healthy without any complications. I want my daughter to start speaking. And finally, I just want to know that Dallas is okay, wherever he is."

"All in good time."

I buried my face into his broad shoulder and whispered, "Thank you, Raven."

"For what?" he asked, half laughing himself.

"For just being you." I hugged him even tighter.

"Well, it's a hard job, but someone has to do it." We both started laughing. "Come on, we got a show to go to."

"I still have to get dressed," I reminded him.

"Oh yeah." Raven let go of my hand and ran back toward the lodge. I followed him, trying to keep his stride.

"What is it?"

"I got you something today." He picked up a white box from the ground. "I dropped it when I saw you running toward the cliff. I hope it fits."

He helped me open the box. I held up a beautiful dress. It was black and had tiny sequins and beads around the collar, with a feminine fringe around the handkerchief hem. My mouth dropped in awe. "Oh, Raven, thank you!"

"Yeah, well, flannel is only sexy for so long."

"Oh, shut up." I kicked at him teasingly. "It's beautiful. Thank you."

"Well, don't keep a man waiting. Go get ready, woman."

I hurried into the lodge. On my way in, I saw the old man still sitting on the porch, minding his own business. I stopped, leaned over, and kissed him on the cheek. He never flinched or uttered a single word as I continued into the lodge.

I hurried to fix my hair and used some of Harley's makeup if for no other reason than to hide my puffy red eyes. After a few minutes of digging through her already cluttered closet, I luckily found a pair of her high-heeled black boots that looked good with the dress.

"Hey!" Raven knocked at the door. "Be thinking of a song you want to sing. It would really mean a lot to the girls if you surprised them."

I knew he was right, and I wanted to do something for my girls. I came out of the bathroom and twirled around in front of Raven. "What do you think?"

"Very nice. You clean up pretty good," he joked with his cocky, crooked grin.

"Well, thank you, sir. You don't look too shabby yourself," I stated as he rose from the chair, allowing me to get a full look at him. He was wearing white jeans that seemed to have been melted around his butt and a black shirt that he purposely left untucked. The top buttons were left unbuttoned, exposing his bold chest that I had come to admire. He sported a white jacket and topped the ensemble off with his black hat. "Not too shabby at all," I stated, admiring the man before me.

"Everyone else already left. Max and Monica took Nyte with them and said they would meet us there."

"How are we supposed to get there?" I asked.

Raven opened the door, allowing me to view the snowmobile parked in front of my room. "Your chariot awaits."

"How am I supposed to ride that wearing this?"

"Stop complaining. It's better than riding the horses. Now grab a coat and come on," he instructed with his hands on his hips.

"I guess it won't be that bad." I grabbed my coat and headed outside.

The ride to the auditorium didn't take long, but it was a cold one. I had tried to sit sideways on the snowmobile and hold on to him, but that wasn't working. So I did the most unladylike thing I could've done; I straddled the machine and held on tight. When we stopped, I had to shake to lose snow out of my dress. Raven seemed to get a kick out of seeing me shiver.

The auditorium was decorated with stars hanging from the ceiling and a few larger ones above the stage. I found the man over the music, and he helped me find the song I wanted to sing. He graciously told me that I could go on stage first, allowing the other acts a few minutes to warm up.

"Great!" I replied, suddenly feeling nauseous. Raven was quickly at my side as if he could somehow sense my anxiety. "There are so many people here. I can't do this!"

Max walked up with Nyte as I was talking to Raven. "Sissy, you got up in front of more people than this in Texas. Remember when we went to the information center and—"

"Yes, yes, I remember," I annoyingly stated, waving my hands toward Max. I didn't want to be reminded of that. "I also remember that during my singing, an aftershock hit and someone died."

Max just shook his head in disapproval.

"Your singing didn't have anything to do with that, and you know it. You just have stage fright. And you may as well get over it because I think he's about to call you on stage now." Raven pointed to the man on stage.

"Good evening, everyone!" His voice boomed over the microphone. "For those of you who don't know, I'm Clayton Wolfchild, son of Chief Wolfchild." Clayton pointed to the old man sitting in a chair on the side of the stage. The growing crowd cheered as the old man raised a hand, acknowledging them.

"He's the chief?" I softly questioned. The same old man who had somehow connected with my daughter on Christmas and had seemed to be able to read my mind was the chief. Raven gave my shoulder a squeeze.

Clayton continued, "We have been blessed to have some new people come into our lives recently. When they heard of our New Year's Eve show, they couldn't wait to get involved, which only shows how much they can contribute to our community. I would like for you to welcome Ms. Ashley Reese." Clayton extended his hand and motioned for me. I felt Raven give me a little nudge.

Walking up onto the stage, I peered down at the skinny old man. "You're the chief?"

The old man looked up at me. "That's what they told me." He just shrugged his shoulders.

"I don't know if I can do this."

"Just put your heart into it, and you can accomplish anything," he said, looking at me with years of wisdom reflected in his eyes.

I only nodded and continued on stage. Clayton handed me the microphone. I looked across the crowd of people and found Harley and Kat standing between Max and Raven. Kat was holding Raven's hand. It nearly broke my heart to see that they, too, had grown close. I knew this was it. I had to sing for my daughters and for Raven.

"Good evening. How are y'all doing today?" Everyone cheered. "My name is Ashley Reese. I'm sure I have met some of you good people. I want to thank you with all my heart for taking my family and me in." I took a deep breath. "Most of you know my situation, so this song is for Dallas." I nodded to Clayton. A piano started playing. I expected the music to come from a stereo and speakers. I looked down, and Marcus was playing for me. I started singing a song by Evanescence entitled "My Immortal." It was a soft song about being able to feel the presence of a loved one after death, the pain of feeling that presence while attempting to move forward with life, as well as being left behind to deal with life and the effects of losing a loved one. I felt that it was appropriate to say goodbye and to let everyone know that I was telling him goodbye.

I closed my eyes and tried hard to imagine Dallas standing in front of me, but I couldn't. Every time I tried, I saw Raven and his crooked grin. What did this mean? It had been so long I could barely remember what Dallas even looked like. I sang with a strong and definite voice that rang clear and, to my surprise, in tune. When I finished, I dragged out the last sentence of the song.

I looked up, and there was a small spotlight on me, and the lights were dimmed. I had no idea when that happened since my eyes had been closed almost the entire time. I had tears streaming down my face, and my hands were shaking. I looked across the silent crowd and found Dallas's mother. She, too, was crying and nodding in an approving tone. She started smiling and then clapping. The rest of the crowd followed her lead and began applauding. I let a gasp of relief as my breath quickened. Clayton was at my side quickly to rescue me. He hugged me and thanked me.

I left the stage and found Raven waiting for me with open arms. "That was awesome."

"Where are the girls?" As soon as the words left my mouth, Harley and Kat was at my side.

"Mama, thank you so much! That was beautiful." Harley stated with a tear in her eye. She and Kat hugged me tightly.

"Don't cry. You will ruin your makeup." I looked at my daughters. "Thank you, girls."

"Harley, come on!" a small thin girl shouted from the door.

"I gotta go. I love you," Harley stated proudly. "Raven, take care of my mom. Come on, Kat." Harley took Kat's hand, and the two disappeared through the large double doors leading behind the stage.

Max came over to greet me with a hug. "That was great, sissy. Good job."

"Thanks, brother. Where are Monica and Nyte?"

"Oh, they're sitting over there." Max chuckled. "Nyte is being passed around like a hot sack of potatoes. I swear, you're never gonna have to buy that kid shoes, because her feet are never going to touch the ground."

We laughed together as Marcus came up to me. "Marcus, thank you so much for playing for me."

"You're welcome. I just wanted to tell you, not that you need my permission or anything, but I just wanted to let you know that I'm okay with this." He pointed to Raven and then me. "You deserve to be happy, and after everything you have done for me, I couldn't be upset with you for moving on with your life." He shuffled his feet and looked at me.

"Thank you, Marcus. That means a lot to me." I grabbed him and hugged him tightly. "And it doesn't mean that I loved your dad any less."

He brought his arms up and hugged me back. We embraced a moment. He left without another word.

"All right, I think our next act is ready," Clayton said as he handed the microphone to a young man. There were drums on the stage of all sizes and young men behind each one.

"Hey, I'm Shane, and as Clayton said, we have had some new people come to be with us. They bring with them a different culture and a readiness to learn ours. Ms. Harley Reese has worked very hard to learn one of our tribal dances." Harley waved from the stage. "We blended our culture with a more modern one. We didn't do this to offend any of the elders, only embracing the changes that came our way. So I hope you enjoy it and our differences." Shane placed the microphone back in its stand and returned to the stage.

I looked but couldn't see Kat anywhere. Raven and I moved closer to the center of the audience so we could have a better view. Harley was dressed in a tribal dress that was adorned with colorful feathers and beads. The drums sounded softly at first and then grew with ferocity. The teens danced what appeared to be a traditional dance. Harley, keeping up with the others, never lost a step. Then the music stopped. There were a few stray claps, and the drums boomed as the music changed to Gwen Stefani's "Hollaback Girl." Harley was center stage as she quickly stripped off the native attire to reveal a short black miniskirt, a strapless red shirt, and of course, black boots. The outfit revealed that she, too, had a new figure. I wasn't sure, as her mother, I liked it though. They danced to the song as the rest of the teens in the crowd cheered and moved closer to the stage. I just laughed as Raven slid behind me and put his arms around me. There was a swear word in the song that was repeated over and over. Every time it came up, Harley and the others on stage would cover their mouths and let out a small *shh* sound.

Her dance classes had paid off because she looked great. She was moving around and looking fine doing it. I had to admit that even though it was a little more provocative than I had liked, my little girl was growing up, and she looked awesome. I glanced around, and the entire crowd seemed to be enjoying it. Looking at the chief sitting to the side of the stage, he was nodding to the beat and even tapping his toes. I couldn't help but smile. Max and Monica grinned and clapped for Harley, and I followed suit by cheering her on with a smile from ear to ear. I was so proud of her. She had taken everything thrown at her and dealt with it like a champ. She was indeed maturing into a wonderful young woman. A tear streaked down my cheek.

Raven tapped my shoulder. "I'll be back." He placed a tender kiss on my forehead and quickly went through the crowd.

When Harley's dance finished, I joined the crowd with a roaring applause. She went backstage with the rest of the teens. I wanted to see her coming through the crowd to me with open arms, but it was Raven who captured my attention on stage. I stood by myself in the crowd facing the center of the stage as Raven sat down on a stool with his guitar. He grinned down at me. His eyes sparkled in the spotlight.

"How y'all doing tonight?" The crowd cheered. Raven laughed and adjusted his guitar. "Me too. A few months ago, I met a woman whom I found to be the most annoying person I have ever met. She was invasive, and I did several mean things to her to attempt to make her run away as fast as she could. If you had told me then that I would be on stage singing a song to her tonight, I probably would've punched you. But this is where fate has led us. I've grown to love her like no other. She's a beautiful person with a big heart, and she's gone through a lot. I have seen her at her worst, and tonight, I saw her at her best. This one's for you, sunshine."

I laughed at the sound of my nickname as he began playing a Hootie and the Blowfish song called "Hold My Hand," a song that says we can take on whatever the world throws at us as long as we are together. It was very fitting to what we both felt, and he sounded great. A young man came on stage and took a place at the drums and began keeping Raven's beat. Another came out with a different kind of guitar and played a backup sound. Raven looked over his shoulder at the two young men, smiled, then turned his attention back to me.

I felt embarrassed standing there alone in a crowd of people, but my eyes stayed glued to my friend. I felt his love fill my heart as it lightened and fluttered in my chest. I smiled at his words, his song choice to me. He was right. We could do anything as long as we worked together side by side. That was a place I wanted to be, right by his side. I closed my eyes and imagined every image of him I had placed in my memory. I saw his expression looking down at me when he was trying to teach me to ride that beast horse of his. I saw his face through the flames of our campfire as he sang to me, his eyes of concern when I was shot, and relief when I woke up. We had been through hell the last few months, but we went through it together and came out just fine. I nodded in agreement at Raven as he finished his song. He stood up, shaking the young men's hands who had helped him complete the song. He handed over his guitar to one of them. He turned to me and jumped off the stage. The crowd of people made a path for him as he walked over to me with a cocky stride and placed his arms around me. "I love you," he stated.

I hugged him tighter, holding his body close to mine. I wanted to say those words to him so badly. Why couldn't I just go with my gut instinct? Everyone was clapping and cheering as the next act came on stage. It was another tribal dance performed by some older men of the tribe. A young woman came on stage next and sang a song. I knew I had seen her before, but I couldn't place where or who she was. I had been such a basket case this past week I was surprised I even knew my own name. I stood with Raven and watched as the next few acts came and went. Everything seemed to be winding down when Monica came up to me.

"Ashley, look, it's Kat," she stated in almost a frantic tone, trying to get my attention.

"Where?" I looked all around for my daughter.

"On the stage." Monica pointed to Kat standing center stage with one hand behind her back.

My heart jumped. Kat was indeed in the center of the stage dressed in a cute denim skirt and vest with a white shirt. "What is she doing?" *Did she get left on the stage accidentally?* I inched my way closer to the stage. "Kat," I tried to whisper. Her eyes found me as she looked down at me and smiled. "Kat, come on, baby." I was standing right at the stage, holding my arms up to her. An expression of shock crossed my face as she shook her head. "Come on, baby, the music is starting." Again, she shook her head no. I looked at my daughter as a hush fell over the crowd that was now staring at my daughter on stage. Kat moved the arm she was hiding behind her back, revealing the microphone as she brought it up to her little mouth. She opened her mouth, and the most beautiful sound escaped as she began to sing. I stood with my mouth gaping open in awe. My hands cupped my mouth as my entire body started to shake. There was my baby girl who hadn't made a sound in months on stage, singing to me.

"Are you breathing?" Raven asked as he put his arms around me from behind to help support the weight of my weakening body.

"Did you know about this?" I was crying now, unable to take my eyes off my child.

"Nope. She's full of surprises. It sounds like someone is trying to tell her mama something." Raven lightly kissed my head.

For the first time, I stopped listening to the sound of her voice and concentrated on her words. I let out a small laugh and smiled big to my daughter. She was singing "You Had a Bad Day" by Daniel Powter. The past few months, I had been telling her that we just had a bad day because she didn't speak that day, and now she was saying the same thing to me. Tears streaked down my face, mixed with smiles and laughter. She was the most beautiful image I could possibly fathom at that moment. I had almost forgotten what her voice sounded like. It was a perfect moment in time, and she was the star of the show.

"One out of three ain't so bad!" I heard Raven exclaim, referring to the three things I had told him I wanted that he couldn't give me.

"It's perfect! She's so beautiful. That's my baby girl." I wasn't even trying to stop the tears now. I let them flow and land where they wanted. The only thing that mattered in the world was the fact that my daughter was talking, even singing. Her voice was strong and clear, meaning she had obviously practiced. I looked around and noticed Harley standing next to the chief. She had a big smile on her face as she watched her sister steal the show. The old man tapped his foot and clapped for Kat. They were the only two who knew Kat's little secret. They were in on the secret to help her pull it off and surprise me. This was the one thing I needed more than anything in the world. I felt my body relax into Raven's arms as he tightened his grip to support me.

Kat hit the final chorus, and I was in a fit of tears and laughter. I nodded to her to show my approval and understanding. She had come out of whatever frame of mind she had been in for so long and was back with a ferocity that only a mama could appreciate or understand. She belted out the last of the song with attitude and pranced around the stage, feeling comfortable.

The song ended, and she held the microphone. "I'm sorry I made you worry, Mama. I love you." She walked to the edge of the stage.

I met and caught my daughter as she jumped off the stage and into my arms. We collapsed to the floor as I bathed her in hugs and kisses. "I love you. I love you so much" I didn't realize the crowd of people had gathered around us.

Kat pulled back. "Now we need to sing one together, Mama." She took Raven's hand. "All of us." She gave him a smile.

"I'm up for it if she is." Raven motioned toward me.

"I wouldn't know what to sing." I still had tears in my eyes as Raven helped me up from the floor.

"I do." Kat found Clayton and whispered something in his ear. He nodded, and Kat made her way back over to me. "Come on, Mama." Kat began pulling me back to the stage. Raven jumped up on stage, then helped me up. Doing my best to wipe away my tears,

I was positive my makeup was totally rubbed off by now. I probably looked like a haggard mess, but no one else seemed to notice or care. The music started, and I knew immediately the song Kat had chosen—Carrie Underwood's song "Jesus Take the Wheel." Kat loved to hear me sing it when we lived in Texas. She would ask me to sing it while we cooked supper. It's a song explaining what little control we actually have in our lives. We should turn our lives over to Jesus and let him deal with all the pain and hardships we encounter. My voice was shaky from all the crying, but I still belted out a fabulous song to do my daughter proud. I stood on stage with my family joining me in the chorus. Kat jumped forward and sang the second verse on her own. I looked at her with admiration and awe when she hit the high notes. We all joined in the second chorus. I finished the song alone. At that moment, singing, I realized that was exactly what I had to do. I had to stop trying to control so much of my life and just go with it, dealing with one thing at a time, allowing whatever was going to happen just happen, because there was nothing I could do to stop it anyway. Life has a funny way of biting you in the butt when you least expect it. All you can do is roll with the punches and do your best and sometimes bite back.

We finished and accepted all the applause that followed. I waved to the crowd and bowed my head to them. It had been a perfectly crazy and emotional night. We were leaving the stage when Frances came up to us with Nyte.

"Ms. Ashley, that was beautiful," she said, smiling.

Raven took Nyte from her. "Thank you, Ms. Frances." I looked around. "Where are Max and Monica?"

"That's what I was about to tell you. Monica's water broke while you were on stage. Max took her to the hospital," she said in a calm voice.

"What?" I almost yelled.

"Yes, it looks like we're going to have a baby tonight."

"Oh my god." I looked to Raven. "How can we get there? We all can't fit on the snowmobile.

The old man, now standing behind me, dangled a set of keys over my shoulders. "It's the old blue truck out front. Be careful. The roads are icy."

Raven took the keys and headed out the door with Harley and Kat on his heels.

I stood staring at the old man. "Thank you so much for everything." He only nodded in response.

I ran out of the auditorium and found the blue truck. Raven had it running and waiting for me. Kat sat in the middle, holding Nyte, while Harley and Marcus got in the back. Throwing my coat to them to help keep them warm, I was thankful we didn't have far to go.

It didn't take us long to get there. Barreling out of the truck, we entered the hospital through the emergency entrance and were quickly pointed in the direction of the maternity ward. Entering the room, Monica was already in bed with Max and Dannie at her side. She was breathing deeply, attempting to control her pain.

"Why didn't you say something?" I asked, going to her side.

"I wasn't sure at first. Then when I knew, the show had started, and I didn't want to miss it." She looked at Kat. "You were wonderful, baby."

Kat smiled proudly as she took a seat in the room by the window.

"You all looked so good up there. Harley, your dance was great." She took a deep breath. "And Ashley..." She stopped to moan as another contraction hit her.

"Shh, just breathe," I told her, taking her hand.

She breathed through the contraction, squeezing my hand a little. "You were awesome," she finished.

"Yeah, sissy, it was great. I'm glad you decided to do it."

"I am too," I agreed.

The doctor came in and asked us to leave so he could examine Monica. We entered the hallway only to be greeted by the old man, Ms. Greta, and Ms. Frances. I didn't know how they got here. These old people seemed to be able to teleport anywhere they wanted and appear at a moment's notice.

"Oh, Ashley, it was a wonderful show. Thank you for helping out," Ms. Greta said with gratitude.

I was a little dumbfounded. "I didn't do anything but sing two songs."

"If it's okay, I'll take the little ones home and get them in bed. It may be a while before this baby is born."

"I appreciate it, but I think I want to be with Nyte for a little while. I haven't spent much time with her, and I know Dannie wants to be here when his little brother or sister arrives," I explained.

"Well, I'll make a big breakfast and bring it up here then." She smiled. "And don't tell me no because you know I'll do it anyway."

"Breakfast will be great. Thank you."

The doctor came out and allowed us back in the room after saying our goodbyes to Greta, Frances, and the chief.

"Well?" I looked at Monica in question.

"He said everything is fine and progressing nicely." She exhaled slowly. "We're going to have a baby tonight."

I let out a breath of relief. "I'm so glad it's here and not out in the middle of nowhere."

We listened to the radio for a while. Dannie and Kat fell asleep in the hallway. Harley and Marcus had pushed some chairs together and were slumped down in them, resting but still awake. Raven sat in the chairs and stared at me as I held Nyte. She was asleep in my arms as she curled her little fingers around mine. Looking around at my family, it had been a perfect day. When I thought of everything I had lost and gained, I realized that the most important thing was all around me—my family. Raven was included in that. He was a part of the family now, and he was a part of me.

After what seemed like forever, the nurse came out of the room quickly and ran down the hallway. I stood up in fear. Soon, she came back down the hall toward Monica's room with the good doctor hot on her heels. I did notice the nurse was smiling, so at least that was a good sign. They dashed into Monica's room and shut the door. I tried to press my ear closer to the door to hear something, but just then, it opened, and I almost fell with Nyte.

"Are you Ashley?" the doctor asked.

"Yes."

"She wants you." The doctor opened the door.

I handed Nyte over to Raven and went in. Monica was crying and trying hard to control herself. The monitor she was connected to appeared to be monitoring earthquakes rather than contractions. "Monica, what is it? I'm here."

"I want you to do it!" she exclaimed.

"Do what?" I asked.

"Deliver the baby." She groaned loudly and grabbed the bed rails. "The plan all along was for you to deliver the baby. You need to do this," she explained.

I knew exactly what she was talking about. Monica thought I needed some sort of redemption to rid myself of the guilt I felt over the death of Nyte's mother. "Monica, I don't know if—"

A hard contraction hit Monica, and her body propelled forward. Monica looked at me sternly and spoke with a tone that would've made the devil cringe, "Get down there and catch this baby." It scared me enough that I sprang into action. The nurse was right there handing me gloves and a gown to put over my clothes.

I quickly got ready and in position. I looked over at the doctor who was standing next to me, poised to talk me through the procedure. "Don't go far, Doc."

He smiled slightly. "I'll be right here."

I stood at the end of the bed and checked Monica. The baby's head was crowning. "All right, next contraction, push hard."

Monica immediately started pushing. The doctor started giving me instructions, which I followed. Monica did great. The baby came out into my awaiting hands. I held the slippery little booger tight. I sat on the small metal stool and cleared the nose, mouth, and throat. She took that first breath and screamed loudly. I let out a sigh of relief and began crying. I looked at Max and Monica as the doctor took over and cut the cord. The nurse helped me quickly clean off the baby and wrap her in a blanket. I took her over to Monica. The baby still crying was a golden sound. I looked down at Monica. "Hey, Mama, do you want to hold your daughter?"

"It's a girl?" she said, surprised.

"A beautiful baby girl," I said, placing the baby into Monica's anxiously awaiting arms, and hugged my brother, allowing the doctor to finish the job. I helped put the bed back together and change the linens with Monica still in the bed, gently rolling to one side then the other, as Max took his turn holding his daughter.

When everything was cleaned up and in order, I opened the door. Everyone was standing and waiting on the edge of their seat. I looked at them. "It's a girl. You can come in now."

Dannie wasted no time. He went right to his mama and crawled in bed with her. Harley, Kat, and even Marcus went right over to the bed to get their first look at the baby. Max stood proudly over them. Raven came up to me and handed Nyte back to me. He went over and took a look at the baby and shook Max's hand and kissed Monica on the head. "You did a good job, Mama."

"Thanks, Raven."

He strutted back over to me and whispered, "Maybe I'm biased, but I think she's prettier." He pulled back Nyte's blanket.

I laughed. "You're the daddy. You're supposed to say that."

Raven stood beside me, draping his arm around me. "Hey! Two out of three ain't bad." Again, he reminded me of the three things I wanted. He looked at me with a grin.

"Not bad at all." I smiled as I watched my happy family around me.

The door opened again, and Ms. Greta bounced in with a plate of iced cinnamon rolls and a thermos of coffee. "Where's the little angel?"

The next hour, we made over the baby and passed her around. The kids were exhausted, and so was I. Ms. Greta offered to take Dannie back to the lodge so he could sleep and give Monica and Max a break too. I felt it was a good time to make our exit. I told the kids to go get in the truck. I hugged Max and Monica. "I'll be back later on. Y'all get some sleep."

I exited the hospital and found Raven standing under the awning, holding Nyte. He was watching some commotion in the street. A crowd was forming. I saw Marcus bolt from the truck and take off running toward the commotion.

"Was there an accident?" I could see Kat and Harley getting out of the truck as well. Then I saw for my own unbelieving eyes what the commotion was. I sucked in a quick short breath. "Oh my god, it's him."

"Who is it?" Raven asked.

My breath quickened, and I could feel the tears welling up.

"Ashley?" Raven said, trying to get my attention.

I looked quickly at Raven. "How does three out of three sound?" The only thing left on my list was to know that Dallas was safe.

I didn't notice the color fade from Raven's face as I tore off running toward the street. He saw me and held his arms open wide. I ran straight into Dallas's awaiting arms, immediately wrapping my arms around him, crying. "You're okay. You're okay."

I felt his arms embrace me. "Thank you so much for taking care of Marcus."

"You're okay!" This was the moment I had longed for, to see him, to know that he was safe, and to have him take me in his arms and hold me tight, yet I felt nothing. Then I noticed neither of us had said "I love you" or kissed. He had thanked me for taking care of Marcus. Something was definitely unusual with this picture-postcard reunion. I opened my eyes and noticed Marcus in a strong embrace with his mother. I noticed even though she was embracing Marcus, her eyes were on Dallas. She was watching us. At that moment, I felt that I had a pretty good understanding about what had happened. "Oh my god, Makayla!" I let go of Dallas and ran to her. I hugged her after Marcus. "Thank God, you're safe."

She was crying now too. "Ashley, I can't thank you enough for keeping *my* son safe." She emphasized the word *my* as if to assure me that she was back and ready to take back what was hers.

I only nodded. Her words rang true. Marcus was her son, not mine. I had known that all along, but she was making an outward claim to him. Dallas was busy saying hello to everyone that had gathered. He hugged Harley and Kat. I stood back and watched at the reunion as if I weren't a part of it. Suddenly, I realized my actual true feelings. I didn't want Dallas anymore. I saw Raven getting into the truck. I wanted to reach out to him, to introduce the two men in my life. How awkward would that introduction be? The moment I had waited so long for was upon me, and all I wanted to do was get away from the spectacle that was unfolding.

Grabbing Dallas's shirt sleeve, I briefly interrupted him, "I know you're busy. I'll meet you back at the lodge." I excused myself. I was elated to see him, but I couldn't ignore the fact that I was about to pass out from being so tired.

I got the girls and got back into the truck. Raven never said a word, but he had a worried look etched onto his face. I wanted to say something, but I wasn't sure what the right thing was. Just a few hours before, I was saying goodbye to Dallas, and now he was back. Where did that leave Raven and me? What was going to happen next? Why didn't I feel anything when I hugged Dallas? Too many questions raced through my mind.

We got back to the lodge quickly, and I got the girls tucked in, then went to my room. Raven tucked Nyte in and covered her up, then sat in the world's most uncomfortable chair as I lay on the bed.

"I wish you would say something," I said, breaking the silence.

"I don't know what to say." He sat forward and slowly rose to his feet. "I think I just need to sleep." He went to his own room instead of lying next to me. I know it would have been inappropriate for Dallas to come in and see Raven and me in the same bed. Raven probably had the same thought. The fact was that I wanted Raven there with me. I saw him leave the room, closing the door behind him and shutting it on my heart. I buried my face into my pillow and cried again. I had cried so much in the past twenty-four hours that I was sick of it. It wasn't long before I fell asleep.

I didn't know how long I slept when I heard the door open. I jumped up and saw Dallas entering the room like a dream with a cup of coffee.

"Hey," he stated.

"Hey," I repeated to him.

"Big day." His words were short and to the point.

"Yeah."

"Lots of changes." He glanced over at Nyte lying asleep in her crib.

"Yeah." I looked at the cup of coffee. "Is that for me?" I reached up for the cup.

"No, but I'll go get you one if you want me to." He started for the door.

"No, it's fine." I couldn't help but think to myself that Raven had never woken me up without having a cup of coffee ready for me. "Have a seat."

Dallas sat on the edge of the bed. "I've been in the kitchen with Mom. She filled me in on a lot that I've missed."

I looked at him. "Yeah, seems like you need to do the same thing with me, because I know I have missed a lot."

He hung his head down. There was something he didn't want to tell me or something he didn't know how to say. I felt for sure I knew what he was going to tell me.

"Look, just cut the shit and answer one question truthfully and honestly. I think I deserve at least that."

Dallas looked sharply at me, unfamiliar with my tone of voice. "I'll try."

"Are you and Makayla together again?"

"It's not as simple as that."

"Well, please fill me in. I feel that's the least you can do after I spent the last few months thinking my fiancé was dead only to have you show up with your ex-wife watching me like she wants to tear out my throat for hugging you." I scooted forward in the bed, taking his cup of coffee away from him and began drinking it.

"You're right. You deserve to know. I just don't know where to start."

"Try at the beginning," I said smartly.

"Okay." He hesitated, trying to find his words. "I was hurt in the quake. I had a concussion and a few broken ribs. I woke up in a military hospital camp. When I was able, I walked back home and found your note. I went looking for Makayla and found her hurt in a hospital tent. She was so happy that Marcus was with you and safe. I waited until she was able to travel, then we headed up here. All we had was basic camping gear. We hitched a ride with the military when we could, but otherwise, we were on foot. That's what took so long."

"And along the way, you fell back in love with her?" I asked.

"Well, along the way, we remembered why we fell in love to begin with. It may be something we want to explore, but it's definitely not something we planned. God knows I don't want to hurt you."

"Hurt me?" I almost yelled. "I don't give a shit about myself, Dallas. What am I supposed to tell my family? I'm the one who convinced them to come up here because it's where you told me to go, and now I have to go tell them we have to leave. They just had a baby, for Christ's sake!"

"No! I've already talked to the chief and the elders, and they all agreed that you can stay as long as you want. In fact, they asked that if you decide to leave that you wait at least until spring. No one is forcing you to leave. You are more than welcome to stay here," Dallas explained.

"So that's it. We're through." I was finding that I wasn't upset since I knew we didn't have to leave.

"I'm sorry, Ashley. I don't want to hurt you."

"I'm not hurt," I said bluntly and looked up at him. "Now that I know we can stay here, I'm fine with it. I'm not upset at all."

He leaned over and looked at me. "Are you okay?"

"I'm fine. I'm great actually." I had to explain to him about Raven. "The truth is, things have changed for me too. This whole trip, I had fallen in love with Raven, and I kept those feelings pushed back because of you. Now that this, us, is over, I can be free to be with him and not feel like I'm cheating on you. I've wanted to know that you were safe. Now that I know that, frankly, my dear, I don't want you anymore."

His expression changed to one of shock. "Huh?"

"I love Raven." I took a moment to realize I had said those words out loud. I looked at Dallas. "I don't love you. I love Raven."

"Well, I'm not even sure who Raven is, but it sounds like he's a lucky man." Dallas rose to his feet. "I'm a little confused though. We are okay, right? You're not mad at me?"

"No, Dallas, I'm not mad at you. But I do need your help to explain things to Max and Monica. I want them to be reassured by you that we are welcome to stay here.

Dallas nodded. "I can do that."

I jumped up and started getting dressed. I threw on a pair of jeans that I couldn't tell were dirty or clean and didn't really care. I knocked on Raven's door, but there wasn't an answer, so I invited myself in. "Raven!" I called out. There was no answer.

I went around to the main house. "Ms. Greta, have you seen Raven?"

"I think he went back up to the hospital, dear. Are you all right?"

"Yes, ma'am. Can you watch Nyte for me? I'm going to the hospital, and I'll be back soon."

"Yes, dear, I can do that."

"Thanks," I said as I bolted toward the door. Dallas was standing with Makayla on the porch. I couldn't help but smile at them as she jumped when she saw me. "Hey, you ready?" I asked Dallas.

"Yep." He looked at Makayla. "I'm taking her to the hospital to explain things to her brother and sister-in-law." Makayla glared at me with green eyes of jealousy.

"Oh my god, please, do you have to explain every move you make?" I looked to Makayla. "Look, he's all yours, okay. I don't want him anymore, and he's being a gentleman by giving me a ride to the hospital. So get over yourself and give me a break." I grabbed Dallas by the shirt. "Now come on."

It was a short ride to the hospital. I entered Monica's room. They jumped in shock at the sight of Dallas. "Oh my god!" Monica exclaimed.

"Dallas, where the hell have you been, buddy?" Max shook Dallas's hand.

"Long story, I'm afraid." Dallas smiled.

"Yeah, a story he can repeat later. The deal is, Dallas and I broke up so he can be with Makayla and—" I began to blurt things out, then took a good look around. "Where's Raven?"

"He didn't come see you this morning?"

"No, why?"

338

"I think it's starting to make sense now." Max sat beside Monica. "Raven came in this morning and said he was leaving. He said he was homesick and wanted to go home." It didn't make sense at the time, but now seeing that Dallas is back, it all makes perfect sense."

"Well, not to me. I'm confused!" I shouted. I felt a tear escape my eye.

"He knew Dallas was back, and he left because he wasn't going to be able to stand to see you be with Dallas. He said he was going to tell you goodbye, but maybe he couldn't."

My breathing was fast and furious. The room seemed to be spinning. "How long has he been gone?"

"He left here about an hour ago," Monica explained. "He was on his horse."

Dallas grabbed my shoulders and spun me around. "Ashley, listen to me. I can see it in your eyes. You love him, and he only has an hour head start. You can still catch him. Go after him."

"Sissy," Max got my attention, "go." Max gathered my hands in his. "I'm your brother, and I know you better than anyone. If you don't go after him, you're going regret it."

I started crying and nodding in agreement. "I love him." I fell into Max's shoulder.

"You ain't telling me nothing that I don't already know. However, I think you need to tell Raven yourself though."

I nodded in agreement.

"You gotta go, Ashley. Go get him and bring him back." Max hugged me a final time and released me. "What is it?"

"I'm trying to figure out why I'm still standing here." I took off running out the doors, down the hallway, and through the front sliding doors. I didn't have a car, truck, horse, nothing. How in the hell was I supposed to catch up to him on foot? I heard a distinct jingle of keys and looked down.

The old man sat on a park bench outside the hospital. He dangled the snowmobile keys at me. "Need these?" he asked.

I ran over to him. "Old man, I don't know how you do what you do, but I love you for it." I snatched the keys and got on the snowmobile. It roared to life, and I quickly got a feel for the machine and accelerated the gas. I made my way out of the reservation with a trail of dogs on my tail. I sped up the machine, pushing it to the limit. I had a whirlwind of thoughts racing in my head. I had to find Raven fast. I gunned the machine again and raced around the corner, slinging snow in every direction.

I drove for a long time with no sight of him. I had just about given up hope when finally I rounded a bend and saw him in the distance. The sky was getting dark as I grew closer. I went around, getting in front of him, throwing on the breaks, slinging the machine sideways to a stop, then jumped off. Raven dismounted his horse and stood there looking handsome as ever.

"Do you mind telling me where the hell you're going?" I stated with attitude.

"I thought Max and Monica would tell you."

"They did," I interrupted him. "They told me you're going home. What kind of shit is that?" I slapped his arm.

"You don't need me anymore since…" Raven paused and rolled his head. "Well, since he's back." He couldn't look at me.

"You're right. I don't need you anymore." I walked over to him and took his hand in mine. "I want you." I took my promise necklace out of my shirt. "You made me a promise, remember? What about Nyte? How can you just leave her?"

He looked like he was crying. "Ashley, I can't sit by and watch you with him. It hurts too much." He pulled his hand free of mine. "Can't you understand?"

"There is one reason why I drove like a madwoman to catch up to you and one reason only."

"What's that?" His voice was quivering.

I decided if I were ever going to let go and act on instincts, this was the moment. Hooking my fingers tightly in his belt loops, I forcefully pulled him close to me. "Because I love you." I stopped and looked at him. "I love you. It's over between Dallas and me. Hell, maybe it was over before that rock fell from the sky. I don't know. But I do know that I love you, and I want to be with you. I want to raise our child together. I want to grow old with you. I want—" I didn't get to finish when Raven grabbed me and brought his face down to mine and kissed me forcefully. We fell to the snow-covered ground in a feverish tone. We kissed with a hunger that couldn't be satisfied.

Finally, he pulled back and looked at me. "Do you mean it?"

"I wouldn't have said it if I didn't mean it. The only way you're going back to Nebraska is with me and my family. We leave the same way we got here, together." He kissed me again, this time gentler and more passionate. He stopped and looked at me, smiling and stroking my cheek with his finger. "You were right," I told him. "I know you meant that kiss. It definitely wasn't just an accidental passing of the lips."

He smiled, looking down at me. "I love you."

"I love you too." I looked up and saw the most amazing sight. "Raven, look." I sat up, pushing him back.

The night sky had grown dark around us. Raven quickly looked up. His eyes lit up with the amazing sight above us. "Well, I'll be damned." We sat in the snow and watched in amazement at thousands of stars twinkling overhead.

I laughed out loud.

"What's so funny?" he asked with his own smile.

"Your kiss made me see stars." I laughed again with him joining me.

We sat quietly holding each other. Somehow, the sky had cleared, allowing us to see our stars that we had longed to see for many months. We sat for a long time just staring into the sky. I looked on with a greater appreciation in what goes on in the universe around us.

We rode back to the hospital and talked with Max and Monica for a while, feeling it was only fitting that they knew I had found Raven and we were indeed together. I kissed my new niece, Summer Rayne, and rode back to the lodge with Raven on horseback. I checked on my girls and tucked them in. Kat sounded like an angel when she said, "Good night, Mama. I love you."

"I love you too, baby." Closing the door, I continued to my room. Raven was there looking over Nyte. I closed the door behind me and pulled the curtains closed. I went over to Raven. He enveloped me in an embrace and kissed me with a fiery passion that could have melted the great glacier peaks of Montana. We lost ourselves in what was sure to be the first night of a long future for us. No matter what the future held, come hell or high water, we would tackle it together.

EPILOGUE

AS SPRING CAME, so did a new visitor. A young man rode onto the reservation asking for Harley and was quickly pointed in the direction of the lodge.

We sat on the porch of the lodge enjoying the fresh sunshine when he rode up. It took Harley just a moment, but then it hit her like a ton of bricks. "Ricky!" she screamed as she bolted from the porch. Ricky jumped free from his horse and caught Harley in his arms, spinning her around. The two shared a kiss. They obviously didn't care if anyone saw or not. Harley was crying and holding on to him. We all greeted him with hugs.

"It's good to see you all again." He hesitated just a moment, taking in our excitement.

"Ricky, how are your parents?" I asked.

"They are fine. In fact, they sent you a letter." Ricky handed me an envelope. "I, um, have something for Max."

Max stepped forward. "Well, I can't imagine anything being better than seeing a familiar face." Max looked on in question.

Ricky only smiled. "I have been holding on to this for you." Ricky opened his saddlebag and took out a puppy. "It seems that your Rocky and my Baby got a little too close for comfort. I felt it was only right for you to have the only male pup out of the bunch." Ricky handed a boxer puppy to Max.

Monica immediately started crying. She hugged Ricky. "Thank you so much. You have no idea what it means to us."

Max held the little pup up and examined him. The pup's ears perked up as he looked at Max with his big chocolate-brown eyes. A tear ran down my brother's face as he brought the pup down into a childish embrace. "Ricky, thank you."

Raven and I read the letter aloud to everyone. As it turned out, Jacob and Rose didn't like Canada. They were ready to make the trip back whenever we were ready.

Raven and I looked at each other, and we knew what we had to do. We talked things over with Max and Monica and made the decision to go back to Nebraska. Raven and I wrote a letter back stating we were going back to work the farm and they were more than welcome to come home with us. There would be plenty of room.

Ricky stayed for a few days, then reluctantly left with our letter in tow. He assured us he would be seeing us soon. Harley hated to say goodbye again but knew next time she saw Ricky, he would be here to stay.

We stood out in the yard waving to Ricky as he rode away. Nyte was crawling across the yard. Raven scooped her up and threw her into the air, catching her. She laughed and giggled the whole time. I stood back and took it all in. I had come to realize the word *home* was more than just a building of wood and nails. It was the contents under the roof that made the home; more specifically, family made the home. I stood back and watched my family enter the lodge. With the exception of Marcus, who would stay on the reservation with his parents, we had all agreed to take on another long journey, but we would do it together as a family. I knew in that moment that no matter where I was, I was home.

Part II

PROLOGUE

S PECIAL AGENT BENJAMIN Presley stood guard outside the heavy oak door. A proud Marine, husband, and father of two, he knew the decisions made in the next few moments could quite possibly change not only his life but forever change what was left of this rattled nation as well. He couldn't wrap his brain around what the secretary of Homeland Security, Martin Lee, had told him. "The president is compromised. He is not acting in the best interest of the country. We are going to take him out, and we need your help."

Benjamin had sat and listened intently to everything that Martin Lee had to say, and even though some of it made perfect sense, he couldn't help but feel that it was all wrong. His job was to protect the president at all cost, even if it meant giving his own life in the process. Benjamin had been guarding President John Michael Mallory III for almost a year. He had seen him at his best and at his worst. Benjamin saw President Mallory struggle for months to come up with a way to divert the comet. He recognized the pain Mallory felt when he was advised not to tell the public about the impending disaster the country was facing. The agony in the president's eyes when their missiles failed to destroy the comet was unbearable to watch. It was Benjamin who witnessed President Mallory cry as the comets hit, instantly killing countless numbers of innocent Americans. In that moment, all Ben could do was place a calming hand on the president's shoulder in a feeble attempt to show that he wasn't alone in his pain. Benjamin knew the president had done all within his power, everything that he was allowed and advised to do in order to protect the American people. Things weren't adding up, and he was running out of time. He had agreed to help the secretary of Homeland Security in the assassination plot, but only because he didn't know who else to go to. He had struggled over this dilemma in his head all week. However, his mama didn't raise a fool. He knew right from wrong, and he knew what his heart was saying.

Right now, at this very moment, the president of the United States was in a meeting with the secretary of Defense, Vincent Flemming, and if Benjamin didn't act quickly, both the president and the secretary of Defense would be killed, leaving the secretary of Homeland Security in control of the country. He didn't understand how deep this plot was or who was involved, but everyone else in line for the succession for president was dead or missing. He knew what he had to do. Benjamin turned and quickly opened the door, interrupting the meeting.

"Benjamin?" John Mallory stated in question as he rose from his chair.

"Mr. President, I'm sorry to interrupt, but it's a matter of life and death. Your life, as a matter of fact." Benjamin explained about the meeting that he was called in on, sputtering the facts of the impending assassination attempt that was about to transpire. "I'm sorry I didn't say something before, sir, but it's imperative that we move you now."

"Where is he supposed to go?" Mr. Flemming inquired.

"My suggestion is to leave now with Agent Williams and Corban and go to either Colorado or Wyoming. There are underground bases there that you will be able to take refuge in. Once you're there, you will be able to regain control and do what you have to in order to make this county safe again. Mr. Lee plans to take over as president after your death. You are going to have to put him back in his place." Benjamin looked at his wristwatch. "You have to move quickly, sir."

"Mr. President, Mr. Flemming, I have transportation waiting. I advise we move now," Bret Corban stated briefly. "What do you intend to do, Benjamin?"

"I'm going to stay here and give them the show they want. I need for you to do something for me, Bret." Benjamin took a small locket from his pocket and placed it gently into Bret's hand. "Find my wife and tell her that I'm sorry for not being there for her and my kids as often as I should have but that I'll look down on them from time to time." Benjamin quickly wiped an escaping tear from his face. "Above all else, keep these men safe. They are the only hope if this country is going to have any future at all."

Bret Corban nodded affirmatively and quickly ushered the president of the United States and the secretary of Defense to the awaiting SUV driven by Special Agent Nicolette Williams. Within moments, they were gone, and Benjamin walked over to the desk and carefully removed the bomb that had been placed there previously by Martin Lee's other unknown accomplice, checking and double-checking the mechanics of the bomb.

It wasn't long before he heard heavy footsteps quickly approaching. Special Agent Raymond Alfred burst through the door with his service pistol and looked around, confused.

"They're gone, Raymond. I tipped them off, and they are far away from the harm that Mr. Martin Lee wants to do." Benjamin stood firm in his spot so Raymond wouldn't see the bomb sitting on the desk.

"You told the son of a bitch? Why would you do that?" Raymond Alfred blurted.

"Because it's wrong. Lee is a power-hungry mongrel that is only looking out for his own interests, not what's in the best interest of the country. I was sworn to protect the president, not kill him. President Mallory is a good man and is doing his best to protect this country."

"I can't go back and tell the secretary of Homeland Security that I failed. Failure is not an option." Raymond waved the gun around, still expecting the president to jump out and say boo.

"Don't worry, Raymond. You're not going to tell him anything. They will find two bodies. Your good name will go untarnished for a while." Without hesitating a moment longer, Benjamin turned sharply, placing his hand on the square bone-white button. "God bless the USA." He gently pressed the button and inhaled his last breath as the south wing of the president's quarters at Fort Leavenworth, Kansas, exploded into a mass of fiery fury.

President John Michael Mallory III watched from the safety of the SUV as his office exploded, killing Special Agent Benjamin Presley and Special Agent Raymond Alfred. The two agents with Mallory had been listening over their headsets, keeping the president informed of what was happening inside the office. He had the confirmation he needed. There was indeed an assassination plot not only for his life but also for the life of his friend, the secretary of Defense, Vincent Flemming, under the command of the secretary of Homeland Security, Martin Lee. He knew when the smoke settled, two bodies would be found. Lee would assume it was their bodies for a while. Until then, they were under the protection of Special Agent Bret Corban and Special Agent Nicolette Williams, and they were on the run in a world full of chaos and despair.

Bret Corban was the youngest of the agents. At twenty-six years old, he was the son of a poor fisherman from Bar Harbor, Maine. His mother had died when he was only six years old. His father, wanting more for his son, encouraged him to join the Army right out of high school. Mallory never questioned Bret's loyalty or ability to do the job and the way he conducted himself. By getting both of them out of harm's way reiterated his sense of duty and respect.

Nicolette Williams, the only female assigned to the presidential protection detail, was a twenty-nine-year-old single mother of one little girl named Mandy. Mandy lived with Nicolette's mother and father in Baltimore. She had joined the Navy after she had Mandy in order to support her daughter. She never intended to do so well or make her military experience a lifelong career. Once, on Easter, President Mallory got to meet little Mandy at the White House Easter egg hunt. She sweetly presented him with a picture she colored of her mother and the president. What Nicolette didn't know was that colored picture was still in the top drawer of the Resolute desk, wherever it was.

"May God bless you, Benjamin Presley." President Mallory turned his attention forward. "Let's go, Mrs. Williams." The SUV pulled away undetected because of the pandemonium unfolding from the explosion. They would make their way west to the safe confines of an underground base in an attempt to restore order to a country in turmoil.

CHAPTER 1

A S I LAY in bed with my head resting firmly on Raven's chest, the moonlight danced through the curtains, giving the room a soft blue glow. Nyte slept peacefully in her crib as my breath synchronized with Raven's. My mind pondered aimlessly over the bizarre events that had transpired over the last six months. A comet had hit and killed thousands, if not millions, of people. I was sure they would never have a definitive account of the lives lost that dreadful day. My family and I had set out on an expedition to Montana to seek refuge on the Blackfoot Indian Reservation. Dallas, my fiancé at the time, was Blackfoot and informed me during our last conversation before all hell descended upon Earth that we would be taken in and given food and shelter if we could make it there. Dallas had been injured in the quakes that followed the impact of the Alpine comets. Coincidently, I inherited Dallas's son, Marcus, when he couldn't find his mother, Makayla, in the collapsed rubble of the hospital she worked in. Hesitantly we left our homes without Dallas and made the long trip to Montana with everyone eventually believing Dallas to be dead.

Along the way, the gas ran out as expected. Our family met Lou and Raven. Lou was nothing short of a miracle. He provided real wagons in exchange for allowing him to make the trip with us. Lou had secretly revealed to me that he was dying and wanted to make the trip as he had in his younger years working cattle drives. Raven wasn't thrilled about but came along for the ride. Raven had been a thorn in my side from day 1. He was a mean, hateful smart-ass and nothing would have made me happier than seeing him strung up and horsewhipped. However, a strange and unexpected occurrence happened along the way. I fell in love with him.

Along the journey, Lou was lost as he succumbed to cancer. Rocky, Max's beloved big dumb boxer dog, died when he protected Max's wife, Monica, and son, Dannie, from a vicious wolf. Harley, my eldest daughter, had nearly been raped, and I was shot in the shoulder. The trip wasn't all bad; treasured souls had been gained along the way. Jacob, Rose, and their son, Ricky, joined us and quickly became great friends.

Then there was Nyte, the child I helped deliver on a cold winter's night. Her mother was in labor, and the baby was breech. The only thing that would save the baby was a cesarean. I felt in no way competent to handle such a procedure and explained the risk to the impending parents in detail. The end result was a beautiful baby girl being brought into this cold, cruel, decaying world, her mother dying, and her father running off in the middle of the night with no clue of what to do with a baby. He left behind what money he could and had never been heard of since. I had contemplated on giving her up for adoption since she wasn't mine to keep in the first place, and I honestly couldn't see myself attempting to raise another baby. It was Raven who convinced me to keep her. He had lost his wife and child in the birthing process years ago and longed for a child. Finally, I gave in to him and agreed we would raise the child together.

My youngest daughter, Kat, had been traumatized by the earthquakes and spent the trip in silence. It wasn't until the talent show on New Year's Eve at the reservation that she surprised everyone by singing a song, in which she directed at me. Harley had also found love on this journey. She fell hard for Jacob and Rose's son, Ricky. He had gifted her with a promise ring. After his family went their separate way, Ricky came back to find Harley on the reservation. And the plan hatched for the entire family to make their way back to North Platte, Nebraska, to Raven's homestead. We planned to work the farm with Jacob and Rose and live together.

"Everything happens for a reason." That was Lou's favorite saying. Dallas and his ex-wife, Makayla, showed up being very much alive only hours after I allowed myself to admit I had feelings for Raven. Dallas and Makayla were also very much *together*. I should have been devastated knowing I had traveled all this way only to have my fiancé coupled with his ex-wife, but I wasn't. It allowed me to be with Raven.

Exhaling slowly, allowing the exhilaration fill my heart, I sighed heavily as Raven wrapped his arm around me. Noticing multiple shadows cross the window out of the corner of my eye, I sat up with senses alert. A soft knock rapped at the door. Getting up quickly and throwing on a robe, I answered the door as Raven sat up, putting on his pants and boots. Opening the door slowly, I saw several men standing before me, smiling.

"We want Raven, and we want him now."

I was relieved when I saw the men in question were my brother, Jacob, and a few men from the reservation. Jacob and his family had made it into town just this evening. "What's going on?" I asked, crossing my arms over my chest.

"It's close to midnight, sissy, and you're not going to see each other till he sees you walking down that aisle," Max stated firmly with his hands resting on his hips.

Scoffing at him, I rolled her eyes. "Aren't we a little past traditions, Max?"

"Nope, and you better move aside. Don't make us get loud and wake the baby. Raven, grab your clothes, son, and come on." Max pushed his way into our room.

Raven was smiling the whole time; he quietly got his clothes together.

"What is this, Max, a bachelor's party or something?" I said in a whisper.

"Have you seen a strip club on this reservation? No, I don't think so. It's a few of us guys sitting around a campfire with nothing but a few buffalo chips and the moon to keep us company." Max was trying to hold himself with authority. "Now tomorrow is a big day, so I expect you to get some sleep and be totally rested."

"Yes, sir." I gave him a sarcastic salute as he exited the room.

Raven stopped in the doorway; his smile was gone. "Are you okay with this?"

"Get out. You're cutting in on my beauty sleep," I said, laughing while pushing him out the door. "Have fun."

"I suppose I'll see you at the altar?" he asked with his cocky half-sideways smile.

"I'll be the one in a dress that makes me feel completely awkward." Smiling, I kissed him on the cheek. "I love you."

"I love you too." Raven tipped his hat, turned, and leaped off the porch of the lodge like a kid, chasing behind the other men.

Closing the door, checking on Nyte, who was sleeping soundly, I lay down once more and had no trouble falling asleep. I felt safe and secure in knowing Raven was in safe hands. We were getting married tomorrow, and everything was where it should be in the world.

Somewhere in Western Kansas

"Where do we stand, Mr. President? What shape are we in?" the secretary of Defense, Vincent Flemming, asked, taking another sip of his coffee, and warmed himself by the fire.

President Mallory shook his head. "We are in bad shape, Vincent, very bad shape." Mallory thought of a good place to start explaining. "When I declared a state of national emergency and active martial law, I set forth a chain of events. That son of a bitch Martin Lee has me blocked. He has made sure he is the one in charge by killing off anyone above him in the chain of succession except the secretary of the Interior, who wouldn't qualify to be president because of his age, and of course, you, Vincent. But that's only because you were with me. It's my belief that Lee plans to use this monstrous disaster to allow the Alpha-Omega Group to implement a New World Order and basically take over the world. He has attempted to push this before and met nothing but brick walls. Now he is the one who has the control."

Secret Service Agent Nicolette Williams gasped at the president's words. "He couldn't do that, could he, sir?" Nicolette knew of the Alpha-Omega Group. Mostly comprised of political pawnbrokers and industrial titans, they were a covert network of elite families who had been controlling world events behind closed doors for years. The group was nothing short of a human machine that combined military, diplomatic, intelligence, economic, scientific, and political operations. They held secret meetings to expand their influence. All preparations were concealed, and if they made a mistake, you would never read about it in the headlines.

"With the world in such a state right now, it just may be possible. I have to admit, if it were going to happen, there wouldn't be a better time than now to attempt it," Mallory explained.

"Sir, what about the secretary of state, Leland Dixon? He's still alive, sir," Bret Corban stated.

"The last I heard, he was in Germany. It's probably in his best interest to stay there. If he comes back, Lee will only have him killed, and that's only if the Germans haven't done it for him already." President Mallory buried his head in his hands. He was so tired yet his brain refused to shut down. "Martin Lee is now the acting president. With me gone, everything, from Fort Knox to the transportation department, is under his control, everything." Mallory tipped his cup over, pouring out his coffee. "I don't want anyone to think badly of me. However, if I don't get some sleep, I'm not going to be much use to anyone."

"Of course, sir, we have your tent set up. I'm afraid you and Mr. Flemming will be roommates till we find more suitable accommodations. We will take turns standing watch. Sleep well, sir." Bret Corban pulled back the flap of the tent, allowing President Mallory inside, then returned to the fire.

"We are going to have one major problem," Nicolette spoke up, "gas. We are never going to have enough to get to Wyoming or Colorado."

"We are going to have to ditch these suits and get civilian clothes, or we are going to stick out like a sore thumb. No one will probably recognize us. We can be normal citizens and find out for ourselves what that bastard Martin Lee does for the populaces of the

United States." Vincent Flemming disposed of his coffee as well and went into the tent.

Corban and Williams looked at each other. Neither of them knew what their future held, but both understood getting President Mallory back in power was the one mission that couldn't fail on. The fate of the entire country rested on their shoulders.

The next day on the Blackfoot Reservation in Montana

The sun rose with a brilliance radiating down on the tiny reservation. I awoke with a smile when Monica busted into the room with Dannie and Summer in tow.

"Happy birthday, Aunt Ashy!" Dannie held out a breakfast tray with apples, eggs, and toast and juice. Laughing, I looked at Monica in confusion.

"I tried to explain about the wedding, but we are having cake, and he associates cake with birthdays, so just grin and nod," Monica explained.

"Thank you so much, buddy," I said, taking the tray from his little hands. "Have you seen Aunt Ashley's wedding dress?"

Dannie got this deer-caught-in-the-headlight look. "Mom, she's asking about the dress?"

"Oh no, you don't. You are the one who gave Frances and Greta full control over the wedding, and you're not going to ruin it for them." Monica shook her finger at me as she got Nyte's clothes together.

"Yeah, but don't I at least need to try it on before the wedding? What if it doesn't fit? What am I going to do then?" I asked, taking a bite of the toast and making a face at Dannie.

"You need to have faith. Everything is going to be just perfect. I know you didn't want a big affair, but we are all so happy for you. This whole thing is special for us too." Monica fiddled around in the bathroom.

Dannie peered around the corner then back to me and patted my leg lightly. "Don't worry, Aunt Ashy. It's perty."

"Dannie, I heard that!" Monica exclaimed.

Dannie smiled big and let a belt of laughter roll as he ran from the room when Monica came back around the corner.

"Now you eat and take a shower. I'm taking the girls to Greta's, and I'll be back to help with hair and makeup. Harley and Kat are with Frances, helping her. You have the whole day to yourself except for me dictating your every step." Monica hugged me tightly and was gone like a hot summer breeze.

For a moment, I regretted giving up control of this wedding, but it was quickly gone. I didn't really care about the details. I simply wanted to be married to Raven and didn't care what kind of crazy dress I wore or what food was served. I was going to be surrounded by family and friends and marry the man I loved. Nothing was going to ruin this day.

Being a good girl, I did as I was told and was waiting in my robe when Monica returned to do my hair and makeup. I wouldn't see any of my children, friends, family, or Raven till I got ready to go down the aisle.

Monica found a CD player and put on some music while I sat quietly with my eyes closed as Monica worked her magic, as she called it. When she was done and I was allowed to open my eyes, I had to admit, I looked great. My makeup was nothing short of a work of art—a well-blended foundation mixed with smoky eye shadow that made my eyes stand out. The hairstyle was an amazing half updo with loose curls that flowed down my back. A few loose strands of hair remained, framing my face, and adorned with a hair clip that had a few colored feathers hanging from it in the back.

"You did an amazing job, Monica. Thank you so much." I hugged her in gratitude. "Now I get the dress, right?" I inquired giddily.

Monica just rolled her eyes. "The dress will be here when it gets here. I'm going to finish getting ready myself and check a few details. Do not leave this room. Do you understand?"

"Yes, Mother," I said in a sarcastic tone.

"I mean it. Don't make me go bridezilla on your ass," she said, laughing, as she opened the door. "Good to see you, Clayton. Make sure she doesn't leave this room." The door shut behind her.

My mouth fell open as I darted to the door, opening it quickly. I found Clayton Wolfchild standing before me, holding a walkie-talkie. "Ashley, get back in there. Don't make me call for backup."

"There is a security detail? Are you serious?" I questioned.

"We just want to make sure this day goes off without a hitch. Now get back in there before it gets ugly." He had a smile from ear to ear but was very serious. He would call for backup if he had to. He had unlimited permission to use whatever means necessary to keep me in this room till it was time.

"Is everything okay over there, Clayton?" a female voice called over the walkie-talkie.

Clayton made a face of certainty at me and pressed the talk button. "Yes, the package is secure." Clayton motioned for me to go back into the room.

Again, doing as I was told, I shut the door and retreated back into my domicile of perpetual waiting. "It's my wedding, dammit," I growled in frustration, wondering if they were keeping Raven pinned up like a rabid dog as well.

I must have dozed off because before I knew what was happening, Monica opened the door and happily bounced in, holding up my wedding dress and a white box. I looked in awe at the garment before me. It was all handmade—a long off-the-shoulder, handkerchief hem white dress covered in lace with a yoke bodice. It had lace sleeves that went the length of the arms and a *V* neckline with delicate fringe hanging from it. Tiny sequins had been sewn into the neckline.

"That's not all," Monica said as she produced a white cowboy hat, obviously used but still in good shape and spruced up to precision. The hat had a lace trim around it and a tulle veil that would drape down the back. "And Raven made you these." Monica took a pair of white dress boots with a small heel from a box. The sides of the boots were see-through lace and laced all the way up.

A tear welled up in my eye as I thought about all the effort put into this wedding. The dress alone must have taken many painstaking hours to complete. Then there were the decorations, the food.

The love I felt at that very moment from people who just a few months ago were complete strangers was overwhelming.

"Oh no, you don't. Don't you dare cry and ruin my masterpiece. You hurry and get dressed. We don't have time to fiddle around. People are already starting to show up," Monica barked her instructions as I commenced to getting dressed.

Monica helped me with the zipper then with the hat and veil. Sitting on the bed, I eased my foot into the dainty lace boots my husband-to-be had made exclusively for me and laced them up snugly. Standing before Monica, patiently awaiting her approval, I stammered, "Well, what do you think?"

Monica stood speechless for a long time with her hands cupped to her mouth. "Absolute perfection." She walked to me and made a few adjustments. "I wish your mom could see you right now."

I dropped my head at the depressing thought of my deceased parents. "I like to think she can. Daddy too."

Monica looked as if she wanted to cry too. "They can, I'm sure of it, and right now, they are smiling down on us." Monica took a deep breath and steadied herself. "Now you stay here, and I'll make sure everything is in order. The next time someone knocks on this door, it will be time for you to take your vows." She quickly left the room again, leaving me alone with my thoughts.

Sitting on the bed, I looked around the room, thinking quietly to myself. Eventually, my thoughts shifted to my parents. *Mama, I know you are still looking out for me. And if possible, please help me and guide me through the day. I would give anything in the world to have you here with me, just to see you one more time. Daddy, I wish you were here to walk me down the aisle, to meet Raven and see for yourself that he's a good man. I love you both so much and miss you even more.*

A knock at the door interrupted my personal moment. "Sissy." The door slowly opened, and my brother stepped inside.

My mouth gaped open at the sight of my brother. "Damn, Max, you clean up pretty good for a country boy." He was dressed in black jeans and white shirt with a blue tie. His hair was slicked back and trimmed, and most importantly, he had shaved. Max had been growing a hellacious beard that Monica hated. She had threatened to shave him in his sleep several times.

"I could say the same to you, country girl." He sneered at me and enveloped me in a tight hug. Pulling back gently, he said, "Are you ready?"

"Yes!" I said enthusiastically.

"No cold feet, second thoughts?" he asked, looking at me through concerned eyes.

"Oh, my feet are hot as hell," I said, exposing my boots with pride. "And the only thing I'm giving second thoughts to is allowing everyone else handle every single detail of this wedding."

My brother kissed me on the forehead and looked at me, grinning. "Don't worry. It's all going to be perfect." Max offered me his arm. "This way, my lady."

"Lady?" I stated in question. "Boy, this dress really is deceiving." I laughed and took my brother's arm, allowing him to gallantly escort me onto the porch.

The sun was beginning to set behind the mountains, casting a beautiful glow. Blue and silver tulle decorated the railing that continued to flow onto the ground, creating a path all the way to the altar. Mason jars with candles dotted along the pathway. Large halved logs sufficed as pews. They were filled with family and friends. It appeared that most people from the reservation were in attendance. Kat was ahead of us, dressed in a beautiful blue dress with silver embellishments. Nyte had a matching dress and was being pulled in a decorated wagon by Kat, and they tossed flower petals on either side. Harley, as my maid of honor, had a silver dress with blue embellishments and had already made it down the aisle and was awaiting her sisters. Marcus had a keyboard set up connected to speakers. Max gave him a quick nod, and he began playing a traditional wedding march. My grip tightened around my brother's arm as everyone rose to their feet to witness my descent down the aisle. Max looked at me, smiling, and lovingly patted my hand.

Two large tree trunks rested on either side of the large boulder I had come to call my thinking spot. The trunks had been shaved down and hand-carved with hearts of all sizes. Draped tulle of silver and blue flowed down and around the trunks, with beautiful floral arrangements in the center of each one.

Chief Wolfchild leaned on the boulder as I made my way down the path, politely smiling and nodding to our friends who had come out to take part in our special day. Greta and Frances stood proud and quietly clapped their hands with excitement. From the moment I relinquished control, they had sworn the entire community to secrecy. They had worked so hard on every detail of this wedding. Their expressions told me that everything was going just as it should. Dallas and Makayla were there hand in hand. In just six short months, Marcus would have a baby brother or sister. Jacob and Rose were standing side by side with grins from ear to ear. Ricky, on the other hand, had never diverted his eyes from Harley. Then I saw him standing at the end of the aisle. Raven was dressed in black jeans, brilliant blue shirt, and as always, his black hat. He had a well-groomed mustache that dribbled onto his chin. For a man, he was strikingly handsome. My steps quickened to hurry to his side. His cocky sideways grin and sparkling eyes received me with anticipation as Max and I came to the boulder. Everyone took their seats.

Marcus wrapped up the music as Chief Wolfchild stepped forward. He nodded to everyone. "Who gives this bride to this groom?"

In a simultaneous movement, every person in attendance stood and stated two words in unison, "We do."

The chief nodded again as everyone took their seats as he continued, "It is agreed on by many that if ever two people were meant to be together, it is the two of you."

Max tenderly kissed my cheek. "You look beautiful, sissy." He then took his place as Raven's best man.

Chief Wolfchild began, "It gives me much happiness to see the numerous faces that have come to witness the joining of Raven and Ashley. It has been brought to my attention that you have prepared your own vows. Ashley, you may begin."

My hands shook as I opened the small piece of paper I had written my vows on. I knew there was no way I could look Raven in the eye, or I would break down crying. I could picture Monica jumping up to fix my mascara. In a small shaking voice, I began, "Raven, in the past few months, I have been terrified, relieved, scared, determined, sad, and angry, but never alone. You have been by my side for all of it. You have seen me at my best and my worst, and you never wavered. I promise to stand by your side and face any and every opposition that tries to tackle us. I dedicate my heart and soul to you, and I promise to work every day toward making a better life not only for us but also for our children. I love you."

The chief nodded to my beloved husband-to-be as he began to speak. Raven didn't have a paper; he was going straight off the cuff. "I'm not real good with words or standing up in front of people talking. But, Ashley, you came into my life like a tornado and turned it upside down. I wasn't always nice to you, and for that, I'm sorry. You are everything I never knew I wanted. You're the reason I get up every morning, you're on my mind all day, then I come home to you and our family, and I can't imagine life being any better than this. And I know in my heart that you're the woman for me because you're everything I'm not. And without trying to sound corny, you complete me. And you make me a better person. And I promise to spend the rest of my life loving you, providing for you, and being the type of man you can be proud to call your husband. I love you." Raven exhaled deeply, relieved that part was over.

Chief Wolfchild looked at Raven. "That was a lot of ands." The chief stepped forward and clasped mine and Raven's right hands within his. "Throughout life, we face many hardships and many joyous occasions. However, if we are lucky to find someone we deem worthy to share these events with, then the joy is multiplied and the hardships don't seem to suck so bad. Ashley Reese, is it your wish to join your life with Raven's in good times and bad?"

"I do," I stated in a matter-of-fact tone.

"Raven Malone, is it your wish to join your life with Ashley's in good times and bad?"

"I do." Raven matched my tone.

"Are you real sure?" A bout of snickers fell over the crowd as Raven looked at Chief Wolfchild, a little confused.

"Yeah, I'm positive." Raven then looked at me, smiling.

"Well, okay then, this couple before me wants to unite. Is there anyone here who believes that this should not happen?"

All the men in the crowd stood up and cocked a gun as if to quickly rid of anyone who dared to protest the union, and another louder bout of laughter escaped the crowd.

The chief's voice grew louder. "Then so shall it be. I join you, Ashley, and you, Raven, in faith, love, and life." The chief placed my hand into Raven's. "Now Greta and Frances have nothing short of smorgasbord over there, so will you kiss your bride so we can go eat?"

Laughter rose from the crowd, along with a few claps. That was all the encouragement Raven needed as he removed his notorious black hat and threw it into the crowd. He grabbed me, wrapping his arm around my waist, pulling me close to him. He was smiling, and I was laughing as I reached up and trailed my fingers down the side of his cheek. He brought his lips down to mine, and he enveloped me in our first passionate kiss as husband and wife. Raven picked me up and swung me around as the crowd were wild with laughter and clapping. A few shots were fired into the sky in celebration. We all but ran down the aisle, dodging bird seed that was being thrown. We received well-wishes and congratulations with smiles. Max and Monica each hugged me and, of course, welcomed Raven into the family as if he weren't already a part of it.

We then made our way into the main hall of the lodge, which was completely decorated in blue and silver. One table was reserved for the bride and groom. We each fixed a plate of food and sat down to eat just as Greta ushered us over to the cake table to cut the cake. This was the first time I noticed someone taking photographs. We followed instructions and cut the cake, then drank punch with our arms intertwined. Neither of us cared for this part, but Greta and Frances had worked so hard we weren't going to deny them the pleasure they wanted. We played along and eventually got to eat a little bit.

Harley called for attention on the small stage area. "Can I have your attention, please?" All eyes and ears fell on her. "My sister and I have worked on something, and we want to sing it for Mama and Raven." Kat walked onto the stage and joined her sister. Marcus jumped to the piano and began playing as each of my girls took a microphone. The girls began singing "Lean on Me," and before they knew what was happening, almost everyone joined in. Hands were up in the air, people singing along. Someone grabbed a guitar, and someone else started beating on the tables as if they were drums. Even Greta and Frances bumped hips in rhythm. Everyone had a blast, which continued for over an hour with song after song. Raven and I danced and enjoyed watching our family have fun. Max danced around, bouncing Nyte and Summer on each hip. But all good things must come to an end. After a while, it was dark, and people started leaving.

Max and Jacob pulled Raven to the side as they talked among themselves. I noticed Monica was at the door, holding my jacket.

"Time to go," Raven said.

"Go where?" I asked in confusion.

"It's what we worked on last night. Just shut up and go with it." Raven ushered me to the door.

We walked out onto the porch where one horse was saddled and waiting for us. "Raven, I'm in a wedding dress. I can't ride a horse. Are you serious?"

People started filing onto the porch, waving goodbye. Raven mounted the horse and smiled down at me. Max and Jacob sneaked up behind me and hoisted me up just enough for Raven to pull me onto the horse. I was sitting almost in his lap with both legs on one side. All I could do was shake my head at him and couldn't help but smile. I suppose I should have been grateful he didn't pull me over the other way with my ass in the air. I wouldn't have put it past him, and he probably would have if he had thought about it himself. I simply draped my arm around him and did what he said and sat there and just enjoyed everything. Harley held Nyte as they waved goodbye. Kat was standing next to the chief, who still had a plate of food. I wished I had eaten more. Soon, we were out of sight as we rode off into the darkness.

"Don't worry. You have a change of clothes in the saddlebag. Monica thought of everything."

Nestling my head into his shoulder, I sighed a breath of relief. "It's been such a long happy day. I love you so much."

"I love you too." Raven kissed my forehead.

We stopped in a clearing. Peeking up, I saw a tent had been set up for us. Raven helped me down, and we went inside the tent. Monica must have known we would still be hungry because she had two dinner plates filled, including an extra piece of cake for dessert. We ate, then bedded down for our first night as husband and wife.

CHAPTER 2

THE NEXT MORNING, we rode back into town, and nothing had changed. People waved happily to us from their property; dogs ran freely throughout the streets. I was going to miss this place. In just one short week, we would be leaving to make our long journey back to Nebraska. At least this time, we didn't have the threat of snow.

That night, we sat around a campfire with Rose and Jacob. We decided it would be best to travel south past Billings and into Wyoming then east to Nebraska. The roads should be open more, and more towns should be open for business. We had been on the reservation for nearly four months. Surely the world had come back together in some form of civility. Only one thing bothered me. Every night, I would turn on the radio, and not a single station would come in. Raven told me that it was because of the mountains, but my gut was telling me it was something else.

Everyone laughed and joked around while I sat quietly in Raven's arms.

"Are you okay?" Raven asked.

"Yeah, I'm just a little tired. I think I'm going to head on to bed." Rising to my feet, I said my good nights.

"Can't get enough of the honeymoon, huh?" Raven smiled up to me.

I shook my finger at him. "Don't be crude, Raven. Good night, everyone."

Walking back quietly to the safety of my room, I got ready for bed and quickly fell asleep with Nyte sleeping peacefully in her bed. I wasn't sure what time Raven slid into bed, but he was up before me, holding Nyte and a cup of coffee out to me. "I gotta go to work. I'll be home late this evening. We are running the herd to the north field. I only got two more days of this, then I'm all yours." He quickly kissed me and left.

I had already quit working at the local hospital so I could prepare for the trip. I gathered Nyte and went to the main house to see Greta and Frances.

"There's my baby." Frances immediately ran over and plucked Nyte from my arms. "I am going to miss you so much when you leave."

"No worries. You will have another little one you can spoil soon," I stated with a laugh, reminding her of Dallas and Makayla's impending arrival.

"True, but everyone is different. Even at this age, they have personalities, and this one is special," she said, playing with Nyte. "She has a special purpose in this world. That table of stuff over there is for you and Raven."

Glancing over, I saw a table full of jars adorned with ribbons and bows. "I thought I said no wedding gifts. You all have done so much as it is."

"My dear, they are not wedding gifts. They are going-away gifts, so stick that in your peace pipe and smoke it," Greta stated firmly as she came into the main room. "We told everyone no wedding gifts, but they brought these anyway." Greta handed me one of the large jars.

After close inspection, I noticed it was beans and pasta with seasoning in the jars.

Frances blurted out, "They are meal jars, and with the number of jars you have there, you shouldn't have to worry about trying to find out what to cook for your whole trip."

Walking over to the table, I closely inspected the decorated jars. There were a lot of meal jars complete with instructions, but also jams and jelly, biscuit and cake mixes. Then I noticed a large package with a smaller one wrapped and taped together. "What's this one?"

"This one is from the chief. We couldn't tell him not to give you anything. I know Raven isn't here, but you could go on and open it. I'm sure he wouldn't mind," Frances explained.

"You just want to find out what it is too," I said, looking at Frances, whose lips were pressed together tightly, trying not to smile with her eyes slightly widened. "Okay, I'll open it." Ripping the paper and opening the smaller package first, I held up a very nice digital camera. All the photos taken at the wedding were on the camera. "Oh my goodness, I never thought I would see technology again." I laughed in spite. I ripped open the bigger box and found a laptop computer and a card. Inside the card, it read, "Every journey should be documented."

"This is too much. I don't know what to say." I was almost in tears.

"Well, there is no use saying anything except thank you. The chief wanted you to have it, and he won't hear anything about it."

"Do you know where he is?"

"I think he is waiting for you in your special place," Frances explained, pointing out the window. "We will take care of Nyte today. I know you have a lot to do."

"Thank you so much for everything, both of you." Hugging each of them quickly, I then went outside.

I found the chief leaning against my boulder. "I got the gifts. I don't know what to say but thank you. It's very extravagant."

"You are welcome. I meant what I said in the note. Every journey should be recorded. This is how your generation does things."

"It's still extravagant, and I appreciate it."

"The winds are changing. My bones are getting chilled, and I'm afraid this journey will be more difficult. In difficult times, you must search deep and find your strength from within in order to do the things that must be done."

"Do you think we need to wait, push back the date when we leave?" I didn't want to get caught in another snowstorm. My eyes darted around the sky, looking for some sign of impending bad weather.

"I don't mean the weather, little one. I sense an evil presence in the air. I think you should stick to your plan. But when there are hardships, you will have to be strong to overcome the obstacles." The chief paused as if being in deep thought for the correct words. "But even the hard journeys should be documented so future generations will know what it means for them to be here."

I nodded, showing my understanding of what he was saying. "We are leaving Saturday. Will you be there to see us off?"

"I wouldn't miss it." The chief smiled what little bit of smile he had.

The week passed quickly as we prepared the wagons and packed all our gear. And before we knew it, our last night was upon us. We sat around a campfire with many of our friends from the reservation till well past dark. Soon, the crowd dissipated, and we retired to our rooms.

"Are you okay? You have seemed a little out of sorts lately," Raven asked, squeezing my shoulders as I put the last of our clothes into a tote.

"I think I'm just scared," I stated, looking to him for some sort of comfort.

"Scared of what?"

"I'm not sure. I just have a feeling, a bad feeling. What if something bad happens?" I stated.

"You mean something besides friends dying, Harley nearly getting raped, you getting shot—"

Quickly snapping, I cut Raven off, "Okay, I see your point. Yes, I know we have already been through a lot, but what if—"

Raven interrupted, "Honey, you could drive yourself crazy thinking of all the *what-ifs*. You took a chance the first time, and you got stuck with me. So this trip should be a breeze. We got to take it one day at a time, always keeping safety in mind and hope for the best. Everything will be fine as long as we are together." Raven held me close. I felt so safe in his arms, and for a moment, I believed what he was saying.

Dawn came early. Raven popped into the room, giddy and grinning. "Rise and shine."

I only groaned and instinctively reached out for the cup of hot coffee that I knew was awaiting me.

Raven laughed. "I would've thought that after having to wake you up early for so long that you would have gotten used to it by now."

"I'll never get used to it. I'm a night owl. Always have been, always will be."

"Yeah, it used to drive our mom crazy," Max boasted as he entered the room. "Come on, sleepyhead, time to move it. I'm taking Nyte to say goodbye to everyone and get the girls in the wagon. So suck down that coffee and get a move on, sissy." Max picked up Nyte and took her away with the small bag I had ready for her.

"Sure, Max, come in, get my baby, and leave." I scoffed.

"Oh, come on now, we are all excited and ready to get going. Don't get your panties in a bunch." Raven leaned down and kissed my neck.

"I don't have anything bunched. I'm just trying to focus my eyes," I said, rubbing the sleep from my eyes.

"Well, suck it down, sister. We gotta get to moving," Raven teased.

"Okay, just give me a minute." Quickly sprinting to the bathroom, I splashed cold water on my face. I wasn't looking forward to saying goodbye, not to our friends or to my mountains. A bad feeling was burning a hole in my gut as I looked in the mirror with water dripping down my face. I had to pull it together. My family was all excited. We had a long trip ahead of us, and they needed me. I just had to suck it up; we were leaving. Swallowing the last of my coffee and jerking on my clothes, I left the safe mental confines of the bathroom. Raven was waiting for me with the door open.

"Are you ready for this?" Raven asked.

Picking up my knapsack, I walked over to my husband. "As long as you are by my side, I'm ready for anything." I kissed him quickly and went out the door.

"Mama, look!" Kat called out in excitement as she paraded in front on a horse of her very own. "I don't have to stay cooped up in the wagon all day. I can ride with y'all now."

"Oh, Kat, she's beautiful," I said, patting the horse.

"Chief gave her to me. He said I was old enough and that Monica was going to have her hands full with Dannie and two babies in the wagon. Can I keep her? Please say yes!"

I glanced over at the chief, who was nodding and smiling. "Yes, baby, you can keep her as long as you still help Monica when she needs it. Maybe Dannie can ride with you sometimes."

"Deal." Kat beamed with pride and rode around the yard.

Everything was packed and ready. I removed the digital camera from my pocket and snapped a few photos of our friends. I found Marcus kicking at the dirt. "Hey, you!"

Marcus popped his head up. "Yeah."

"I'm going to miss you. Don't get me wrong, I am glad you have your mom and dad, but I will miss you. I will get you a letter as soon as I know the mail is running," I explained.

Marcus nodded, then looked at me with sadness in his eyes. "I'm glad both of my parents are alive and that you and Raven are happy together, but…" Marcus paused and looked down then back at me. "I'm going to miss you too. You have never been a possible stepmother to me, Ashley. You have always been my friend. When I thought I had lost both Mom and Dad, I was sad, but I all I could think about was, at least I had you. I'm going to miss you too." Marcus reached out and hugged me, laying his head on my shoulder.

I wrapped my arms around Marcus and savored this rare show of emotion from my friend. "Okay, don't get mushy on me. I want to get through this without crying." I patted him on the back. "Stay true to yourself, Marcus. You are a very unique, smart, and multitalented person who can do anything you set out to accomplish. And maybe one day you can come see us on the farm. We will teach you to milk a cow or something."

We both looked at each other and laughed. "Yeah, I don't think so. But I will come for a visit one day."

"I'll look forward to it."

We said our goodbyes and expressed our deepest gratitude to everyone. Monica retired to her wagon with Dannie, Nyte, and Summer. Harley was driving one wagon, while Max drove the other. Rose drove their own, leaving Jacob, Ricky, Raven, and myself to ride and scout.

I mounted my horse as the chief walked over to me. "Just remember what I said."

"I will, and thank you for everything." Reaching down, I shook his leathery hand and watched him walk away.

The wagons lurched forward. Everyone was waving and shouting; some were crying. I brought up the rear, looking back one last time at my thinking spot and my mountain. I couldn't look long, or I would be the next one crying. I probably already had a hundred photos of the mountains, but a few more wouldn't hurt. I never wanted to forget the rugged elegance of the view that the lodge had offered. We drove on through town, waving to everyone as we passed, and all too soon, we were off the reservation and well on our way home.

CHAPTER 3

I HAD TO ADMIT, it was a beautiful day. There was still a brisk breeze steadily blowing from the north. Wildflowers bloomed randomly in the fields as a radiant sun danced overhead. There was nothing but silence around us except for the occasional songbird. Kat rode her horse proudly, like the big girl that she was now. She seemed to have grown a foot and matured a mile since we had left Texas. Harley sat high in the driver's seat of one wagon. She, too, had changed. She had gladly traded in her designer leather boots and popularity status for flannel shirts and horses. I never would have thought my daughter would be happy, but there she was with one of the biggest smiles I had ever seen. Raven led the caravan, being the leader he was always meant to be, and Max was nothing less than content.

The small towns of Cut Bank and Shelby weren't much on our first way through, but now they were even worse. They were nothing more than ghost towns. Windows were boarded up; random bits of trash and debris littered the streets. Abandoned cars, some with the doors left open, lined the streets with dust covering the windshields.

Raven caught me looking around. "They must have all left and went to the tent cities."

"Yeah, but that's just it. I thought there would be more cities up and running. I thought the power would be on by now. Something's not right." I shook my head in concern and rode on.

Just outside Shelby, we pulled off into the woods to camp for the night. Everyone went quickly about doing their job. Quickly camp was set up, and Monica finished dinner while Kat and Harley kept the little ones entertained.

We ate and settled in for the night. I had to admit, I was exhausted, but I took my turn at first watch. Jacob relieved me, and Raven relieved him, leaving Max to sleep all night. We planned on switching out so we each got one full night of sleep every few nights.

Raven woke me the next morning with coffee and a smile. "Good morning."

I could only look at him through sleepy, squinted eyes. "Well, it's a bright one. I'm starting to miss that dust cloud."

Raven only laughed at me and shook his head.

I quickly got myself and Nyte dressed and joined the others for breakfast. Before I had finished eating, everyone was packing up and getting ready to go. I quickly washed my plate and cup and delivered them to Monica. "You doing okay?"

"I'm fine. I'm just figuring out what to fix for dinner and constantly trying to come up with creative ways to keep the kiddos occupied." Monica sounded exasperated.

"Do you want Dannie to ride with Kat for a while?" I offered.

"No, we better save that excursion. I just got accustomed to everything being so wide and open. It's going to take a few days to get into a rhythm," Monica said, wiping her brow.

"Well, just let us know. We appreciate everything you do and want to make it as easy as possible on you."

"Thank you, Ashley. I'll let you know," Monica said.

We were soon on our way again. I was constantly and carefully scanning the tree lines. I so desperately wanted to see some sign of life. We hadn't seen anyone since we left the reservation. It was as if we were the only people left in the world. Raven rode proud with Kat at his side. They stayed in near constant conversation. I would have saved him from Kat's chatter, but he seemed to be oddly enjoying it. Harley drove the wagon, and Ricky watched her. Jacob would occasionally entertain himself with what was all too often a one-sided discussion with his son. Ricky's attention always fell back to Harley. I, on the other hand, even though I paid attention to everything going on around me, stayed mentally in my own little world where I knew something was horrifically wrong in the world.

Somewhere near Bennett, Colorado

"The base in Denver is under the control of our new so-called government. Those bastards have even gone as far as flying a new United States flag," Bret explained to the president after he and Nicolette returned from their scouting mission. President Mallory looked at him in question. "Sir, the flag is red, white, and blue, but the colors are displayed in sideways rectangles with one black star in the center. The place is crawling with military. There is no way you are going to walk in there and say who you are without being killed. However, the good part to seeing the flag is that it will make it easier to identify who can be trusted."

Nicolette nodded in agreement. "I say we keep moving north. There are going to be local militias that would be more willing to hear us out and actually listen. But I am afraid there is more to this New World Order." Nicolette's head dropped. President Mallory probed her to go on. Nicolette took a deep breath and made an attempt to get comfortable as she went into explaining the current betrayal of America.

From the beginning of this disaster, Martin Lee knew exactly what he wanted to do. He had always been an opportunist, and this was the biggest opportunity of his life. Finally, after all the years of political bullshit, ass-kissing, and backstabbing, he would have the biggest payoff in his life. The United States had become too free, especially free-minded. The peons of this land had no idea what was good for them, so the decision to decide needed to be removed from them. In Martin's world, there would be one religion, one currency; there would be no armed citizens. They would live where and how they were told. They would work hard from dusk till dawn and, in return, given food and shelter. If anyone refused, they would simply be removed from the equation. He had the full support of the U5. The civilian concentration camps had been set up and started to receive its labor force. Although some people would resist at first, they had the lab set up at the underground base in Denver in order to change their minds. Martin sinisterly chuckled to himself as he pictured hardworking blue-collar Americans strapped to a cold metal slab engulfed with headgear that would brainwash them into accepting their new way of life. And if it failed, and he was sure there would be some cases that it would, the wayward soul would be imprisoned and eventually incinerated for their resistance. The plan was to sweep the military through the plains, wiping out major areas. He had secretly and discreetly secured troops along the northern border to begin the sweeps south and to the south to sweep north. As well as the bases he had acquired in his new leadership would patrol centrally. Civilians would be loaded into boxcars and shipped by rails that he now controlled to the nearest concentration camp. His plan was indeed coming together nicely, and now that he had successfully removed that arrogant, constitution-wielding idiot Mallory, nothing was going to stop him.

President Mallory held his head in disgust. "I think I'm going to be sick."

"You actually saw our military loading normal everyday citizens onto trains?" Vincent asked.

Bret and Nicolette both nodded. "It was horrible, sir. I believe Nicolette is correct. We have to keep moving north. There is bound to be somewhere we can start."

Vincent broke in, "What about Texas? I know they have a militia."

"Texas would be a good choice, except the coast had severe damage from the tsunami. And now Mexico has issued a public proclamation for its citizens who currently reside in the US, illegal or otherwise, to return to Mexico to protect its borders into the US. I'm not exactly sure going south would be a wise choice."

"Why even bother? At this point, I'm not sure there is anything we can do that would make a difference. This whole thing has gotten out of control." Mallory asked the question that stopped all of them in their tracks.

Nicolette stood up and pointed her finger directly at the president. "Don't you dare do that. Don't you dare give up, or I will hand deliver you to that damn passenger train. Do you hear me?"

Mallory looked up at her in shock. Bret and Vincent looked on, horrified, as Nicolette continued, "I helped you escape, deserted my little girl and my family because I believe in you. I believe in doing what is right. So I'm sorry. You don't get the luxury of giving up. You can suck it up and keep going and do the damn best you can with what we have. If it means wiping your ass on a tree bark, then so be it. I will stand in front of you and fight till my dying breath. But in return, you do not get the advantage of feeling sorry for yourself. You need to take a time-out. Pull yourself together and remember who the hell you are and what you stand for and who you're fighting for. This is hard on all of us, but we can either give up or we can keep going and find someone who will listen and help. And if you're not prepared to do that, then you better let me know right now." Nicolette noticed all eyes on her as she remembered exactly who she was talking to. And if her words alone weren't enough, she was standing in front of the president, shaking her finger as if she were scolding a child. Nicolette felt a quick need to redeem herself, so she quickly added "sir" and sat down quickly.

Vincent was the first to break the dead, eerie silence. "Are you finished with your tantrum?"

"She's right. And the comical thing is, she is the only one who had big enough balls to put me in my place." President Mallory rose and walked over to Nicolette, who was doing everything in her power to keep from crying. He reached down and took her arms, pulling her up. "I promise you right now. I will keep fighting. I will go north. I will keep looking for someone who will listen and will help begin putting this country back together. If you can promise me something, if I ever step out of line, you have to put me back in the right frame of mind. There are too many lives at stake for me to give up. I am the rightful president, and I will fight till my dying breath to take back the position." Mallory did something never witnessed; he pulled Special Agent Nicolette Williams into an embrace. "I promise, you will see your daughter again."

Not even the Hoover Dam could hold back the tears that exploded from Nicolette's eyes. "Thank you, sir." She quickly pulled back and wiped her face. "I'm sorry, sir."

"Don't be. You did what needed to be done. I'm glad I can count on you," Mallory stated.

"Okay, so it's settled. We sleep tonight, and tomorrow we start making our way north. We need to stay off the main roads. We can't take a chance of being caught." Bret took out a map as he started plotting their next journey.

Great Falls, Montana

As we entered into Great Falls, I gasped sharply as I looked around. Only a few months before, this had been a recovering city. I was expecting stores to be opened, but there was nothing. All stores had been closed or burned down. There was no evidence that anyone inhabited this desolate place. Looking to Raven for some sort of support, maybe this would make him realize that something was wrong.

He noticed me staring at him and made his way over. "Don't worry. They are probably at the base."

I looked at Raven, surprised at his childish ability to be naive. "No, Raven, everyone is not at the base. This is wrong. Something is wrong here. Can't you see that?"

"There is no need to speculate and get everyone's feathers ruffled when we don't know what happened. They may have been moved to another town." Raven rode ahead, not wanting to hear my conspiracy theories. He was sure there was a reasonable explanation as to why the town had been shut down. He wanted to keep to the mission at hand. They had to get back to his homestead, and all would be fine.

I noticed Max watching me, and all I could do was shake my head. I knew something was wrong, but I didn't have enough information to make a plausible argument. I looked around at the buildings we had visited on our first trip through town. The general store had been burned, but the bar still stood. This was the place where Raven and I had shared our first dance. As my eyes danced around the buildings, I thought I saw the curtains move in one of the upstairs windows. I stopped and watched intently, wanting to yell out or tell Raven. However, in his current state of mind, he would only say it was the wind. After several minutes of not seeing anything out of the norm, I moved on. I didn't know what it was going to take to make Raven admit that there was something strange going on. However, I knew that I was going to have to have definitive proof of something before I would say anything further; otherwise, I was going to be dubbed the worrywart of the group.

The next few days, we traveled along Highway 89 through the Little Belt Mountains, which ran through the Lewis and Clark National Forest. I had kept quiet for the most part. Even when we passed the base where the massive survivor camp had been, we found nothing. It looked as if everyone had picked up and moved in the middle of the night. I only shook my head and stared at Raven, who seemed to only shake it off by shrugging his shoulders. I was sure he felt something was off if he admitted it or not.

That night around the campfire, everyone was quiet. Everyone was feeling the loneliness of the road and shared in wondering why they hadn't come across another living soul, yet no one mentioned it. I finished my plate and finished feeding Nyte and put her in the tent. I took first watch and was happy to see Max when he came to relieve me.

"Sissy, are you okay?" Max asked.

"Yeah, just tired. Why?"

"You just seem, I don't know, out of sorts. Are you and Raven fighting?"

I scoffed. "Now, Max, you know, if Raven and I were fighting, you would know about it. I just feel like something is wrong, and he doesn't. It worries me that we haven't seen anyone else and that there are no towns open. I mean, where the hell did everyone go? Did the rapture happen? I'm just confused, and Raven is just concentrating on getting us home."

"Well, lately, I have been worried too. It does seem like we should have seen somebody along the way. But like Raven said, maybe all survivors have been relocated. It would make more sense to have everyone in a more central location rather than having to deliver supplies to numerous towns."

So he had talked to Raven too. At least I knew I wasn't alone in my concerns. And maybe Raven was right. It was just the not knowing that was killing me. "I'm tired. I'm just going to get some sleep. I'm sure things will work out."

Max nodded. "I just wanted you to know that things aren't going unnoticed."

"Good night, Max." I hugged my brother tightly and crawled into the tent, curling up to Raven. He had Nyte pulled to his chest. Gently kissing him on the shoulder, I pulled the blanket up. I placed my hand on his hips and pulled myself closer to him, securing the blanket around both of us. I prayed he was right and that I was concerned for no reason. I remembered about just turning everything over to God. Everything happens for a reason, and God would provide and protect us.

The next morning, we made our way into White Sulphur Springs. This town was nothing new. All buildings were boarded up or burned. Only loose remnants of the life that once occupied this area littered the streets. I let out an exasperated breath, then noticed a woman standing in an upstairs window. I stared for a moment to make sure I was indeed seeing what I thought I was. When the woman noticed me staring, she quickly turned away.

"Wait!" I cried out.

Max stopped the wagon and looked at me. Raven had ridden ahead and didn't hear me. "What is it, sissy?"

Pointing at the window, I said, "There is someone up there." I was already dismounting my horse.

"Are you sure?" Max asked.

"Yes, I'm positive, and I'm going to check it out." I removed my pistol and slowly made my way to the building. The door wasn't boarded up or even locked. I looked back at Max, who was getting down from the wagon, and Raven making his way back to us. I proceeded into the building before he could have the opportunity to talk me out of it. Bare shelves hosted nothing but dust. The windows were sparsely covered by tattered curtains. Finding the steps, I made my way up them, attempting to listen for any movement. Reaching the top, I checked the first room only to find it empty. The second was a bathroom, again empty. The third was a bedroom with windows facing the street. This was the room I was looking for.

"Is anyone in here?" Pushing into the room, I saw a slim figure squatting in the corner. Catching my breath, I lowered my pistol. "Are you okay?" No response came from the frail-looking woman as she cowered in the corner. "My name is Ashley. Are you hungry?"

The woman dressed in tattered jeans and shirt looked quickly at me. Taking a moment to look around, there was one small bed in the room that was dirty as well. The room clouded in dust. I could tell that by the woman's response that she was indeed hungry. There was no evidence in this room that she had eaten anything of substance in a while. The woman slowly rose to her bare feet that were nasty, corroded with dirt and grime. "Are you with them?" the woman produced a small meek voice that was barely audible.

"Yes, that's my family down there." I motioned outside the window.

"You're one of them."

"One of who? I don't know what you mean," I continued closer.

"You're a wolf. You're with the wolf pack." The woman's voice grew stronger.

"Wolf pack? I have never heard of them. Who are they? Can you tell me what happened here?"

"Got to run, got to hide, stay out of sight. They will get you. You go away and never come back. No, no, no," the woman rambled.

Nothing was making any sense, but I felt like I had to get more information from this woman. Proceeding with caution, I continued, "Who is this wolf pack?"

"You are a wolf. I see it. I know it. You want to take me away." The woman began pushing herself along the wall. "You're the wolf."

"No, I'm no wolf."

The woman laughed. "They'll come, and they huff and puff and blow you down." She stopped and looked directly at me. "I won't go. No, I won't go."

In a swift, agile move that I wasn't expecting, the woman threw herself at me, knocking me to the floor. My gun went off, but not in a helpful direction before it was knocked from my hand. I watched as it slid across the floor away from me. The crazy woman with oddly unbelievable strength pinned me to the floor and held up a knife. I had no intention of hurting the woman, but now it was a fight for survival. This lady was crazy, and I had to defend myself. Throwing my hands up, I caught the woman's arm. Holding the woman's wrist tightly in one hand, I flipped the woman over onto the floor, simultaneously taking away the knife, and drove it into her chest. Raven busted into the room and yanked me into a stance. For a moment, I stood and watched the knife quiver, sticking out of the woman's chest. I knew from the way the knife moved that it was in the woman's heart, or at least damn close. I stood over the woman and watched the life drain from her.

"Would you mind telling me what the hell just happened?" Raven said, pulling me away from the corpse.

"I saw her standing at the window watching us. I wanted to see who it was and see if she could give me any information."

"And did you find out anything?" Raven asked.

"She called me a wolf, mentioned a wolf pack. I don't know. It didn't make any sense."

Raven grabbed my shoulders. "Of course, it didn't. This chick was obviously crazy, Ashley, and you barrel in here. You're lucky she didn't kill you."

I looked up to Raven and shook free of his grasp. "As you can see, I can handle myself, Raven, and I think you're missing the bigger picture here. Look at her, look at her skin. It's pale, like she hasn't been in the sunlight for months. She was scared I was going to take her away. Something is going on, and you seem to be oblivious to it."

"No, Ashley, I'm not." Raven turned from me and paced the room. "I see it too, okay? I know something is not right, but until I know what it is, I'm not going to put myself in danger in a stupid attempt to figure out what it is. You can't do this."

"So you admit something is strange."

"Yes, but our plan hasn't changed, and until we see differently, I think we need to continue with our plans. We have enough supplies to make it, but we have to play it smart, and you running up here ain't it."

"Well, O powerful leader, if you had simply expressed that you shared my concerns rather than letting me think I was the only one, then maybe I wouldn't have." I was pointing my finger at Raven.

"Okay, yes, I should have talked to you earlier. I just didn't want to worry you any more than what you already were." Raven pulled me to his chest. "Do you have any idea how scared I was when I heard that gunshot?"

"You guys all right?" Max asked, coming through the door, stopping the moment he saw the dead body.

"Yeah, your sister is just expressing her homicidal tendencies again." Raven kissed my forehead.

"Well, she is good at that. What happened?"

I stepped forward and picked up my pistol. "She was crazy. She attacked me, and I defended myself. I didn't want to kill her. It just sorta happened." I walked past the men and made my way back outside.

Max turned to Raven. "Is she really okay?"

"Yeah, she did what she needed to do." Raven left Max in the room with the body.

Max looked at the blood that was now pooling onto the floor, remembering the other lives his sister had taken since the whole mess started. He was proud in a way and scared in another. "She always does." Max turned and made his way out.

Everyone was standing outside, patiently awaiting word that all was well. The expression of relief crossed all their faces when I walked back out. Seeing everyone looking at me, I held up my hands. "We are all fine. I will explain everything tonight over dinner. Right now, I feel like we need to get moving and put this town behind us before we make camp."

Raven and Max rejoined the group, and after making camp several miles out of town, I held true to my word and recounted what happened in that dingy room with the crazy lady.

"It sounds like you were lucky," Jacob stated, finishing his dinner.

"I was, but I'm stilled concerned as to why this woman was so scared. What has happened in this world? What would make her so afraid that she wouldn't even go outside? And I don't know what this wolf pack is, but I know I don't want any part of it," I explained.

"We are going to have to stay alert at all times. No one goes anywhere alone." Raven was speaking to everyone but cut his eyes and looked directly at me. Everyone agreed.

"I just want to go to bed." I washed my plate and cup and put it up in the wagon. I collected Nyte and went into the tent. Raven soon followed.

"I just wanted to check on you."

"I am fine. I just want to sleep. Tomorrow will be a better day." I was clearly not in the mood to talk. I only covered Nyte and myself up and laid my head down.

"Okay, I love you, Ashley." Raven patted my hip and left the tent, leaving me to finally be able to breathe. I snuggled with my daughter, who was already slipping into dreamland. My thoughts shifted to the woman I had killed that day—the look of crazy fear that radiated from her eyes. I didn't know where she had gotten the knife from. She might have had it on her the whole time, and I had simply missed it. Raven was right about one thing—I was going to have to be smarter. I should have waited for someone to go with me. I had hoped that this trip would be easier or, at the very least, that no blood would be shed. I hadn't intended on killing the poor woman; I only wanted information. The image of the knife buried into the woman's chest, the way it quivered in correlation with her fading heartbeat flashed in my head. I shook my head as if to shake the image out. It was all too much to think about. I closed my eyes and pictured my secret spot on the mountain. I wished I was there right then. Things were bad out here, and I had a sinking feeling they were going to get a lot worse. At least I knew now that Raven was indeed concerned too and that I wasn't alone. The need to get home to Nebraska was growing more prevalent, but who was to say it was any better there? What if we got there and things were just as bad, if not worse? What would we do then?

I fell asleep not knowing what our future held, but the chief's words rang in my head. *In difficult times, you must search deep and find your strength from within in order to do the things that must be done.* I dreamed of my peaceful boulder overlooking the mountains and awoke with a sense of peace. I was determined to dig deep and find my inner strength once again to get myself and my family to safety wherever that might be.

CHAPTER 4

OVER THE NEXT few days, we continued south on Highway 89 to Springdale, where we started east on I-90. The state of Montana covered a vast area with an overabundant number of breathtaking views but lacked a variety of roads. We were attempting to keep the wagons as close together as possible, and Raven and Jacob took the lead and rode ahead to scout the area. I desperately had wished I had a calendar. All the days and nights seemed to be running together.

I noticed Raven and Jacob had rejoined the group, so I rode up to them. "How is it looking?"

"More of the same, I'm afraid. There is a semitruck up ahead. You feel like opening it and seeing if there is anything we can use?"

"Sure. How far?" I asked.

"Just over this hill. Come on." Raven took off and motioned to Jacob to stay behind with the rest of the group as I followed close behind him.

The large red-and-black truck was pulled onto the shoulder of the road. It had obviously been there awhile because grass was jutting up through the pavement around the tires. Raven and I dismounted and retrieved our firearms and opened the back of the truck. With no apparent movement, Raven climbed inside. He took a quick look around, then assisted me up. It took a moment for my eyes to adjust to the dim light. Looking around, I saw pallets of blankets and other evidence of life.

"Someone was living in here."

"Someone may still be living here. And frankly, I don't want to be caught breaking and entering," Raven stated as he climbed out of the truck, then helped me down and shut the door. The rest of their party came over the hill as Raven locked the truck back up. We waited for them to catch up.

"Find anything?" Jacob asked, hopeful.

"It looks like someone's been living in here. No idea if they are still around, but there's nothing we need in here, and no one seems to be around, so it's best we just keep moving," Raven explained.

I mounted up and rode on, following my husband and friend. I tried to act nonchalant about things, but the truth was that all this not knowing was killing me.

We seemed to be making good time on the road. By the next day, we made camp in Laurel. Kat and Dannie were running and playing tag while everyone set up camp. Harley and Ricky played with the babies, while Monica got dinner on the fire. Raven and I were feeding the horses when Kat and Dannie came running toward us.

"Mama, there is someone trapped down there!" Kat was shouting in excitement.

"People? Where?" Raven was the first to respond.

"On the other side of the hill," Kat explained and pointed.

Monica was already getting the kids in the wagon as Raven, Jacob, Max, and I grabbed weapons and footed it over the hill. Finally, another person. What would they be able to tell us? We ran in excitement, but what we found turned all our stomachs. A small concrete jailhouse had partially collapsed. One man dressed in an orange jumpsuit had his hand dangling from the window, calling out to us. He was filthy, and as we got closer, the stench that was emitting from this building was wretched.

"Hey, thank God. Can you get me out of here?" the man pleaded.

How could he have survived this long in that cell? Raven and Jacob danced around the rubble, inspecting it.

"What's your name?" I asked. "And why are you in jail?"

For the first time, Raven stopped and took a closer look at the actual structure and began to step back.

"My name is Anthony. I got put in here one night for driving drunk. This place was already starting to fall apart, then an earth-quake hit and finished it off." The man was still reaching for us.

I stepped back and pulled the men to the side. "This is bullshit. He is a prisoner for a reason. We can't prove what he had done to get in here. He could be a killer. And if he has been in there from the beginning, what has he eaten to stay alive?"

Jacob's eyes popped up in horror. "You don't think…"

"Oh yes, I do. There is no way he has survived in there on crack-ers and rainwater. Someone that's been in this situation for this long can't be sane. And if we let him out, there's a chance he is going to follow us and possibly hurt one of us. I don't know about you, but I don't want my family harmed because we tried to do the right thing here," I explained.

"Well, can we at least ask him?" Max asked.

"Sure, Max, go on ahead." This was the only way her brother was going to see things her way. He had to see for himself.

Max walked over to the window with bars. The guy was making every effort to grab ahold of Max, who was doing well to stay out of reach. Raven had his gun ready just in case anything went wrong. "Dude, you have been in here a long time."

"No shit, man. Come on, can you find some way to get me out, please?" the man pleaded.

"How have you survived in here, man? What did you eat?" Max asked, attempting to mask his nose from the putrid smell.

The man suddenly stopped reaching and looked at Max. "Are you hungry? Here, I got food. Just get me out of here." The man disappeared but quickly reappeared, chunking a piece of meat out the window. "Here, it tastes like chicken." The man began laughing.

We looked at the meat that he had tossed in disbelief. Jacob turned away quickly and puked. A bloody crudely severed forearm with an obvious bite lay on the ground before us. When our world ended, there had been more than one prisoner in that cell. This man was the only person left. He had eaten the others to stay alive. The aroma of rotting flesh and months of human urine and fecal matter was what we smelled. Max shook his head and walked away from the window with the man still laughing.

Raven and I looked at each other knowing what had to be done. "Max, if you will, please take Jacob back to the camp. We will handle this."

Max only nodded and took Jacob by the arm. Poor Jacob puked again before they got out of sight. I took out my pistol and walked up to the window. The man still continued to laugh wildly. I felt Raven's eyes on me.

"You know you don't have to. I'll do it."

I only shook my head. "No, there's no need. Remember, I'm good at this part." I took aim as the man looked directly at me.

"Thank you," he muttered as I fired off one shot that struck him directly between the eyes. His head snapped back as bloody brain matter splattered behind him. I put away my pistol and began walking back to the camp with Raven on my heels.

"Hey, wait." Raven grabbed my arm and spun me around. "Are you okay?"

"Why does everyone ask me that after I have killed someone?" I shouted in frustration.

Raven looked at me in shock. "Um, because it's kinda a big deal, and I want to make sure you are okay with it."

"Yes, I'm okay with it. Our kids were playing around here, Raven. There was no way in hell we were going to let him go free, and we couldn't let him continue to live like that and die a horrible death. I did that guy a favor. The main thing that bothers me is that the only two living souls we have seen since we left the reservation have been crazy. What do you want me to say? Do you want to know if the woman you married is a cold-blooded killer with no conscience? No, believe me, I see the faces of everyone I have killed every time I shut my eyes. But I wouldn't do it any differently. I have only killed someone who has attempted to hurt me or my family. Does it bother me? No, because I will do it again and again, over and over if I have to in order to protect the ones I love."

Raven continued to hold me in his arms, then pulled me into a tight hug. "I just worry about you." He held on to me for a while, then let go. "The thing is, I'm not sure I could have done what you just did. I don't think I could just walk up to someone and shoot him." Raven sat down on the broken concrete.

I sat beside him. "Look, you are good in a crisis. You keep your head, and I'm sure if someone was trying to hurt me or any of us that you wouldn't hesitate. Maybe I'm desensitized to blood, guts, and gore. But I can walk away right now and know at least this guy isn't starving to death trapped."

Raven scoffed and looked back at the severed arm. "Don't look like he was starving to me."

I laughed under my breath. "You know what I mean." I patted his leg. "Come on, we have work to do."

"You can do that? Just turn your back and move on?" Raven asked.

I looked at him. I could tell this situation really bothered him. "What choice do we have, Raven?"

Raven stood and hugged me tightly. "You have got to be the strongest woman I have ever met."

"You should have met my grandmother," I stated and walked hand in hand with Raven back to the camp.

Jacob and Max had filled everyone in on what we had found. So when they heard the gunshot, they knew what had been done. Max only looked at me and nodded. Jacob was sitting by the fire, nursing a bottle of water, recovering. He certainly wasn't dealing well with this one.

Everyone sat around the fire that evening in silence. It was really getting old, no one talking. I knew I had to do something to raise my family's spirits. There was one thing I could try.

"Screw this shit." I jumped up from the fire and walked to the wagon.

Everyone stopped and stared at me. Max rose to his feet, half expecting me to totally lose it. Raven had to be thinking the same thing, because at the same time, he jumped and retrieved his guitar from the wagon. I saw him and just smiled, then rejoined our family at the fire.

"You people need to lighten up. All of us have had a hard time the last few days, so maybe this will lift your spirits."

Raven whispered to me for a moment. I only laughed and nodded in agreement. Raven began strumming the guitar as I began clapping out the tune. Max only hung his head down to hide his smile as he immediately recognized the song as AC/DC's song "Highway to Hell." He looked up at me smiling, then began to tap his fork on his plate with the beat as I began to sing. Soon, we were all getting in on it, dancing around the fire, shouting out "Highway to hell!" Fists were pumping, faces were smiling, and feet were moving. I stood back for a moment and took it all in. Monica and Harley danced around with a baby on their hip. Even the babies were smiling, enjoying the moment. At the end of the song, they all fell down back in a circle, laughing.

"Damn, Ashley, only you," Jacob stated between snorts.

"Hey, Raven picked the song." I playfully pushed Raven's shoulder. "By the way, is your guitar okay? You were picking it pretty hard there."

"Yeah, it's been a while since I played that song." Raven drank on his water.

"'Nother one, play again," Dannie said, smiling.

"Oh, buddy, I don't know if I can do that one again," Raven stated, laughing. "But maybe your Aunt Ashley can think of one, a slower one. I'm getting too old for all that."

"Yeah, Aunt Ashee, you sing one," Dannie said as he sat in his mama's lap.

"Something slow, huh?" Ashley thought for a moment and came up with "Take Me Home, Country Roads" by John Denver. Raven nodded and began to play.

I began to sing as everyone settled in and began to sway with the music. I sang the whole song with all eyes on me and Raven. I wrapped it up, and everyone clapped.

"And the country roads are taking us home," Rose stated. "I can't wait to see our new home."

"Well, it's time for our little ones to go to bed." Monica stood up with Summer on her hip and took Dannie's hand.

Just then, Dannie pulled away from Monica and ran back to me and wrapped me in a tight bear hug. "Thank you, Aunt Ashee."

"You're welcome, buddy." I patted his bottom. "Go get some sleep. We got another big day tomorrow."

Dannie ran back to his mama and went into the wagon. I soon put Kat to bed in the wagon, and Harley wasn't far behind her. Raven was holding a sleeping Nyte at the fire. Rose, Jacob, and Ricky had already retired.

"That was nice, sissy. I think we all needed that," Max said as he got up.

"Thank you." I nodded. "Everyone just seemed so beat down. I figured it couldn't hurt to lighten the mood a little."

Max agreed and went into his wagon, leaving Raven and I alone.

"I'll take her into the tent. You take first watch, and Jacob will relieve you, then Max. It's my turn to sleep tonight." Raven arched his eyebrows in anticipation of a good night's sleep. He kissed me softly and took our daughter to bed.

I sat by the fire humming and scanning the tree line. Wolves howled from a distance. I shivered at the thought of the crazy lady calling me a wolf. Still wishing I knew what she meant, I pushed it out of my mind and tried to enjoy my alone time. After a few hours, Jacob relieved me as I retired into the tent, curled up beside my husband, and fell quickly asleep without any bad dreams.

The next morning, we started south, and the day after that, we pushed into Wyoming. It was a welcomed delight when we crossed the state line. It only got better when we made it to Crowley and found a few people out and about. Most of them were skittish and ran for cover at the sight of strangers making their way into the town. Raven and I dismounted and entered the store. There might have been four patrons in the store, but they all quickly dispersed when they saw strangers. Raven and I just looked at each other in question. Out of the four, three of them were men with scraggly beards. One lady was wearing a dress that was once very nice; however, time had taken its toll on it as well. The one thing that I noticed was the woman's hairy legs. It looked as if they hadn't seen a razor in months.

"How can we help you?" the shop owner called from behind the counter. The one thing that captured our attention was that the shop owner only displayed one hand. He was purposely hiding the other. Raven and I both knew he had a gun on us.

"We don't want any trouble. We are traveling from Montana, and y'all are the first open store," Raven explained.

"Who are we kidding? You are the first people we have seen since leaving Montana. Can you tell us what's going on?"

"The military wolf packs are going from town to town rounding people up. I heard they were putting them in boxcars and shipping them by rail somewhere," the shop owner explained, relaxing just a little.

"Wolf packs? Oh my god." Understanding what the crazy lady was trying to say, now I felt the hairs on my neck stand on end. "The president ordered this?"

"Which one, lady?" The shop owner scoffed. "You got one guy over in New York who is claiming he's the president, another at Fort Leavenworth, and another in Seattle, not to mention Texas is fighting to succeed. They will be their own country soon. The real president was killed, assassinated. The world has gone to hell in a hand basket, and we are all fighting for survival. Now is there something you need to get?"

"No, but thank you for the information. We will leave you be." Raven guided my arm.

"Hey, if you're smart, you will stay off the roads!" the shop owner called out to us as we left the store.

We quickly got on our horses and directed our family out of the town. Pulling off the road and into the woods around Basin, we camped for the night. We shared the information with everyone around the fire that night.

The next day, we made it to Worland, Wyoming. Riding past the municipal airport, Raven called out, "Hey, hold up! I want to check out the airport. I don't suppose any of you hillbillies know how to fly, do you?" Raven laughed. We circled around to the front gate.

Raven and I were voted to go inspect, while Max and Jacob stayed with the wagons.

We stepped around large army-green containers marked MRE; they were all empty. Large tents danced in the wind. Cots lined the walls of these tents, along with a few IV poles. This was all evidence that this area had been a refugee center. He went over to one of the planes and stopped abruptly. I slowly came up beside him. "Oh my god, Raven." Bullet holes sprayed along the length of the plane. Blood stained the pilot's door. As we looked on the ground, we found hundreds, if not thousands, of shell casings. There had been a bloody fight here.

"I think we need to get the hell out of here," Raven said, looking around cautiously.

"I think you're right." I turned and led the way out with Raven close behind me.

Jacob waved them down as they came out the gate. "Y'all find anything?"

"Nothing good," I said. "We need to go now. We need to find a safe place to camp tonight."

Jacob looked to Raven. "We can explain later, man. She's right. We need to get the hell out of here."

"The map says there is a river not far from here. I'll scout ahead and see if there's a good place to make camp," Jacob said as he took off on his horse.

Raven helped Harley turn the wagon around, and we were off again. We didn't have a choice but to take the main street right through town. Raven rode in front of their wagon, and I rode in front of Max. This once sleepy little town was now in a coma. Shop windows were busted and falling in; all had been raided of any supplies long ago. But the one thing that didn't get past any of us were the bullet holes that riddled every vehicle that was on the side of the street, as well as the brick-walled buildings. There had been a gunfight here as well. I was going to take a wild guess that the wolf pack was responsible. We crossed the railroad tracks, and a tingle went up my spine as I thought about humans being the cargo that last traveled these tracks. Was that why there was no one left in this town or any of the other towns we had passed thus far? Soon, we were relieved to see Jacob as he directed us to the camping spot off the road and near the water.

When we arrived at the site, Raven talked to Monica, and they decided to serve dinner from the wagon so they wouldn't have to start a fire. Raven was afraid a fire would be seen and draw unwanted attention. Raven then talked to Max and Jacob and explained what we had seen at the airport. There would be no singing around the fire tonight. Everyone would stay in their wagon or tent. I allowed Nyte to sleep in the wagon with Rose. It was decided that there would be two people on watch at all times. No chances would be taken with the safety of the family. The need to be vigilant was never so clear. Raven and I were in our tent with the map, attempting to plan out the best route to get our family off the main roads. We saw one point on the map we had to stop. It was only a half day of riding to get there. Even though we had to plan for safety, we had to plan for the health and well-being as well, and this one place would be good for all of us. At least that was the excuse we used in order to plan this stop.

CHAPTER 5

D AWN CAME EARLY with brilliance. We quietly ate breakfast, cleaned up, and started on our way without many words. We only had a half day's ride before we were going to stop. We stayed alert and vigilant. Max's new boxer pup that Ricky had given him, named Tyson, was walking proudly beside him. Even the dog seemed to be on high alert. My stomach churned at the thoughts of what possibly happened in the aftermath of the Alpine comet. I had wished that we could find the military and get definitive answers, but the way the shopkeeper talked, we needed to avoid the military at all cost. I knew we didn't have the firepower in our small arsenal to take on the military. It seemed I was the only one with the balls to actually kill someone, so I wasn't sure, if an actual fight happened, how much help anyone else in my family would be. I felt sure Raven would stand his own, but I didn't know about Max or Jacob.

We found Thermopolis without incident. Thermopolis, a natural hot spring, held sacred by Native Americans, was thought to have healing powers. The water was a constant 104 degrees surrounded by colorful rock walls. There was an actual park with several pools or hot, inviting thermal water. Once a tourist town with museums, it was now like all the others—deserted. We chose a spot on the outskirts so we could take cover quickly if the need arose.

We got camp set up and had lunch. Monica and Rose got dirty laundry washed and set it out to dry while we still had the sun. The kids played, while Raven and I stood watch. Jacob and Max went around to the old business to see if anything had been left behind that could be useful. I didn't like doing this, because to me, it felt like looting or grave robbing. As expected, they came back with nothing other than a horrified look.

Max walked up to us. "There are shallow mass graves behind one of the buildings."

"I don't know what happened to this old world," Jacob said, taking a seat.

I only looked at him. "This isn't the old world anymore, Jacob. This is the new one. We are going to have to adapt and overcome, or it's going to suck us in too."

Later, I stood watch over the women while they bathed and bathed the kids. Nyte loved the water. The men ate while we bathed, then Raven stood and watched as they bathed. Being on the reservation had spoiled us all, and I had to admit, we stank.

That night, everyone sat around an imaginary campfire, talking among ourselves. I excused myself to go bathe. Removing my clothes behind a large rock, making sure my pistol was within hand's reach, I slid into the hot water. It felt so good against my skin. I closed my eyes and took in all the healing waters had to offer. Dipping my head back into the water, I felt as if I were being watched. Opening my eyes quickly, Raven surprised me by grabbing me and pinning me against a rock. His lips quickly found mine as he enveloped me in a passionate kiss.

"You, my dear, are going to have to be more careful. Anyone could have sneaked up on you." He smiled down at me. "There are many bad things that could happen to a woman like you."

Reaching up, I trailed my fingers down his face. "Oh, I think I can handle myself." My finger continued trailing down his chest and under the water. With both hands, I grabbed his ass, pulling his hips to mine. "Would you care to demonstrate some of those bad things for me?"

Raven smiled as his head tilted back, allowing his eyes to roll. He groaned heavily. "You, my dear, are incorrigible."

Smiling up at him, I brought my arms up and crossed them in front of him as if they were tied up. "Sounds like I need to be punished." He needed no other encouragement as he grabbed my waist and lifted me up. I wrapped my legs around his waist and my arms around his broad shoulders. We made love under a full moon.

We stayed in the water longer than we should have, but it was so inviting neither of us wanted to leave. Raven helped me wash and rinse my hair and watched me shave my legs. How something so simple could feel so erotic dumbfounded me.

We made it back to the camp hand in hand. Everyone else had gone to bed. Max and Jacob were going to stand watch first, then Raven and I would take over.

"So did y'all use all the hot water?" Jacob said jokingly.

"No one likes a smart-ass, Jacob," Raven joked back. "Wake us for our watch." We went into our tent and held each other till we each fell asleep.

All too soon, Jacob woke us for our watch. The night air had a slight chill. I wished we had a fire, but I also understood why we couldn't, so my coat would have to suffice for now. I couldn't even nestle with Raven. We had to stay alert.

Raven took the north and east, and I took the south and west watch. And it was something in the south that caught my eye. "Raven, look." He came over and looked in the direction I was pointing. On top of a ridge that was several miles away, there was a light. "Is that a campfire?" I asked.

Raven grabbed his binoculars to get a better look. "No, look, there are two lights."

Taking the binoculars and looking for myself, I noticed for the first time that there were indeed two small lights pointed in our direction. "Headlights?" I questioned.

"Yeah, someone is up there with a truck." I felt Raven tense. "Just keep watching them. As long as they are over there, we are fine." For the rest of the night, I watched that area carefully while still scanning all over. My stomach was in knots. Finally, the lights went off. "Raven, I lost them."

"What do you mean?" he asked.

"I mean, I lost them. The headlights went off, and I can't see them anymore. I can't tell if they are still there or not." I felt a panic growing.

"Ashley, it's okay. They are probably just other survivors. If they saw us, they are probably just as scared of us. Don't panic." Raven grabbed my shoulders and pulled me into his chest.

"I'm just so tired of this." I wrapped my arms around him. "I just want to be home." I was almost on the verge of tears. "I wish we had never left the reservation."

"I know it, baby. Don't cry." Raven held me, then pulled back. "You got to hold it together now. Don't give up on me. We will get home, and it will be fine. You will see." Raven kissed my forehead and hugged me again. "It's starting to get light. Let's wake the others and get an early start."

I nodded in agreement. I collected stuff and began to make breakfast as Monica came out and joined me. "I already have biscuits and gravy made." She looked at me. "Are you okay?"

"I saw headlights last night over there on that ridge. It looked like someone was camping out or something. I don't know."

Monica held her head down. "Max told me everything about the airport, bullet holes, the blood stains, mass graves. I have to admit, I'm a little happy I am stuck in that wagon all day."

I laughed. "Yeah, it's mentally exhausting to attempt to stay so alert all the time, but I'll take that over being in a wagon all day. We all have our places, I suppose."

Monica reached up and hugged me. "You do so much, Ashley. I honestly don't know how you handle things so well."

"I keep her in line," Raven said as he came around the corner with two pans of biscuits, and Max followed with the gravy. They set them down on our makeshift table. The smell of food began to wake everyone else up.

"Oh, is that so?" I popped him on the ass with my hand. "You act like you have some kind of power over me, mister."

Raven spun around and grabbed me, spinning me around so my back was to his. He playfully nestled my neck as I laughed. "I'm the master."

"So what does that make me, your slave?" I asked.

Raven stopped and grunted against me. "I have so many naughty images in my head right now."

"Now you're just being sick and twisted." I spun in his arms and wrapped my arms around his neck and kissed him.

He only smiled. "But it could be so much fun."

"Now who is being incorrigible?" I asked.

Jacob came out of his wagon and saw us wrapped up together. "God, you two need to be hosed down or something," Jacob stated, smiling.

"You just shut up and leave them alone. You're just jealous I don't hang on you like that, old man," Rose said as she came out of the wagon.

"Hell, woman, last time we wrapped up like that, we ended up with Ricky. I said never again," Jacob teased as Rose slapped him on his arm.

"Thanks a lot, Dad," Ricky said as he and Harley came around the corner of the wagon. Kat went and sat with Dannie, and they ate quietly.

We decided to stay a half day where we were to allow our clothes a little more drying time, then ride a half day to Shoshoni, where we would camp for the night. The kids would have a little extra outside playtime, which was good for them and Monica. As things settled down, I was constantly looking around for something. I was half scared and half hoping to see that truck again. I was unsure of what would happen if I did. It was as if aliens had landed, and we were waiting to find out if they were friendly or not.

The day passed quickly. Our clothes were dry, folded, and put away as we packed up and started on our way. We all stayed alert and found ourselves not wanting to see anything. If we didn't see anything or anyone, then we didn't have to worry if they were friendly or not.

By that evening, we had found a place to make camp on the edge of a rolling hill with a forest to the east. The terrain of Wyoming was becoming harder to deal with. There were a lot of rocks, and soft ground was harder to come by, as well as forest to hunt in. We got lucky with this forest. Who knows when we would find another area. Monica let the kids run around and play while she finished dinner on the woodstove. Max was watching to the east, Jacob to the west,

I took the south, and Raven watched the north. Kat and Dannie paraded around on her horse.

"Don't go too far, Kat!" I shouted to her.

"I won't." Both she and Dannie laughed and giggled as they rode by me, waving.

"Not too fast either. You're not used to riding yet!" I called out to her.

Harley and Ricky were sitting with Nyte, and Rose was playing with Summer. I saw Monica bringing a cast-iron pot out of the wagon. An eerie feeling came over me. I felt as if I were being watched. I looked around to everyone else who didn't seem to feel anything. Everything from that point on seemed to be in slow motion. Everything fell deathly silent. I didn't even hear the birds or crickets. Nothing. I could no longer see Kat or Dannie. I could only assume they rode past Raven in a large circle. Just then, a deafening boom rang out across the prairie and echoed in the air around us. I spun around to see Raven take off out of sight. Something was wrong with Kat and Dannie. The events that followed changed all our lives forever, as hell was unleashed on our family.

A large jeep leaped from the forest like a monster and ripped through our camp, spraying bullets in every direction. My heart stopped beating and lurched into my throat. Pulling out my pistol, I took aim on the bastard who was firing at my family. I fired once, piercing his skull above his right ear. He dropped the automatic rifle. I ran forward as I saw Monica fall with the pot, screaming. I didn't know if she was shot or scared. Rose was facedown on the ground. I didn't see Harley or Ricky anywhere. While running for the rifle, I heard more gunshots off in the distance. Grabbing the rifle, I saw the jeep was coming back around with a fresh gunman. I stood firmly in front of it and sprayed bullets of my own. I must have hit the driver because the jeep veered off. One man jumped free of the jeep before it crashed into a tree. I ran over and shot him once in the head before he had a chance to recover himself. He couldn't have been over twenty years old. Running for the hill where I knew Raven had been, I heard more commotion behind me, and another large military-style truck pulled right into the middle of our camp. Men began jumping out by what seemed the handfuls.

"We're so fucked," I said out loud as I got to the hill. Kat and Dannie were being shoved into a crude-looking cage. Raven was on the ground, along with two horses. I began firing the gun at anyone who wasn't my family. The only bad thing about firing at people was that sometimes they fire back, and they did. I took cover behind the hill. Hearing Kat scream was the worst feeling in the world. I couldn't get to her without being shot, but I wasn't going to be any good to her shot either.

Once the gunshots died down, I peeked over and saw our kids being driven away in this cage, screaming, holding the wires of the cage, reaching out to me. "Fuck this shit. Today is a good day to die," I said as I took off running and screaming. More gunfire behind made me duck down. I saw Raven on the ground as I scooted past him. He was covered in blood and didn't appear to be breathing. Firing again, I took out two more military men. Each had a red patch on their left arm. Upon closer inspection, a wolf head was on the red patch. This was the wolf pack I had heard so much about, and now those bastards have my kids.

"Stop!" A large man came up behind me and captured me in a huge bear hug, pinning my arms by the side. Another man came and removed the gun. Bucking wildly against the arms restraining me, I began screaming Kat's name while reaching my arms out to my daughter, who by the second was getting farther from my sight. My pain increased as I heard the fear in my daughter's screams echoing across the flatland.

"You need to stop," a gruff voice called to me and roughly shook my shoulders. The man slowly released me, and for the first time, I looked at the brawny man who had been restraining me. "You need to look around. We are not here to hurt you. We are here to help. And if you ever want to see your kids again, you better come with us now." Cyrus was a man of misguidance and direction, or was he? He rose to power quickly because of his keen abilities to make swift decisions and stick to a plan of action. He was not reckless but cunning. His followers needed a leader of strength but, more importantly, a leader who would protect them and get the nasty part of revolution done.

My arms slid down my captors as I looked around at the carnage that had just unraveled our happy existence. There were several men standing around me; all were armed and looking as if I were a caged animal that had just broken free. I turned and stood on top of the hill. Max was on the ground with a gunshot wound to his foot, nothing life-threatening but still painful. Monica was in a hysterical fit of tears and being restrained by another man. Tyson, the boxer, lay dead by one of the wagons. Harley and Ricky were making their way from the edge of the woods. Harley was holding Nyte tightly in her arms, trying to console the crying baby. Rose's and Jacob's bodies were side by side in a pool of blood. Rose had been shot in the head and Jacob in the chest. Both were obviously dead. I stopped resisting and relaxed my body as the man stepped away from me to give me some room. I walked slowly to Rose's body and rolled her over, trying hard not to look at the torn flesh and shredded bone that was once her skull. I found Summer covered in Rose's blood but relatively unharmed. Rose had given her life to protect the child. Picking up the blood-soaked baby, I carried her over to Monica.

"Listen to me," I said, handing Monica her baby. "We are going to get our kids back. I'll make sure of it, but for now, hold close what we have left." Monica nodded, showing she understood, but was still unable to speak. The man holding her loosened his hold and helped her over to Max, who was also being helped to stand. Max hugged his wife and cried, promising to get Dannie back. Max looked at me, and I saw a mixture of fear and rage in my brother I had never seen before.

Ricky quickly made his way over to his parents' bodies and dropped to his knees. Harley stood behind him with her hand on his shoulder, giving the only support she knew how to give. Turning back, I saw Raven's body lying faceup and motionless on the ground with what appeared to be a gunshot wound to the stomach. I couldn't bear to see him this way. I knew in my heart that with the amount of blood loss that he was gone. The world seemed to spin around me as I felt a piece of myself detach from the world. The love of my life was gone, my best friend. My stomach churned while my heart and mind raced with anger. My breath quickened as my eyes found the man who had been restraining me. He seemed to be the leader of this so-called rescue group. I walked up to him briskly. "We will go with you, but we are not leaving our loved ones behind, and we have our belongings in the wagons."

"We will have a few stay behind and have an armed truck come to collect your friends and bring your wagons to the base, but we must move now to get to safety," Cyrus said with authority.

I looked at him harshly. "Fine." Turning quickly to my own tearful brood, I yelled out, "Load up now!" Everyone looked at me in confusion. Stopping abruptly, I reaffirmed my statement. "Do you want to be here when those bastards come back? Because I sure don't. Get in the trucks now."

Max was the one to break the literal dead silence. "Sissy, are you sure?"

I slowly walked over to my brother. "Right now, I'm not sure of anything except those sons of bitches just killed our friends and my husband and stole our children. These bastards could have killed us at any time but didn't." I had my face in his, pointing my finger into his chest. "They say they can help us get our kids back, and at this moment, I don't see where we have a whole lot of options. So hobble your ass to the truck, climb in, sit down, and shut up until we can figure out exactly what the hell is going on." I roughly brushed by my brother and climbed into the back of the truck and assisted the rest of my family in.

A young man with dark hair who looked scared to approach me held up the small little Chihuahua that Kat had named Taco. She had kept him in a saddlebag on her horse. "This little guy was still alive. Do you want to keep him?"

"His name is Taco, and he belongs to my daughter. Yes, I would like to keep him." I rudely snatched the small canine from his hands.

I held on to an overhead railing of the military-style truck as it rode roughly and quickly. A small window separated the cab of the truck from the bed. A young redheaded male was watching me with a goofy smile. He appeared to be in his late twenties but yet had boyish or immature features. I looked at my shaken family. I knew I had to protect them at all cost. Inside, my heart was breaking. I had just left my husband's body laid out on the rugged terrain of Wyoming. I wanted nothing more than to scream and cry at the top of my lungs, but my body lacked the ability. It wasn't my heart that was broken; it was my spirit. I turned to the leader. "Where are we going?"

"When the government broke down and society went to hell in a hand basket, we took over and secured a small underground military base. We have been taking in refugees and performing sweeps like we were today when we found you guys. Some of the actual military stayed behind and became one of us. We are a part of the resistance." The leader looked down at me. "I'm Cyrus, and believe it or not, I'm sorry for your loss."

At this point, I didn't believe him or anyone else, but I suppose introductions were in order. "I'm Ashley. That's my brother Max; his wife, Monica; and his daughter, Summer. Those are my daughters, Harley and Nyte. This is Ricky. He lost his parents today. My other daughter, Kat, and Max's son, Dannie, were the ones taken."

"And the other one you lost was your husband?" Cyrus asked.

I only nodded, not being able to think about Raven right now. "You said you could help get our kids back."

"They usually hold the young ones because they can still be reprogrammed. They keep them in a civilian concentration camp not too far from the base. That's where we will find them, but you can't just walk up and ring the bell. This is a mission you will have to train for. You have to be ready to kill."

I looked at him through cold eyes. "That's nothing I haven't done before."

"I would just take her word for it if I were you," Max added.

CHAPTER 6

"FORGIVE ME FOR** saying this, but you don't seem to know a whole lot about what's going on. Have you been living under a rock for the last few months?" Cyrus asked.

"No, we were on an Indian reservation in Montana."

"Same difference," Cyrus huffed under his breath. They rode in silence a little longer before Cyrus announced their arrival. "We're here."

I looked through the small window that separated the cab and saw a large rocky mountain. It wasn't anything like my mountains in Montana but still considered a mountain. We were heading right for the massive mound, and for a moment, I thought we might crash into it. However, what appeared to be a large concrete door began opening, and our truck drove right through it.

I gave my family what I hoped was an assuring smile. The truck came to a stop, and the back opened. We all climbed down from the truck and took a look around. We were in a garage with other trucks. Cyrus was already giving instructions to another man, then turned to us. "This is our maintenance department. Over there is Salvador and Tank. They are our mad auto scientists. They keep us running. Now if you will follow me, we will go underground."

We quietly followed him to an elevator. I held my breath as he pressed the down button. I kept expecting something to happen. When the doors opened, we stepped out into a series of huge circular tunnels with smooth sides and flat walkways. "There are three levels, not counting the main-level garage. The first level here is living quarters. All the rooms are pretty much the same. You will have one queen or two full beds and a small kitchenette area with a table. The bathrooms are small, and the hot water is on a timer, so you will have to hurry. Nothing is pretty and decorated. It's all pretty basic.

We took the elevator to the second level. "Down this hallway is the cantina." Cyrus pointed. "And down there is the supply room. If you need soap, shampoo, or whatever, just go to the counter. The infirmary is also down here. I think you need to go get checked out, and you can get a tour later." Cyrus spoke to Max, "T-Bone can take you, and we can meet back up in the cantina." T-Bone nodded and helped Max down the hallway. "The day-care area is down there at the very end." Cyrus turned and walked on, and we quietly followed. "We also have a few classrooms for our young ones to go to school. Most of the older ones just go to work. Everyone works around here."

Soon, we were back in the elevator and exited onto the third level. "At the end of the hallway is our arena and training room." We walked to the arena. There was a boxing ring with seats all around and a full gym with every piece of equipment imaginable. "You will be spending a lot of time in here," Cyrus said, smiling.

Cyrus was not a man lusting or craving power or control; he just wanted what the US Constitution on its merits had intended. He felt that many politicians through the years and their political parties and the few very wealthy had very different interpretations of what the document and government place was to further their own wealth and agendas. He felt this power was a coup d'état of all man's rights and the freedom of all.

A young man with lots of tattoos and piercings came up to Cyrus and whispered something I couldn't hear. They both looked directly at me. Cyrus spoke softly yet with authority, "Blade, why don't you make sure they find their way back to the cantina? You can eat, and I'll be up to see you in a little while. I can answer any questions you may have then." With that, he turned and left us. He was a strange individual. I wasn't sure if I could trust him or not, but at this point, I didn't trust anyone.

Once back in the cantina, we got an old cafeteria-style plate and waited in line. "Fresh meat," a very large black man said behind the counter. This man had to be at least six feet, five inches, and I couldn't begin to guess his weight. He was the largest human being I had ever seen in my entire life. He caught me looking at him wide-eyed. I wasn't sure what to say, so I said the first thing that came to my mind.

"Are you calling us names or asking what we want?" I asked.

He looked at me for a moment and then smiled the most gentle smile I had ever seen. "Believe me, the meat isn't that fresh." He began laughing. "Where are you from?" he asked, making light conversation.

"Texas, originally, but we were coming from Montana, until we were attacked today," I explained briefly.

"You lost anyone?" he inquired as he slopped food onto the plates.

I nodded. "Three dead, two little ones kidnapped."

"Don't worry. You are in the right spot. If anyone can get them back, it's Cyrus." The man placed food trays out for us to take. "Everyone calls me Big Mo. Welcome to the cave."

"Bullshit, people call you the fucking pampered chef." I looked behind us. There was a rugged, backwoods-looking fellow, slightly overweight, with a ball cap on backward, and the sleeves were cut out of his shirt.

"Blaine, you hush up now. I don't like you much anyway. I'm liable to give you some not-so-fresh roadkill, you pudgy little bastard," Mo boasted.

The pudgy man was laughing, then abruptly stopped at Mo's words.

I nodded to Mo gratefully as we took our plates and found a seat. We ate in silence, mostly just picking at our food. I don't think any of us had an appetite. After what seemed like forever, T-Bone came back with Max following behind with a set of crutches. His foot was all bandaged. He found us and came to sit down.

"The doctor said I would be fine. I have to stay off my foot for a few weeks. He said he would show me some exercises I could do so I won't have a limp," Max stated as he put his arm around Monica.

"That's great, Max." I was pleased to hear there would be no lasting effects of his injury. However, that did mean he wouldn't be able to play a part in getting the kids back.

"Sissy, you would love the infirmary. You can still use your nursing skills here," Max said.

Just then, Cyrus plopped down beside me. "You a nurse?" he asked.

I only looked at him. There was no way I could concentrate on nursing anyone back to health while our kids were missing. "I was a nurse. Now I'm the one who is going to get our kids back. So when are we going?"

"Slow down now. Like I said before, you will have to train for this. I saw your shooting abilities out in the field, but you can't go in there guns blazing. We will have to go in quietly. There will be a lot of hand-to-hand combat. That's what you will have to train on." Cyrus looked at all of us. "None of you have a clue as to what's going on."

"We only know bits and pieces. Can you fill us in?" I stated.

Cyrus nodded. "It's a long story, but I don't suppose you have anywhere to run off to." He chuckled. "When the comets hit, there was a series of earthquakes, tidal waves, and aftershocks. To sum up the damage, the United States is in three pieces. The New Madrid Fault shifted and cracked from the mouth of Lake Michigan all the way to the Mississippi River. Los Angeles is its own uninhabited island now. There is nothing left of the Gulf Coast except oily marshlands of glop. You can't even eat the fish. Most major cities have been evacuated, and those who chose to stay behind will kill you for the shoes on your feet. There's nothing but pirates and pillagers out there."

Big Mo set a plate of food down for Cyrus.

"Thank you, big man."

Mo only smiled to the rest of us as he patted Cyrus on the back.

"Now as if all this weren't bad enough, our own president screwed us over the most. You see, when he declared a state of emergency and initiated martial law, the Department of Homeland Security pretty much took over all the day-to-day operations of evacuations, rescues, things like that. However, that wasn't enough. They wanted more, so they assassinated the president in cold blood. Now everyone else in the line of succession was either killed off or, if they are alive, they haven't stepped up yet. So that leaves the secretary of Homeland Security as the acting president. He wants to use the U5 to implement a New World Order. He has everything at his disposal, and let me tell you, he is one ruthless son of a bitch. There is a whole list of executive orders he has signed. Everything, from transportation to oil reserves, even our military, is in his control. He thinks Americans have become too free. So that bastard has made it to where all of us are to be rounded up and housed in concentration camps. We are supposed to work where we are told, no longer being able to choose our own jobs. He has total control of your life if you are caught. Now they like to catch the kids because the kids are easy to brainwash. If they catch them young enough, then this is the only way of life they will remember, and they won't protest. They will try to brainwash older people using psychotropic drugs. If they are unable to change their way of thinking, then they shove them into a boxcar they have rigged up to an incinerator. The U5 group, the original five members of the United Nations, is fully backing Homeland Security. No one here knows if they actually know what's going on or if they are being lied to as well."

Cyrus took a bite of food and got a drink. "Now there is one group in New York that disputes the presidency. They have their own president, but since they are on the other side of the gorge, we don't know for sure how they are living. There is one man, a very rich, eccentric man, who has no claim to a presidency, but he is more of a czar over what is left of California. He has the resources and means to take care of a large amount of people, and they love him for it. For now, that system is working for them. What's left of Texas has succeeded from the union. They are their own country now. They have commenced to building a fence between them and Mexico. The real funny thing is, Mexico is helping them build the fence because they don't want people migrating over to Mexico." Cyrus took a moment to laugh at this.

"I think I'm going to be sick," I said as I pushed my plate away.

"Well, the thing is, our illustrious military is making sweeps, rounding people up and shipping them off to concentration camps. That's where we will find your kids. There is a camp not too far from here, so that's probably where they have been taken. We got lucky. There were only a handful of us when we took this place over. It was a confusing time, and most of the military just joined us."

"That's because we didn't like what was going on." A young man with black hair and striking blue eyes sat down. "We have always had the right to refuse an order if we felt it was wrong and could justify it. But our own brothers were being shot and killed for refusing." The young man stopped and looked at our disheveled group. "I'm Mason. It's good to see some fresh faces around here."

A large group of people began filing into the cantina, laughing and pushing each other around. They noticed us sitting there lost in our worries and quickly quieted down. Some were pointing at us as if we were a circus sideshow. They all got in line to get their share of Big Mo's cuisine.

A young lady dressed in cutoff camouflage shorts and a mid-riff-bearing tank top entered the room and whispered in his ear. He only nodded. "Are you guys finished eating? Your rooms are ready."

"I never had too much of an appetite to begin with," I said, looking to my family, who were all pushing their plates away. Monica and I gathered everyone's plates and emptied them into the large garbage cans. We followed behind Cyrus.

"I just wanted you to be aware that we have buried your friends. We don't make a fuss over funerals anymore."

Max and Monica were given their room first. Theirs was only two doors down from mine. I entered my room with Harley and Nyte. It was a simple hole that had been burrowed into the side of the mountain with smooth stone walls. There were, of course, no windows. Two beds with a nightstand on each side lined one wall. It looked pretty much the way I remembered a cheap hotel looked.

Harley checked out the bathroom. "It's small, but at least it's not five-gallon buckets." She tried to giggle but failed as she wiped a dripping tear from her eye.

A door opened from the side, and Ricky walked through it. "Oh, I guess my room connects with yours." Harley jumped to his side and hugged him tight.

I sat Nyte down on the bed and looked around. All our belongings had been delivered. It looked like everything had been brought to my room. I would have to get up with Monica later to make sure they had their clothes.

"Mama," Harley called out.

"Yeah, what is it?" I had a feeling where this conversation was going to lead.

"I know how you feel about things, but if we leave the door open, can I stay with Ricky tonight?" Harley looked at me through tearful eyes.

I exhaled a long, exasperating breath. As long as we were out on the road, I had been able to keep these two young bodies apart, but I no longer had the strength to fight about it. I found myself not really caring about what happened or how. "Harley, Ricky lost his parents today, and I'm sure he could use some company. I'm too tired and worn out to fight about things. I honestly don't have it in me anymore. I will need your help with Nyte while I'm training. All I ask is that"—I felt a little dizzy as I sat on the edge of the bed—"just don't screw up and get pregnant, Harley. This is not the world you want to raise a child in." I looked at Nyte, and even though I loved this child with all my heart and she was my last connection to Raven, I had to wonder what the world would be like as she grew up. She would never be able to play in a yard or play on a front porch. It was going to be an evil, cold black world for her to grow up in. She would never know how good things once were. I started to doubt if saving her life was even worth it or if she would grow up hating me for it.

A knock came at the door, disrupting my thoughts. Harley opened the door, and the girl from the cantina in cutoff shorts was standing there with a portable crib.

"Hi, I know it's not much, but it doubles as a playpen and a bed, so I thought it would be helpful." The girl invited herself in and set the crib down and set it up quickly as we just stared at her. "I gave one to your sister down the hall too."

"I appreciate it very much." Rising from the bed, I wobbled on my feet a little.

"Whoa, it's okay. You don't have to get up." The girl pushed my shoulder and gently eased me back down to the bed. "I can only imagine what you guys have been through today." Her smile was like a ray of sunshine; her eyes were big and round. "I'm Lita." The muscles in her arm were well-defined. My head swam in huge circles as the whole room twirled around. I never noticed when my eyes rolled in my head as I fell backward onto the bed.

"Mama!" Harley cried out as she ran to my side.

"She's okay. She just passed out. It's been a long day. Why don't you pull back the bed? Harley did as she was told. Lita carefully removed my clothes, leaving me in my bra and panties only. Placing one arm under me, she pulled my limp body up in the bed and covered me up. "Your name is Harley?" Harley only nodded in response. "Why don't you take the baby, and y'all sleep in the other room? If it's okay, I'll sleep over there and keep a watch over your mom. You all are going to need some sleep."

"How do I know we can trust you?" Harley stated with her hands on her hips.

"How do you know you can't?" Lita only smiled. "I understand your concern, but really, we are underground with nowhere to run. I was new here once, and I know how hard it is. Someone was nice to me when I got here, so I'm just paying it forward," Lita explained.

Harley nodded as she took the baby bed to Ricky's room, then quickly came back for Nyte. Lita was putting a cool cloth on her mother's forehead. Even though she didn't know this woman, she didn't feel like she meant any of them any harm. "Just come get me if she needs anything."

Lita nodded politely at her. "Your mom will be fine. She is just exhausted, but I will let you know if she needs anything."

"Thank you." Harley went into Ricky's room, leaving the door open as promised.

My eyes fluttered open. Attempting to focus, I wasn't sure where I was. Sitting up on the side of the bed, I noticed a woman on the other bed, asleep. I remembered her name was Lita. I slowly got up and walked to Ricky's door. Harley was asleep in one bed, and Ricky was asleep in the other. "Good girl," I whispered. Nyte was sleeping peacefully in her new crib. I quietly found me a change of clothes and went to the bathroom. While in the shower, it all came back to me. We were all so happy one minute, then the next, our world was turned upside down. I had lost Raven. He had been taken from me so quickly. I didn't have enough time with him. I remember everything happening so fast and bullets flying. I remember Kat screaming for me, reaching her hand out to me from across the field. My body began to tremble. I wasn't crying; I was pissed off, angry. I wanted the bastards who took my baby and killed my husband. I wanted their blood, and nothing was going to satisfy me till I got it. Shutting off the water, I quickly dried off and got dressed in my jeans and flannel shirt. I was going to have to find something other than flannel to wear, but that was the least of my worries. Opening the door, I saw Harley and Lita sitting on the bed.

"Mama." Harley came to me almost in tears. "I was so worried about you." She hugged me. I could feel her arms around me, but at that point, I didn't care.

I pulled her away from me. "Harley, you need to stop. I am fine. I was just tired. You need to be tougher than this." I brushed past her and shook Lita's hand. "I appreciate everything you did last night. I don't think I needed a babysitter, but I'm sure Harley liked having someone else around. Now I need a cup of coffee. Harley, your job for today is to sort through the totes and give Max their stuff and put everything up in here and watch Nyte." I opened the door and left our little hobble in search of the cantina.

"Hey, wait up." Lita was right behind me. "I'll go with you. I know it's none of my business, but she was really worried about you last night."

"You're right. It's none of your business." I stopped in the hallway and looked at Lita directly. "Look, I appreciate you staying, but Harley is going to have to learn to have more of a backbone and be tough. If she stays soft, she is going to get killed in this world."

Lita only looked at me through confused eyes. "Okay, I get it." We stood there looking at each other for a brief moment. I had to admit, I admired her body. She was in great shape. "So let's go get some breakfast."

We entered the cantina. Max and Monica were already there, eating.

"Morning, sissy."

"Is it? I can't tell," I said sarcastically as I took a seat and ate quietly. The place was packed with mostly men. I knew I was going to have to work extra hard to show these men I was every bit as good as them and twice as tough. Max watched me, and I found it a little annoying, but I decided it wasn't worth a fight. We finished up, dumped our plates, and started out of the cantina.

Monica stopped and handed Summer over to Max. "Now where was that training area at?" she asked.

"What are you doing?" Max asked her, taking the baby being pushed into his arms.

"I'm going to get our son back. You are in no shape to fight, so hobble your ass back to our room and take care of the baby and leave the hard stuff to me. I'm not about to let your sister risk her life to bring back our son. I'm going to be right there beside her, and if you don't like it, tough shit." Monica turned to Lita and asked again, "The gym?"

"Right this way." Lita was smiling as she led the way.

I brushed past Max, who was standing in shock on crutches, holding his daughter, unsure what to do. "If you need anything, just ask Harley."

We entered the gym, and Cyrus was there waiting for us. "'Bout time. All right, first thing is, we need to see where your weak spots are."

Monica and I didn't waste any time. After about an hour, Cyrus pulled us out and explained that we both needed to work on our upper-body strength and endurance. I knew that was right, because I was wiped out. Monica impressed me though; she was right there with me doing the same thing. Everyone looked up as Ricky entered the gym. He quickly found his way to me. "What can I do?" he said as he hitched his thumbs in his belt loop.

"Go back to the room and take care of my daughter, Ricky."

"No, those bastards killed my parents," Ricky stammered.

"That's right, and they won't hesitate to kill you. Do you understand that? I don't want to see Harley go through that if you die. It will devastate her." I knew I had to make him understand. I stood up in front of him. "Ricky, I am the only parent Harley has left. I can't let you do this. If she were to lose both of us, it would kill her. I need to know that if anything happens to me that at least she will have you. I'm sure there are other things you can do around here to help out. But I need to know Harley will be taken care of. Can you do that for me?" I asked, putting my hand on his shoulder.

Cyrus spoke up, "Big Mo has asked for some help. If you want, you can report to him. I'm sure he will put you right to work."

Ricky was obviously not happy about it, but he nodded. "I will take care of her, Ashley, no matter what."

"Thank you, Ricky. That takes a lot off my mind," I said, almost mocking him. He left the gym, and I took a swig of the water bottle.

"Lita, why don't you take Ashley and Monica into town and see if you ladies can find something more suitable for her to wear and work out in? This flannel crap isn't going to cut it."

"Yes, sir." Lita jumped up off the crate she was sitting on. "Follow me."

We went up the elevator and into the garage. "Tank, my darling," Lita said, hugging the broad-shouldered man. "What do you have for me today to make a run?"

"What are y'all going out for?" he asked.

"A lady has to look her best," Lita said, shaking her hips a little.

Tank only rolled his eyes. "Take the little mule." He dangled the keys as she jerked them from her hand. "Be careful with her. I just got the roll bars welded back on."

"You know me," Lita said, dancing around.

"Yeah, I know you, all right, and like I said, take it easy." He was smiling, but we could tell he was serious as we loaded up in the dune buggy-looking device.

We headed out. The landscape wasn't much to brag about, but at least I was getting to see the sun again. The thought of being underground didn't appeal to me, but at least we would have a momentary reprieve. Lita was driving fast; the wind was blowing through our hair.

"There's no seat belts!" Monica yelled from the back.

I only laughed and brushed the hair from my face. "That's what these are for." I grabbed one of the overhead bars. "I call them 'oh shit' bars."

Lita busted out laughing as she jumped a hill. Monica screamed out "Oh shit!" and grabbed the bar to steady herself for the landing.

"See, it works!" I shouted as we all laughed. We settled down as we reached town. Lita scanned the area and pulled up behind a small strip mall. The door had been pried open, and we entered cautiously.

"Okay, it's clear." Lita secured the door. Knowing we didn't have long, Monica and I each grabbed a shopping bag. We found some tank tops and shoved them by the handfuls into my bag. There didn't appear to be a wide assortment of shorts, but I found some cargo pants that would work if I cut them off. Monica found some sweats."

"Y'all hit the store next door too. It's an old army surplus. They don't have many supplies left, but they have plenty of clothes.

We left and went next door and ran through the store like a timed shopping spree. I found a field jacket, and even though it would be too warm to wear right away, I would save it. I grabbed some camouflage pants and a few other things before Lita came around the corner and, in a shouting whisper, said, "We got to go."

My senses were on high alert. "Come on." We ran past Lita, who was now holding an assault rifle. I had no idea where she got it but was happy to see it as a caravan started rolling past the store, loaded with men and more weapons.

"Is that them?" Monica stated bluntly.

"Yes, that's them, but now is not the time. We are outnumbered and outmanned and outgunned. We fall back to the mule and wait, then haul ass."

"They have my son," Monica said.

I stepped up. "And my daughter. But our kids are not on that truck. We are not going to do them any good if we get shot here today." I shook Monica, who was staring directly at the passing trucks. "Do you understand?"

Monica only nodded and retreated back to the mule. I knew all too well the way she felt. I wanted nothing more than to walk into the street and shoot every single one of those bastards down. If we were going to win this war, we would have to be smarter and quicker than them, and right now, we didn't have the advantage. Lita ushered me out, and when she felt it was safe, we left. She drove even faster going back. I wasn't in a hurry to go back underground, but I understood the urgency.

When we were within sight, she pulled a radio from her pocket and shouted, "Tank, the gate!" We could see Tank and Salvador run out to the gate and open it. Lita was smiling again, because seeing the guys meant we were safe. She pulled into the garage and skidded to a stop.

"Damn, girl, take it easy," Tank scolded Lita.

"I'll take it any way I can get it, Tank. You know that." Lita laughed and led the way out of the garage and to the elevators.

"There's something wrong with you, girl!" Tank hollered behind us.

"You love me!" Lita yelled back just as the elevator doors closed, lowering us back underground.

"You two can get your stuff put up, and I'll meet you back in the cantina for lunch."

"I'm not really hungry," I stated.

"I didn't ask you now, did I? You are going to have to eat to keep your strength up, both of you." Lita waved a finger at each of us. "See you in a few."

I only rolled my eyes knowing she was right. "Come on." Monica and I put our things away, checked on the kids, and quickly went to the cantina. I knew Monica and Max must have had words because her eyes were red and she was angry. We ate quickly and went to the gym.

"Use that anger," I whispered to her.

She only nodded and stiffened her stance as Cyrus came into the room. He was just a normal guy. I didn't see what was so great about him, but everyone seemed to come to attention when he entered a room. We trained for the rest of the evening, learning different holds, where the pressure points were, and how to use them to our advantage. Time passes quickly when you're being thrown around on a wrestling mat.

We retired to our room, showered, and dressed for dinner. We met up with the rest of the family in the cantina. I had to admit, I was hungry. Ricky was behind the counter with Big Mo serving up the food. He wasn't happy about it, but he was doing his part.

"You did good today, girl," Mason said, slapping me on the back and taking a seat.

"Yeah, for a girl," the pudgy man said, taking a seat behind me.

"Shut up, Blaine. I can't wait to watch her take you down." Mason rolled his eyes.

"When that happens, I will kiss Big Mo back there!" Blaine shouted.

Big Mo pointed a spatula at Blaine. "Boy, don't you bring me into this."

Harley came into the cantina looking exhausted, holding Summer on one hip and Nyte on the other, and took a seat. Max soon followed on his crutches. I guessed she had been taking care of both of the babies while Max wallowed in self-pity.

"Y'all have a nice stage area up there," Max said, pointing to the stage. I continued to eat. Monica brought Max a plate and set it down.

"We haven't had a chance to use it yet. None of these guys can play the piano or carry a note in a bucket," Mason said as everyone laughed. "But the karaoke machine is back there with everything you can imagine."

Max only looked at me. I pretended I didn't see him. "My sister sings. She's damn good too even though she won't admit it."

I stopped eating and stared at Max with hate in my eyes. Singing was something I did with Raven.

"Really? Well, it's about time someone showed up that can sing," Mason said, leaning back on the table.

I only shook my head, glaring at my brother. "No, don't do this."

Blaine shouted out behind me, "Maybe you sing better than you fight! Come on, girl, sing for us!"

"I don't sing anymore." My eyes never left Max, who was smiling at me. He was obviously proud of himself for putting me on the spot like this.

Mason spoke up, "Yeah, come on, just one song."

I looked over at Mason, who was holding up his hands in a mocking prayer.

"She ain't gonna do it. She's chicken!" Blaine shouted out again.

"You know what"—I slammed my fork down onto the plate—"I hate you." I pointed at Max. I turned and grabbed Blaine's mullet. "And the only thing I'm afraid of is that we may one day have the same barber, you obnoxious bastard." I slammed his head forward into his mashed potatoes, then walked on stage.

Harley looked excited as she positioned the babies where they could see. Max had a huge smile on his face. Monica had her arms folded in frustration with her husband. Lita entered the cantina and stood in the back as I found the music I wanted, the one song that stated my current frame of mind. It was an oldie but goodie. Mason ran forward and plugged in a microphone. It squawked as Cyrus entered and stood in the doorway. I looked out into the cantina and thought to myself, *I must be crazy.* I was giving Max what he wanted, just not in the way he wanted it. The days of me singing the soft, mushy, heartfelt songs were over. It was time to rock it. As I hit Play, the music of Twisted Sister titled "We're Not Gonna Take It" began to play. It wasn't far into the song when Lita joined me on stage. She must have seen how uncomfortable I was and didn't want me up there alone. It was a gesture I appreciated. My heart wasn't in the song, but we put on a show for the guys. Max soon got up and started for the door. I smiled knowing he didn't approve of my song choice, but too bad.

Cyrus stopped him. "Is there anything she can't do?"

"I haven't found anything yet." Max smiled at me. I was attempting to show him attitude, but at least I was up there. "She's pretty amazing up there," Max said as he left the cantina.

"Yeah, she is," Cyrus agreed as he watched me sing the rest of the song. I got the whole cantina involved in the song. Even Big Mo shook his hips and shoulders behind the counter. Everyone clapped as the song ended, and I left the stage quickly.

"You do sing better than you fight. That was great!" Blaine shouted out.

I only sneered at him. I just needed to get out of this room. I left my plate of unfinished food where it sat and walked out of the cantina. I had no idea where I was going, but I just had to get away. I walked around for a while, rode the elevator, and found a doorway past the gym. I entered, and I was in heaven. Wall to wall was nothing but different guns and ammo. I found a strange-looking rifle. I picked it up, looking at it curiously.

"It's a double AR-15. It's really more of a novelty, but it suits you. It matches your boots," Cyrus said from the doorway with a smirk on his face. "What are you doing in here?"

"I just had to get out of there. I never wanted to sing. That is something I did with my husband. But he's gone now, so that's like pouring salt in an open wound. It hurts." I bit my lip.

"I get that, but pushing through the hurt makes you stronger." Cyrus was blocking the doorway. "We have all had things to overcome and work through."

"I'm tired of working through shit. I want my kids, and I want to get back to a normal life," I snapped.

"You're never going to have a normal life again. I hate to tell you that, but I think you are smart enough to know that already." Cyrus started to leave but turned back. "The way I see it, you have two choices: you can sit back and try to fight the way things are, or you can accept them and make it work for you. You kicked ass out there on that stage even though you didn't want to. You have to do the same thing in life, or it's going to be the one that kicks your ass." Cyrus quietly walked away.

I took another look around. I knew he was right. I made a big deal about singing a song. I made the decision right there that no matter what, I wasn't going to let Raven's death be the most important event in my life. He was gone, and I couldn't bring him back no matter what, so I was going to somehow suck it up and move on. We were safe here, and we were going to make the best out of things.

Maybe one day would come when we could live aboveground again, but until then, at least we were safe and had other capable bodies to help protect what we had. It wasn't much, and it wasn't what I had in mind, but for this time, it was home.

CHAPTER 7

MY HEAD BOUNCED off the mat as Blaine laughed. "Dammit!" I shouted, slapping the mat with my hand in anger.

"You can't touch this, singer girl." Blaine laughed again.

I picked myself up. "Believe me, you pudgy little bastard, I wouldn't touch you with his dick. I pointed at Blade, the bald, tattoo-covered, skinny guy.

"Now that's hurtful." Blaine swung for me as I dodged and smiled. I waved him forward to come for me.

"You want hurtful? Come on." I wanted to get him in a submission hold. I wanted him to submit to me. It wasn't enough for me to beat him; I wanted him to give up. We were in the ring. Blaine swung for me, and again, I dodged it, immediately kicking sideways, landing my kick on the side of his head. It was a good kick, but not strong enough. Blaine caught my leg and fell to the mat, bringing me down with him. Landing on my stomach, Blaine twisted my foot and bent my leg behind me, sending my entire leg into excruciating pain. I had no choice but to tap out and let him have the joy of me submitting to him.

"Okay, that's enough for today!" Cyrus called out. "You guys hit the showers."

Blaine, still laughing, let go of my leg. I got up quickly, glaring at him with hatred. "I hate that guy."

"And he knows that. And he's using it as a distraction to whip your ass. You let him get to you. You have to block him out. When he had you down, all you thought about was that it hurt. You missed the important thing," Cyrus explained.

"Yeah, and what was that, Cyrus?"

"You still had one leg and two arms free. He was using his whole body to cripple one of your legs. You still had the advantage and couldn't see it. Monica, come here. Help me a minute." Monica entered the ring and followed his instructions. "When he has you down like this, he is using his body to hold you down and leaving himself wide open. When he is twisting your leg this way, roll with it and clock him with your other leg. He will let go, believe me, then you are free to kick his ass because you have the shock factor on your side." Cyrus let Monica up and turned to her. "And you, when someone grabs your arms like this"—Cyrus grabbed me and pinned my arms behind me—"what do you see?"

"The legs are free?" Monica stated in question.

"Exactly," Cyrus stated.

I quickly stomped on his foot, and in his shock, he let go of me as I planted a solid kick in his gut. Cyrus doubled over, and I punched him with a forceful uppercut, sending him staggering backward. "Is that the shock factor you were talking about?"

"Yeah, that would be the one," Cyrus said as he climbed out of the ring. "Damn, would you please do that to Blaine next time? I would almost pay to see it."

I laughed. "I will certainly do my best."

"Good. Now y'all go get ready for dinner. I'm going to see Big Mo and get some ice."

"Sorry!" I called out to him as we left the gym.

"No, you're not, but that's okay," Cyrus said, rubbing his jaw.

I took my time getting a shower and getting ready for dinner. I really didn't want to be around those guys, especially Blaine. I took a few minutes and put some things away and fiddled around for a little while before finally taking off to the cantina. However, there were still plenty of people around, including Blaine.

Big Mo saw me come in and fixed me a plate. "Have a rough day?"

"Yeah, you could say that. Thanks, Mo." I took the plate gratefully and took a seat. I sat quietly, picking at the food on the plate.

Calling it food was a stretch, but I suppose Mo did the best he could with what he had, and I needed to be grateful for whatever I was given. The sound of men laughing all around me distracted my thoughts. It was late, and I had hoped everyone had cleared out, but I couldn't get that lucky.

"Aw, what's wrong, Ashley? Are you still licking your wounds?" Blaine's drunken words slurred as he rudely sat down on the table in front of me. I looked up to see his ass crack. Quickly losing my appetite, I pushed my plate to the side.

"Bullshit, Blaine. This girl don't have a mark on her and would have kicked your ass if you hadn't pulled that chicken shit submission hold." Mason patted me on the back and sat at the other table behind me. Glancing back, I noticed he held a bottle of Jack Daniel's. My mouth instantly watered for it.

"Yeah, keep making excuses." Blaine laughed loudly, then threw back a bottle of Crown Royal, staggering just a little. "Here, Ashley, have a drink." He slammed down the bottle in front of me.

Where the hell was the liquor cabinet? These guys have been holding out on me, I thought to myself. I quickly noticed Lita standing in the doorway with her hands on her hips in disgust of the way Blaine was acting. I glared at Blaine. I really didn't like him, and I knew I had to do something, or he would become nothing more than a schoolyard bully.

"What, you don't want a drink? Can't handle the hard stuff, huh?" He took another drink and sat down again. Standing seemed to be becoming too much of a challenge for him.

I dropped my fork and stood up and faced Mason. I leaned over and snatched the bottle of Jack Daniel's from his hands and turned to Blaine. "I would rather be over here with a man named Jack than over there with the pussy and a crown." I threw back the bottle and welcomed that smooth warmth down my throat. "Cheers, motherfucker."

The other guys shouted and cheered.

"Are you going to sing for us again?" Mason asked.

"Maybe after some more Jack. You guys have been holding out on me." I drank again from the bottle and passed it back to Mason.

Mason refused to take the bottle. "Take all you want, sister. I enjoyed you singing last time, so if this is what it takes, hell, baby, I'll get you drunk every night."

"Sissy, are you drunk?" Max asked as he came into the cantina.

I only looked at my brother. I could see he was worried about me, but at that point, I didn't care. "Not yet, but I'm working on it."

"Ease up, Max. She is just letting off some steam," Lita said, patting Max's shoulder.

"No, she's hiding inside a bottle," Max said.

Monica walked into the cantina, and everyone stopped and stared at her. She had cut off most of her hair and had changed her clothes. "It's no different than hiding behind a song, and this makes you feel better." Monica took the bottle of Jack Daniel's and took a drink. "Don't you have a baby to be taking care of?"

Max stared at his wife in total confusion. "What the hell is going on?"

"I cut my fucking hair. It was getting in my way, so I cut it. Move on!" Monica shouted out as she took a seat at the table.

"I don't get it. You are the one who has always held us together, Ashley. You're letting it all fall apart," Max said as he hung his head down.

"Aw, does baby want me to sing about it? Fine." I got to the stage and found a song. I grabbed the microphone from Mason, who was smiling from ear to ear as he handed me back the bottle of Jack. I only pointed to him and winked as the music started. I sang Halestorm's "Hate It When You See Me Cry." Everyone cheered me on as I sang with a bottle in my hand. Max only looked around as if he had no control of the situation, and the fact was, he didn't. I was tired of being the strong one for everyone. There were plenty of strong people here. He backed out of the cantina, shaking his head, not knowing what to say to any of us.

Cyrus met him in the hallway. "She just needs to cut loose every once in a while. Don't worry. I'm watching her."

Max only looked at Cyrus. "Yeah, and that's just one thing that bothers me. I don't know that woman in there. Hell, I don't know either one of them."

"The women you know are still there. They are just suppressing them to get into the frame of mind they need to in order to do what they are going to need to do." Cyrus patted Max on the back. "When your kids are back, you will see those women again. Trust me."

I finished up the song and needed some air. I went up to the garage and climbed a ladder to the observation tower. Lita followed me.

"You did that rather gracefully with a bottle in your hand." She laughed as she sat beside me.

"Well, thank you. I lay back on the ground. The coolness of the earth soaked through my shirt as I looked up at the stars. They reminded me of Raven. I closed my eyes and pictured him lying beside me. I could feel tears welling up, and I knew I couldn't have that, so I forced myself to sit up. Lita assisted me, and I hadn't realized her hand on my leg. It felt so warm against the coolness of the night air.

"Are you okay?" she asked.

"Yeah, it takes more than this to make me polluted." I giggled as I lay my head on her shoulder. "I love it out here. It's so quiet."

She put her arm around me and kissed me on the forehead. We sat together and watched the stars for at least an hour and finished our bottle before we made the descent down the ladder. I didn't do it as gracefully going down.

"Whoa, sister, come on, let's get you back to your room." She guided me back to the elevator and to my room. She opened the door and pushed me into the bed. I laughed and lay there, unable to move. Lita removed my shoes. "I don't do this often, but this is twice I have put you to bed." She unbuttoned my pants and grabbed the hem and yanked them off, then covered me up.

"But you do it so well." I laughed again.

Lita stood over me with her hands on hips and shook her head. "You have no clue, do you?"

The room was spinning, and Lita was becoming a blur. She leaned down and tenderly kissed me. She whispered in my ear, "I'm gay, Ashley."

I knew I was on the verge of passing out, and I couldn't come up with anything else to say. I only looked at her and gave her a thumbs-up sign and said, "Good for you. You go, girl."

The next thing was Cyrus shaking the bed, waking me up. I rolled over and looked at him through blurred eyes. "Come on, girl. There is a gym waiting for you."

I only moaned and wished I was somewhere else. "Do the doors around here lock?"

"Not for me. Come on, you got to get to moving. I want you in the gym in five minutes. Here's a cup of black coffee. Shake it off and come on." Cyrus clapped and jerked the covers off me.

"You fucking jerk." I jumped up and attempted to cover myself.

Cyrus leaned forward and face-to-face with me. "Don't flatter yourself, chick. You ain't got nothing I haven't seen before, and besides, I like my women with a little more meat on their bones. Now get up and get dressed." Cyrus left without any further argument.

I was well awake even though my head throbbed horribly. I threw on some clothes and went to the cantina. There was no way I could eat, but at least some juice. Big Mo only smiled at me. I had no idea why, but I just smiled back at him and swallowed the juice in a hurry to get to the gym.

I started with the weights, then moved to cardio. I wished there could be music playing. Monica was working out as well. Blade was at her side, talking her through every move, giving her encouragement along the way.

"Kenny Wayne, I'll take you driving later on, not now." Cyrus shook his head as he came in the gym.

"Who's Kenny?" I asked.

"That little good for nothing is Kenny Wayne. He comes and goes. He's a little on the special side. He don't mean any harm though. Some days he is here, and others, he just goes missing. Nobody knows where he goes. I take him out driving, and that's what he wants to do now, but we don't have time right now."

The same little man I saw on the day we were rescued was sitting on a weight bench, eating a piece of chocolate. He was actually wearing more than he was eating, but he looked like he was enjoying it. He smiled at me with chocolate all over his face. He was a simple person. I wasn't sure if he was mentally challenged, but he was definitely slow-minded. Cyrus walked around and talked me through a grueling workout. I almost felt it was punishment for getting drunk the night before, and I suppose it could have been. But it felt good, so I didn't mind.

We broke for lunch, and I checked on the kids. Harley had pretty much taken on the responsibility of taking care of the kids while Max sat around feeling sorry for himself. It made me sick the way he was acting, but I appreciated Harley for stepping up and helping out.

"Mama, can I talk to you tonight about something?" Harley asked.

"Sure, baby, right after dinner, okay? I gotta go. I love you both." I gave Harley and Nyte a quick kiss and was out the door, heading back to the gym.

The day went without incident. Cyrus was tied up elsewhere, so we didn't spar. He liked to be there when that happened so he could see how well we were developing. Blade helped Monica and me with knives. Monica was actually pretty good at throwing them, while I was better with brute force stabbing. We moved out to the shooting range and practiced. Monica was getting the hang of shooting pretty quickly. I felt guilty because we shouldn't have kept her cooped up in that wagon while out on the road. It wouldn't be taking us so long to prepare if she already knew a few things. *All things happen for a reason.* Lou's words rang in my head. The thought made me want to cry, so I quickly pushed the thoughts out of my head.

We finished training for the day and went to the cantina for dinner. Lita came in soon after I got there. She smiled and waved to me. I returned the gesture, remembering what she had whispered to me right before I passed out the night before. I didn't really care that she was gay. She was a good person, smart and caring. There was no reason to think otherwise of her.

"Hey, girl, have a good day?" she asked as she took a seat beside me.

"Yeah, it was good." I continued to eat as everyone talked around us.

"Lita, what do you do around here?" Max asked.

Lita swallowed her food. "Well, I work in supply, and I go out on runs so we can find things we need."

"How convenient is that?" Max said snidely.

"It is convenient, because if you ever pull that stick out of your ass, I can replace it with a tampon," Lita dished it out as quickly as Max.

We finished eating, and I returned to our room with Nyte in tow. She clung to me. I knew she missed me and that I needed to make an attempt to spend more time with her. She had noticed that Raven wasn't around and that must have confused her. I stayed in my room instead of going back to the cantina with everyone else. I gave Nyte a bath and played with her for a while before bedding her down for the night. She had been sleeping in the room with Harley since she was the one taking care of her.

"Mama," Harley called from the doorway.

"Yeah?" I went into my room where Harley was waiting for me.

"I wanted to talk to you."

I could sense that Harley was nervous. "Just say what you need to say, Harley." I was secretly praying she wasn't about to tell me she was pregnant.

"I want to get married to Ricky." She paused for a moment and looked at me as my jaw hit the floor before she continued, "You know it's been our plan to get married."

I could only shake my head. "Harley, you're too young, much too young."

"Please hear me out." Harley put her hand out, stopping me. "Nothing has changed for Ricky and me. But you are about to go out on a dangerous mission to get my sister back. You may not come home. You can't promise me that you will come home. With Daddy gone and Raven gone, I want at least one of my parents at my wedding. This will be my only chance to have that."

"Harley, no, you're too young and too immature."

"Immature? Seriously, Mom, you're gonna go with that one? I'm here every day with two babies doing everything while you and Monica are in that gym busting your butts. Uncle Max is depressed, so he isn't much help. Ricky is working with Big Mo. I'm here by myself handling it, and I'm doing it rather well, I think. I don't want to get pregnant. I don't want to have sex. I just want my mama to walk me down the aisle and give me away to the man I love."

"You have no idea what you're asking for, Harley. Marriage is a big deal. I know you have stepped up and pitched in, and honestly, I couldn't be in that gym working if it weren't for you. But marriage?" I was shocked by Harley. "If I had known that would be the result of you sleeping in the same room with Ricky, I wouldn't have allowed it. You can move your stuff back in here starting tonight."

Harley only shook her head. "No, Mama, it stays this way. I'm not moving in here. I'm staying with Ricky. A long time ago, it was normal for girls my age to get married."

"It's not a hundred years ago, Harley," I argued.

"Look around, Mom. In a lot of ways, it is. I love Ricky, and we are going to be married. And before you go off and get yourself shot and taken away from us forever, you need to decide if you want to be at the wedding or not." Harley walked into her room and shut the door. I could hear her crying. I had to get out and get some air.

Leaving my room, I went to find the ladder Lita and I had used before. I went out and sat on the cool ground. It wasn't long before Ricky joined me.

"I see Harley talked to you," he said, not bothering to take a seat.

"Yes, and I don't appreciate this, Ricky," I stated gruffly. "I told her she had to move back into my room tonight."

"It's not my idea." Ricky finally felt brave enough to sit beside me. "She just wants you there, Ashley. She is scared to death something is going to happen to you and she won't have anyone in her family left. Nothing else will change. I'm not going to pressure her into sex just because we are married. And if you want her to stay in your room, I don't have a problem with that. She just wants the wedding experience with at least one of her parents there. I can sympathize with that." Ricky held his head down.

I had almost forgotten about Jacob and Rose. Ricky had lost both of his parents. His mother and father would never see their son grow up into the man he was becoming. I felt so tired. I was beginning to understand where Harley was coming from. "I will think about it." I patted him on the back. "I don't like it, but I will think about it."

"That's all she wants. I'll let her know." Ricky quietly got up and left me in peace to entertain my own thoughts.

It wasn't long before Lita joined me. "What's up, chick?"

I looked at her and smiled. "Harley wants to get married."

"Whoa," Lita said, watching me. "And how does Mama feel about it?"

"I think she's too young and has no idea what's she getting into," I explained.

"Do any of us?" Lita held up her hands. "I mean, seriously, when you got married the first time, did you have the slightest idea what you were doing?"

I thought of Aaron and realized how young and stupid we were. We were so in love with the idea of being in love we didn't realize how much work a home and family would be. "I suppose not, but that's the thing, Lita. She just wants me there. She is scared I'm going to die and she won't have any parents left to walk her down the aisle. She wants the wedding experience before I die. She has assured me that she doesn't want kids right now and not even interested in having sex. She just wants me there."

Lita placed her hand on my leg. "Girl, I'm going to be honest with you. If all your little girl wants is to be able to have her mama walk her down the aisle before she goes out on a mission that she may not come home from, then it's pretty selfish of you not to give that to her."

I thought about it for a while. I knew I had to give this to Harley. It might very well be my last gift to her. There were no promises in life; that was one lesson we had all learned.

"We could have the wedding in the cantina. Mo can cook a cake, and Preacher can marry them," Lita explained.

"Preacher?" I questioned.

"He oversees the supply room. He is a real-life preacher. He even conducts church on Sundays in the cantina. I know he would do it."

I knew what I had to do. "Shit," I said in a long, dragged-out breath. "Fine, I give up." I threw myself back onto the ground. "Uncle, isn't that what you're supposed to yell when you're down? What kind of mother have I turned out to be?"

Lita leaned back on her side, resting her head on her hand. "I think you're pretty great."

Lita had realized at an early age that she was different. She went through high school as an athlete just so she could be in the girls' locker room. She found great pleasure in watching the other girls even if it wasn't proper for her to say so out loud. She knew it wasn't the normal thing to do. She tried to be interested in guys her age. She went to the prom and parties with dates, but it always disgusted her when they attempted to kiss her or feel her up. When she was in college and was hard-strapped for cash, a girl in the dorms took her to a strip club. It was there that she learned how much cash could be earned in one night. She talked to the manager and started the next night. That was where she had met Andrea. They started seeing each other and quickly found love. Lita finally had someone in her life who understood her. They combined their money and bought a house. Lita finished school and got a job in a TV studio doing traffic reports. To everyone else, they were roommates. For years, her mother questioned her about finding a man and having kids. She never had the courage to come out to her mother, and a part of her thought her mother always knew. Her mother went to her grave still waiting for those grandchildren. Lita and Andrea lived together happily for years in their little house until the day the comets hit. Andrea had been killed when an earthquake tore their home out from under them. Lita had been dug out of the rubble and taken to a medical camp. When she was better, she set out on her own, and that was when she met up with Cyrus. She had never thought about loving another woman until she saw me.

I caught Lita staring at me, smiling. "I am anything but great. In fact, I'm almost positive that I'm pretty fucked up." I sat up, laughing, and noticed a truck driving in circles outside the fences. "What are they doing?"

Lita looked up and laughed. "Oh, Cyrus is letting Kenny Wayne drive."

"What's his story?" I asked.

"Who, Kenny Wayne?" Lita shrugged her shoulders. "He is like our mascot. He is everyone's little brother. He comes, and he goes. Nobody knows where he goes when he leaves, but he always comes back and always wants chocolate. He will find little things and want to trade for chocolate. Whoever was taking care of him died, and he's just on his own."

"So tell me, do you know where there is an abandoned store where I can find my daughter a wedding dress?" I asked.

"Oh, you're going to let her do it!" Lita squealed in excitement. "I will find a shop and make sure it's safe before I take you there. I'm sure I can find something. It's not like wedding dresses are in big demand."

"I don't see that I have much of a choice. I still don't like it, but I do understand it." I shoved my hands in my pockets. "I will talk to Mo and Preacher and get everything organized. I guess I should go talk to my daughter."

I left Lita and went to find Harley. She was so happy. It made me happy to see her so excited over something. She didn't care about a dress, a cake, or decorations. She was just happy she would have pictures of me at her wedding. She and Ricky thanked me and retired for the night. I went to bed knowing I had made my daughter happy even if I wasn't sure it was a good thing. If I died, I knew Ricky would take care of her and protect her till his last breath.

Monica woke me up the next morning. "Hey, get up. We got to eat and head to the gym."

I groaned loudly. "I really have to get a lock for that door." Monica was throwing my clothes at me. "Why are you here so early?"

"I got tired of being in that room with your asshole of a brother," Monica stated as she sat down.

"Oh no, what happened?" I asked as I dragged myself from the bed since it was evident she wasn't going anywhere.

"He is just upset that I'm not being my usual quiet, meek, sub-missive self. It's not like he can do anything to get Dannie back, so

I have stepped up, and I will do what I need to in order to get that accomplished. I want my son back, dammit, and if he can't understand that, then fuck him!" Monica almost yelled.

My eyes bulged a bit at her language. I had never heard her talk like that. It would have been funny if she weren't so upset. "Look, you're right. We need to suck it up and do what we have to in order to get our kids back. Max will forget everything as soon as Dannie is back. Now let's go get that breakfast."

Over breakfast, I explained about Harley getting married and the wedding. Monica was happy for them and thought it was about time they got married. We ate and went directly to the gym, forgetting about weddings. Our morning was filled with cardio and weight lifting. Monica went to the gun range while I hit that mat with Blaine.

The level of disgust that followed Blaine had no limits. He was always running his mouth. We locked up, and I brought my knee up to his midsection. He crumpled a little, allowing my right fist to land to the side of his head. To everyone's amazement, including mine, he went down. My internal victory was short-lived when he latched onto my leg, pulling me down. He was attempting to get me into the ankle lock submission. I was fighting him with everything I had and saw Cyrus watching on as he shook his head. I wasn't fighting smart. I was wasting too much energy and not doing anything. I allowed Blaine to get me into position for the submission. He was spouting off at the mouth, and everyone was around the ring, yelling. Blaine applied the hold as I yelled out in pain but kept my eyes on Cyrus as he nodded. Rolling with the hold, I clocked Blaine again in the head with my free foot, shocking him enough to drop the hold. On my back and using both feet, I kicked him in the upper chest and quickly got up and pounced on him, punching him repeatedly in the face. Blaine's eyes swam in his head as his body rocked on his knees. He didn't know what planet he was on. I went behind him and pushed him forward as he fell onto the mat face-first. I jumped on his back, wrapping my arms under his, latching my fingers around the back of his neck, and brought his upper body off the mat, putting pressure on his back. Blaine cried out in pain. I kept the hold, wanting him to submit. "Do you give up?" Blaine only moaned as he attempted to pull my arms free. I put more pressure on his back by pulling him up a little more. His cries grew louder. "Come on, Blaine, do you give up?"

"Yes, yes, I give up." Blaine was relieved when I released him, scooting away from me in the ring. "Damn chick."

"That's right, asshole, and this damn chick just whipped your ass." I was proud of myself. I felt exhilarated and full of energy.

We went to the cantina for lunch, then returned to the gym. I felt like I was ready for anything. I quickly found out how wrong I was.

Cyrus was in the ring with me. "I know you are happy with yourself right now, but you have to learn to keep those emotions buried, especially in a fight. Ashley, you and Monica have learned a lot, so I want you to show me what you have learned. So without further delay, Ashley, here is your opponent for this match." Cyrus moved away and pointed at Monica. My mouth dropped open as Monica climbed through the ropes and entered the ring.

"No, this is wrong. I won't fight her. I will not be a part of this sideshow, Cyrus. I'm sorry, but I refuse to be your entertainment."

Out of nowhere, Monica hauled off and kicked me in the back, knocking me to my knees. She latched onto my head and pulled backward. "Whatever it takes to get our kids back, remember? Let's do what we have to and get this over with." Monica slammed me forward onto the mat and stepped back, looking at me.

I could only stare at her. She wanted this. She had worked hard on her training as well, and she wanted to prove to everyone, including herself, that she could handle this. I smiled at her. "Okay, let's do this."

I got up slowly, then met Monica in the middle. We were both in the best shape we had ever been in. I had no idea how this was going to end, but she wanted a chance to prove she could handle a fight. We stepped around each other, sizing each other up. A few punches were thrown before I landed one square in her face. I wanted to run to her and say I was sorry. It was that moment when I had my elbow dropped that Monica saw her opportunity. She landed a right hook that took me completely off my feet. It shocked her as well as I took a brief moment to spit out the blood that was pouring from my bottom lip. I stood and smiled at her and nodded. We locked up again in the middle and pushed off toward the ropes. Monica brought her knee up to my side as I grabbed her around the waist and applied pressure to her spine. She arched her back in pain. I wrapped my left leg around her right and leaned her back enough to knock her off-balance. Using my hip, I flipped Monica over, and we both went down. My plan was to be on top when we landed. Somehow, in the mix, Monica rolled and was now on top of me, plowing away at my head. Keeping my arms up in an attempt to block her blows, I thrust my hips forward, knocking Monica over. I wasn't counting on her having her legs wrapped around my hips, so I went with her, but now I was on top, with her legs wrapped around me. Using some of my newfound upper-body strength, I stood up with her still attached and slammed myself onto the mat, pinning Monica to the ground under me. As I slid my body up, Monica latched onto my arm and held it to her body as she rolled onto her stomach, pulling my arm between her legs. I flipped over, disoriented, not sure if I was up or down, but I was greatly aware of the pressure in my arm and shoulder. Monica let go of my arm and threw herself onto me and stopped. Everyone grew quiet. I opened my eyes enough to see Monica sitting on top of me with a knife to my throat. I would have been dead. She could have killed me. There was no doubt about it—Monica had just won. Blade started clapping as Monica began smiling. She was proud of herself. Hell, I was proud of her. I didn't even know she had a knife. Monica got up and ran to Blade as he swung her around.

Mason pulled me out of the ring and allowed me to regain my balance. "Are you okay?"

I was still smiling. "Yeah, I'm great." I watched Monica enjoy her moment and climbed back in the ring. Blade put her down, and she walked over to me. Everyone was watching, not sure what was going to happen. I stuck out my hand to shake hers. "Good job."

Monica had a grin from ear to ear. She had earned her moment of glory. She reached out and hugged me. "You're not mad?"

"Hell no, you did great. I'm proud of you." I hugged her, then allowed her to have her time to shine.

Cyrus was standing there, waiting. "You know as well as I do that you could have gotten out of that."

"Maybe, but she won fair and square, and you're not taking that away from her," I scolded him.

"Don't worry. I get it. It seems I'm going to have to come up with another way of testing the two of you to make sure you're ready," Cyrus explained.

"You do what you need to, Cyrus. We just want to go get our kids. She is a better shot now. We are both better fighters. I don't know what else you want, but whatever it is, we will give you, because not you or anyone else is going to stand in our way. Because if you try, keep in mind that you are training the two people who will only see you as an obstacle standing in their way, and you, too, will be taken out." I brushed past him, leaving Monica behind to revel in her victory.

CHAPTER 8

OVER THE NEXT two weeks, Monica and I trained in the gym in order to prepare for whatever test Cyrus was going to come up with. We were getting a little fed up with his stalling. We felt like we were ready, and we wanted our kids. We also knew we couldn't do it alone. We needed the group for backup. I was thrilled when Lita came into the gym to see me. We had been spending a lot of time together. I wasn't sure if it was a good thing or not, but I enjoyed her company.

She came up to me and dangled her arms around my neck. "I have a surprise for you."

"Really, what is it?" I inquired.

"I found a dress shop. We can go now and be back before dinner." She dangled a set of keys in front of me.

"Are you serious? Oh my god, are you serious?" I hugged her in my excitement. Every mother wants to see their daughter in the perfect wedding dress. "I want it to be a surprise for her though."

"It will be. Now let's go." Lita grabbed my hand and led me out of the gym.

We found the little ATV fueled and ready for us. "You go get that little girl a pretty dress, Ms. Ashley. You ladies be careful out there."

"We will, Tank, and thank you." It seemed like everyone had heard about Harley's wedding and was excited for her, or perhaps it was just an excuse to have a party.

441

They opened the gate, and Lita punched the accelerator. We were cruising over the hills in no time. I was so grateful to be topside again. I had decided when the kids were back and safe that I would ask to go out on salvages so I could get outside more. We were riding for almost an hour before Lita slowed down. I could see her scanning the area to make sure it was safe. We were driving slowly through town when I saw an abandoned Volkswagen Beetle on a side street. I laughed to myself remembering the game Harley, Kat, and I once played. I reached up and lightly punched Lita in the arm. "Slug bug." She only looked at me like I was crazy. It was little things like this that I missed so much. Since the comets hit, we had lost so much. The one thing that I found scary was that we were losing who we were. The world was changing so fast around us, and we had done well to change with it. My fear was what we were changing for. What kind of world were we evolving for our children and grandchildren?

Lita backed the ATV into an alley. We went in through the side entrance. The store looked virtually untouched. I suppose there hadn't been much demand for wedding dresses. Lita and I searched the racks of dresses and pulled out several different styles in Harley's size. We both loved one particular dress, and we could both see Harley wearing it. We double-bagged the dress to keep the road dust off it and made our way out.

We made it back to the cave without incident. Tank was happy to see us in one piece as he took the keys from Lita. I grabbed the dress and followed her to the elevators. She went with me to my room. She wanted to see Harley's face when she saw the dress. I entered the room and yelled for Harley to shut her eyes. I opened the box and held the dress up. "Okay, open them," I instructed.

Harley's mouth dropped open. "Oh my god, Mama, are you kidding me?" Harley marveled at the dress. "You went out there to get this?"

"I couldn't have done it without Lita's help. She found the store and took me, then helped me decide which one to get."

Harley looked at Lita. "Thank you so much."

"Not a problem. We are all so happy for you and want you to have a great wedding." Lita hugged Harley and excused herself.

We hung the dress up and gathered the babies and went for dinner. We ate and went back to our room to finish finalizing arrangements. Mo was going to fix a cake. Preacher had already talked to Harley and Ricky and agreed to perform the ceremony. Mason and Blade were going to set up a backdrop. Lita was our unofficial photographer. Everything was going to come together in just two days.

We had just settled in for the night when someone began beating on my door. I opened it to find T-Bone staring at me. "Ms. Ashley, you gotta come with me right now."

"What is it? Is someone hurt?" I was totally confused.

"No, nothing like that, but Cyrus said to come get you. It's urgent."

Dressed in only pajama pants and tank top, I took off behind T-Bone. We went up to the garage and climbed the ladder leading outside. I found Cyrus using binoculars staring at the gate. Then I heard someone screaming my name.

"Do you know this guy?" Cyrus handed me the binoculars.

I peered through them and tried to make sense of the scene unfolding before me. "Oh my god, yes, I know him. Open the damn gate." I slid down the hill and ran for the gate that was now opening. "Marcus!" I screamed.

Marcus stood before me, exhausted and spent. He was thin and weak and obviously dehydrated and very dirty. I grabbed him and hugged him close. "Marcus, what are you doing here? How did you find us?" Marcus collapsed in my arms. Without hesitating, I threw him over my shoulder and carried him back to the garage, whereby that time Tank had a stretcher waiting. We got him down into my room and put him on the bed.

T-Bone brought a few bottles of water. "Mo is going to bring some soup for him."

"My question is, who is he?" Cyrus said, looking at me.

"His name is Marcus. He is my ex-fiancé's son. I left him on the reservation with his mom and dad when we left. I have no idea why he is here or how he got here."

"Mama," Harley called from her doorway, wondering what was going on.

"Harley, get me a cold cloth, please," I stated as she hurried to the bathroom and returned with a cloth. She sat on the other bed as Ricky came in and sat beside her.

Everyone but Cyrus left. Marcus slowly came around and was glad to see friendly faces. "I made it."

"It's okay, Marcus. You are safe here. Sit up and see if you can drink some water." He sat up and was a little shaky but took the water gratefully. He drank half the bottle before coming up for air. "Can you tell us what happened?"

Marcus finished off the water and got another bottle. "Ashley, it was awful. People with guns showed up at the reservation and killed everybody. It was a slaughter. Mom, Dad, Grandmother, everyone. Even the chief is gone. If it weren't for the chief, I wouldn't be here. He showed me a place to hide in the barn. He told me to go south, and I would find you where your horse ran behind the gate. I had no clue what he meant, but I did as he said, and I found you." Marcus took another half bottle of water.

"They killed everyone." I buried my head in my hands.

"Who are they, Ashley?" Marcus asked.

"It's a long story, but the same people who killed everyone on the reservation are the same ones who have kidnapped Kat and Dannie," I explained as Marcus looked around for the first time, noticing that they weren't around. "They also killed Rose and Jacob and Raven." My voice quivered.

Marcus looked up suddenly. "Raven? Oh my god, Ashley, I'm so sorry." His attention turned to Ricky. "You, too, Ricky, I'm so sorry."

"So you have been out walking around trying to find our horses?" I asked.

"When it got quiet and I knew the soldiers were gone, I left the barn and quickly grabbed what I could. I got a rifle even though I wasn't sure how to shoot it. I grabbed a knife and a little food, a jacket, and one change of clothes. I ran out of there and headed south. I just tried to stay quiet and out of sight."

"Seems like you just got lucky finding those horses," Cyrus said as he stood up. "Ashley, looks like you can handle things from here. I'll bring down a change of clothes so he can get a hot shower.

"Thank you, Cyrus. That's kind of you," I said as he left the room, closing the door behind him.

"We will go back to bed. Marcus, I'm glad you are here," Harley said as she and Ricky left the room.

Mo knocked on the door and opened it, holding out a large hot bowl of soup. "I heard someone was hungry," he said, handing the bowl over to Marcus. "If you need something else, just come find me."

"We will be fine, Mo, and thank you." I closed the door and turned back to Marcus, who had forgotten every table manner he ever had. He had the bowl up to his lips, sucking the soup down like a siphon. I could only giggle at him. "Take it easy. There will be plenty. Eat it slow."

"You have no idea how happy I am to see you," Marcus said.

"I can only imagine. We are happy to have you. I just wish it were under better circumstances. I'm sorry about your mom and dad."

"I prefer not to think about it. I have bad dreams now. It's like I see it all happening again. It's worse if I think about things too much," Marcus said, shoveling in the food. "Chief told me I would be safe and that I would find you, and I did. Can you fill me in on what's going on?"

I sat and explained everything as best as I could to him, starting from when we left the reservation and ending with Harley and Ricky's upcoming nuptials. Marcus was turning green. "Why don't you get a shower and get cleaned up?" He agreed and retired to the bathroom. Cyrus brought the clothes as promised and said Lita and I could take him into town tomorrow for more. Marcus came out of the bathroom and collapsed onto the bed and fell fast asleep. Taco came out from under the bed, jumped up with Marcus, and curled up with him.

The next day, we spent decorating the cantina for the wedding. Marcus said he felt well enough to play the wedding march on the piano that no one ever used. I took photos of people decorating. They all seemed to be having a good time. Even Cyrus delightfully watched everyone float around with enthusiasm.

"I hate things happened the way they did, but I am so glad you and your family came here," Cyrus explained as he finished off his evening coffee. "You guys have really livened things up around here, and we needed that."

"Well, gee whiz, Cyrus, I am so happy we could be of service to you." I paused and looked at him intently. "So have you decided when we are going to get our kids?"

Cyrus just dropped his head, snickering in exasperation. "I have one more test for you ladies, and if you pass, we can go get your kids."

"And when do you plan to give us this test?" I asked, never dropping my eyes from him.

"After the wedding, okay? Let your daughter have her night, then we will worry about the other stuff," Cyrus explained.

Reluctantly I agreed and retired to my room. I lay across my bed. It wasn't long before I heard a commotion coming from Harley's room. I went to the adjoining door and opened it. Several of the guys were wrapping Ricky up in a sheet and carrying him away.

"Just what in the hell is going on?" I asked Mason as Big Mo threw Ricky's wrapped body over his shoulder like it was a sack of potatoes.

"Relax, little Mama. We put some stuff together for a bachelor party. We will make sure he is in place tomorrow, dressed and pressed." Mason watched as I folded my arms in protest. "He can't see her before the wedding. It will be bad luck."

They were just looking for any excuse to party, so who was I to take it from them? "Fine, but you make damn sure he is there on time."

"No worries. We are underground. Where the hell are we going to go?" Mason snapped with a huge smile on his face. He took Ricky's clothes, and they all disappeared down the hallway. Harley sat on her bed and looked around as she sat alone for the first time in several weeks.

"Are you okay, baby?" I asked her as I sat beside her.

"Yeah, I'm fine. I just really miss Kat. When she was around me all the time, I felt like she was so annoying. Now I would give anything to have her annoy me. I'm getting married tomorrow, Mama, and my sister should be here to share that with me. It just seems unfair," Harley explained.

"We can always postpone the wedding and wait till Kat is with us again," I encouraged.

Harley looked at me with horror in her eyes. "No, Mama, you said we could do this. You can't go back on your word now. We have done too much work on this wedding."

"Relax, Harley." I patted her leg. "Baby, I'm not going back on my word. I only thought if you wanted to wait, I wanted you to know that you could."

"I would love to have Kat with me, Mama. But I want you there too, and there is no way I could choose between you two. So I'm getting married tomorrow, and my mama is going to be there. And when my sister gets home, maybe we can have another cake or something."

I hugged Harley and assured her everything would be fine. Harley crawled into bed, and I tucked her in for the last time as my little girl. "Get some sleep. You got a big day tomorrow." I gently kissed Harley's forehead. "Good night, baby."

"Night, Mama," Harley said softly as she rolled over and shut her eyes.

I eased back into my room and looked at Nyte sleeping in her bed. I had no idea how she could sleep through all the noise and commotion that sometimes surrounded her. I suppose somewhere along the way, she had simply learned that if it were important, I would wake her up.

I lay down in my bed. I tossed and turned most of the night. My thoughts raced with thoughts of Harley as a baby and toddler. It was a simpler time, a happier time. In my thoughts, I relived her first two teeth and how they shone when she smiled. Her first steps as she tenderly let go of my finger and took those all-important steps unassisted. Her first day of school, I witnessed some children screaming and crying as teachers attempted to pry them from their parents' grip. Harley sat quietly at her seat, coloring. She looked up and saw me standing at the door. She flashed me with a huge smile now full of teeth and waved bye to me. I knew then she was going to be just fine. As her mother, I had done everything in my power to protect her from the cold, cruel world. Now the cruel world had been thrust upon all of us. We all seemed to have adjusted. I wanted so much for Harley. I knew in that moment that she would never attend college. And if the best I could hope for was a happy marriage to a man who loved her and would never abandon her, as a mother, I was lucky she had found a man whom she could work side by side with and a man who would take care of my little girl. I would have preferred if this wedding had been put off for a few years, but I also understood Harley's dilemma of wanting at least one of her parents at her wedding. Her father was already gone. I could never deprive my daughter of this experience.

Somewhere between imagining her walking down the aisle and me playing with my grandkids one day, I feel asleep. When I awoke, Harley was in the shower. In preparation of the wedding, everyone had the day off. These nuptials had become the talk of the base, and everyone was excited for the kids. Lita and Monica came in with coffee for me and breakfast for Harley. They descended on her like a few vultures, doing her hair and makeup. I was lucky to have family like this. I left the security of our domicile and walked down the hall. Everyone greeted me by name. I walked into the cantina and gasped at the decorations. When we had left the previous night, we had a few bows and pretty tablecloths. Big Mo was setting the cake on the table, and he saw me looking around in awe.

"The boys done it, Ms. Ashley. Mason, Blade, T-Bone, Tank, even Blaine came in here last night with Lita and rearranged the tables and chairs and set up the altar. I think it means a lot to everyone for the little girl to have a nice wedding. The cake is done." Big Mo waved his hand to display a three-tier camouflaged cake.

"It's beautiful, Mo. Thank you so much. Harley is going to love it." A tear began to well up into my eye as I looked around. Camouflage netting was draped over and around a wooden altar Mason had built and put into place. All these strangers had gone out of their way to make sure my daughter had a perfect wedding. I had to leave before I got too emotional, and no one needed that. I went back to my room and reveled to Lita how great everything looked.

From that point on, it was everything we could do to keep Harley in the room. I took time to get myself dressed and ready, then got Nyte dressed.

Max hobbled into my room a short time later with a cane. He was dressed nicely in pants and shirt. He hugged Monica then me, then he turned to Harley. "I know I'm not your daddy, but I was there the day you were born, and I just wanted to take a moment to tell you that you look beautiful and that your daddy would be so proud of you right now." Max lightly kissed Harley on the cheek and took a seat.

Before Lita left, I gave her my camera. "I know it may seem silly, but please take as many photos as you can. You have fresh batteries and plenty of room on the memory card."

She only smiled. "Don't worry, Mama. I will capture all those sweet little moments." She took the camera and disappeared down the hallway.

"Has anyone seen Ricky?" Harley asked.

"I saw him last night. He is fine and will be there at the altar waiting for you in about ten minutes. Are you ladies about ready to get this deed done?" Max asked as he offered Monica his arm. They had been fighting so much since we arrived at the base I was worried if they would overcome their problems. However, seeing them today looking at each other, I could see their love reblooming between them. We collected Summer and Nyte and took the elevator down to the cantina level.

Mason met us as the elevator doors opened. He handed a small basket of flower petals to Monica and Max. "These are for the little ones to throw as you walk down the aisle. You can go on in. Marcus is playing the piano."

I grabbed Mason's arm. "Everything is beautiful. Thank you so much."

Mason patted my hand. "We just love an excuse for a party." He winked at me, and he walked into the cantina ahead of me.

I looked back at Harley. She was absolutely gorgeous dressed in a strapless white dress. The only adornment was a silver Western-looking belt and, of course, her boots, which showed so well with the dress's high-low hem. Her hair was down and curled. Monica had finished off her makeup perfectly. I offered my daughter my arm that she graciously took. Marcus began the wedding march, and everyone rose from their seats to capture their first look of Harley in all her glory. Harley caught her breath as she noticed all the added decorations and everyone who showed up. The entire cantina was packed full of people. I felt Harley's grasp tighten around my arm. I just patted her hand and looked at her. "They are all here because they want to be. All you have to do is keep your head straight ahead."

Then she saw Ricky for the first time standing under the camouflage-draped arbor. I felt her grip loosen around my arm, and I knew my daughter was going to be just fine. I elegantly escorted her down the aisle with Lita jumping in front of us to take photos. We got to Ricky, and I reached for his hand.

"I am so sorry your parents couldn't be here to see this day, but I know they are smiling and so proud of you right now." Ricky only nodded to me. "Take care of my daughter, Ricky." I kissed his cheek and placed his hand into Harley's, then politely took my seat next to Max, who put his arm around me.

Lita buzzed around like a busy bee taking photos. Preacher conducted the ceremony and quickly pronounced them man and wife. Ricky kissed my daughter gently in front of everyone and laughed at her when she blushed at the public display. Preacher asked everyone to stick around for the reception party. Lita took photos of all of us with Harley and Ricky. They cut the cake and finally sat down to eat.

Cyrus gave them a key and explained that it was to a private room for the night. Again, Harley blushed. I sat back and watched my daughter dance with her husband. I caught the looks of love and admiration exchanged between them.

"Looks like you could use this." Mason produced a bottle of whiskey.

I took the bottle with gratitude. "You have no idea." I threw the bottle back and took a good long drink.

"I know she is the bride, but I wanted to say that you look really nice tonight." Mason flashed his sparkling eyes.

"Thank you, Mason. I'm still not sure I agree with all this, but with the world coming apart around us, who am I to deny my daughter a little happiness?" I explained. Mason only nodded in understanding.

Soon, Ricky and Harley were ready to leave. They thanked everyone for coming and helping them celebrate, then excused themselves to their room for the night.

Harley turned back and ran to me, throwing her arms around me. "I love you, Mama."

"I love you too, Harley." I embraced my daughter and patted her on the back. "Go to your husband and have your special night. I promise, you will never forget it."

By the time I awoke the next morning, all wedding decorations had been removed, and it was business as usual. Lita found me and gave me my camera. I went immediately to my room. I couldn't wait to see the photos. In my excitement, I forgot to close the door to my room. I sat at the little ledge and loaded up the laptop. The photos began to flash on the screen. They weren't just of Harley's wedding. They were of mine too. Images of Raven and his mystic eyes stared at me hauntingly from the screen. My heart shattered into million pieces. It had been so long since I had seen him or even allowed myself to think about him. I began to cry, and there was no stopping it. I attempted to stand and walk away but fell onto the bed, barely able to catch my breath. Nyte was in her playpen, awkwardly watching me.

I heard someone at my door. "Kitty cat." Then nothing. A few seconds passed and then "Kitty cat, Dan Dan."

I opened my eyes and saw Kenny Wayne standing in my doorway. He was watching my computer. A photo of Kat flashed on the screen, and again, he said, "Kitty cat."

Sitting up on the bed, I looked him over and noticed his bracelet. "Oh my god." I started toward Kenny Wayne. He must have thought he was in trouble, or maybe I just scared him, because he turned and started running away. I chased right behind him. "Kenny Wayne, come back here. I just want to talk to you." He only squealed and ran faster. I pursued him into the gym, where he ran behind Cyrus, using him as a human shield.

"What the hell is going on?" Cyrus yelled out.

"She's mad at me. She chased me," Kenny Wayne said, pointing at me.

At that point, we had everyone's attention. "No, Kenny, I'm not mad at you. Do you know someone named Kitty Kat and Dan Dan? Did Kitty Kat give you that bracelet?"

Monica climbed out of the ring and looked at Kenny's arm. Her breath quickened as she grabbed at her chest.

I turned to Cyrus. "I was in my room, and I had the door open. My computer was cycling photos, and he was saying Kitty Cat and Dan Dan every time a photo of Kat and Dannie flashed on screen. And Kat had a bracelet just like that one."

"I didn't steal it. Kenny don't thief from no one," Kenny said, staying behind Cyrus for protection.

"But did someone named Kat give it to you? Did you see that girl who was on my computer screen somewhere?" I looked at Cyrus to help me out here.

"Kenny, answer the lady," Cyrus demanded and moved to the side, exposing Kenny Wayne.

Kenny just looked at everyone staring at him. "Kenny some-times sleeps at another place. That's where Kitty Kat and Dan Dan are."

Monica gasped and grabbed for my arm. "Oh my god, Ashley, he knows where they are."

"Kenny, honey, no one is mad at you. We are excited, and I am sorry if I scared you. We are going back to my room to look at pho-tos, and if you want to look at them with us, you can." I took Monica by the hand, and we walked to my room. The computer was still cycling the photos. We were both nearly in tears when Kenny Wayne showed up at the door. Cyrus slowly followed behind him.

"Come sit down, Kenny." I patted a chair next to me.

Kenny cautiously sat down and pointed to the screen. "That's my friend Kitty Kat."

I scrolled through more photos and stopped on a photo of Dannie and looked at Kenny.

"That's Dan Dan. We play go fish," Kenny said. "I win a lot of games."

"Kenny, are they both okay?" Monica asked, fighting back her tears.

"Dan Dan is okay. Kitty Kat has a white tree trunk on her leg. She let me write my name on it. She's real nice to me," Kenny said, smiling.

"Can you show us where they are? It would have to be a secret," Cyrus asked, standing in the doorway.

"Sure can. It's not that far." Kenny darted for the door. "Can I drive?" he asked.

Cyrus only smiled. "Maybe next time, buddy." Then he turned to us. "Let me take him out with a few others, and I will be back to let you know what we find."

"We want to go too!" Monica stated, rising from her seat. "They are our kids."

"That's why we don't need to go," I said. "Be honest, Monica, if you saw Dannie, could you be still, or would your first instinct be to run toward him? I know what I would want to do, and people may die in the process," I explained. "Let them go, and when they come back, we will make our plans to go get our kids." I looked to Cyrus. "I'm putting my faith in you to keep your word."

Cyrus nodded. "If they are where I think they are, you will have your kids by the week's end, I promise." He quickly disappeared down the hallway.

I got up and hugged Monica. "They are going to find them. We are going to get them back."

"I guess Kat has a broken leg. It sounded like Kenny was describing a cast." Monica wiped a tear from her eye.

"That's my guess, probably happened when the horse went down." I could not sit and go crazy waiting for Cyrus to return. "Why don't you go tell Max what's going on? I'm going to the gym. I feel like I need to hit something." I attempted a smile at Monica, but she understood totally.

I walked out of my room and found my way to the gym. I donned a pair of boxing gloves and began to work over a punching bag. It didn't take long for me to grow tired, but I continued punching and kicking. Images of Raven and his crooked grin, Kat's angelic eyes, and Dannie's innocent face flashed in my mind. I saw the kids playing, laughing, and smiling. I imagined Raven on our wedding day. I was not entirely sure how long I had been working out, but it was Mason's voice that brought me back into reality.

"Ashley!" he yelled. "You need to stop."

My chest heaved with every breath, and my hands were shaking. A fine white powder drifted in the air around me. Everyone in the gym was watching me. Mason approached me with his hands up in caution. "Just breathe," he instructed.

"I'm fine," I said, using my teeth to remove a glove.

"Fine? Hell, you busted the fucking bag. I have never seen that happen before," he said with a slight chuckle.

Looking around, I couldn't help but smile a little at my destructive accomplishment. "I'm sorry. I'll fix the bag." Taking a seat on a metal bench, I finished removing my gloves.

"We're not worried about the bag. I have never seen you like that. You were fixated on that thing. I'm not sure what you were thinking about, but that is the fire and passion you are going to need. I wish Cyrus could have been here to see it," Mason said, handing me a bottle of water. "I would hate to see that bag if you actually had a weapon in your hand."

"Yeah, well, I'll save that for the bastards who took our kids and killed our people." I sat quietly for a few moments. Mason must have felt my exasperation radiating from my body. He raised his hand and patted me on the back. My reaction was a quick jump with my fist pulling back.

"Whoa, girl, it's okay," Mason said as he stood up.

"No, it's not," I snapped at him. "I feel like a fucking pinned-up vampire. I'm trapped underground. My emotions are all fucked up. My family has been ripped apart, and those sons of bitches took my kids from me. They have taken everything. They took Raven." A tear welled in my eye. "I'm not okay. I'm fucking pissed off. And the only thing that is going to satisfy me is having their blood run through my fingers like a raging river." I was pacing in a circle. "The thing that scares me the most is, I think I like this feeling. I just need to be alone for a little while."

I got up, and Blaine was blocking my exit. "Sounds like little sister has grown a pair of balls." He laughed hard.

I truly detested this man. "That's right, you pudgy bastard. I just wear mine on my chest." Before I knew what I was doing, I punched Blaine. He fell like a ton of bricks onto the floor with his mouth bleeding. Looking down, I noticed a smear of his blood on my hand. Bringing it up to my mouth, I licked his salty essence from my knuckle. "For now, your blood will have to tide me over. Stay out of my way, Blaine."

"You crazy bitch, you knocked out my tooth." Several guys were helping Blaine up as I walked right out of the gym without looking back.

I skipped dinner that night. Harley had agreed to keep Nyte for me. It would give me some alone time. I lay across my bed and replayed the image of Blaine's expression when I punched him over and over in my mind. I felt someone watching me and jumped up to find Cyrus standing in my doorway. "Are there any doors that actually lock around here?"

Cyrus only shook his head and halfway smiled. "I just talked to Monica. You'll have your final fight tomorrow night. Are you up for it?"

"You found them then? Our kids, you found them, right?" I asked, hopeful.

Cyrus nodded. "Kenny showed us where they are. We saw them with our own eyes. They seem fine."

"They are not fine. They are little, alone, and scared. Who knows what lines of bullshit those bastards have told them," I spouted.

"I only meant that they appear to be in good health. The little girl has a cast on her leg, but other than that, they appear fine." Cyrus took a seat at the small table. "You got to get a grip on yourself."

I took a seat across from him. "Cyrus, I feel like I'm going to burst. Working the punching bag over helped, but I feel so much rage."

"Good, now direct it in the right direction. You have to be smart and use that anger instead of letting it use you," Cyrus explained. "You and Monica have both come so far. Tomorrow night is your last opportunity to prove that you're ready for this. We will have to go in quietly to get the kids. There will be a lot of hand-to-hand. I don't want to be the first ones to fire a weapon. If it comes to that, we will be prepared. But we would rather do this quietly. I know the chances are slim, but that's what we are striving for. I don't think you want your kids caught in the crossfire if things go south."

"No, of course not." I could tell that Cyrus was worried about my mental state. "I will keep myself in check. I will do whatever you want. It may be our kids, but this is your mission. I will follow your lead."

"Glad to hear that." Cyrus rose from his chair. "And if it's not too much to ask, please don't beat Blaine up again."

I made a face. "You heard about that, huh?"

"Not much goes on in this place without me hearing about it. It's a curse really." Cyrus hitched his thumbs in his belt loops. "I have to admit, I was proud when I heard you knocked him on his ass. I know he probably deserved it. But he's a good man, and when shit hits the fan, believe it or not, he's one you can count on."

"I hope you're not asking me to apologize because I won't. However, I will attempt to play nice." I tried to force a smile.

"That's all I can ask for. So you need to do whatever you need to do. Your final test is tomorrow night. I think you will be intrigued with what I have planned for you two." Cyrus turned to leave with a wicked grin.

I had no idea what he had planned, but I knew it wasn't going to be easy.

I found my family in the cantina having dinner. Monica was full of smiles and excitement. Max looked like he wanted to cry. Harley was tending to the little ones, while Ricky worked the dinner shift. I got a food tray and took a seat.

Lita soon came in and found me and took a seat next to me. "You wanna sing tonight?"

I just looked at her. "Have you lost your mind? I never want to sing. I get trapped or tricked into it."

"Bullshit," Max spouted out loud. All eyes fell on him. "You love to sing. You are just in a foul mood and have been since we got here. You're using it as an excuse not to sing."

I glared at my brother, and finally, I had my gut full of his selfish bellyaching. "Max, you don't want to get into this with me."

"Оннн, I'm so scared." Max wiggled his fingers childishly. Monica rolled her eyes at his behavior.

I rose from my seat. "Max, you can pick on other people if it makes you feel any better, but you are the one sitting there wallowing in pity. You got hurt, and you can't do your fatherly duties to go get your son. You hate it, so you are taking it out on everyone around you. I honestly don't know how Monica is putting up with you. She has shed her fears and stepped up to do what she needs to in order to get her son back, and instead of giving her your support, you give her grief. I choose not to sing because it reminds me of my dead husband, a man I didn't get to spend enough time with, and it hurts. It seems to me that you're the one that's full of bullshit. Do you want to see me hurt? Do you want to see me in pain? Fine!" I went up on stage and motioned for Lita to join me.

I chose another song by Halestorm entitled "Tell Me Where It Hurts" since that was the only hard band I could identify with that had a female singer. The song was hard and fast and gave opportunity to show some attitude. The guys loved it. Even Blaine danced about the room with a bruise on his jaw. Big Mo danced in the kitchen with Ricky, and Harley bounced Nyte on her hip. Lita and I danced around each other, and I suppose it must have looked a bit provocative. Cyrus entered the cantina and watched Lita and I on stage with his arms folded. As the song wrapped up, Lita wrapped her arm around me and pulled my body to hers and engaged me in a deep, passionate, yet awkward kiss. It caught me totally off guard. The guys showed their testosterone with all sorts of hoots and hollers and catcalls. I saw Cyrus's eyes widen. I wasn't sure what to do. Max glared at me; his eyes were becoming bloodshot red, and finally, he got up and headed for the door. I didn't know where he went, nor did I care at that moment. I didn't want to embarrass Lita, but I definitely wanted to move forward. I scanned the room, and Mason had my favorite bottle in front of him, along with a huge grin. I found a different song by Luke Bryan called "Country Girl [Shake It for Me]." I whispered my plan to Lita, "Just change the word *girl* to *boy*."

As the music started, I went over to Mason and took his bottle. "I need this more than you right now." Then I returned to the stage. "Get off your asses and shake 'em for me!" I yelled into the microphone. It was a fast song. I would call it a country rap. Lita didn't seem to enjoy the country music. She didn't sing as much on this song. Blaine moved to the front of the stage and backed his ass up to it and began to shake his massive butt in front of me. I couldn't help but laugh. I put my boot on his butt and gave him a slight push. I saw Blade run in and whisper something to Cyrus, and they both left quickly. I figured if it were something important, they would have interrupted us. I wrapped up the song and took a good long drink of my whiskey.

The guys wanted another song, but I refused. Harley took the babies back to the room. Monica stayed with us for a while. She really didn't want to go back to her room. She knew Max would be there waiting for her. I offered for her to sleep in my room, but she declined. Even though my brother was being an ass, she loved him. I had tried not to make eye contact with Lita. I didn't want things to get strange between us. I knew eventually I would have to talk to her about it. Soon, I was tipsy enough to stagger safely back to my room.

In my room, my computer was still cycling photos. They were on the photos of my wedding. Raven's face screamed my name through the screen. I swear I heard his voice. A cold chill went up my spine. Setting the bottle down, I figured I had enough. I lay on my bed and watched the photos change. I lay there thinking of all the songs we had performed together. Soon, I felt the heat on my face from the tears that were streaming down my cheeks. "Damn you, Max! Damn you to hell." I wiped the tears from my face and noticed Lita standing in my doorway. "I swear to God I'm going to find some way to lock that fucking door."

"Do you want me to go?" Lita asked.

Shaking my head, I said, "No, I think we need to talk."

"I'm sorry. I got caught up in the moment. I like you, Ashley, but I would never force anything on you. I was out of line." Lita sat on my bed. "Can you forgive me?"

"Lita, there's nothing to forgive. I just don't want you to have some sort of crush on me. I am so fucked up in the head right now. There's no way I could return any sort of romantic feelings to anyone, male or female. I love you, just not in that way. You're my friend, and I want to keep it that way."

"Understood. So it's not going to be weird between us?" Lita asked.

"Nah, hell, if anything, I should be thanking you. If the men think we are together, I probably won't have anyone hitting on me." I laughed and hugged Lita.

"That's what you think. There is always one asshole who thinks if you're a lesbian that he will be the one to flip you." We both looked at each other and laughed, and simultaneously, we said, "Blaine." Then we laughed in unison.

CHAPTER 9

CYRUS GAVE MONICA and me the next morning off so we could prepare for our final test, but it was Max who showed up at my door early.

"Sissy, can I come in?" he asked, standing in my doorway.

"Depends on what you want." I stood firmly with my hands on my hips.

"I wanted to say I'm sorry. Monica and I talked last night. I understand that I haven't been very supportive of either of you. Maybe I was feeling sorry for myself. I don't know. I just want you to know that no matter what, I do love you, and I'm scared for you and Monica to gear up and go out there. It's going to be dangerous, and I don't want to lose either of you. I don't know what I would do if one of you didn't come home tomorrow," Max explained as he sat at my small table.

"I understand that, Max. But you have been a total ass to Monica. She don't like guns, and she has learned to shoot. She's always been mild and meek, and she has stepped up. You should be proud of her. She can really hold her own now." I patted my brother's hand.

"I am proud." Max exhaled deeply. "It's just hard to see her like this. And I have told her all of this too, and she understands. I just wanted to tell you."

"I appreciate it, Max. Are you coming tonight?" I asked.

"It will be one of the hardest things I have ever done, but yes, I wouldn't miss it for anything." Max smiled at me.

My brother and I hugged each other. Before he left, he turned to me. "Can I ask you a question?"

"Yeah, what is it?"

"Are you and Lita…" Max stopped and looked uncomfortable.

"We are just friends. She took things a little far, but we are cool. No worries. The world may be changing before our very eyes, but I'm still straight, little brother," I explained.

Max, looking more relieved, only nodded and went back to his room.

After eating lunch, I went for a run around the base. It was a nice day. The air was still crisp, but everything was in bloom. I stopped abruptly at the mounds of disturbed ground marked with small white crosses. Some had names, and some didn't. This must have been where Raven, Jacob, and Rose were buried. I had no idea which grave was Raven's, so I just picked one and sat beside it. I felt a little stupid talking to a mound of dirt, but it made me feel better. "Hey, honey, I miss you. Nyte is good. She's growing so fast. She misses you too." I paused. "The bastards who killed you took Kat and Dannie. We have new friends now, and we are going tomorrow to get them back. It's going to be dangerous. I wish you were here. I need you to hug me and tell me it's going to fine." I wrapped my arms around myself and squeezed. "I'm going to kill again. I'm going to kill all of them if I can, and if I die in the process, then at least I get to see you again. So who knows? Maybe I'll see you soon, baby. I love you." I got up from the ground and started back to the base.

I noticed Cyrus standing on the hill watching me. I didn't bother to wave. With the mood I was in, I probably wouldn't have used all my fingers. I simply went back to my room and got a quick shower. I dressed in camouflaged shorts with a white T-shirt tucked in. I pulled my hair back into a braided ponytail. My heavy hiking boots were about the only thing I wore these days. I put on some mood music of heavy metal. Harley had been keeping Nyte for me, so I turned it up loud. I headbanged around the room and just danced it out. A loud banging distracted me. I looked up to see Lita standing in my doorway. I was going to have to find a way to lock that damn door.

"What's up?" I asked, turning the music down.

"I brought your dinner to you. I thought you may want to eat early before the fight tonight." Lita sat the tray down on the table.

"Thanks. I hadn't planned on eating dinner," I admitted.

"Yeah, I figured as much. You got to eat. You need the strength. Who knows what Cyrus has planned for you. He is keeping it all hushed, and he hasn't let anyone into the gym all day," she explained.

"Well, we will find out soon enough. Personally, I'm ready for anything that man can possibly throw at me," I said, and Lita sat with me.

"Is it okay if I'm in your corner tonight?" Lita asked. "You need someone, and I thought—"

I interrupted, "I would love to have you in my corner, girl. You and Mason are just about my best friends, and it would be an honor." Lita only smiled back at me.

We sat and listened to music for a while. Lita massaged my shoulders to keep me loosened up. Soon, Mason came to the door. "Are we ready? Cyrus has opened the doors to the gym, and people are already filling it up."

"Did you look inside?" Lita asked.

Mason's eyes dropped to the ground. "Yeah, I did."

"Well?" Lita probed him for more information.

Mason looked at me. "It's a fucking cage. He has like a giant shark cage around the ring. He has chairs set up all around it. I have never seen anything like it. I think he's lost his damn mind. I don't know what he expects from you."

"But who am I fighting?" I asked.

"Really? That's what you want to know? This doesn't bother you?" Lita asked.

"No one knows yet. Cyrus is keeping it quiet."

"I wouldn't have expected any less. Cyrus likes the shock factor, and he loves a good show. So I'll give him one. If you two are through pussyfooting around, let's get this done." I was in a mood. I was ready to prove myself and to put this night behind us. This was the last obstacle standing in our way to get our kids. Nobody was going to stand in my way.

After everyone else was in the gym and seated, Cyrus acted as the master of ceremonies and introduced Monica and then myself. I walked into the gym and kept my eyes forward. The cage was huge, but I didn't want anyone to see that it intimidated me. I walked around and entered the cage. Max was already on his feet at the cage, telling Monica to call it off and get out of the ring. He looked at me, and I only shook my head. He sat back down and hid his face. Harley and Ricky were there, but the babies were left in the day care. Ricky was holding Harley's hand, but they were smiling at me, giving me what encouragement they could.

Cyrus came back on the microphone. "And tonight, they will team up against the biggest motherfucker we could find. Give a big round of applause for Big Mo." The crowd's cheers echoed in the room. I spun around to see Big Mo making his way to the ring in a pair of shorts, then turned back to the metal bars.

"Oh, Ashley," Monica said softly.

Everyone was cheering and yelling. I looked over the crowd. Mason looked at me and nodded.

"We got this, Monica." She looked at me, shocked. "We get to work together. Cyrus wants to see how we can work together. Remember the simple rules of fighting. If they can't walk, they can't fight. If they can't see, they can't fight. Now because he's so big, I doubt we are going to get a submission hold on him, so we are going to incapacitate him. He's a cook, for God's sake. He hasn't been in this gym every day busting his ass. We have. Cyrus wants a show, so let's give it to him."

Monica nodded in agreement. "The bigger they are, the harder they fall."

"That's right." We high-fived. "Just don't be under him when he falls." We couldn't help but laugh.

"Hey, Ashley," Monica said, looking at me, "can you promise me something?" Monica placed her hand on my arm gently. "Don't kill him."

Mo entered the ring. He looked scared and displaced. For a moment, I felt sorry for him. Even though he was a tall, broad-shoul-dered man, he wasn't a fighter. I didn't know if Mo had a mean bone in his body, but he had evidently pissed off someone to be thrown into this ring.

The bell rang, and Mo let out a roar and slapped at his own chest like a big black gorilla. Monica and I both slightly bent our knees in a defensive crouch. We looked at each other and grinned wickedly. At the same time, we took off running and plowed like a wrecking ball into each of Mo's knees, which immediately buckled under him. The big man let out a howl as his body hit the mat. I was instantly on him, hammering my fists into his head. He was trying to shout or talk, but I wasn't paying any attention to what he was saying. I was starting to feel a little confident, but then I felt Mo's large hands latch onto my upper arms. I was quickly tumbling across the mat as he threw me off like a nagging fly. He got up to his feet, and I smiled when I saw Monica leap onto his back. Her feet were perched on his massive hips while her arms encircled his neck, cutting off his airway. Mo shook and twisted his body, attempting to fling Monica off, but she was holding on for dear life. I cringed when Mo flopped down on the mat, pinning Monica's body and knocking the breath out of her. He rolled and got back to his feet, then looked at me. It wasn't a look of anger or determination; it was one of concern and worry. He held his hands up defensively and shook his head. He obviously didn't want to be here. Cyrus had his hand extended through the cage and was slapping the mat, yelling at Mo.

Monica was beginning to stir, her hand still clutching her chest. It wouldn't surprise me if she had a few cracked ribs. However, she dug down deep and found the strength within herself to get to her feet. She glared at Mo. Rays of determination and anger radiated from her eyes. I had never seen that look in her before. I smiled and ran toward him, stopping short, dropping, then sliding into his left knee with both of my feet. His knee buckled under him just as Monica lunged herself into him. Mo fell to the mat with a thud with Monica still attached. She began blasting him with punches to his head. He attempted to roll and deflect her blows. I grabbed his leg and twisted his ankle. He howled in pain, deflecting his attention, allowing Monica to land a few significant blows. She was tiring quickly. Mo found the strength to kick me off his leg, then flung Monica off. He straddled her, grabbed her shoulders, and yelled, "Stay down, please!" Mo turned to me, grabbing my arms, and stared into my eyes. "You don't understand what's going on." The crowd was on their feet and cheering. Cyrus was glaring at Mo with hatred and contempt.

I didn't know what Mo had done to piss Cyrus off enough to throw him in this ring, but that wasn't my problem. "I understand that right now you're standing in our way to get our kids back, and even though I like you, I can't have that. I'm sorry." I quickly raised my knee and planted it firmly into Mo's groin. He doubled over in pain, attempting to hold his aching nut sack. Mo's head snapped back as I brought my knee up again, landing a hard blow to his nose. Blood began pouring from his nose. His eyes began to roll back in his head. Taking the opportunity, I began punching him repeatedly. He staggered backward in a daze and fell onto his ass in a sitting position. He fell over in a slump as I landed a massive kick to the side of his head, opening a large gash over his left eye. A small puddle of blood began to form under his head. Straddling him, I continued a relentless series of blows. Blood covered my hands and his face. His eyes were swollen; he was breathing hard. He was done. Monica was getting to her feet, yelling my name.

Something bumped my knee, distracting me. Cyrus was standing on the outside of the ring looking at me with his hands on his hips. "Now finish him."

Looking down, I noticed a large knife beside my knee. Cyrus wanted me to kill him. Taking the knife in my hand, the crowd fell silent. It seemed like a dream. I could hear Monica shouting my name, but she seemed far away. Max was on his feet and beating his fist against the ring, shouting. "No, sissy, you don't have to do this!" Harley had her head buried into Ricky's shoulder, unable to watch anymore of this spectacle.

Cyrus only watched me. He was the leader, the boss. Everyone just did whatever he told them to; it was just expected. He was the one who was going to help us get our babies back. I didn't want to disappoint him or damage our chances of a rescue mission. I took the knife into my hands and raised it above my head, set to plunge it into Mo's body.

I looked down at Mo, who was now crying real tears. "It's okay, Ms. Ashley. You do what you need to. You go get your babies."

This man was willing to sacrifice his life so we could go get our kids. My breath quickened. I knew whose side he was on. He had never once punched Monica or me. He had only attempted to defend himself. He wasn't the enemy. I looked up at Cyrus, who nodded at me. He wanted me to kill him, and there would be no consequences for me taking Mo's life. I looked down at Mo. He shut his eyes and let out a long breath, as if he were readying himself for the death blow. My hands were shaking as I let out a scream and brought the large knife down only a fraction of an inch from Mo's head. I whispered into Mo's ear, "You will live another day, my friend."

The crowd cheered at my decision. Monica and Max looked relieved. Cyrus only took a seat and began shaking his head. I plucked the knife out of the mat and walked to the entrance. "Open the damn door!" I shouted. The door was unlocked, and I kicked it open. People were patting me on the back and congratulating me. My entire body was quivering. My hair had come out of my ponytail and was matted with sweat and blood, Mo's blood.

I made my way over to Cyrus. In a swift motion, I straddled him as he sat in the chair. I grabbed a handful of hair and snapped his head back and placed the knife to his throat. His hands went up defensively in shock of my actions. Everyone stepped back, not knowing what I was about to do.

Leaning closer to him, I whispered, "I don't know what he did to piss you off, but he's not a fighter, and I'll be dammed if I'm going to do your dirty work. I didn't kill him because he's not the enemy. He was willing to sacrifice his life. The way I see it, you're the one standing in our way. So you tell me right fucking now. Did we pass your little test, or do I still need to prove to you that I'm not afraid to kill? When do we go get our kids?"

Cyrus glanced around, noticing that no one was coming to his aid. "Tomorrow, we go tomorrow."

Pressing the knife ever so slightly into the side of his neck, breaking the skin, I smiled as I saw his bright red blood dripping. Cyrus grunted at my actions. "Go back on your word, and next time, it will be your jugular." I lifted myself from his lap and turned away from him. Everyone was staring at me. Mason had everyone backed up. Monica and Max were in the ring, attending to Mo.

Mason was the first to approach me. "Are you with us? I thought we had lost you mentally there for a minute."

There was actual fear in people's eyes as they looked upon me. "I'm fine. Cyrus has agreed. We leave tomorrow to go get our kids. And I don't think he will be going back on his word. Meet me in the cantina in fifteen minutes." I made my way to the exit and found a bathroom.

Looking at myself in the mirror, I could understand the looks of fear. I looked like a monster. My hair was a mess and matted and caked with blood.

Lita came in behind me. "Are you okay?"

"Yeah, I'm fine," I replied as I turned back to the mirror.

"Let's get you cleaned up a little before heading to the cantina." Lita began wiping the blood from my hair.

"Yeah, I would hate to freak people out." I smiled.

"Oh, honey, I think that ship has sailed." We laughed together and continued to get me cleaned up.

When I entered the cantina, again everyone cheered. I didn't want any glory; I just wanted my daughter. Kenny Wayne sat beside Cyrus. I made my way over to them. "Good evening, Kenny Wayne. How are you this evening?" I smiled and appeared to be happy. I noticed Cyrus had a large Band-Aid covering the small slice I had made on his throat. "Kenny, are you ready to be a big hero tomorrow?"

He nodded, showing he was eager. "When Kitty Kat and Dan Dan get here, can I play with them all I want to?"

"Of course, you can. Now do you know your job tomorrow?"

Again, he nodded. "Yes, I find them and tell them that you said they were just having a bad day. Kitty Kat needs to take Dan Dan to the outhouse, and their day will get a lot better."

"That's right, buddy, and once they go into the outhouse, what do you do?" Cyrus asked.

"I leave, 'cuz you may start shooting, and I don't want to get hit," Kenny explained. "And I don't tell anyone about you guys. It's going to be a surprise."

"That's right. Good job. Now I want our hero to go get a good night's sleep. We will go over the plan again tomorrow." Cyrus patted him on the back.

"Okay." Kenny waved goodbye to everyone and gave a few hugs, then left the cantina.

"You think he can handle this? I hate knowing the rescue of our kids lay in the ability of someone who is on the quote special side of life," I explained.

"He will be fine. He's excited about them coming here. I think I'm going to hit the hay too. We got a long day tomorrow." Cyrus left the cantina.

I sat there and looked around at all the guys. They laughed and joked around with one another. They were a family. They were all going to put their lives in danger in order to help get our kids back, and not a single one of them were giving it a second thought. I got up and went on stage and retrieved the microphone. Turning it on and giving it a little tap, allowing it to echo, I grabbed everyone's attention. "If I could have your attention, I wanted to say a few words." Taking a deep breath, I continued, "We are going tomorrow to get our kids back. I shouldn't ask any of you to come with me, but I am. When I first arrived, I noticed something. Your group was like mine. You had come to trust, even love one another. I have come to trust you and even love a few of you. I want people I know, love and trust with me. I know it's a dangerous thing we are doing. I understand the risk I am asking you to take, and I just wanted you to know that I appreciate everything you have done to help Monica and me get ready. I also want to thank you in advance for your help, so thank you."

"Are you going to sing?" Blaine asked out loud, and a few people cheered.

"Oh god, fine. I knew you were going to ask, so I already had it planned out, Blaine." Turning to the music, I chose my song—Halestorm's "Here's to Us." The music started, and I sat on a stool in the center of the stage. I sang the song to all the guys in the room.

They loved it. Mason brought me a bottle of Jack Daniel's up on stage. During the song, I made eye contact with Blaine, who raised his glass to me. I raised my bottle up to him. It somehow showed a mutual respect that we had acquired for each other. I finished the song, and everyone cheered. Many of them hugged me or patted me on the back.

I decided to turn in early. I knew the next day was going to be a long, hard, trying day. I went to my room. Peeking in on my newly married daughter, she had Nyte sleeping between her and Ricky. "Best birth control in the world," I whispered to myself.

A soft knock on my door surprised me. Usually, people just open it and walk in. I opened the door to find Marcus standing there. "Hey, kiddo, what's up?"

"I didn't know if I would get a chance to see you tomorrow. I just wanted to say thank you and please be careful." Marcus looked up at me. "I know you're not my mom, but I don't know if I could handle it if anything happened to you too. I have lost everyone."

I knew Marcus was never one to show emotion verbally or physically, but I took a chance. I grabbed him and hugged him. It took him by surprise, but after the shock wore off, he returned my embrace. "Don't worry. I'm coming back. You will always have a family here. We love you." Marcus just nodded as I released him from my bonds, and he quietly walked away. I shut the door and fell across the bed, pulling a light blanket over me. I tried for what seemed like hours to go to sleep. When I finally did, I spent the rest of the night flipping, flouncing, and flopping around on the bed.

It was Harley who woke me up. "Mama," she called out softly.

"What?" I said.

"I brought you some breakfast. And Nyte wanted to see you," Harley explained.

I rolled over and saw my two girls looking at me with smiles. I sat up and picked at my breakfast. I fed more eggs to Nyte than I ate, but that was fine too. I knew Harley wanted to say something. She wanted to get all mushy before I left. I cut her off before she could get started. "You know what's going on today. We all know the risks. You also understand that it's something I have to do. I need to ask you to

469

be an adult. If something were to happen to me, you have two sisters to raise. Can I count on you to handle this?"

"Yes, Mama. You don't have to worry. I will make you proud." Harley looked at me knowing very well this might be the last time we get to talk.

"You already make me proud every day. I love you, Harley," I said, taking her hand.

"I love you too, Mama. Just be careful and bring my sister home safely."

"I will." I kissed my daughter's cheek. "Now why don't you take this little monster and get her all cleaned up?" I had a small tickle session with Nyte. I loved hearing her giggle. When they were gone, I quickly got dressed in a pair of camouflaged cargo pants and army-green T-shirt. I pulled my hair back out of my face and put on a base-ball cap, tucking my hair under the hat. Not knowing what terrain we would be stomping through, I put on my hiking boots. They were durable enough to handle anything.

At ten o'clock, I walked into the garage and joined the guys. It looked like everyone had shown up. Hand shaking and pats on the back were being dished out left and right. I found Monica leaning on a truck.

"Hey, girl, are you ready for this?" she asked.

"About as ready as I can get," I stated, hugging my sister-in-law.

Cyrus stood up on top of one of the trucks. "Can I have your attention, please?" A hush fell over us, and all eyes were diverted to him. "We all know why we are here and what we are going to do. We all have firearms, but we don't want to use them. We want to go in quietly. If Kenny does his job correctly and without trouble, we should have an easy time getting the kids out. If you are confronted, attempt to diffuse the situation quietly. Everyone should have a knife. If you do hear a firearm discharge, be prepared for hell to come off the hinges. Do your best to make your way back to the trucks. The wolves are well stocked and well trained. Monica and Ashley, we want you up front. The little ones won't know any of us and may be afraid to go with us. We want your faces to be the first ones they see." Monica and I nodded in understanding. "Be smart and be quiet. I don't want to lose any of you. Let's roll!"

Everyone cheered and began loading up into the trucks. Guns were already loaded up, and we each had one on our hip. The trucks began leaving. We looked back and saw Max, Harley, and the babies waving, watching us leave. Monica grabbed my hand, and we waved and smiled. If this mission went badly, we wanted their last memory of us to be smiling. Depending how this all went down, this might very well be our last memory of them as well. I saw Harley hug her uncle. Even from that far away, I knew she was crying. I turned away from them. I didn't want all that emotional crap running through my head. Harley was a grown married woman now. She knew the hazards and risks of me leaving. I had to concentrate on the job we were here to do.

We drove for at least thirty minutes before the truck lurched to a stop. We began to file out. We were in a small wooded section on the base of a hill. We belly crawled up the hill and used binoculars to view the compound where our kids were being held. Just like Kenny had said, it appeared most of the kids were outside playing around. Scanning the grounds, I found Kat and Dannie sitting in the dirt. "There they are," I said quietly, handing the binoculars to Monica. It took everything inside me to keep from sprinting toward them. They were so close yet so far away.

"Thank God they are safe," Monica said, relieved.

"Yep, now let's keep them that way," Cyrus stated. "Kenny Wayne, you know your job. Don't say anything about us. Get Kat and Dannie to go to the outhouse, then you get the hell out of there."

"Yes, sir." Kenny gave a salute, then got up and began walking toward the compound.

He did well. He didn't even look back toward us. Once he was inside the compound, Blade, Blaine, Monica, and I started making our way to the outhouse. Blade used a crowbar to pry one of the boards off the back of the structure. They then moved back, allowing Monica and me to be up front while they positioned themselves to stand watch.

"Okay, little mama, here they come," Blaine whispered to us and gave us a thumbs-up sign.

Monica and I had our backs plastered to the back wall of the outhouse when we heard the door open then close.

Dannie's sweet little voice sounded from the outhouse, "But, Kat, I don't have to go pee right now."

"Shh, Dannie." Kat noticed the missing board. "Mama, is that you?"

Feeling elated, I turned, peeking into the outhouse. "You bet your sweet ass it is." I saw their excited little faces light up. "Shhhh." I put my finger up to my lips, indicating for them to be very quiet. Monica replaced me at the opening. "Climb up on the seat, baby. Just don't fall in."

Dannie did exactly what he was told. He didn't make a sound, but the smile on his face was shouting with excitement. When Dannie was out safely, Monica hugged him tightly. "Listen to me. This is Blade. He is a good friend of mine, and he is going to take you to the truck, and we are going to get out of here." Blade picked Dannie up and took off running to the truck.

"Go with him," I said, putting my hand on Monica's shoulder. "We've come too far to be separated now. Go!"

Monica smiled and took off behind Blade and Dannie.

"Mama, we have a problem," Kat said, quietly standing inside the outhouse. "I don't think I'll fit through there."

The one board Blade had removed wasn't enough for Kat to fit through. Looking back, Blade and the crowbar had just made it over the hill. I pulled my knife and began working another board free. We were so close. Blaine pulled his knife and started helping me. We were making more noise than we wanted, but at this point, we didn't have a choice. The board finally came free when the guard knocked at the door. "Hurry up in there."

Kat tried several times to climb up onto the seat, but the cast on her leg wasn't allowing her to bend it enough to achieve the leverage she needed. I could see the fear and apprehension building up inside her little mind.

"Sit on the seat, and we will pull you through backward," Blaine instructed just as the guard opened the door and saw what was going on. Kat lunged forward into Blaine's arms. He pulled her through the opening, shredding the flesh from her lower leg against the rough wood as they fell onto the ground. The guard dove at the opening. With my knife in hand, I jabbed just as the guard dove, embedding my knife into his eye socket. He let out a yelp as his body collapsed and began twitching, with his legs protruding from the outhouse. It was a matter of seconds before someone else noticed what was going on.

Turning to Blaine, who was helping Kat up, I yelled in a whisper, "Get her the hell out of here." Blaine swept my daughter off her feet and took off running. I could hear a thunder of commotion behind us as another guard discovered the body. For a fat man, Blaine ran fast. He had a huge head start on me. Soon, he disappeared over the hill. I knew they were safe.

A large hand grabbed me from behind and yanked me backward, slamming me into a tree, scraping the side of my face against the bark. "Where are you going, you little slut?" My head was yanked backward as a large knife was pressed roughly against my throat. He told me not to move. His body pressed against mine, pinning my body between him and the tree. His other hand wrapped around my body and worked upward, latching onto my breast. "I need to show you what happens to little girls who rebel out here in the wild." He spun me around, keeping my body against the tree and knife to my throat. I looked up at this monster and began laughing, taking him by surprise. "What the fuck are you laughing at, you crazy bitch?"

Leaning my head forward, I roughly kissed my captor on the lips, gently biting it and totally blowing his mind. "If you're going to rape someone, you better make sure they don't like it rougher than you do, you son of a bitch." Bringing my knee up to meet his groin, he doubled over, dropping his knife. I picked it up and buried it into his throat. He lay on the ground with his blood volume pumping out of his body.

Dannie and Monica appeared on the tree line. Dannie walked over to the dying man and looked at him. "I told you my Aunt Ashy was going to kill you." He gave the man a hard kick. Dannie evidently knew this man from the compound.

"Come on, let's get out of here." I grabbed Dannie and ran for the truck. I lifted him up and threw him up to Blaine, who was waiting to receive him. That was when the gunfire started. They knew we were here and not very happy about it. I helped Monica into the truck. She dove in and lay on the floor with Dannie and Kat. Blaine also lay down to help shield their bodies. Blade flipped open the top flap and produced a large cannon-looking gun. He began returning gunfire in a spray of bullets. I grabbed ahold of the truck just as it began to pull forward. I removed my pistol from my hip and noticed Mason slumped over in the corner. "Mason!" I yelled.

"They got him with one of the first shots. It went right through the truck!" Cyrus shouted.

"I'll live. Just get me home," Mason said quietly, holding his shoulder.

I lightly kissed him on his forehead. "Thank you, my friend." Looking around, I found Lita. "Lita, hold pressure here." Lita stumbled over and began to hold pressure on Mason's shoulder. "Blade, are they following?" I asked.

"Not yet," he returned. "Just let 'em try." He looked down at me with a wicked grin.

I perched at the back of the truck to help fight off anyone who tried to follow. I watched as the captives of this compound began to fight back. The last thing we saw before we went over the hill was the back half of the fence falling to the ground as someone else took over the tower and began shooting at the wolf pack. We had given these people a means to help themselves. Even though we had achieved our goal of setting free two children, we had succeeded at possibly liberating the whole camp.

Cyrus pulled into our gates and skidded to a stop in the garage as we began to file out of the back of the truck. I grabbed Kat and hugged her tight, taking in everything. My heart was beating fast, and I could feel the tears starting to build up. I had my baby back. I must have looked like a horrific mess with bloodied hair and face, but I never wanted to let go. "Are you okay? Did they hurt you?"

"I'm fine now, Mama. I broke my leg when they took us, but they put a cast on it. If anything, I'm hungry."

"Well, little sister, we can feed you." Blaine swept Kat off her feet and yelled out, "To the cantina!"

Everyone cheered as we made our way to the elevator and down to the cantina.

Dannie took my hand. "I knew you would come for us."

Picking him up swiftly, I hugged him tight. "It hasn't been the same without you, buddy. A lot of people played a part in getting y'all back."

Dannie quickly pulled back and looked at Monica; he made a weird face and raised his eyebrows. "Mama, you got a haircut."

Everyone was still laughing as we entered the cantina. Marcus and Ricky were in the kitchen. They quickly started fixing plates for the kids. Mason was taken straight to the infirmary.

Blaine shouted out, "The only thing that would make this any better would be if Ashley would sing for us." The growing crowd cheered, and the kids' faces lit up.

"Anything for you, Blaine," I said, choosing a song. I had expected Max and Harley to be here, but they were nowhere to be seen.

I stepped on stage with my hair in a tattered mess, large scratches on my face, and my enemy's blood soaking my clothes. But the music started, and Pink's "Raise Your Glass" blared from the speakers. I shouted along with the music. Blaine and Lita danced along in front of the stage. Monica bounced Dannie on her hip. By the second chorus, I was dancing on the tabletops. I got Kenny Wayne up with me and danced with him for a moment. He was funny as he shook his butt in front of everyone. The entire cantina was bursting with singing and dancing. People were shouting and singing along. I was in the middle of the cantina on top of a table when I saw Harley enter the room with Nyte on her hip. Her face and eyes were red. She had been crying. My heart began to sink.

"Blaine, kill it!" I shouted as Blaine ran over and jerked a plug from the wall. The music stopped abruptly. I stared at Harley, who was visibly shaken, as her hand went to her mouth. I couldn't imagine what had happened in the short time we were gone that had upset her so much. I used the people's shoulders for support as I stepped on tabletops. As I got closer to her, I looked up to see that she was smiling through her tears as Big Mo and Max entered the room with Raven's arms draped around theirs as they helped him into the cantina. He appeared weak but very much alive.

I dropped the microphone as my breath quickened. I couldn't believe it. I couldn't understand how. I slowly made my way over to him, not taking my eyes off him in fear he would vanish like a mirage. Max and Mo had a huge smile.

Raven lifted his head and produced his crooked little half smile as his crystal eyes shone beneath his long black hair. "Hey, good-looking."

I was in complete confusion. I raised my hand up and touched his face, expecting him to crumble into a million pieces. This couldn't be real; it had to be a dream. But he didn't crumble or fade away, and he wasn't a mirage. He was real flesh standing before me. I quickly wrapped my arms around him. Months of worry and madness flowed from me in the tears I spilled on his chest. I was not sure how long we stood there hugging and crying, but Max and Mo held him up so he could wrap his arms around me as well.

Looking up at him, I said the only syllable I could muster, "How?"

"They've been keeping me locked up in the infirmary. They kept me drugged up."

My eyes found Cyrus knowing this had to be his doing. Cyrus was leaning against the wall in the corner of the cantina. He had a proud smile on his face. "You're responsible for this?" I asked.

"You can thank me at any time," Cyrus said proudly.

"Thank you for what exactly, lying to me?" I could feel the rage filling me up. My hand began to shake. "You have known he was alive all this time and you didn't tell me?"

Cyrus let out an exasperated sigh. "I knew you would fight harder if you thought you had nothing left to lose."

The clarity hit me like a ton of bricks. Turning to Mo, I said, "You found out about him, and that's why he put you in the ring to fight us." Mo only nodded. I attempted to shake the confusion from my head. Cyrus had known my husband was alive and kept him hidden away. He had put me through hell, and there was no way I was letting him get away with it. I looked around, and people were staring at me nervously. Blaine was shaking his head in disbelief. Blade had his arms crossed in disgust. Lita stood with one hand on her hip. I made my way over to Cyrus. "So you did all this to help me. You lied to me. You put me through hell. You were willing to let me kill Mo to hide your secret."

"Like I said, you can thank me at any time," Cyrus said smugly.

I let out a little laugh as I stuck out my left hand to shake his. I could hear that gasps fell across the crowd behind me in disbelief. Cyrus smiled and took my left hand in his. In a swift motion, I pulled my pistol, pressing it firmly under his chin. "You were warned not to piss me off, you son of a bitch. You won't be doing me or anyone else any more favors." I saw his horrified eyes cut down to me, realizing his final fatal mistake. I gently pulled the trigger. Blood sprayed, and his body crumbled to the floor around my feet. Blood began to pool around my feet as I looked back at Mo. "Can you help Raven get to our room?"

"You got it." Mo softly nodded as he and Max left the cantina with Raven. I collected Harley, Nyte, and Kat and ushered them out of the room. I saw Blaine and Blade pushing a mop bucket into the cantina as everyone else started leaving. I didn't care who did what. I was going to my room with my husband and my kids. I wasn't sorry for killing their so-called leader. He was a cold, cruel man on a power trip who didn't have any business leading a group of any size.

I got Kat tucked in that night and kissed her forehead. She was so happy to be home. At this point, I wasn't sure how much longer we could call this place home. I was sure they would vote me and my entire family out of the compound for killing Cyrus. We would be exiled. No one had said anything to me yet, but I knew it was coming. It was just a matter of time. I crawled into bed next to Raven and wrapped my arm around him. He opened his eyes and looked at me. He brought his hand up and brushed the matted hair from my face. "Looks like you saw some action. Do you want to fill me in on what the hell happened around here?"

"I wouldn't know where to start." I tilted my head and kissed his hand.

"Try at the beginning, unless you got somewhere else to be," Raven stated, half smiling.

I took a deep breath and began telling him about the raid on our camp and coming to the base. I explained about my friendship with Lita, Mason, and even Blaine. I told him about the extensive training I had gone through to prove myself to Cyrus. I told him about Monica and Max fighting and her cutting off her hair and learning to fight and shoot. I told him about Marcus arriving and the raid on the reservation. I went into detail about our rescue mission to get the kids back. He lay there and listened to every word, soaking it in like a sponge.

Raven explained that when he woke up, Cyrus had told him that everyone else had died, and for a while, he welcomed being doped up and injected with drugs, because it made the harsh reality easier to deal with if he could just sleep through the pain. But then one evening, he woke up and heard me singing, and he knew they were lying to him. When he met Mo, he pleaded with him to help him break free. "I'm glad you killed him. It saved me the trouble," Raven said.

"Even if it means we may have to leave this place?" I asked.

"Yes, I will take my chances out on the road rather than stay here with the likes of him." Raven pulled me closer and held me tight. We eventually fell asleep enveloped in each other's arms.

When I opened my eyes, Raven was not in the bed. I sat up quickly and started calling out for him. When he stepped out of the bathroom wrapped up in a towel, I was so relieved to know I wasn't crazy and dreamed the whole thing.

"It's okay. I felt strong enough to stand in the shower and needed one. You were still asleep, and I didn't want to wake you."

I made my way over to him and hugged him tight. "Sorry. I just thought I was dreaming."

"You need to get a shower too." He picked through my blood-matted hair. "Eww."

"Yeah, I guess I do. Wait for me, and we can go to breakfast." When I exited the bathroom, Raven was sitting on the bed playing with Nyte. Harley and Kat sat on the other bed watching him, laughing and playing with each other. I stood in the doorway, towel drying my hair, taking it all in. He was really alive; he was here playing with our daughters. He was weak from the drugs Cyrus had been keeping him doped up with, but his only real injuries had been a gunshot wound, which had mostly healed, and a few cracked ribs. It would take a while for him to get back to 100 percent, but he was going to make it.

This was the first day since I came to the compound that my day wasn't planned out for me. We went to eat breakfast, then quickly returned to our room. I was uncomfortable with people staring at me. The word had spread, and everyone knew I was the one who killed Cyrus. I ventured out long enough to see Mason in the infirmary. He was happy for me and glad to hear of Raven's survival. He swore he didn't know anything about Cyrus hiding him. I had no choice but to believe him or kill him, so I chose to believe him. He had been a good friend, and I felt like I could trust him.

Raven slept through lunch but awoke in time to go to dinner. We opened the door to our room. Mo and Blaine were waiting for me on the other side.

Mo spoke up, "Mrs. Ashley, there are people at the gate asking to speak to the leader."

"So why are you telling me?" I asked them.

"Well, we all kind of took a vote, and well…" Blaine said gleefully, throwing his hands up in the air. "You won!" Blaine shouted with a nervous smile.

"You got what Cyrus never had—a heart. You are a good lady, and you're strong."

I interrupted Mo, "I'm no leader."

"But you are. You just don't realize it yet. Please, we don't know what to tell the people at the gate."

"All right, fine, damn. Mo, make sure my family gets to the cantina."

"You got it."

Blaine followed me to the guard wall. I was pissed off. No one consulted me about being a freaking leader. No one asked if I even wanted the job. I used the binoculars and peered through them, at the four bodies waiting at the gate. The two in front stood with a stance and faced forward. The two behind were more apprehensive and looked worried.

"Fuck it," I stated as I marched down the hill and made my way to the gate. "State your business," I barked at the four.

It was the woman who spoke up. "Forgive our appearance. We have been out here a long time. We have been searching for the right group to help us. We witnessed your raid on the wolf pack camp yesterday, and we think your group is the right one."

"The right group for what?" I snapped.

A man from the back spoke up and began to step forward, "To help restore this country to what it used to be, the land of the free and home of the brave."

"My name is Special Agent Williams, and this is the president of the United States." Her hand went out as if to present the president to me.

I looked him over. He was supposed to be dead. But this was indeed the man who was on television reporting about the comets. He was a bit scruffier, needed a shave, and thinner than I remembered, but it was him all the same. I stood quietly for a moment, knowing that this meant the world was going to change, again. "Well, hell, I guess like anyone else who shows up at this gate, you are hungry and in need of a hot shower. Don't expect special treatment just because you got a title. But you will be safe." I yelled behind me, "Open the gate!" I extended my hand to meet the president's in a handshake. "Just one question, sir."

"What's that?" he replied.

"What the hell took you so long?" I smiled and slapped him on the back. The two agents looked relieved and actually relaxed at little. I shook each of their hands and introduced myself. "Please bear with me. I just found out about ten minutes ago that I had been nominated as the leader here, so forgive me if I don't meet your standards."

I escorted the four inside the base. They ate and quickly found quarters and got their first good night's sleep in months.

The next morning over breakfast, I got the scoop on what had happened and how the attempt on the president's life was foiled. I sat and listened quietly, taking it all in. Word had spread throughout the compound about our special visitors, and the cantina was packed. Ricky and Marcus had pretty much taken over kitchen duties as I wanted, if not required, Mo by my side. Blade and Blaine also sat with me, intrigued over the president's story.

"We know your group is highly capable of handling this task, and we will pick up other groups along the way. We are hoping that as we go, members of the actual military will join our forces. We will need as many trained fighters as possible," the president explained. "So can we count on you?"

I sat for a moment and looked over the cantina at all the faces. These were faces who had nominated me as their leader. For some reason, they saw something in me, and they knew they could trust me. This was a big decision that was going to put us in danger. I got up and went up on stage and found the microphone and turned it on. "If I could get your attention, please." All eyes fell on me. "It was brought to my attention that there was a vote, and I was nominated as your leader. As most of you have probably heard, last night, special visitors arrived at the gate. We all have been under the impression that our president had been killed. He sits before us today, very much alive. He has asked something of us a decision that involves all of us, a decision that I can't…" I stopped and rethought my words. "I shouldn't make for all of us. He wants our help to retake this country one wolf camp at a time." The crowd began to cheer. "No one will be forced to fight. There is plenty here to do to keep our base going. There will be fights, there will be bloodshed, and I'm sure there will be lives lost on both sides. The president of the United States just asked us to help him. Who wants to tell him no?" The crowd cheered, beat on tables, and made as much noise as humanly possible. "I will keep you all posted on any details as they arise." I stood before them and nodded, looking at President Mallory. "Sir, you have your army."

He returned my nod as I went back to the table. "Your crew is right. You're a natural leader."

I just rolled my eyes at the president. "Okay, guys, I know there are parts of this base I haven't seen, so it's time to feel me in. What resources do we have?"

Mo started, "We have a big garden going that will hopefully provide us with fresh vegetables for a while, lots of potatoes."

"I go out on runs with a few others and scavenge for auto parts, medical supplies, clothes. Just about anything we need, we look for," Lita spoke up.

Blade interrupted, "I think she wants more hard-core information." He looked around, and everyone nodded, as if giving him permission to go any further. "We have the control room. It's one large room on another level that controls our water and lights. We also have a computer room. There is intermittent internet, and we have a hard line. Then there's the monorail. It's like a high-speed subway that connects with another base in Colorado. We trade whatever we can with them for gas and other supplies. Cyrus and I were the only ones who ever went."

I looked around the table. "That's the kind of information that I need." I let out a long, exhausting breath. "Okay, any good leader is going to have advisers. Mo"—I looked at him—"you have showed that I can trust you with my life. I appoint you over the security of my family. Protect my kids. You need to know where they are at all times. If trouble comes, your only job is to get my kids to a safe and secure location."

"It would be an honor, Ashley. Thank you." Mo turned and left the table to immediately begin his new detail.

"Lita, can I count on you to provide me with a weekly update on how we are doing on supplies and if there is anything special we are in need of?" I asked.

"You got it, sister. I will put my crew on notice. Preacher and I will do an inventory." Lita walked over and kissed my forehead. "See, you are already doing a great job as our leader." She snickered and hurried away as I swatted at her.

"I will put Ricky and Marcus in charge of food and the garden." I looked up to Blaine and Blade. "It will be a while before Mason and Raven are 100 percent. Blaine, you have been a thorn in my side ever since I arrived here. You have pissed me off more times than I can count." He held his head down in shame. "But when it came down to it, you had my back. You protected my kid. You put yourself in harm's way for me. You have proven that even though you're annoying at times, I can count on you, and you are definitely someone I want on my team. I want you to be my shadow, my right hand, if you will. Where I go, you go. Can you handle that?"

Blaine popped his head up in surprise. "Baby, when you fart, I will be right there to tell you it smells like roses."

I only rolled my eyes at Blaine's response. "Blade, since you visited the other base with Cyrus, I would like to ask for you to do the same with me and Blaine, of course. I want you to be like an ambassador. I think in the next few weeks to months, we will be in closer contact with them, and I want someone I can trust to run interference."

"You got it, boss," Blade said happily.

"The crew that's been running the control room and computers need to continue. I will meet them one day soon. Blade, how long does it take to get to the other base?"

"About an hour," he quickly replied.

"Really?" I stated in surprise.

Blade snickered. "It's fast, real fast."

"I think we need to make a run down there. I need to introduce myself and fill them in on what's going on. Do they have a fighting force?"

"They sure do." Blade rose from the table. "Wanna go now?"

I nodded in response. "Mr. President, I think it's best if you remain here for now. I'm not sure how they will respond, and I don't want you in danger."

Without giving him a chance to respond, Blaine and I followed Blade to the elevator. We began our descent. When the doors opened, Blade stepped out and reached for a red phone mounted to the stone wall. "This is Blade from North Base, is the rail clear?

Great. Have Bear waiting for us. We got news he will want to hear." Blade looked at me, smiling big. He ushered me into the large white cylinder-shaped train car. We took a seat as he began to strap himself in. "You will want to buckle up for this."

I struggled with the straps, and finally, I was securely restrained.

"Ready?" Before I could respond, Blade slapped a large red button, and the train took off like a bullet. Pure energy forced my body into the seat. Blaine squealed like a baby pig. I was barely able to lift a finger, but no force could stop my face from producing a large grin. It was a total rush. I cut my eyes over to Blade, who was sitting back with his eyes shut. I couldn't believe we had to ride an hour like this. I hoped that Blaine didn't scream like a girl the whole ride.

After what seemed like forever, we began slowing down and finally stopped. We unstrapped ourselves and stood at the door. Blaine wobbled on his feet. The door opened slowly, revealing three people on the opposite side.

Bear (otherwise known as Logan Boyd before the comets) stood six feet tall, bald-headed, and sported a face of iron. To his left was his lady, Charlotte, a small-framed lady with frizzy black hair, dressed in tank top and very short shorts. She was too busy smacking her chewing gum and filing her nails to notice anything. She obviously didn't get out much. To his right was a short yet stocky man named John. His arms were large. It immediately reminded me of someone who had used steroids. His head seemed too small for his body.

Bear looked us over, then stared at Blade. "Where's Cyrus?"

Before Blade could say anything, I responded, "I killed him." I couldn't tell if I caught Bear off guard just by his expression that he was trying to hide. Now all their eyes were on me.

"It's true. This is Ashley. She has been voted as our new leader. I was bringing her to meet you. She has some news to share," Blade explained.

"How did you kill him?" John stated, crossing his bulging arms.

My eyes were fixed on Bear. He was their leader; he was the one I needed to do business with. "I shot him in the head in the cantina."

"Why?" Charlotte whined.

"I warned him not to piss me off. He didn't listen." I looked at each one of them. "Any more questions about Cyrus, or can we get down to business?"

Bear stood strong, looking me up and down, then finally busted with laughter. "Serves that bastard right. I never liked him anyway. Come on, girl." I stepped off the train with Blade and Blaine at my side. We were on a concrete loading dock. We took seats at a picnic table.

"There has been a development that I think you may be interested in," I started.

"You mean besides North Base being ruled by a woman?" John boasted.

"Don't piss me off. Bad things happen when I get pissed." I glared into his eyes to let him know I was serious. I sat back and looked at Bear. "The president of the United States, John Michael Mallory III, is alive and well and wants to put together a rebellion to take back this country from the current tyranny it's being molested by. I want to know if we can count on you and your team to help fight the wolf pack. We want to go camp by camp, and hopefully, actual members of the military will recognize their commander in chief and turn their backs on the wolf pack. We need help getting the word out, and anyone who wants to fight needs to show up to a rendezvous point. I just want to know we can count on you or if you need to be the first base we take over." I never looked away from Bear.

Bear was silent for a few moments. "You're a cocky little bitch, aren't you?"

I shook my head. "No, I'm just honest and realistic."

"You're serious about all this. He's really alive and ready to fight and take back his place."

"Come back with me and see for yourself," I offered.

"Oh, hell no. I hate riding that train. Last time, it took a week for my nuts to go back into their rightful spot." Bear laughed.

"Tell me about it," Blaine said, adjusting the crotch of his pants.

Bear rubbed his chin with his fingers. "All right, you name the day and place and details, and we will be there."

"Thank you for the support. President Mallory will be happy to hear it. I will have Blade contact you with any information."

We went back to the train to begin our ride home. It took a little convincing to get Blaine back on it, but finally, he succumbed.

Bear stuck his hand out to shake mine. "You're all right."

"You too." I nodded in a mutual respect as the doors closed.

CHAPTER 10

THE NEXT FEW months went by in a blur. There was one battle after another, with more camps being freed from their deceptive imprisonment. When the news spread that President Mallory was alive, many camps laid down arms and opened the doors of their respective camps, allowing citizens to come and go freely. Many of the men dedicated themselves to securing our country by joining the military. Many families just went back to their home, taking what supplies could be spared for their journey. It was a time of uncertainty, but things were looking up as the wolf pack's numbers slowly diminished.

When President Mallory was returned to official command, things went a lot quicker. His first action was to have the secretary of Homeland Security, Mr. Martin Lee, publicly executed by firing squad for treason. His second action was for radio operators putting out the word on the air waves that he was alive and back in command. He humbled himself and asked for help from any of our allies to get back on our feet as a county. His pleas were answered by numerous airdrops of much-needed supplies at the camps from countries all over the world.

My family and I conjoined in the cantina for a family meeting. There was a major decision to be made. This had to be a family decision and not one that I could make for everyone.

I started, "The past year or so has been hell. Now that things are returning to a bit of normalcy, we need to decide something. Do we stay here, or do we return to Raven's ranch?"

Raven stood and wrapped his arms around me. "Just so you know, I am good with anything y'all decide."

Heads turned as everyone looked to one another. No one wanted to speak first. This wasn't an easy decision. If we stayed here at the compound, we would have friends and resources at our disposal. It was convenient, but it would never be "our home." We all wanted a place to call our own. We wanted to raise our own crops and animals and be self-sufficient.

It was Kat who broke the silence. "I want to go home to Raven's."

Max smiled and nodded at Monica. "I second that motion. Wherever we are is home as long as we are all together, but I think we will all be more comfortable in our own place."

There were nods all around. Everyone wanted to leave. The decision was unanimous. The kids were excited and danced around, shouting and cheering.

"Okay, everyone, settle down. I have things to do here before we can just leave. We will have to get with everyone and announce it and get things planned out. But we are going home!" I cheered and hugged my family.

The next morning during breakfast, I made the announcement. Everyone was disappointed. People voiced their concerns and asked their questions. It was determined that the first thing that needed to happen was to hold an election for a new leader. From there, he or she would take over, freeing my family and me to return to Nebraska. I sent a message to the president, notifying him of our departure plans, and thanked him for his service and dedication to the country.

The next week was filled with packing and planning out the route home. Blaine, of all people, was widely elected the new leader. He shockingly accepted the position with pride and honor. He elected Lita as his second hand. Mo made the decision to accompany me to Nebraska. He would be a grand addition to our family. Marcus would, of course, be joining us as well.

The morning of our departure, there was a knock on my door. It was Lita saying there was a package for us at the front gate. Raven and I went to the gate hand in hand, followed by the rest of the family. None of us were able to sleep. The anticipation of leaving kept us all awake. When we got to the gate, we stood there with mouths dropped open. Before us was a large truck with a horse trailer and all the gas we would need to get home, along with a few other supplies. A young man handed an envelope to me. Without even looking, I knew who it was from.

> Dearest Ashley,
>
> Your country can never repay you and your family for the love, loyalty, and dedication you showed. Please accept this gift as a show of my undying gratitude.
>
> I hope you find your way *home*.
>
> President John Michael Mallory III

Raven and I held each other tight and looked into each other's eyes. Raven gave me a kiss on the forehead and said, "Let's go home."

ABOUT THE AUTHOR

Photo Credit to Nancy Wilson at Nancyannphoto

C. A. BAILES is a lifelong resident of Southeast Texas. She is a mother of two daughters and a grandmother to her first grandson. She began creative writing in the second grade and never stopped. She has been a certified nurse aide for thirty years. She has worked for the Christus Health system for the past sixteen years. She loves her extended emergency room work family. She loves spending time with her grandson, Tobias; her husband, Gator Bait; and fourteen rescue cats. In her spare time, she also enjoys making quilt tops and gardening.

Ingram Content Group UK Ltd.
Milton Keynes UK
UKHW010058100623
423095UK00016B/82